FLY INTO FIRE

Susan Jane Bigelow

[Extrahumans Book 2]

First edition published 2012.

For information, address
Candlemark & Gleam LLC,
104 Morgan Street, Bennington, VT 05201
info@candlemarkandgleam.com

Library of Congress Cataloging-in-Publication Data
In Progress

ISBN: 978-1-936460-18-2
eISBN: 978-1-936460-17-5

Cover art and design by Kate Sullivan

Book design and composition by Kate Sullivan
Typeface: Candara

Editors: Ray Stilwell and Kate Sullivan

Proofreaders: Karla Bowdring and Sarah LaBelle

www.candlemarkandgleam.com

For my mother,
who always believed
I'd write books someday

[PRELUDE]
2107

UNION TOWER, SLENDER AND FORTY STORIES tall, dominated the skyline of Queens: a landmark in a city that had precious few of them left.

The sun rose low in the January sky, its light reflecting off the skyscraper's glass surface. Birds perched on the high fence surrounding its base. The hundred or so extrahumans who lived within were just beginning their days.

It started as a low rumble somewhere deep inside the Tower. The birds, startled, took to the skies.

A moment later, fire burst from the windows. Shattered glass rained down on the gardens and sidewalks below. Then, the Tower cracked in half, and, with a terrible groan, collapsed in a mountain of fire and dust.

[PART ONE]
THREE YEARS LATER

[CHAPTER 1]

THEY HATED HIM, AND SOME PART OF HIM knew he deserved it.

Sky Ranger drifted through the dank cargo ship's corridors, trying not to see the sour expressions of the people he passed. Everyone on board was running from the Reformists who ran the Terran Confederation with an iron fist, and they despised him for collaborating with them.

Three years of fighting his former allies hadn't done much to change their minds. It stung far worse than he wanted to admit.

He caught the glance of a tall young woman with black hair and intriguing brown eyes. He smiled at her; to his shock, she smiled back. She was about to say something when the ship jerked and shuddered, and everything went dark. Sky Ranger felt himself tumble end over end as people all around screamed. Then his face smacked into the wall, and he knew nothing more.

◆▷►◄◁◆

He came to slumped on the floor, head throbbing. Weak emergency lights had come on; he could see them, illuminating a hallway full of bleeding, moaning people. The air felt thick and hot, and Sky Ranger's lungs burned as he struggled to breathe. He was no expert on space travel, but he knew that meant the ship was in serious trouble.

He exerted a small amount of energy and rose, coughing, a few inches off the floor. The headache was making flying a little more difficult, but he'd manage.

He floated down the hall and into the stairwell--he never used elevators if he could help it. He quickly made his way up to the top deck, and exited to the bridge.

The bridge was a small room crammed with instruments and screens. Portable emergency lights had been placed all around, and nervous crew members studied readouts, entering commands into their terminals. A large screen at the front of the room showed a motionless starfield. They'd come out of hyperspace.

"What's happening?" he asked. A few heads turned his way, and he heard some frustrated sighs.

"What are *you* doing here?" someone asked.

"Checking on the situation," Sky Ranger insisted. "I might be able to help!"

"I doubt that," snapped the first mate, who didn't even bother to glance up from his terminal.

"Arnold," warned the captain. "He's just trying to help out." The first mate said something foul under his breath.

Sky Ranger drifted over to the captain's station. "Jackie?"

Captain Jackie Nabors shook her head, her breath labored. The air here was worse than below. "You can't help, I'm afraid, unless you know how to fix the power regulators. *Three* of them broke, and the safety systems were tripped. Which is why we're out of hyperspace, and running on minimal power. We have one working regulator left, and no spare parts." She wheezed out a sigh. "If we're lucky, we can make the nearest system."

Sky Ranger shook his head. "I'm sorry."

"Me too," said the captain. "But this isn't a young ship, and it's been a while since she's been in good repair. It's almost surprising that it took this long for something bad to happen. We were due."

"So where are we headed?"

"Well, not to Räton space, that's for sure. Can't make it. Power wouldn't last us."

"Ah?" he said, trying not to panic. Stuck inside a metal box with no air to breathe. He couldn't think of much worse than that.

"However," she said, "I think we can make the Seera system." She brought up a schematic. "See, we're less than two light years away. Not bad, really. We could be there in a couple of days if we baby it, and if that regulator holds."

"Still in Confederation space, then. What do we do when we get there?"

"I have no idea. We'll figure it out. Now get lost, okay? I think Arnold's going to mutiny if you stick around any longer."

"Right," Sky Ranger said, pushing away his hurt as he flew off towards the door.

He'd lost everything. His home was gone, and his people were dead. So many extrahumans lost, now: Doc, Crimson Cadet, Strong Rex, Lucky Jane, and most painful of all, Michael Forward, who had died to send Sky Ranger a message.

All he had left now was the fight.

He'd fought the Reformists as only he could, but in the end they were far too many. Not even flight, near invulnerability, and great strength were enough to even the odds. He'd done some damage, but in the end, they'd chased him to the farthest corners of Earth. There, in a bar somewhere in Nova Scotia, he'd found Jackie. She'd been suspicious of him at first, but when he told her his story she had, for some reason, believed it. She'd offered him a place on her ship, which was taking off on another run to Räton space the next day. She made a living ferrying former UNP members, political dissidents, criminals, and anyone else who wanted to escape the Reformists' tightening grip to the relative safety of Reilis, a Räton planet just across the border.

It had seemed like a godsend. Sky Ranger had desperately

needed to get away from Earth, and accepted the offer without hesitation. That had been almost a month ago.

Now it seemed like Räton space might not be a possibility after all. He touched down on the metal deck plates at the bottom of the stairwell and sat, feeling the muted thrum of the ship's weak power. Then, he felt it start to shift and surge. The crew must have figured out what to do with the remaining regulator.

The ship heaved and groaned as the engines returned to life. The lights brightened ever so slightly, and Sky Ranger could feel a slight breeze as the fans and filters of the life support system sputtered back into motion. The air started to cool.

Then there was a jolt as the ship transitioned into hyperspace.

Sky Ranger exhaled. They hadn't exploded, and the lights were still on: Both of those things were good signs. Maybe life was finally about to get better.

◂▸▸ ◂◂▸

The hills of Valen were green, greener than the lushest forest Penny Silverwing had ever seen on Earth. She swooped gracefully through the air, squinting as the hot blue-white light of Valen's sun flooded her eyes, barely feeling the cold of the higher altitudes. The broad vista of the LaCouraine Valley spread out before her like a painted canvas. Then, with a twinge of regret, she angled down and came in for a landing in a small field outside the tiny hillside village of LaNant.

A blue-clad figure waited for her there with a crooked smile on her face. Penny broke into a wide grin as she recognized the woman. "Monica!"

Monica waved cheerily. "Penny! Hi! I finally found you!"

The two women embraced awkwardly. Monica looked good in the deep blue leathers of the Order of St. Val. The black dye had long since grown out of her hair, and she had cut her deep brown locks short; her face was tanned and her body taut and muscled.

"You've been out walking," Penny observed.

Monica spread her arms, as if taking her lean, athletic body in for the first time. "I have. They gave me journeyman status for some reason, so I'm out here hiking from village to village providing services for people. Life's been good to me since we got here."

"Happy to hear," said Penny.

"So how are *you*? I haven't seen you since you left with Ian. How long ago was that, now?"

"Almost three years," Penny said. "And I'm well enough. I go from place to place doing odd jobs. I've been here in LaNant for a little over six months. Good place; a little town where no one minds me and no one asks questions. I might even stay."

"That does sound nice," Monica said, too quickly. "Hey. Want to go for a walk? I need to talk with you."

"All right," said Penny, curious. It wasn't as if there were many people around to overhear them here. "Let's head out to the field."

They walked in silence for a few minutes, out past the grassy fields where cows grazed. LaNant was a farming village, despite the fact that the alien soil needed constant treatment to make Earth plants grow well.

"So. What's happened?" Penny asked as the village receded into the distance.

"What makes you think something's happened?" Monica said innocently.

"The Temple sent you to find me," Penny said flatly.

Monica gave her a crooked grin. "Yes and no. I really did get journeyman status, and they assigned me this route. They also told me that *if* I bumped into you, which they strongly encouraged, I should deliver a message. You know the way it is."

"I see," said Penny shortly. "What's the message?"

Monica pulled a sealed envelope out of her jacket pocket. "This is it. I don't know what's in it." She lowered her voice. "The Temple said it was about Sky Ranger."

The name brought Penny to a dead stop. She could hear her heart pound in her ears.

Sky Ranger. She still couldn't think of him without a blizzard of conflicting emotions. Penny took the envelope, fighting a terrible gut-wrenching dread. Why would the Temple send her letters about him?

She opened the envelope and read the letter's contents carefully. Then again, to be sure. A stone settled in her stomach.

"What is it?" Monica asked.

"Sky Ranger left Earth for Räton space on a refugee ship," Penny said. "But his ship never arrived at Reilis. ...He's missing."

Monica's eyes widened.

"They're presuming he's dead," said Penny, and it was like falling out of the sky.

[CHAPTER 2]

THE BLUE STAR SEERA BEAT DOWN MERCILESSLY on Sky Ranger's bare, tanned shoulders as he flew his morning patrol. He swept out from the camp in a ten-mile arc, overflew the broken, twisted remains of the ship, and continued on from there until he could see the foothills of the mountains far to the south. Then he traced a massive circle to the north and east, and, upon reaching another outcropping of rock north of the camp, circled to the southeast, and then southwest again, turning back to the camp at the first sight of the mountains. He kept his gaze fixed on the endless gray sands below, but he never saw any signs of human encroachment on the desert.

He had tried to find the nearest town back during the days just after the crash, if only to gain a source for more supplies. But he hadn't discovered so much as a road or a farm, or even an aircraft in the sky. They were the only people he knew of for thousands of kilometers around.

Seera Terron was inhabited, he knew, but he had no idea where the other people were, or how many of them remained. The crash survivors were essentially on their own.

Fortunately, the vast desert was dotted with oases. Sky Ranger had been able to find one for the survivors to head for the day after the crash. He had helped carry all the food and supplies he could from the ship to their new camp at the oasis. He had even carried several people too infirm or elderly to make the grueling ten-kilometer walk from the ship.

The others at the camp had rewarded his efforts by shunning him, just as they had when the vessel was in space. All except for one.

◄►►◄◄►

Renna swept her dark brown hair, once close-cropped but now at that point where it was just long enough to get in her eyes, away from her face as she spotted the black pinprick of Sky Ranger against the white-blue sky. Marsha, short and formerly squat with tiny, beady eyes and a permanently sour expression, sighed and nudged her. "Stare a little more, why don't you?"

"I'm not staring," snapped Renna. "Look. He flies. I never met a man who flies. That's all."

Plus, he looked great without a shirt on.

"He's still who he is," Marsha said. "You know what he did. For all we know, he'll come leading a pack of troops right to us. I bet he's out there looking for them every day."

Renna ignored her. A surprising number of the refugees believed Sky Ranger would find a way to get them all killed, despite the fact that he'd been stuck on a refugee ship with them, the Reformists hot on his tail. Hadn't he been branded a Public Enemy by the government? Shouldn't that have been enough?

"Eh," said Marsha. "Screw it."

Renna had been lucky to survive the crash. She had been in a small berth with her friend Amy, and both of them had scrunched themselves into the tiniest little balls possible to try and avoid injury. When the crash came, they'd been thrown around the compartment so violently that Renna had been knocked out when her head collided with the bulkhead. When she came to, she was lying on top of Amy. Or, rather, what was left of Amy.

Renna tried not to think about it, but when she did, she was forced to the conclusion that Amy had been caught between a ballistic Renna and the wall. Amy had been crushed while Renna was saved. Pure dumb luck.

And that was as much as she allowed herself to think about it. Renna was practical; she didn't want to waste her energy dwelling on the past. But she still turned around and half-expected Amy to be there with some inane story, or some stupid joke.

Sky Ranger was coming in for a landing, and she watched as discreetly as she could. He touched down just outside the oasis, kicking up a cloud of gray dust. He was, noted Renna, still shirtless.

She stood, decision made.

"Where're you going?" asked Marsha.

"Just for a walk. And I need to go find the washing tub for later," Renna said.

"Oh. Well, hurry back," said Marsha. Renna mentally made a rude gesture in return. She would have to be marooned on a strange desert planet with a bunch of jerks.

She meandered along the edge of the pool. The oasis was a small lopsided bowl with a head-high ridge of rock running along the northwestern edge about a meter or two away from the water. The southern and eastern sides of the oasis sloped gently up to the rest of the desert, and were covered with a riot of blue, leafy plants. Tall, thin, flexible trees grew in clusters around the clear, deep pool of water.

All of the tents were clustered on the northwestern edge of the pool, under the rocks. They had originally been all around the pool, but the first sandstorm had made them rethink that. Sandstorms—there had been two so far—seemed to come from the west, as did the wind in general.

She walked faster, angling away from the tents. She waved to a teenage girl and a waifish, blonde young woman sitting together in the shade. "Hi, Dee! Hi Willow!" Now, Dee she could stand. She was friendly and had a great sense of humor. Still, she didn't like Sky Ranger much either, though Renna couldn't quite figure out why. Dee waved back. Willow, who never said anything, cracked a tiny smile.

Ordinarily, she would have sat down in the shade with them, but Renna was a woman on a mission.

Sky Ranger was talking to the guy who was technically in charge of the camp, Karl. He'd been part of the crew, so people followed him. Renna suspected he'd been a cook. Karl said something and Sky Ranger's too-open face fell. Probably some insult. Karl was nothing if not a horrible person. Sky Ranger nodded and walked off. Renna sprinted after him.

"Hey there!" she said brightly as she pulled up next to his broad shoulders. Renna was very tall for a woman, but Sky Ranger was taller still. She felt gloriously tiny next to him.

He broke into a wide, heart-stopping smile. "Renna!"

She grabbed his hand. "Karl giving you trouble?"

Sky Ranger shook his head. "He's being shortsighted again. We talked about the food problem; he refuses to see it or care. He thinks we can hunt. Hunting!" Sky Ranger glowered at the horizon. "There's nothing to hunt."

"Well, that's him," Renna said quickly. "So. Wanna go for a walk?"

He glanced around. They were already out of sight. "Lead on."

They'd started going for walks not long after the crash, when Renna was the only person who would even look at Sky Ranger.

They walked under the hot, blue light of Seera, their ragged shoes crunching gray sand beneath them.

In the beginning, they didn't speak much. Renna had no idea what to say to him. She never did. But she was glad for his company, every day, for at least a few minutes.

Often they'd make polite scraps of conversation, just passing the time. "I've seen those before," he'd say, pointing to a small, flat creature sunning itself nearby. "I tried to kill one, but they have hard shells. They seem indestructible. I've only seen a very few."

Renna made a face. "I bet they taste horrible."

"Dry," he agreed. "Like everything else." They'd laugh. They repeated that conversation every few days.

Other people back in the camp were good subjects, too. "Mick's a good man," Sky Ranger would say, or "I wonder about Marsha." The conversation would pick its way over the rough ground from there, in fits and starts.

One time, he asked her if she remembered what they said about him, back home.

"It's nothing flattering," she warned him.

"Still. I'd like to know."

So she told him. He sighed.

There was a night when she slipped out of her tent to find him waiting. How had she known he'd be there? Was he there every night?

Once they were away from the oasis and out into the desert, she grabbed him and drew his lips to hers. He tasted like sweat and promise. He didn't resist.

It's desert sex, she thought through the fog of riotous plea-sure as he grunted and groaned below her. *Nothing but desert sex. It means nothing!*

Still. I'm having sex with a demigod! She cried out in ecstasy. It was better than she'd ever dreamed.

The next day, they went for their walk as usual, and said nothing of it until she took his hand. He squeezed back.

"It was..." she began, but had no words to continue.

"Yeah," he said.

Awkwardness intruded, and they detached.

"Ah," he said. "The moss here is a little different. I wonder if it burns better?"

"Only one way to find out!" she said.

That night, she'd warred with herself. Should she go to him again? At last, as her tentmates snored away, she crept out of the tent and searched the oasis by the light of the little solar-powered lamp someone had set up.

He wasn't there. She only found Dee, sitting by the edge of the water.

"Hey kiddo," she said. "How come you're up?"

"Why are *you*?" Dee shot back.

"Couldn't sleep," Renna said.

"Same," Dee sighed. She chucked a rock into the pond, where it landed with a plop.

"Don't throw stuff in there," Renna said automatically.

Dee shrugged. "Whatever."

"I'm going to take a walk," Renna said. "I'll be back later."

Renna walked around hopefully, but Sky Ranger was nowhere to be found. She wondered if she was more disappointed or relieved.

Now they talked easily, and if sometimes her hand drifted down to his and held it, or if they found a little, cool place to spend a very pleasurable half-hour or so, then so what? It meant nothing. Right?

They were trapped in the desert. And he looked and smelled so, so good. She could tell from his expression, too, that she wasn't the only one who needed it. She was water for his parched throat. He drank, and she gave herself willingly.

It occurred to her that Sky Ranger might not be so thirsty for her if he knew more about her past. But that was neither here nor there. He didn't know, and it didn't matter anyway. She told herself she felt nothing for him.

◆➤ ◄◆

Today they rested in the shade, looking up at the vast blue-white dome of the sky overhead. Renna shrugged her shirt back over her head. "They're going to wonder someday," she said.

"We're careful," Sky Ranger said. "And what if they do?"

She almost told him. But what did he care if everyone else shunned her right along with him? He'd probably be glad for the company. She sighed. Maybe it wasn't worth fighting over. "Hey," she said instead. "I have a favor to ask of you. Okay?"

"A favor?"

◆➤ ◄◆

Renna held tightly to Sky Ranger's back as they skimmed over the desert floor, adrenaline pumping through her. Ahead, on the horizon, the hulking wreckage of the ship loomed.

When they crashed, Renna had been carrying a little pack full of stuff with her from Canada, and she had asked Sky Ranger if he'd fly her out to the ship so she could find it. He agreed, and off they went. She climbed on his back, and they leapt up into the sky. She braced herself, clinging tightly to him, utterly exhilarated.

They flew low, and Renna suspected they weren't going anywhere near Sky Ranger's top speed. She fought the perverse impulse to kick him like a horse and cry "Yah! Faster!"

At last they came to the ship—Sky Ranger hovered over the sand so she could drop off. She didn't know he could hover like that, parallel to the ground.

"Thank you!" she said, wobbling a little as she stood. Her heart was racing. "That was really cool."

He grinned. Clearly, he loved flying. "I'll be right here," he said. "You're sure you don't want me coming with you? It's dangerous in there."

"I'll be fine," Renna promised. She didn't want him anywhere near her when she found the bag. Too many questions.

The ship was at the end of a long, shallow furrow carved out by its own skidding, destructive impact, and looked more like a twisted wrapper than a ship. Yet somehow, enough of it had stayed intact for as many people to survive as had, and for Renna to go back inside to retrieve what she needed.

Inside, the ship was hot and stuffy. There was no light, so Renna picked up one of the flashlights they'd left at the only usable entrance.

Despite all their efforts to remove and bury the bodies, it stank of death. There were places no one, not even Sky Ranger, could get to.

Renna made her way gingerly through the wrecked corridor, paranoid that any wrong movement could bring a thousand tons of steel down on her head. The ship stirred and groaned whenever the wind moved it.

She didn't have far to go. Here, in the tiny room where she'd...

Where Amy had...

She squeezed her eyes shut and breathed for a second.

Shut it out. Don't think about it. She waited until the feeling and memory had drained from her, and sifted through the small, battered footlocker lying against the wall. *Don't think about the stains. Don't think about that corner there. Don't. Just get what you need and go.*

Ah. She pulled on the strap, and the little pack came loose. This was what she'd come for; her past. She opened it up and pulled out the contents.

Magically, everything seemed intact. There, a little notebook her mother had given her. Here, a ring from Amy. Amy.

And of course, at the bottom, a torn piece of paper.

RAMON FERNÁNDEZ SILVA, it read. OCTOBER 10TH, 2090. MALE.
SONORA DEL NORTE GENERAL HOSPITAL, TUCSON, ARIZONA, MEXICAN CONFEDERACY.

Why did she still have this old thing? In these times it was dangerous to hold on to the original, but... her mother had wanted her to have it, so she kept it. Her mother was sentimental to a fault. Renna didn't have space for sentiment, but she carried it anyway. She stuffed it back into the pack along with the other knick-knacks and mementos. She could figure out what to do with it some other, better day.

She shouldered the pack and rapidly retreated from the horrible room, back into the ship's main corridor. *Out. Must get out.*

The stench was overwhelming. No. This way. *This way.* She turned around, humming to keep herself from losing her lunch, and ran out. She didn't care if the ship fell on her. She needed to be gone from there.

At last, blessedly, she emerged into white-blue light, and stumbled onto the gray sands. She took a few moments to breathe the fresh desert air, vowing not to turn around or look at the ship again.

Sky Ranger waited nearby. "Got what you came for?"

She nodded.

"What was it, if I may ask?"

She looked away. "Personal stuff."

"Ah," he said. "Like what?"

"Like, it's *personal*," she shot back. "Can we get going?"

"Sure," he said, frowning in clear confusion. She sighed. "Let's go."

She climbed onto his back, her pack firmly bound in place. He leapt into the air. *Wherever we go*, she thought as they flew over the deserts of Seera Terron, *we carry the past with us.*

[CHAPTER 3]

THE DAYS WERE LONG AND SWELTERING. One of the more mathematically inclined refugees had figured from the position of hot, huge Serra that they were nowhere near the equator, and that they should be glad of it. Of all of the habitable planets humanity had either discovered or been given by the Rätons, Seera Terron was the second worst in terms of hot and dry. Only Polarisar, which had a single, tiny habitable zone at the south pole, was worse.

Better heat than the alternative; Seera Trikon was supposed to be a snowball. Renna had lived in Canada long enough to despise the cold.

She still expected to see beige sand and brown rocks stretching out before her. But this desert's sand and rocks were brownish-gray. The scraggly, spidery plants were deep purple or red, and the sky was too pale.

Sky Ranger was off patrolling, so Renna skipped out on washing and mending to go bug Dee.

She found her sitting by the water, in full sun. Dee was maybe thirteen: the youngest survivor. Both of her parents had been killed in the crash.

"Hey, kiddo," she called.

Dee waved. She had curly, sandy brown hair, hazel eyes, and fair skin that hadn't even tanned. Renna envied her. Her own family was from Mexico, and liked to joke that they never burned, but Renna's cracked and painful skin said otherwise. She had no idea how Dee spent as much time in the sunlight as she did; it was like she absorbed heat.

"Want to go for a walk?" What else was there to do?

Dee shrugged. "Sure." She stood with as much grace as a gawky-looking teenager could manage—which, thought Renna, was a surprising amount—and picked her way over to where Renna waited.

"Which direction?" said Renna.

Dee looked around, and then pointed off to the southeast. Had they been that way before? Maybe. It hardly mattered. They'd get away from camp for a while, and that was the point.

They set off. Renna made sure to tell Karl, who made it his business to keep track of everyone, that they were leaving. He was arguing with Allison, who was the most belligerent and angry person in the camp. Renna liked her, too.

"Okay," he said gruffly when Renna said where they were going. "Just come back soon. You never know when weather will blow up." He turned back to Allison.

"Right," Renna said, barely paying attention. When a sandstorm was on its way in, they knew, because Sky Ranger would warn them. He'd seen one coming when it was over four hours away, last time. They'd be fine.

They strode up the hill and out into the desert. Gray sand crunched beneath their feet. Renna kept an eye out for the sorts of little pests that filled the deserts she'd known back on Earth, but saw almost nothing. This planet simply didn't have that much life.

Renna had expected animals to come down to the watering hole to drink, but none did. No birds landed there. No lizards or bugs crawled into their tents at night. It was very strange. She kept exploring, looking for some answers. It was, at least, something to do.

This time, she followed Dee's lead as they trudged down a massive dune and towards yet another large rock outcropping. She had to run to keep up with Dee, who always had an incredible amount of energy.

"Hey, kid, slow down," she huffed and puffed after a while. "Come on, have pity on me."

"Old lady," Dee taunted. "Keep up."

But she slowed down a little anyway, to Renna's quiet relief. She kept an eye out, constantly peering left and right, but saw no animals or even plants. What a rotten, lifeless dustball this was!

"I hate this planet," Dee said, echoing Renna's thoughts.

"Oh, sure," Renna agreed. "But at least the air is clean."

Dee snorted. "We had clean air at home. We had food and electricity, too."

"There is that," Renna allowed. "But it's not all bad."

"How?"

"Well," Renna said. "Look around."

Dee did. "Sand and rocks."

"Sure. But do you see any black flags? See any ConFedMilPol agents? Any pictures of Peltan?"

ConFedMilPol, or the Confederation Military Police, were the regime's secret police; they were the ones who swept through cities arresting "enemies" of the state. Renna remembered when they'd come to Toronto, when she and Amy had fled. She still could hear the boots on the stairs, and the heavy pounding on the doors.

Dee said nothing, lost in her own glowering thoughts.

"It may not be much fun, but it's freedom," said Renna.

"Great," said Dee. "We'll starve to death in freedom."

"That's the spirit," Renna encouraged as they approached the rock face. They hadn't been to this particular cluster before—Renna could tell because no one had stripped the rock bare of the flammable brown moss yet.

Dee was already peeling off the nearest strips, and loading them into the sack she carried with her. Renna took out her own sack and started putting moss in it. What would they do when the moss was all gone? They were already having to wander farther afield to find it.

The rock face had a good amount of moss on it now, though, more than they could carry back. They'd have to return for the rest tomorrow. Dee closed her full sack, slung it over her back, and started to climb up the rocks. Renna took an exploratory walk around the edges. The rock seemed unusually smooth and uniform. She ran her hand along the surprisingly smooth surface. It was cool to the touch, except where Dee had been working. There, she felt the remains of a little warm patch.

Her head jerked up. Had that been Dee calling?

"Renna!" she called again. "Come on over here!"

Renna trotted around the side to where Dee squatted, poking at something at about knee height.

"What is it?"

"Look," Dee said. "Actually, listen." She rapped on the rock. It clunked.

"Metal," said Dee with satisfaction. "Metal!"

"Seriously? You're kidding." Renna moved in closer. Yes, there was a discernible change in coloration and material at about the height of her kneecap. A straight line, below which was darker gray. She reached out to touch it. Much cooler than the stone. She rapped it lightly, and was rewarded with another metallic clunk.

"A door in the rock face," said Dee.

"That's nuts," said Renna, "But I think you're right! How did you find it?"

"I kicked it," Dee explained. "I got lucky."

"A door," Renna said, shaking her head. "This place is weird."

"It's kind of low," said Dee. "Isn't it?"

"Maybe the sands covered it up," said Renna. "Wanna try and get inside?"

Dee's eyes lit up. They scrabbled at the sand for a few minutes before giving up.

"This is crap," said Renna. "It'll take all day."

Dee's face fell as she sat panting on the gray sands.

Renna had an idea. "Hey," she said. "Who around here has super-strength and needs something to do?"

◄►► ◄◄►

It turned out to be a great plan. Once they explained, Sky Ranger nodded, grabbed a shovel and followed them out to the site. Sand started flying not long after. At some point, he stripped off the dusty, sweaty shirt he had been wearing, which made Renna rather glad she had stayed. Dee simply rolled her eyes and stalked off to examine some dirt. She still didn't like him. Renna hadn't asked.

Sky Ranger labored quickly and mechanically, and gradually the hole deepened and the door was revealed. He dug rapidly through the hot surface down into cooler, darker sands below, hollowing out a pit in front of the door and a ramp leading down to it. The whole process took him about half an hour.

"Done," he called.

"That was fast," Renna said, impressed and distracted.

He shrugged. "I'm strong." Somewhere along the line he'd developed an annoying knack for understatement, Renna realized. Her memories of him from videos were full of boasts and demonstrations of power. Maybe he'd had enough of that.

Too bad, she thought with a little internal sigh.

They scurried down into the pit and took a long look at the revealed door. It was taller and thinner than most normal human doorways. A series of faded white markings climbed the side of the door. They were either letters or numbers; Renna couldn't tell which.

"Rätons," said Sky Ranger, running his hands over the symbols. "I forgot they were here, a long time ago."

"Oh, right," Renna said, dragging out dusty history lessons from the cobwebby corners of her mind. The Rätons had deeded a dozen worlds they couldn't populate or care for to humanity as part of a treaty in 2069. This, clearly, was the ancient remains of something they'd built when they were here.

There was no handle, keypad or any other apparent means of entry.

"How do we get in?" asked Dee suspiciously.

Sky Ranger smoothly levitated out of the pit and returned a second later with the pick. *I'll never get used to that,* Renna thought to herself. It was both unnerving and fascinating; men just weren't supposed to lift off the ground like that. "I could try this," he said, holding up the pick.

Renna shrugged. "Go ahead. Can't hurt, I suppose."

"Stand back," he said to them. They clambered out of the pit. Sky Ranger drew back, and drove the pick forward.

THUNG.

The metal door rang and vibrated. Sky Ranger looked a little shaken. He put the pick down and examined the door.

"Only a little dent," he said. "I suppose this could take a while."

Renna was about to agree when the door creaked, groaned, and slid open.

[CHAPTER 4]

THE RÄTON BUILDING TURNED OUT TO BE just a large, circular room with a few pieces of broken, dusty equipment scattered around on the floor.

Still, Dee was beside herself. She rocketed around the room, picking up pieces of debris and squinting at the walls. "This is amazing!" she gushed. "An alien house! I've never seen any Räton stuff! I wonder if Reilis is like this! All round and smooth."

"It's just concrete," Renna said, not trying very hard to conceal her disappointment. "Humans can do that, too." She wrinkled her nose. The place had a stale, musty odor, like what Renna believed tombs must smell like.

"But this is *different*," Dee exclaimed. Renna had to admit she was right. The equipment didn't look like anything one would find on Earth. The ceiling was higher than she would have expected, and the whole place had a sense of *other* to it. A long time ago, people from an alien species had lived here.

She had to remind herself that she had been headed for a wholly Räton planet. What would *that* have been like? How would she have survived on a whole planet full of *other*?

Sky Ranger stood in the door and glanced around suspiciously. "There must be power somewhere," he said. "The door opened. It must be powered."

"What's a Räton light switch look like?" Dee asked. "I don't see anything anywhere like I'd think it'd be."

"I don't know," said Renna. "I don't even see any lights on the ceiling. Hang on." She found a button mounted on the wall near the door, at about head height. "This?" She pressed it.

Nothing happened.

"Maybe it only had power to open the door and nothing else," Dee suggested.

Renna picked up one of the pieces of equipment from the floor. "I wonder what this stuff is? And if any of it still works."

"Maybe we should go back and get some of the others," Sky Ranger said. He paced around the debris-strewn room, nudging bits of plastic and metal with his boot. "I don't see anything that looks like communications equipment, but I'm not an expert in this stuff."

"Okay," said Renna. "We'll wait here."

He hesitated.

"We'll be fine," she said, shooing him off. Sky Ranger nodded and backed out of the doorway.

The door promptly shut, plunging Renna and Dee into total darkness.

"Hey!"

The door slid open again. "Sorry!" Sky Ranger said. "It reacts to proximity, I guess." He seemed a little embarrassed. "I should have thought of that."

"Really? Okay, we'll come out, then."

Renna had to physically drag Dee out of the Räton building back out into the sunlight. Sky Ranger took off and rapidly disappeared.

"So how come it didn't open when we got near it the first time?" Dee asked.

Renna shrugged. "All the sand?"

"Maybe... we just got lucky," Dee said. A very slight shadow seemed to pass over her features.

◄►► ◄►◄►

"We should head back to camp," Renna suggested after a while. Where the hell was Sky Ranger? Shouldn't they be getting back inside this thing already?

"Why? There's still all kinds of stuff in there to look at."

"It's nothing but crap," Renna said, feeling annoyed and tired. "And I'm getting hungry."

"You go," Dee said. "I'll stay here. I want to see more of what's in there."

"Dee," Renna said, putting a hand on her hip, "You saw it all already. You need to come back to camp!"

"Says who? You?" Dee plunked herself down on the sand. "I'm gonna wait for the others to come."

"Fine." Renna snapped. "See you back at camp."

"Okay," said Dee, lying back on the sand. She hummed a little tune to herself. Renna scowled and started back for the oasis.

◆>►◄◆►

Night fell and the temperature started dropping rapidly. Renna remembered this from when she'd lived in Arizona; the desert got *cold* at night. One normal thing, at least.

No one in the camp bothered to light a fire and waste any fuel. They could find enough warmth under the blankets in their respective tents, especially if someone else was in there with them. Renna shared a tent with Marsha, and she'd quickly discovered that she was a lousy roommate. She snored loudly, farted nonstop, hogged the blankets, and complained whenever she woke up. Renna dreamed of murder, and stayed up late.

She stared up at the stars, trying to pick out something she could identify. The patterns were all wrong. She often thought she might be able to spot the sun, but so far hadn't had any luck. She had found what looked like a yellow star down low near the horizon, but couldn't be sure. Was Earth there, eighty light-years away? If she looked through a powerful enough telescope, she might be able to pick out the planet as it had been more than eighty years before. She might be able to see her home as it was before Damien Peltan and all his howling Reformists in their mobs, before the Rätons came in their ship *Mathapavanka*, and even before the Last War had destroyed so much of the planet that the survivors had agreed to a single world government. Better days, maybe. That's what everyone said.

She glanced away from the endless starfield, and picked out Sky Ranger's tent. It was set up apart from the others, and he slept there alone. He'd volunteered to share with someone, but Karl had given him his own tent. No one had complained.

She wondered if he'd like company. He seemed to enjoy being solitary, but maybe that was because she had never seen him be anything but. She was about to head back to her tent when she saw Willow waving her arms at Renna. She jogged over, eyes wide.

"Renna, have you seen Dee? She didn't come back to the tent, and I can't find her anywhere! It's freezing." She shivered. "I can't get warm when it's only me. Have you seen her at all?"

"Not lately," said Renna. "The last time I saw her was at the Räton outpost this afternoon."

Willow looked on the verge of crying. "I haven't seen her all day, not since this morning. Did she even come back from the outpost? You don't think she *stayed* there?"

Renna shook her head, her guts twisting. "I don't know." Was this her fault? Should she have insisted harder that Dee return with her? She looked around the darkened camp. No one else was stirring, not that she could see. "We should tell Karl."

Renna made sure to make enough noise outside of Karl's tent that he didn't take more than a minute or two to finally open the flap. He had a tent by himself, a fact that made Renna see sparks.

"Karl," Renna said, "Willow can't find Dee. She didn't come to the tent tonight."

Karl glared at her. "So?"

"So she could be *lost* or worse!" Willow seemed on the verge of panic. "Karl, we have to keep track of each other! We can't not know where she is! We just—we just can't!"

"Calm down," Karl said. "Gah! Fine! Okay, we can look for her in the morning."

"Karl," Renna said, drawing out his name warningly.

"What? What should we do, turn everybody out of bed?"

"For starters," Renna said.

"And then we need to search."

"At *night?*"

Willow, normally so quiet, exploded. *"One of our people is missing! You're so busy jerking off that you don't even give a f—"*

Renna cut her off. "Willow! Knock it off. But Karl, she's right. We need to find Dee. Let's go get everyone up. She's just a kid; if she's lost out there we may never find her."

She drew herself up to her full height, looming over the diminutive Karl. He actually shrank back a little.

"Fine," Karl said, giving in with a tremendous sigh. He glared at Willow. "Give me a minute." The tent flap dropped.

"I hate him," Willow said, voice high and trembling.

"Clearly," said Renna snapped in frustration. "Next time, try and keep your stupidest comments to yourself."

Willow's eyes widened, and she stormed off, hurt. Renna sighed.

Where could Dee have gone?

There was a rush of air, and Sky Ranger landed next to her with a soft thump.

"What is it?" he asked.

It was a measure of how worried she was that she barely reacted to his presence. "Dee didn't come back to Willow's tent,"
she said. "Did you see her earlier?"

He frowned. "She came back to the camp with you this afternoon, right?"

"No," said Renna. "She said she wanted to wait there."

"Oh," He looked off to the southeast. "Oh, no. She wasn't
there when we arrived. We didn't see any sign of her. We assumed she'd gone with you."

"Oh, God," said Renna, feeling like someone had punched
her in the gut.

Dee had been gone for *hours*. How were they ever going to
find her now?

Karl finally pulled himself together enough to walk up and
down the clustered row of tents, calling for everyone to get up.
A lot of grumbling and cursing ensued, but finally everyone had
gathered themselves in a little open area just south of the tents.

Karl cleared his throat. "Uh. Is Dee here?"

No one answered.

"Well, that answers that," Renna said, folding her arms over
her chest. "You idiot. She's missing!"

"Dee is *missing*?" asked an older man, Raul. "When did this
happen?"

"This afternoon," Sky Ranger said.

"And what do *you* have to do with it?" Marsha spat. "Did
you take her somewhere?"

Sky Ranger's eyes drifted upward.

"Marsha!" Renna snapped. "Give it a rest, already! We need
to split up and search the area. Dee might be hurt or lost."

"It's night," Allison observed helpfully.

"So?"

"So I can't *see*, damn it!"

Renna was about to say something not in the least complimentary when Marsha chimed in, "She's right. I can't see a thing. Dee could be right next to me and I wouldn't see her."

"Are there flashlights?" Raul asked.

Karl shook his head. "No, the ones we managed to salvage from the ship are running out of batteries. We need to save them."

"But we have to do *something*," Willow said. "Like Renna said, she could be hurt or lost or scared..."

Sky Ranger cleared his throat. "If I may—"

"You may *not*," Marsha snapped.

"Let him talk!" roared Renna, failing to keep a lid on her temper.

"Just because you think he's cute with his shirt off—"

"You are *such* a—!"

The rest of the survivors began shouting all at once.

"*Enough*," boomed out a voice from above them. Sky Ranger hovered a few feet off the ground, arms folded over his chest. Renna's jaw dropped. "This isn't helping! We can't do much that's useful tonight, but we should scout the camp thoroughly. Look all around the water. Dee might be hurt or unconscious. In the morning, I'll go out looking for her in the areas past the Räton structure. I can cover a lot more ground than any of you. The rest of you will search the immediate area."

Marsha stepped forward. "And how do we know you'll do as you say? This could be a trap to separate us from one another! Dee could be a prisoner right now."

"Look, Marsha—" Renna started, but Marsha cut her off.

"No, *you* look! The Black Bands and ConFedMilPol, that's what they did to the people from my UNP committee. They made sure to lure a few of us off one at a time. Then they captured the rest when we went looking for them. I almost didn't escape! *None* of the others did." She pointed an accusing finger at Sky Ranger. "And *he* is one of *them*."

An unsettled murmur ran through the crowd. They remembered.

Sky Ranger's eyes flared.

"I am *not* one of them!" he said. "I *was*, once. But not now! I did more to fight them over the past three years than *any* of you! I promise, I am not trying to trick or mislead you."

"How do we *know* that!" Marsha cried. "We don't know at all!"

"You will have to *trust* me," he said, voice cold and hard. Renna's heart rate doubled. But..." he held up a hand before Marsha could say another word, "The more we argue, the later it gets. We should search the camp now. Unless one of you has a better idea."

The tension remained, but no one had anything else to say. Sky Ranger nodded and settled back down onto the ground. Renna gave him a quick smile, and he nodded gravely back at her.

"All right," Karl said. He looked relieved to have something to do. "Let's do that. The search thing."

An hour later, it was beyond clear that Dee was not anywhere in the oasis. Devon was the first to retire from the field, muttering to anyone who would listen that the whole thing had been a waste of time, she'd probably turn up in the morning, and this was either her own stupid fault or, somehow, Sky Ranger's.

Seera Terron turned quickly, so the night was mercifully short. Renna was out of her tent at the first hint of daybreak, dragging a grumbling Marsha behind her. Several others were also up.

"Figures *he* isn't out here," Marsha said, glancing meaningfully at Sky Ranger's tent. Willow wordlessly pointed up at the whitening sky, where a small black dot was rapidly receding from the camp.

"He was up before us," Willow said. "I don't think he even slept."

"I doubt that," grumped Marsha. Renna managed not to kick her. It was a start.

"We should head out soon," Renna said. "We want to have as much time to search as possible. Raul, you and Vlad head north. Willow and Allison, go west. Marsha and I will go to the Räton outpost. Karl and Paska, go east. Mick, can you to stay here and let the others know where we've gone when they get up?"

Mick, an older man who had trouble getting around, nodded. "You can count on me, no worries."

"Good. You can organize the remaining parties. Everyone grab some rations and put them in a bag. Get some water, too. We should plan on being out all day. Clear?"

Everyone was clear.

"Right. Let's go."

◆▷▸◂◁◆

The sun had peeked above the distant horizon before Renna and Marsha made it to the Räton outpost. The wind was picking up, blowing the gray sands across the desert in billowing drifts.

"You think she's really here? That she came back here in the night or something?" Marsha asked.

"I don't know," Renna answered. "She could be anywhere. But this is a pretty likely place. She could stay inside and be okay all night if she wanted. And she seemed really interested in it."

"Why would she have gone off?" Marsha said. "I don't understand. It could be dangerous out there!" She waved an accusing hand at the desert.

"She's a kid. I was like that, too, when I was thirteen. Completely reckless."

"Huh. Not me," Marsha said. "I wouldn't have done something stupid like this."

They reached the outpost. Renna again laid a hand on the cool, smooth stone of the outside. "Dee!" she called. "*Dee?*"

No answer. She circled around to the door, which was shut tight. She clambered down into the pit Sky Ranger had dug, to find that the wind had already filled some of it in. Would the door open if there was sand blocking it? She banged on the metal surface. "Dee! Are you in there? *Dee!*"

Again, nothing.

"She isn't here," Marsha said doubtfully.

"She could be inside. Maybe she can't hear us. I think we need to clear the sand away. Did Sky Ranger leave the shovel?" She fought her way out of the pit. The wind was stronger, now, and sand blew into her mouth and eyes.

"I don't see it," said Marsha.

"Help me, then!" Renna jumped back down into the pit and began throwing sand out. Marsha held back for a moment, then joined Renna at the bottom of the pit.

Working frantically together, the two women cleared the bottom of the doorway in just a few minutes. But still, the door wouldn't budge.

"Come on," Renna cried, exasperated. "Open! Dee!" She pounded her fists on the door. "*Dee!*"

Nothing. The door stayed tightly shut.

"What made it open yesterday?" Marsha asked.

"I don't know. I thought it was just being close to it, and having the sand cleared away. But... I don't know, now." She leaned heavily against the cool metal, panting.

"Now what?" asked Marsha.

"If she's in there, she's probably safe," Renna said. "But if she isn't, we still need to find her."

Renna stood back up, pushing her doubts aside. They had to do something. When in doubt, her father had always said, *act.* Better something than nothing.

"Okay. Let's go," she said.

◄➤► ◄◄►

They trudged wearily back into camp at around midday, having fruitlessly combed the desert for hours. The wind had picked up considerably, and they were tired, dusty, and windblown.

"Hey!" Mick came hobbling up to them. "Hey, you're all right."

Renna nodded, trying to catch her breath. "Yuh."

Marsha shook her head. "We didn't find her."

"Well, no kidding," said Mick. "Sky Ranger brought her in a little over an hour ago. He found her off to the east."

"Seriously?" Renna asked, relief washing over her in a flood. She was too tired to be angry. "Oh! That's good news to hear."

"He did, huh?" Marsha scowled. She obviously still had some strength. "I could kill him! Didn't even bother telling us to stop searching. I could have come back to the tent an hour ago!" She stalked off, muttering to herself.

"Where is she?" Renna asked.

Mick pointed to a tent they used for supplies. "She's lying down in there. She was all scraped and bruised. I guess she had a hard night."

"Where did she go? And why?"

"I have no idea. Ask her." Mick sighed wearily. "There's still two more groups out there. Sky Ranger is going to head out and look for them soon, I think. He's in with Dee now."

"Okay," Renna said. "Good. I'm going to go collapse, now."

◄➤► ◄◄►

Sky Ranger had looked north, first, and had flown far, far beyond his usual range. He knew somewhere in the back of his mind that Dee wouldn't have been able to walk so far, but he flew on anyway. Then, finding nothing, he turned east in a wide arc. His search pattern had been aimless and inconsistent at best, and he knew it. He'd never been much good at methodical searches. That had been Crimson Cadet's department.

He'd been lucky to spot her. He'd had an itch in his leg, and he pulled up to give it a good scratching. While he was hovering in midair, he happened to look directly below. There was Dee, collapsed on the sand. The wind had blown enough sand over her that she and her clothes looked a little gray. No wonder he hadn't been able to pick her out from farther away.

He dove to the surface at once. She was alive, and except for a few bumps and bruises, she wasn't injured. He breathed a sigh of relief, and hoisted the unconscious girl into his arms. She groaned and stirred a little, but didn't really wake up. Good. That would make things easier. He took off as lightly as he could. Hopefully they'd be back at camp before she awoke to find herself a thousand feet up in the air.

She was awake, now, although she still seemed a little disoriented. Mick had pronounced her fine, with just a need for some rest. Sky Ranger wasn't confident in Mick's diagnosis, and had stuck around.

Her eyes focused on him. "Sky Ranger," she croaked. "Did you... where is this?"

"Camp," he said. "I found you out in the desert, off to the east."

Her eyes widened. "Oh. Oh. Camp?"

He nodded. "Why were you out so far?" he asked. "Why didn't you come back yesterday? Did you get lost?"

She stared back at him, mouth open a little. He was surprised to read fear on her face.

"What is it?" he asked. "What's wrong?"

"I have to go," she said nervously. "I can't stay."

"What? Why?" he asked.

"I have to go. I *have to*. Please." She started to struggle to her feet. "I have to get *away*."

"Wait," he said, confused. "No. I just got you back! You have to stay here. Please promise me! Dee?"

She moaned a little, but lay back down on the bed. A second later, he heard her snoring softly. Saved by sleep...

He thought for a moment. He'd seen that sort of behavior before, hadn't he? That sort of sudden paranoia... but where?

Then it came back to him. Lucky Jane.

◆❯ ► ◄ ◆

They didn't bring Lucky Jane with them too often. But this time, she'd presented herself for the briefing, as if she had always been assigned to go. They didn't question it. They knew better than to go against her instincts.

And it had come in handy, again. They'd been investigating a small house somewhere upstate near Poughkeepsie, trying to find a rogue extrahuman with devastating fire abilities, when all of a sudden Lucky Jane had run from the house, shouting "I have to get out of here!" at the top of her lungs. Crimson Cadet had quickly ordered everyone else out.

The house burst into flames a few minutes later. Someone had set a trap for them.

◆❯ ► ◄ ◆

She'd lost her luck, later, and had left the Union. Sometimes it happened; people lost their abilities. Sky Ranger had let her go. He knew where she lived in Yonkers, and figured that, powerless, she wouldn't be able to do much harm.

She'd died in a fire set by an angry mob during the worst of the anarchy following Black Rock. Definitely out of luck. But before then, her instinct had always been right on. She could do no wrong. She always came out on the right side, always escaped danger.

He stared hard at Dee.

"Are you one of my people?" he whispered softly.

She slept on, her chest rising and falling rhythmically as before.

He let the enormity of that possibility wash over him. *Another extrahuman.* Maybe not a particularly strong one—they might classify her as Type I, the lowest level of power. But *another... If it was true... One more. There's one more.*

If it was true, what had she been trying to tell them? Why had her instincts led her away from the camp?

Wind ruffled the sides of the tent. It had been getting stronger all day.

Wind. She'd been heading *east.* Sandstorms always came from the west.

He bolted from the tent and took to the air.

He forced himself through the sky, as fast as he'd ever gone. A massive headache had started to build, and he could feel the weariness creeping in around the edges of his body. No time to stop yet. Where was it? He scanned the western horizon, fighting the west wind. Where?

There. A little puff of gray haze, far away. He dared to get closer, and the haze grew into a terrifying, howling beast of a storm, stretching hundreds of miles north and south. This one was bigger than any he'd yet seen on Seera Terron, and it was heading straight for the oasis.

Dee knew. She'd known it was coming, somehow, and now Sky Ranger had dragged her right back into the thick of it.

He turned back for the camp, the wind driving him forward at breakneck speed.

<>►<◄>

The gusts had picked up again. Renna sat with Dee, who drifted in and out of panicked wakefulness and fitful sleep, and worried a little about Karl and Paska, who still hadn't returned from the search.

A *whoosh*, and Sky Ranger ducked his head into the tent.

"We all need to get to the Räton outpost," he said. "Sandstorm."

"Why the outpost?" Renna said. "We stayed in our tents the last time, and we were fine."

"This one is really big," he said, slouching a little in exhaustion. Was he panting? She'd never seen that before. She didn't know he could get tired. "Huge. Hundreds of miles across. It's a killer. We need to be indoors."

Renna's heart skipped a beat. "But we couldn't get in. We couldn't! Marsha and I tried, but we couldn't get the door to open."

Sky Ranger nodded at the sleeping Dee. "Take her. It'll open. But we need to get everyone there *now*."

She nodded briskly, then gasped as she remembered. "Karl and Paska!"

"What about them?" Sky Ranger said, irritated.

"They're still out there. They didn't come back from the search."

Sky Ranger looked briefly annoyed. Renna arched an eyebrow in surprise. She'd never seen him show much of any emotion. "Okay," he said, exhaustion clear in his voice. "Just... Just get everyone to the outpost. I'll find them and get to you as soon as I can."

He took off, leaving Renna alone with Dee.

<>►<◄>

At first, they didn't believe her.

"So?" said Allison, munching on a ration bar. "We rode out the last two here at camp. Why should we go anywhere?"

Marsha shook her head. "He's just saying this to get us out of camp. What evidence do we have of any sandstorms?"

"Sky Ranger *was* right before," Renna said. "And he did bring Dee back."

"Fine," said Allison, tossing the bar away. "Whatever. Let's hike our asses out to the outpost."

Soon it became clear that Sky Ranger had been telling the truth as they struggled against the fierce, now howling wind on their way to the Räton outpost. Sand got in their shoes and eyes, and filled their mouths and ears. Each person carried only what he or she could manage, but a lot was simply dropped on the way.

Renna supported Dee, who was struggling to walk. At times, she carried her.

About halfway there, they caught the first glimpse of the monster. A low gray haze appeared all along the western horizon, growing fast.

"It's huge!" Mick shouted. "It must go on forever!"

"We need to get inside!" Renna commanded. "Everyone move as fast as possible!"

Visibility was next to nothing when they finally made the outpost. They were, Renna reckoned, lucky to have made it at all. The pit had started to fill in again, and Renna moaned. They had to get it dug out, and quickly.

Dee, though, struggled out of Renna's arms and fell down into the pit. She hit her hands against the door once, twice... and then it slid open.

"Come on!" Renna called. Twenty-four people raced past Dee, and into the dark, cramped outpost.

Renna stood in the door, keeping it open, for as long as she dared, as the wind and the sand swirled around them.

Sky Ranger didn't come.

At last, when the winds were too fierce and sand was beginning to stream into the dark, debris-covered room, she stepped away. The door slid shut, plunging the room and the refugees into utter darkness. Everyone fell silent. The only sound was the muffled howling of the wind.

Renna sank down next to the door. They could do nothing but wait, now. No one saw the tiny light behind a pile of old, useless Räton equipment come slowly to life, and start blinking.

[CHAPTER 5]

SKY RANGER SAT ALONE, EXHAUSTED, IN THE middle of the desert. Off to the northeast, he could still see the haze of the massive sandstorm as it receded into the distance. Behind him, the sun had begun to set.

He had no idea where he was. The storm had forced him higher than he usually dared go, just to escape the massive, choking clouds of sand and dust. The winds up there, if anything, had been worse. It had taken all of his strength to stay aloft in what must have been gale forces.

Eventually, his energy draining away, he had been driven to the ground. He somehow managed to get behind a large rock, where he squeezed himself into as tight a ball as he could and put his head down to escape the sand. He still figured he'd swallowed about a pound of the gray stuff, and he'd been coughing ever since.

The storm had been fierce, even blotting out the sun for a brief time, but by the end of the day, it had finally passed. Coughing and sputtering, a filthy Sky Ranger emerged to a completely unfamiliar landscape.

Worst of all, he hadn't been able to find Karl and Paska. He hoped they'd managed to find some sort of shelter, but he knew the odds weren't good.

He coughed again in a great wracking spasm, and spat out

more sand. He needed water. He had to fly.

He steeled himself and *willed* himself off the ground an inch or two—only to collapse, coughing, onto the sand a second later.

This, he realized dimly as the world spun around him, black spots forming in his vision, was very bad.

"Hey," someone said.

Sky Ranger coughed and gingerly opened his eyes. It was night; the stars were out overhead, and everything was dark—except for the roaring fire and the red-clad man sitting in a beach chair next to it.

Sky Ranger blinked, trying to clear his vision. "What?" he rasped.

"Hey, Sky," the man said, raising what looked very much like a can of beer at him.

"Crim?"

"How are ya, buddy?" Crimson Cadet grinned, and took a long pull from his beer. Sky Ranger watched, his throat feeling like ash. "Been a while."

"What—what are you *doing* here?" Sky Ranger managed to say.

"Ha! Wrong question," Crim said.

The gears in Sky Ranger's head clicked and whirred. "You're dead," he finally said. He pulled himself, with some difficulty, into a sitting position. "You died a long time ago."

Crim spread his hands in a half shrug. "Guilty."

"So this is some sort of hallucination. You aren't really here."

"There's my smart boy," Crim said. "Got it in one."

Sky Ranger coughed again, staring at the image of his old friend. "...It's good to see you again."

"You, too."

Sky Ranger crawled on all fours over to the fire and sat. The fire gave off no heat, but its light danced weirdly on Crimson Cadet's face.

"Nice planet," Crim said. "Why'd you pick this place for your vacation? Seems a bit out of the way."

"Not my choice," said Sky Ranger.

"No? What happened to you?"

"Crashed. The ship I was on."

"Ah, right. You're on the run, I forgot."

Sky Ranger said nothing, but stared into the fire. Sparks of green and blue shot up into the night. He couldn't quite make out what was actually burning in the center. Something other than wood.

"What a damn sorry state of affairs," Crim said. "The great Sky Ranger the Third, leader of the Extrahuman Union, running from the law like a common criminal, and now marooned on a desert planet with a bunch of useless refugees. How the hell did you let it come to this?"

Sky Ranger remained silent.

"Let me spell it out for you, then," Crim said mercilessly. "You screwed up. You screwed up in a *big* way, and now you're paying for it. Except, of course, that you *aren't* really paying for it—you're just running away again. That about right?"

Sky Ranger shook his head. "No! I mean, *yes*, I screwed up. I worked with the Reformists. But I did what I did for us... for our people."

Crim frowned as the strange firelight drew strange patterns on his face, but said nothing.

"I didn't know what they were," Sky Ranger finished lamely. "How could I have?"

"Please. Everyone knew," Crim said quietly. "How could you miss it? They made no secret of what they were. It was right there in front of you. You just didn't *want* to know."

"That isn't true!" Sky Ranger protested. "Crim, you know me. They seemed... they seemed to make so much sense. And after what the old government did to you..."

"Don't make *me* your excuse," Crim said. "The old government, the UNP, they used us, imprisoned us, tested us, and yeah, that led to me getting shot. They didn't like us, sure. We knew that. That was them, that was how it had been for decades. But the Reformists? They *hated* us. We were nothing but freaks to them, something that should never have been allowed to exist in the first place. Peltan even *wrote* about it. The old government wanted to contain us. The Reformists wanted us all *dead*. God, Little Hawk, you should have known! You had to have seen that."

"I didn't see it, so sue me," Sky Ranger wheezed. "And don't call me 'Little Hawk'."

Crim laughed. "Oh, *names*. How many did you have? 'Little Hawk' when you were a kid. Then 'Sky Cadet' when the old Sky Ranger adopted you as his heir. Then 'Sky Ranger' when he died. So which one is really you?"

"Sky Ranger," he said. "That's who I am."

"You're the Sky Ranger of an Extrahuman Union that no longer exists," Crim pointed out. "The words are meaningless."

"Not to me."

Crim shrugged. "Suit yourself."

"I never understood why you cared so much about your original name," Sky Ranger said. "It isn't like it matters that much what people call you."

"No," said Crim, leaning forward in his chair. His can of beer dropped, empty, to the sand with a dull *ting*, and rolled away down the hill. "But it matters what I call myself. You know, in the old stories, back from before extrahumans even existed, the superheroes would always have a secret identity. They hid a little piece of themselves from the world, and that was who they really were under all the powers and the funny name and title. That's what I wanted. I was always just Crimson Cadet. I was the guy in the Law Enforcement Division who wore red. But what else was I? I never knew." He grinned and sat back in his chair. "Then, right at the end, I remembered."

Sky Ranger remembered, too. They'd carried Crim back to the tower, bathed in his own blood, and laid him on the bed. Lucky Jane had tried everything she knew how to do to save him, but her medical skills and her luck weren't enough.

"Jack!" he called.
They stared at him, speechless.
"My name is Jack," he said, a smile growing on his face. "I remember it now."
He died, smiling still.

"And then you..." Sky Ranger said, his eyes welling up with unaccustomed tears. "You left me to deal with it on my own. And then Sil left..."

"Now *there* was someone who understood how powerful names can be," Crim cut in. "Silverwyng. What did she call herself after she left? 'Broken'? That's a great name. Very descriptive."

"Yeah, I suppose."

"A strange girl, really. Always so aloof, even when she was happy. But I liked her. As did you, for a while." He wiggled his eyebrows. Sky Ranger ignored him. "She hated being in the Law Enforcement Division, you know. She hated doing what we did. Catching non-registereds and either dragging them to the Tower or killing them... I can't blame her. I hated it, too."

"It was necessary work," Sky Ranger said. He'd said that line a thousand, a hundred thousand, times. It rang so hollow now.

"Why? And don't give me that crap about *protecting* them.

The Union was a prison. A zoo. That's all it was."

Sky Ranger shook his head. "You and I have had this argument before." He stared at the fire. In the middle, twisting and burning, was the cracked spindle of Union Tower. He blanched and looked away.

"She only joined because of you, you know."

"No, she didn't," Sky Ranger insisted, horrified at the idea. "She wanted to serve. That's what she said."

"Well, believe it," Crim said. "She joined to get close to you."

"That isn't what she told me."

"Heh," chuckled Crim. "She didn't tell you much, then. Tell me, did you even bother to go after her, when she left us?"

"I don't need this from you," Sky Ranger said, anger building up in him.

"You forgot *all about* her," Crim accused. "My God, Sky, she was your lover! She served in the LED with us! And you just *let her go*."

"I didn't *forget*," Sky Ranger began.

"Right," Crim cut him off. "You had other priorities. Like joining the Reform Party."

"I told you, that was a mistake!"

"Yes, it was," said Crim. "And thanks to you, the whole Union is gone. The Tower blew up. Remember?"

"That wasn't my fault," Sky Ranger said desperately. "It was the government! They planted someone in there—"

"The Reformists controlled the government. And you were in bed with them, while they were busy stabbing our people in the back," Crim said. "You never saw it coming, did you? All the things they said, all the hate they spewed. You *really* never saw it coming?"

"How could I have?" Sky Ranger said miserably, his anger subsiding. "I thought everything would be fine if I worked with them. If we were useful to them."

"Not just that," Crim pressed relentlessly. "You liked be-ing popular. You shook hands with the president; you were on screen campaigning for them. You went on missions for them. You *served* them, while they schemed ways to destroy us."

"Why are you doing this to me?" Sky Ranger cried. "Crim, you were my friend!"

"Because of you, the Union is gone. My home. Our people... *wiped out*. We were unique; nothing like us existed anywhere else. Now nothing like us exists at all. All because you let the Reformists get what they always wanted. Good work."

"I know," Sky Ranger said miserably. "I know. And I'm all that's left. I *know*."

Crim shook his head. "You aren't the last. Sil is still out there."

"Yes."

"She remembered her name, you know."

"I know."

"'Penny.' It's funny, it really doesn't fit her at all. But that's her *name*. Penny Something-or-other. You know that she's on Valen, right?"

"I think so," Sky Ranger said. "I haven't heard from her in a while, but..."

"But she's *out there*. Alive. And then there's that girl back in camp. Dee. She's one of us. You know she is."

Sky Ranger looked back at the fire. Dee was there, leaping and playing with the flames. They did not burn her. He looked away again.

"I don't know," he said. "She could just be lucky. She might not be what she seems."

Crim laughed. "Oh, *come* on, Little Hawk! You know she is. How many people did you test? She's just like Lucky Jane was when she was her age. Stuff *happened* to her. Dee is an extra-human. It's probably why she and her parents were on the run.

And there's more to her even than that. You'll see." He leaned close. "Our people aren't gone. There are just fewer of us, now, and we're a lot harder for people like *you* to find."

"And it's my fault," said Sky Ranger dubiously.

"Yes. So you know what you have to do."

"No, I don't!" said Sky Ranger. "Crim, I haven't seen you in a decade! You're *dead*, and all you can think of to do is come here and insult me!"

"You forget," Crim said, holding up a finger and wagging it at Sky Ranger. "I'm just a hallucination."

"Oh," Sky Ranger whispered, head spinning. "I did forget. You seem so real."

"Imagination is a powerful thing," Crim said. "I think for us it's even more so."

"Did you ever find out what you wanted to know about us?" Sky Ranger asked. "You were always searching for the reason why we exist, where extrahumans came from. Did you ever find out?"

Crim smiled his sad little smile. "Yes. I found out. But I can't tell you yet. Not for a while."

"Why *not*?" Sky Ranger demanded petulantly. "You're my hallucination, you should do what I tell you to do!"

Crimson Cadet laughed, and Sky Ranger's anger exploded again. "This isn't funny! Damn it, Crim! You— Look, all you are is the last random firing of my neurons before I die of thirst out in the desert! That's it!"

"Oh, Sky," Crim laughed. "You're so dramatic. I may not be real, sure, but there's one thing I do know."

"And what's that?" Sky Ranger seethed.

"You aren't going to die. At least, not right now. You have some work to do, first."

Before Sky Ranger could respond, the fire roared and exploded, engulfing Crim, Sky Ranger and the whole desert, the whole *world*, in its wild heat.

Somewhere off in the distance he thought he heard Penny Silverwing laughing.

◆▷▸ ◂◁◆

Sky Ranger opened his eyes. His throat was a dry riverbed, and sand had filled his mouth, nose, and ears. He coughed violently and spat some of it back out. He could barely swallow. He blinked, and his vision cleared. Two bright stars shone overhead, bouncing and...moving closer?

He realized that he wasn't staring at the sky, but off towards the horizon. The two lights were drawing closer. A vehicle's headlights! He tried to raise his arm, to shout, but found he couldn't.

He heard the whine of the unknown vehicle as it approached, and squinted as the lights blinded him. The engine cut out.

"So," an unknown voice said after a while. "Where did *you* come from?"

Sky Ranger passed out again.

◆▷▸ ◂◁◆

The storm had almost entirely obliterated the camp. Renna and the others had staggered back in the early morning, following a very uncomfortable night spent in the Räton outpost, to find devastation. The wind had scattered the tents, leaving half-buried burlap and tent poles littered all over the oasis. Only a few of the tents, those closest to the rock face, had survived—and even those were in bad shape.

The worst news seemed to be that the tent where all the rations had been stored was also gone, but Dee had simply gone over to a certain spot in the sand and started digging. To everyone's relief, she turned up a buried mound of ration bars.

The other refugees wandered shakily around the camp asking questions to which everyone already knew the answers. No, we can't get more tents from the ship. This was it. No, there's no sign of Karl or Paska. No, there's only the ration bars Dee discovered. Yes, it's about a third of what we had before. Yes, the level of the water is down. Yes, we'll be able to drink it again, eventually, when all the sand settles to the bottom.

Renna answered their questions as best she could, but wondered what would happen next. Their situation had gone from bad to much, much worse literally overnight. They were lucky they had Sky Ranger, Renna knew. If they'd been caught in this, the results could have been very bad indeed.

No one had seen Sky Ranger, though, and despite the fact that he had saved them from the storm, no one seemed to care much. Renna burned and fumed about it, feeling helpless.

Mick sought her out in the late morning. "We have maybe enough rations for a few more weeks," he said. "But after that... I don't know. We have nothing. I don't know what we'll eat."

Renna nodded glumly. "Yeah. We'd have to come to this eventually. We can try hunting, but we'd have to find something to hunt, first."

"What would we hunt with?" Mick said. "We don't have any weapons. There weren't even any still working on the ship."

"Huh," said Raul. "But there was metal..."

Marsha came up to them and sat. "I heard you talking," she said. "And I think you're right. We have to hunt. We need to learn how to survive here."

"We have some time," Renna said, stalling. "We have a few weeks to test this before things get desperate, time to see if we can find some animals, *something...* "

"Maybe we ought to move the camp back to the outpost permanently," said Tricia, who had joined the growing crowd around Renna.

"I agree," said Renna. "We should."

"Yes," Willow said. "And post a guard at night to make sure nothing bad comes."

"Hmm," said Mick. "We should start moving now, if we can. What do you think?"

Everyone looked at Renna expectantly.

"All right," she said without hesitation. "Then let's do that. Raul, go with Willow and Vlad back to the outpost. Take Dee—she seems to be the only one for whom the door will work reliably. If you can't jam it open, find a big rock. But try to think of a way to close it if we need to."

"Okay," said Raul. "This should be interesting."

"Marsha, can you and Tricia round up some people to start moving ration bars and anything else we can scavenge back to the Räton outpost?"

"I can do that," Marsha said.

"The rest of us... will try to figure out a way to hunt," Renna said, looking around. Almost the entire group of survivors had joined them. "Does that work for everyone?" she finished lamely.

People nodded.

"Well, let's start work," she said. The group broke up.

Marsha corralled a few people, and they started extracting the ration bars from the ground and putting them into their bags. Mick, Willow, Vlad, and Dee filled up containers with sandy water and set off for the outpost.

They all slept in the outpost that night, and every night after that. A patrol kept watch on the oasis, but of course no animals approached it. They did notice with some apprehension that the water level seemed to be diminishing. Renna started to consider some sort of expedition to find more water, although Sky Ranger had never mentioned seeing other oases. She wished she could ask him directly.

It turned out not to matter. On the morning of the fifth day after the sandstorm, a Confederation Fleet ship came from nearby Seera Trikon.

[CHAPTER 6]

SKY RANGER WOKE IN A COOL, DRY, DIMLY lit place, and for a moment thought he was back in his rooms in Union Tower. His first thought was that he should ask Blue Blur, who sometimes served as a runner to the kitchens due to his tremendous speed, to bring him some coffee.

In the next instant, he remembered that Blue Blur was dead, and the Tower gone. He grimaced and coughed. His throat felt like someone had scoured it with steel wool, and his eyes were having trouble focusing.

"You're awake," someone said. "Excellent. Drink."

Cool liquid pressed against his lips. He drank, but his throat rebelled and he coughed most of it out.

"Mmpf. Try again. Small sips."

The water returned. Sky Ranger did as he was told, and managed to get much of the water down.

"Good. You'll have more in a minute," said the gravelly, lightly accented voice. Sky Ranger's vision finally cleared. A slight old man with a wisp of white hair perched precariously on his scalp stared intently down at him. "Hello."

"Who—?" Sky Ranger began, but couldn't finish the words before he started coughing again.

"Broussard. Don't try to talk. You must have swallowed a liter of sand. What were you doing out in the storm? That was foolish of you." He held up a hand. "Don't try to answer, now. You've been asleep for more than a day, and you need water and food to get your strength back first. Here. More water."

A day...

Sky Ranger gratefully accepted the proffered cup, and lay back on the pillow. His eyes widened as the old man refilled a glass jar of water from what looked like a tap in the wall. "This? It leads to the cistern above. Convenient, yes?" Broussard set the jar down next to Sky Ranger, and sat in a chair set along the nearby rock wall. "So. You're in my home. This is the southern reach of the desert, near the mountains. I found you nearly a hundred kilometers away to the northeast. You're very lucky. I was watching the storm through my telescope, and I thought I saw a man flying through the air, struggling to stay aloft. That was you? Nod yes, don't speak."

Sky Ranger nodded.

"I would ask how a man can fly, but I know what Extrahumans are. You're one of those?" Sky Ranger nodded again. "Hm. I saw you crash, so I came to have a look when the storm was done. You should be dead. You must be very strong."

To that, Sky Ranger had nothing to say. He looked away from the old man.

"Drink more," said Broussard. "Here." Sky Ranger drank. "Good. Soon, perhaps, some food. Then rest."

◂▸▸ ◂◂▸

By the next morning, Sky Ranger was feeling much more like his old self, although he still found it difficult to rise from his prone position in the bed. It grated on him. He was rarely injured and healed quickly, and so he wasn't used to lying around helpless. When Broussard came to talk to him, he hazarded speech.

"How... why are you out here in the middle of the desert?"

he asked.

Broussard fixed him with a speculative look. "I could ask you the same. Where did you come from?"

Sky Ranger smiled weakly, coughing. "You first."

Broussard shrugged. He seemed to shrug a lot, and he did so in a peculiar way, with his eyes closed and a strange twist to his lips. "I live here. I've lived here for twenty years. Before that, I lived in the town on the shore of the big lake."

"The town," rasped Sky Ranger. "How far?"

"Oh, thousands of kilometers. Far. On the other side of the world from here."

Sky Ranger's heart sank. No wonder no one had come looking for them. "Are you the only one living here?"

Broussard nodded. "Oh, yes. As far as I know, I'm the only human in the desert. Except, of course, for you."

He waited. Sky Ranger realized that it was his turn to explain.

"You saw me," Sky Ranger said. "But you didn't see the ship crash? It would have been about six weeks ago."

Broussard frowned thoughtfully. "No. Six weeks? No, I saw nothing then. But I wasn't looking. Which direction?"

Sky Ranger half-coughed, half-laughed at that. "I have no idea. North somewhere."

"The entire desert is north. Hm. I saw a dark haze to the northeast that week. I had thought it was another sandstorm. That may have been your ship. Are there other survivors?"

Sky Ranger hesitated.

"I see." Broussard offered him more of the pungent, tangy broth he had served him the day before. "Eat this."

"What is it?" Sky Ranger asked.

"A soup made from the *lyski* moss, which grows on most rocky surfaces here." He smiled apologetically. "It's one of the only foods there is out in the desert. Get used to it."

Sky Ranger drank the broth obligingly. Strangely, it didn't

taste half bad.

◀▷▶ ◀◁▶

Some time later, Sky Ranger experimented with sitting up in bed, and, after a few failures, finally managed it. The next step was walking. If he could do that, then soon he'd fly again. The sooner he flew, the sooner he could return to the camp.

Then what? He'd failed to find Karl and Paska. He doubted the others would be glad to see him again. Even Renna, who for some reason often defended him, might not want him to return.

Dee was there, though. *Dee.*

He swung his legs out, and touched the cool, rock floor with his bare feet. Broussard's home, he realized belatedly, must be a cave of some sort.

"Feeling better, are we?" Broussard said, ambling into the room.

"Yes," Sky Ranger said. "Much."

"Good," said the old man. "I don't like to play nursemaid. If you can walk, come sit down with me in the next room. I made us tea." And he left.

◀▷▶ ◀◁▶

They sat at a small table in the center of a large room. The walls here were rock, with several windows carved into them. Glass panes allowed the purplish light of setting Seera in. No decorations or coverings graced the walls, and there was almost no other furniture to be seen.

"So," Broussard said. "You're the first visitor I've had in years."

"Thank you for your hospitality," Sky Ranger said, mustering his politeness. "I appreciate all you've done for me."

"Hmph." The old man waved Sky Ranger's thanks off. "You were foolish to try and fly during a storm. Why did you do that, anyway?"

"I got caught," Sky Ranger said. "I couldn't get back to shelter in time."

"And where were you sheltering? Was it a cave?"

"A—a Räton outpost," Sky Ranger said, unable to come up with a convincing lie.

Broussard looked at him, a shrewd expression on his face. "Ah. Yes, there are more than a dozen of those spread throughout the desert."

"Oh," said Sky Ranger. He had hoped the old man would be able to help him locate the outpost, at least. No such luck.

"Did the people from the town come to visit you? You said you had visitors once." Sky Ranger said quickly, trying to change the subject.

"Sometimes," Broussard said, sipping his tea, which also seemed to be made from the ubiquitous *lyski* moss. "Sometimes the people from Trikon come, doing surveys. But I haven't heard from either in a long time."

"Do you think they forgot you're out here?" Sky Ranger asked.

Broussard shrugged again. "I hope they did. I want nothing to do with them, and they know it. But that's me. I'd like to know about you. Tell me. Why were you in a ship near Terron in the first place? Where were you going? What happened to your crew?"

"As I said, we crashed," Sky Ranger said calmly.

"Hm. And where were you going?" Sky Ranger said nothing. Broussard nodded. "I thought as much. On the run, are you? That's why no one has come looking for you in what, six weeks?"

"Surely the tracking station would have seen the ship go down, though," Sky Ranger said.

"What tracking station? The one in town?" Broussard shook his head. "No one has manned it in years. Why bother? The only ships are from Trikon, and they come on a regular schedule."

Sky Ranger was taken aback. "What if a ship from Seera Trikon goes off course?"

Again Broussard shrugged in that maddeningly casual way of his. "Then Trikon will know, and take care of it." He set his tea down. "You have to understand how things are done here, which is to say that they are barely done at all. There are maybe a few dozen humans living on this world, and all but you and I are in the town. They mine, they farm, and they fish. Except that the mines fail because the Rätons took all the good ore centuries ago, farming here is poor because of the soil, and there are very few fish to speak of in the lakes. Therefore, life here is a losing proposition. Everyone is simply waiting, getting by, until they can leave. Which, eventually, they all will. Why stay on a pointless planet?"

"You seem to be staying," Sky Ranger pointed out.

"I'm stubborn," said Broussard after a moment. "And I'm old. I can be contrary if I wish."

"I know what it's like," said Sky Ranger after a pause, "To be the last of something. To be an end."

Broussard nodded. "Yes, I suspected. I'm not cut off, here. I can access news feeds from Trikon. I know there are no more extrahumans. Which means you're the rogue Sky Ranger of the old Union, yes?"

Sky Ranger nodded.

"So. Drink your tea, Sky Ranger. It will help you get stronger. When you're stronger, then you can leave."

Sky Ranger got the message. "I'll leave soon."

◄❯► ◄❮►

But he found it remarkably easy to stay. The next morning, Broussard woke him to say that he was leaving for a few hours, to check on his moss farms. "They grow in caves in the mountains to the south," he explained. "So that's where I'll be. Don't leave before I get back. I'll bring some moss for you to take."

Sky Ranger waited, and explored Broussard's home to pass the time. It was carved into the side of a massive lump of gray rock rising out of the desert. The rock's outer face was festooned with black panels and antennae. The panels, Sky Ranger surmised, were for collecting power from Seera's harsh rays. That made sense. The antennae were obviously communications equipment, even though Broussard had said he wasn't interested in the outside world. Maybe the old man was lying.

Six large funnel-shaped objects perched on the very top of the rock. Sky Ranger suspected that those were for water collection. He had seen something like that once in a documentary about desert living.

The cave was a surprisingly comfortable place to live. It stayed cool in the day, yet didn't get too cold at night. Perfectly pleasant.

When Broussard returned, he invited Sky Ranger to have dinner with him. He fried some of the moss in a pan, and seasoned it with some sort of blue leaves. The result was bitter and chewy, but edible.

Then, of course, there could be no flying at night. So Sky Ranger stayed.

◆▻▸◂◄◆

Late one night, after several days had passed, Broussard told Sky Ranger a little of his past.

"I was one of the first to come to this system, forty years ago," he said as they sat just outside Broussard's rocky home, watching the stars slowly rotate past. "I came with my father and brothers. We were the first ship of colonists to come here after the Rätons gave us this system, and many others, in the treaty. We thought they were being so generous! But they gave us a useless desert world, and a freezing lump of ice and rock. They gave us other, better worlds as well, but only because they never had the population to settle them. The Räton population has been in decline for hundreds of years. Did you know that?"

Sky Ranger nodded, although he hadn't known. He had never cared to know much about Rätons.

"They had never done much with this world. They mined what ore they could, did some studies, left their rock-and-concrete outposts scattered around the desert, and left. But they found a few interesting things, which they passed on to us. Did you know, for instance, that this world used to be much wetter and cooler than it is now?" He continued on, not waiting for Sky Ranger to respond. "It's true. The Rätons found fossils of fish and other aquatic animals here in the desert, and they found petrified forests up in the mountains. This was once a lush world, filled with life."

"What happened?" asked Sky Ranger.

"There are theories," Broussard said. "Some of them are my own. I was a scientist in the town for a long time, and I studied the Seera system extensively. You know the asteroid belt between this world and Trikon, yes?"

"No."

Broussard looked mildly annoyed. "Well, there is one there. I believe that it was once another planet, and that Trikon is actually the fourth planet from Seera instead of the third. The mass of the asteroids suggests a planet maybe a fourth the size of Terron. But something, perhaps a comet or other large object, smashed into it and destroyed it. There is a definite geological line where much of the water on this world simply disappears;

perhaps a billion years ago. I believe it happened because the third planet was destroyed. The shock waves caused Terron's orbit to move closer to Seera, and the temperature of the planet was raised. The weather patterns shifted."

"You studied this? It was your job?"

"Actually," Broussard said, "I was a geologist. My job was to find ore to mine. I either wasn't particularly good at it or there wasn't much left to find, so I studied other things in my spare time."

He drifted into a thoughtful silence.

"You said you were one of the first to come to this system," Sky Ranger prompted.

"Yes," Broussard nodded. "I was. I grew up on Earth, and came here with my father when I was in my twenties. My stepbrothers were little at the time, and needed someone to watch them. So I did. My father had the honor of being the first human to set foot on this planet. Heh. I think he wanted to be in the history texts of generations of future Seera Terron schoolchildren. The joke is on him! There are no schoolchildren here. My stepbrothers were some of the only boys to grow up on this world."

"Are they still here?" Sky Ranger asked.

Broussard sighed. "They left; went back to Earth a long time ago. My father left, too, although he is now dead. All of the original colonists decided that Seera Terron wasn't worth their while, and migrated elsewhere. I'm all that remains. The colonists here now are transients, mainly."

"Is that why you live out here?"

"Partly," Broussard said. "But partly because I hate the town. My father built much of that town, and it's falling to ruin. The people who live there now don't like this planet, and anyway, I can't stand their noise and stench. Here in the desert, everything is clean. There are no other humans." He narrowed his eyes at Sky Ranger. "There *were* no others, at any rate."

"I'll be gone soon," Sky Ranger promised.

"You said that four days ago."

"You kept saying I could stay."

Broussard allowed a small smile to creep onto his face. "True."

They sat in silence for a moment.

"This desert is a poor place to run to," Broussard said. "I can barely keep myself fed, and I never have enough water. I haven't eaten meat in years. Run somewhere else, if you can."

"I was trying to," Sky Ranger admitted. "But my ship crashed."

"Hmpf. A strange place to crash."

"Our power regulators blew out," Sky Ranger explained. "We had no choice but to come to this system. We hoped to land outside the town here on Seera Terron and get replacement parts."

"There are no replacement parts here," Broussard scoffed. "There is nothing in the town."

"It hardly matters now," said Sky Ranger. "The ship is destroyed."

"Yes, so I gathered."

"Is there any way off this planet?" Sky Ranger asked. "What if I go to the town? Are there any ships there?"

Broussard shook his head. "No. You don't think I'd leave if I could? The ships that come from Trikon are the only ones. You won't be able to get aboard without permission."

"Permission from who?" Sky Ranger asked.

"I don't know," Broussard said. "Someone on Trikon, I suspect. The military."

"Huh," said Sky Ranger, deflating.

"Trikon is mainly a Fleet base," Broussard said. "You shouldn't go there. The Confederation Fleet is not the same thing it was a decade ago. They won't treat you kindly."

"I know."

"But... better that than staying here?" Broussard said softly.

"I don't know. I think so."

Broussard nodded. "I've thought the same myself, sometimes." The stars shone bright overhead. "Maybe it's time."

The next morning, Broussard burst in on him before he was quite awake.

"Broussard?"

He displayed a small, intermittently bleeping piece of equipment. "One of the Räton outposts started transmitting its beacon five days ago, during the storm," he said.

Sky Ranger stared mutely at the receiver.

"But that isn't what you're hearing. That's the transponder of a Confederation Fleet ship from Trikon, here to investigate."

Sky Ranger sat bolt upright. "Where?"

"It landed near the Räton beacon about half an hour ago. To the northeast, about four hundred kilometers."

Dee. Renna. Sky Ranger threw his clothes on and sprinted for the door. "I have to go!" he called. "I'm sorry! Thank you for everything!"

"Good luck!" called Broussard as Sky Ranger took to the air.

He flew as fast as he could through the cool morning air, expending as much energy as he dared. He struck out in a general northeasterly direction, and, after five hours in the air, found a few landmarks he had noted on his patrols before. He altered his trajectory and made for the oasis.

But when Sky Ranger finally arrived at the camp, no sign of

the other survivors remained.

[CHAPTER 7]

RENNA AND TWENTY-THREE OTHER REFUGEES
sat crammed knee to knee and back to back in the tiny hold
of the Confederation Fleet patrol ship Semper Idem, while the
soldiers who had captured them watched them through windows and cameras. They hadn't moved in hours. Renna had lost
all feeling in her legs, and her back had started cramping up.
Worse, she really had to pee.

"When do you think they'll let us stand?" someone whispered.

"No talking!" a voice on the intercom shouted, punctuated
by what sounded like giggles.

Just a bunch of kids, Renna thought, disgusted. They'd
been captured by teenagers with guns and a spaceship. How
humiliating.

They'd had no warning. One minute, they were waiting outside the oasis for animals to not show up, and then next a massive metal beast was roaring overhead, bound for the outpost.
Renna and the others with her, Vlad and Raul, had run as fast as
they could, but they were far too late to warn anyone. A dozen
or so Marines had streamed out of the ship, surrounding the
outpost, and suddenly everyone had been captured. Just like
that. They came meekly out of the outpost and stood trembling

where the soldiers ordered, hands in the air.

"Who the *hell* is in charge here?" a Marine with a silver ser-geant's rank pin on his collar had screamed. "Who's in *charge*?! Which of you filthy, *stinking* traitors is in charge?" The other sol-diers, most of whom didn't look old enough to start shaving, had laughed.

Renna swallowed hard and stepped forward. "I am." A rip-ple spread through the survivors. They hadn't expected anyone to claim it.

The Marine had sized her up. "So. Heading for Räton space, huh? Just like all the other traitors." He was clearly enjoying himself. "So tell me—how *many* of you damned Rattie-lovers survived the crash?"

She took a quick look around. "Um. I'm not sure. Two dozen, maybe?" Was anyone missing? Had anyone escaped? She did a mental count.

Dee wasn't there.

When had she left? Renna hadn't even noticed.

"Twenty-four," she said. "I'm pretty sure."

The Marine with the pins nodded at one of the others. "How many we got here?"

"Twenty-four, sergeant," the soldier said.

He nodded briskly. "You're all coming back to the base for processing. And *no funny stuff!* My men will shoot you dead if you make a break for it, *so don't try.*"

A couple of the soldiers sneered and mimed blowing some-one's head off with their guns. Several refugees had started to cry. Vlad, usually a stone wall, had turned white as a sheet. Mick's expression was pinched and resigned, while both Marsha and Willow looked like they were about to have panic attacks.

Renna scanned the sky without even thinking about it. *If you're out there, this would be a good time,* she thought to her-self. But Sky Ranger didn't come.

They were unceremoniously loaded onto the ship, packed into the hold, and that was that. They lifted off, and left the gray sands of Seera Terron behind.

Now, three hours later, she found her mind wandering back to Sky Ranger. Why hadn't he come back? She couldn't bring herself to believe he had been killed in the storm.

Would he find Dee? Would Dee survive by herself? The ration bars would last longer, certainly, but how long...?

She pushed the thought out of her mind. She had more immediate concerns. They'd get to Seera Trikon eventually, and... then what? She had no idea of what to expect. Would they be sent back to Earth? Or, worse, to Calvasna?

Marsha, next to her, leaned over and whispered in her ear.

"Believe in your Sky Ranger now?" she hissed. "You know he told them where we were. That's why he isn't here. That's why he left. You *know* it's true."

"No talking in there!" the loudspeaker barked, followed by another cacophony of giggles and hoots.

Renna sighed and shrugged. Her anger, usually so quick to come to the surface, was nowhere now. She didn't know what to think, but there was little point in believing the worst.

Nothing. *Nothing.* The Confederation had taken them all. Sky Ranger flew to the Räton outpost, just to make sure, and there he found the imprint of the ship's landing pads still pressed into the shifting, blowing sands.

Frantic, he took to the air, trying desperately to see where the ship had gone, but there was no sign of it. He settled back to the ground and leaned against the smooth outpost wall. Now what?

A noise—soft footfalls nearby. He sprang to his feet, ready to confront Confederation soldiers, but instead found himself face to face with a thirteen-year-old girl.

"Dee!" he exclaimed.

"Sky Ranger," she said icily, taking a step back from him.

"You're still here! Did anyone else get away?"

She scowled. "Like I'd tell *you*."

"What?"

Dee's face twisted, as if she was trying desperately to keep herself from crying. "They're *all gone*, the Fleet has them, and it's *all your fault!*"

"My fault?" Sky Ranger took a step towards her, but she backed away. "No, no. Dee, no! I came as soon as I could, but I was caught in the storm. I was injured, I had to get better."

"*Don't* patronize me!" she snapped. "*You* called the ship! *You* told them where we were! How else could they have known?"

Ah, he thought. He shook his head and pointed to the outpost.

"That thing transmits a beacon," he said. "That's how. It started transmitting during the storm."

She scowled at him. "And how do you know that?"

"There's someone else living here in the desert. An old man. He's an original settler. He picked up the beacon, and apparently, the Fleet base on Seera Trikon picked it up, too."

She seemed to weigh that for a moment. "There's no reason I should believe you."

"Is there a reason not to?" Sky Ranger shot back. He instantly regretted it.

She advanced on him. "Like a thousand! I know what you are. I know what you *did*."

He held up a hand. "I didn't know about the Reformists—"

he began, launching into his well-practiced defense. She cut him off.

"Not the Reformists. I know you took children from their families. I know you *hunted down* people who wouldn't go live in the Tower. If they didn't go with you, you *killed* them."

"It—it wasn't like that," Sky Ranger stammered, taken aback.

"Yes, it was," Dee seethed. "It *was*."

"Dee—we had to bring people into the Union. It was the law, and it was for their own protection! People—normal people, other people—they just don't know how to deal with us. With extrahumans. They've killed us before, just for being ourselves. It—it wasn't safe on the outside."

Dee looked at him, eyes narrowed.

"And we never hunted anyone. We just followed the law. The Senate passed the laws, not me. We just enforced them." He knew he was babbling, a torrent of poor excuses flowing out of his mouth. "And we never killed anyone—at least not anyone who wasn't clearly a threat to us and other people. Dee—"

"Save it," she snapped, turning her back on him. "Doesn't mean a thing to me!"

"Dee," he asked softly. "How do you know about this?"

She didn't respond.

"Was someone in your family an extrahuman, Dee?"

Dee started to walk quickly away from him. He took to the air, easily keeping pace.

"Dee, talk to me. Dee! Please. It's important."

She stopped.

"There are no more extrahumans," he said. "We're all gone. The Tower is gone, and almost all of our people with it."

"Thanks to you," she snarled.

"Not—that doesn't matter right now," he corrected hastily. "There is no more LED. There isn't a Tower to take people to. The law doesn't apply, because as far as the Senate and the Party know, extrahumans are extinct."

"So what?"

"So," he said awkwardly. "Uh. Have you ever noticed that you have really incredible luck?"

She sucked in her breath, screwed up her face and started walking away again, hands balled into tight fists. He hovered next to her.

"Tell me, Dee. How lucky are you? Is it like an impulse in your head, a sudden *need* to do something, to go somewhere? What did it feel like when you knew you had to get out of the camp?"

She turned away from him. He whipped around in front of her, blocking her path. "Dee, *how did you escape the ship from Seera Trikon?*"

Dee stopped. Tears were rolling down her face. "My grandma was one of you," she said shakily. "My grandma. She—she always knew when something bad was going to happen. So she could get out of the way. And—"

"...And?" Sky Ranger said softly.

"She could start fires. Little ones. With her mind."

A *firestarter*. Those were incredibly rare. He'd only ever met one—and the LED had been forced to kill him before he burned down an entire town.

"Dee," he started.

"*Go away*," she wailed, and bolted into the Räton outpost. The door clanged shut behind her, reacting as it always did to her presence.

He rather prudently decided not to follow her. She'd have to come out eventually.

◄►►◄◄►

Sky Ranger sat atop the Räton outpost, waiting for Dee to

re-emerge, thinking of all the ways he had managed to screw things up. She had a lot of ideas about the Law Enforcement Division and Sky Ranger himself, probably from her grandmother. She was scared, traumatized, and alone, and he had pushed her. Brilliant, as usual. Guilt sucked at him.

Firestarting was the rarest of the range of abilities that extrahumans could manifest. He wondered if she had inherited it. Sometimes abilities would skip generations before manifesting again. Sometimes they'd disappear entirely. Sometimes they even came and went in the same person over time. Extrahuman powers were a mystery.

Dee had certainly inherited the luck. He wondered about her parents. Maybe they hadn't had any abilities at all, or maybe they'd been extrahumans like her. Hard to know.

He wondered if that had been what they were running from. It must have been a nightmare to have someone who embodied all their worst fears floating around on the same refugee ship. For a brief instant he saw himself as they must have, threatening and unpredictable. Some luck.

"Hey," a voice called. Dee stood outside the outpost, looking up at him. "You haven't called the ship back?"

He spread his hands. "You think I can do that?"

"Yes."

"Well, I can't. I wouldn't even know where to start."

She grimaced and studied the sand beneath her bare feet. "... You really didn't bring them here?"

"No. I really didn't."

She seemed to decide something. "I think I found the thing that's making the beacon. So you aren't lying about that."

He flew down to her. "Believe it or not, I don't have any reason to lie to you."

"I *don't* believe it," she said, backing off again. He kept his distance. "I shouldn't trust you."

"No?"

"Admit it. You did hunt people down when they wouldn't join the Union."

He sighed. "If you like. That was the law."

"And you *did* kill some people."

"Yes. But only when they tried to hurt us, or hurt other people. Believe me, I didn't like doing that."

"But you *did* like rounding people up?"

He considered for a moment. "I... don't know. It was a job. I can't say I liked it or disliked it. I just did it."

She glared defiantly at him.

He took a deep breath. "Dee. I'm... sorry. For what happened. All of that. But... I've been trying to make up for it. I've been fighting the Reformists for three years." He allowed some of the bitterness he felt to come through. "Three long, awful years. I had to run eventually, or they would have killed me. Even I'm not indestructible, so... One more dead extrahuman." He looked away. "*They* killed my people. *Our* people. I woke up then, and I fought back. It was too late... but I could never work with them now."

Dee continued to glower at him. "I still don't trust you."

"I know."

"And I don't like you."

He nodded.

"...I *am* an extrahuman," she said defiantly. "Like my grandmother."

"I know," he said.

"But there is no Tower," she insisted, waving a finger at him. "You can't take me anywhere. I'm free, and I'm going to stay that way."

He nodded again. "Right. Agreed."

"Okay. Good."

They stood there for a moment, staring at one another.

"So," she said at last. "How do we save the others?"

[CHAPTER 8]

PENNY KNELT IN SANDI'S GARDEN, EXAMINING the fragile plants for any signs of the voracious buglike critters that had been eating the tomato crop.

She picked another one off, and flicked it away with her finger. She followed it with her eyes as it hopped around the garden, then leapt up onto one of the other plants and disappeared. At least it wasn't the pack pigs this time.

This planet. She made a face and decided to give up for the day. She stood and stretched, then lifted off the ground to float back to the house.

There was a note for her in the mailbox. An actual letter? How strange. The return address was that of the Temple in West Arve.

Penny looked around, thinking maybe Monica had returned from her wanderings. However, no one in a blue outfit was visible anywhere nearby.

She opened the letter, and scanned its brief contents.

Penny, it read. *Please come to the Temple as soon as you are able. There is a matter of great importance for us to discuss. –Celeste, Prelate, West Arve Temple*

Penny thought about the note for a while, then stuck it in her pocket. Two impulses warred within her: first, to ignore what was basically a summons from the Temple, as her rather contrary nature told her she should; and second, to find out about whatever this "matter of great importance" was, and whether it had anything to do with Sky Ranger.

Curiosity, and the need to know more about her old lover, won out. She started packing, intending to set out soon. LaNant would not miss her.

In contrast to her sister planet, Seera Trikon froze Renna to the bone, even at the Fleet base near the equator. She shuddered to think what the planet must be like farther north or south.

The refugees were marched off the ship and into two wide, poorly heated cells, divided by gender. The guards shut the iron doors with a clang, then withdrew to another, warmer room.

And that was that.

Renna did a quick count. Okay. Then she counted again, and a few times more.

"Well," Marsha said disgustedly. "Now what?"

Renna started pacing around the room. Marsha and her cronies took up a bench over by the wall separating them from the men. They could hear subdued murmurings coming from beyond it. Anna, Luci, and Allison sat on the other bench, on the other side of the room. Willow had taken herself off into a corner, where she had sat on the ground and started crying. Tricia went to comfort her.

"Hey," Tricia said, few traces of kindness in her voice. "Hey, shut up, kid. It's not so bad."

Anna, a Russian woman who almost never spoke, gave a short, sharp laugh. "Huh. It's bad. We won't get away. She's right to cry. This is the end for us."

Her benchmates, Allison and Luci, agreed. "They'll take us to Calvasna, I bet," Luci said. "No escape from there."

"I've heard stories about the military's headquarters. I hear they paint the walls with blood," Allison concurred, with a certain relish. Willow started shaking with terror. Renna glimpsed a small smile on Allison's pinched face.

"Stop pacing," Marsha snapped at Renna. "You'll drive us nuts."

"There must be something," Renna said, more to herself than anyone else. "There must be. It can't end like this."

Marsha shrugged. "And if it does? So what. Look. I've lived with the possibility of death or worse happening to me for so long, I don't even get scared anymore."

Renna looked out at the bars and the gray, featureless hallway beyond. "Yeah. I know what it's like." Every night for months in Toronto, waiting huddled under the covers with Amy... sometimes they'd hear the boots in the hallway, and thank God when they took someone else. "It wasn't legal to be me," she said. "I was always afraid."

It struck her then: she'd left her pack back on Seera Terron. She sat down heavily, crushed, as everyone else jabbered around her.

"I shouldn't even be here!" Willow wailed. "I never wanted to leave! I should be warm and safe back on Earth!"

"Why *did* you leave, then?" Allison snapped. "Just decide to go on a cruise to Räton space?"

Willow shook her head. "N-no. My boyfriend. He—he published something about the Black Bands, and what they'd done. When we were back home in Texas. They—they'd stolen something from people, and hurt them—I guess just because they could. I don't know. Maybe there was a reason. But it wasn't supposed to happen, you know? But my b-boyfriend, he saw it and then he wrote about it, and posted it online."

Someone whistled. "That was stupid," Marsha said. Everything on any network was monitored by sophisticated surveillance programs, everyone knew that.

Willow rocked back and forth. "He was idealistic. So obviously they found out who did it, and we had to go on the run. I was in my third year at college. I was going to graduate, and be a teacher. And now?" She dissolved into sobs again.

"What were you going to teach?"

"Little kids," Willow said bitterly, wiping a wisp of dirty blonde hair away from her face. "I wanted to teach first form—you know, like six-year olds. The kids are so sweet and cute... and fun. And so innocent! *They* don't care about all this stuff. But Ryan, he was so—he wanted to change everything. He said that if people just could know the truth—but no one cared! People barely read it. That was the worst part. No one even said anything. The only thing that happened was that we had to run away." She sniffled and wiped her nose with her arm. "He died in the crash."

Around the room, women nodded. They all had stories like that: Things they'd done, or were suspected of doing. Things relatives had done. People they knew and loved, dead in the wreck of twisted metal and gray sand back on Seera Terron.

Everyone fell silent for a while. Allison got up to use the toilet, which was, embarrassingly, in the cell with them. "What?" she snapped when everyone's eyes got big. "None of you ever been in prison before?"

After a while, a guard came and pointed at Renna. "Come on," he said. "The captain wants to talk to you."

She was allowed out of the cell, which the guard, a kid who had to be no more than eighteen, then clumsily relocked. Allison rushed the door and started pulling at the bars and swearing at the top of her lungs. The guard recoiled, and pointed his weapon at her. "Shut up!" he said. Allison sat back down, face twisted into a terrible leering grin. "Let's go," he said to Renna.

"Are you kidding?" Renna heard Allison saying to the others as she was escorted down the hall. "That's how you get inside their minds. That's how you *mess* with them. You're all such wimps!"

◆➤◄◆

Captain Veselinovich was a skinny, depressed-looking man with a pencil-thin mustache and short, graying hair. His spartan office had one distinctive feature—a huge window overlooking the camp and the wilderness beyond.

"You're the leader of this group we brought in?" he asked in lightly accented English as Renna entered. "Sit down." She sat in a chair in front of his desk. Behind him, she could see an endless, frozen ice field. Her eyes widened a little.

"It is winter, here," he explained, following her gaze. "You've come at a bad time. In summer, which we'll have in a few more years, the ice melts and there is water. It's quite beautiful." He examined a datapad in front of him. "So. Your ship was the transport *Holy Mission of Mary?*"

The lie. The false beacon. A flicker of hope rose in Renna's breast. The captain had made sure everyone knew their cover before they left. "Yes. That's us. We were on our way to Mantillies—"

Captain Veselinovich held up a hand. "Stop. I know it's a lie. The ship is an unregistered Sikorsky-Drummond-600, belonging to Jackie Nabors of Halifax, Nova Scotia, North America. A known refugee smuggler. So you are refugees. Going to the Rätons."

It wasn't a question. Renna didn't say a word.

"You don't have to answer. I know. We scanned you. You're all on file. You, for instance: Ramon Fernández Silva."

Renna flinched.

Veselinovich continued, relentless. "UNP local committee before Black Rock. Took part in a demonstration in Toronto against the government. Sexual deviant. And your close confederate, Amy Delacroix, was an influential member of the Student Alliance, a group on the terror watch list."

Renna said nothing. She'd sat across from men like Veselinovich many times before. They liked to talk, and it was usually best to let them.

"Well, it's all here anyway," he said. "I assume that she died in the wreck. But there is one passenger that you can tell me more about. He was a tall man with dark hair, but you would have remembered him. He could fly, although he may have hidden this from you. He was called Sky Ranger. Do you know of him?"

Renna decided on a mostly truthful path. Safer. "Yes. He was on the ship."

"We know that," said the captain, seeming bored. "Yet we did not find his remains on board, and he's not here. So. Where is he?"

Renna shrugged. "I don't know. He flew off. He was lost in a storm."

"No," the captain said. "Tell me the truth now. Save yourself some trouble later."

Renna's heart jumped into her throat. "What? Are you...?"

He smiled briefly, but it didn't reach his eyes. "Contrary to what you might believe, we aren't monsters. We are Confederation Fleet, still. We won't torture you, if that's what you're worried about. But... other charges may be laid against you if you don't cooperate. It's easier not to lie. So. Tell me the truth."

In Renna's experience, these kinds of men always said they weren't monsters just before acting monstrously. She braced herself.

"I'm sorry to say that I just did," she said, trying to keep her voice from shaking. "There was a huge sandstorm about a week ago. He went looking for two people who were missing. None of them ever came back."

"Well," said the captain. "I suppose that if you're lying, it'll come out when they hook you up to their machines. And then things will be worse for you." He paused, letting that sink in, giving her a last chance. "Very well. So. Since you're the leader, or what passes for it, I'll send this message to the others through you." He glanced at his screen and recited: "You have been detained and charged under the Emergency Law, and are all scheduled for trial for your various offenses, including and especially attempting to leave human space for the territory of a hostile alien government, at the Special Emergency Court on Calvasna."

Renna felt a dull shock of panic run through her. No one came back from Calvasna. She met the captain's sad, brown eyes.

"Please," Renna said, desperately trying to play on his sympathies. "You can't believe we deserve what they'll give us there. Protesting and belonging to a political party didn't used to be treason!"

He shook his head. "It's only the law. My job is to uphold the law."

"How did you wind up posted out here?" Renna asked, trying a different tack. "It doesn't seem like a very prestigious posting."

"That," said the captain sharply, "is none of your business." He looked up at the guard. "Take her back to the cell."

◁▷ ► ◄▷

After Renna had been taken away, Captain Veselinovich sat

and worried about what he should do next. He knew what he was expected to do. He knew his orders, which had come as part of a pack sent to all stations between Earth and the Räton border.

He was a soldier. He should do his duty. Still, he hesitated. What harm would come from not saying anything? There was no way off of Seera Terron.

But if they found out, they'd do more than banish him to the least pleasant station in Confederation space. And if he did his duty, maybe he'd finally get to come home. And it *was* his duty. What was left beyond duty?

We are Confederation Fleet, still.

The captain sighed again and thumbed the communications button on his console.

"Sergeant," he said to the young man who appeared on screen. "Please send a message to Major Vasna at Military Command. Sky Ranger is alive and presumably on Seera Terron."

"Understood," said the sergeant, and the screen winked off. Captain Veselinovich leaned back in his chair. There. He'd done it. Surely they'd reward him. Surely.

He reached into his desk and withdrew a little crystal flask full of amber liquid. He took a swig and leaned back in his chair, turning slowly to stare blankly at the endless ice fields beyond.

They were so beautiful. He took another drink.

[CHAPTER 9]

SKY RANGER AGAIN SAT AT BROUSSARD'S table, drinking a thin tea that the old man had gleefully explained was made by straining hot water through thin strips of *lyski* moss. It was, Sky Ranger realized sadly, almost exactly like the soup, only more watery. He forced himself to drink about half of it before giving up.

Dee and Broussard got along famously. She had been full of questions for the old man ever since their arrival: "How long have you been here? Are those big solar panels? Wow! I've never seen a whole place running on them. Is there any food besides moss? Ever kill a plate monster? Can we take a ride in your car?" And so on. Broussard had been delighted to answer all of her questions in detail, and was even now showing her his water collection system.

Together, they'd flown back to Broussard's rocky home, Dee clinging tightly to Sky Ranger's back. He'd gone as fast as he dared, thinking the experience would surely terrify her. But she'd slipped off his back once they landed and jumped up and down, a wide grin on her face. "That was amazing! I want to do it again! You're so lucky! My power is completely worthless: Why can't I *fly*?"

He was glad to see her in a better mood. She hadn't been

happy when, after she asked what they could do to rescue the others, he shrugged and said he had no idea. *That's a shitty plan,* she had snapped angrily. And he agreed. It was. But he had no better ideas, so after arguing for a few minutes, they'd given up and flown to Broussard's. At least it was a direction. Fortunately, she and Broussard had taken a liking to one another instantly, and both had been visibly happier since.

It made him feel a little left out, actually.

He sipped his moss tea and grimaced, trying not to think about coffee, bacon, or anything else he actually considered food.

"Hey," said Dee, bouncing up the stairs. "Did you know you can *eat* that moss stuff we were finding everywhere? We were just *burning* it! Isn't that incredible?"

"Yeah," said Sky Ranger gloomily, setting his "tea" down. "It sure is."

"Trikon isn't easy to get to," Broussard commented over a meal of steamed, rolled moss and ration bars salvaged from the campsite. "First, you'll need a ship. Terron doesn't have many, sad to say. I knew of a few old ships at the settlement, but I doubt they're still there—or if they were, that they still fly. And then you'll need to actually get there, and land, without being shot out of the sky."

"Right. Then we'd need to get into the base, free our friends, get out, and get away into hyperspace," said Dee. "What's so hard about that?"

Broussard and Sky Ranger just looked at her.

"You're kidding," Sky Ranger said. "You know it's impossible, right?"

"Please," said Dee airily. "Aren't you some sort of incredible flying man with great strength and tons of combat experience? Can't you do it?"

Broussard chuckled.

"I really doubt it," said Sky Ranger after an uncomfortable pause. He wasn't feeling particularly incredible at the moment. "Maybe, if I was on my own, I could sneak in there. Maybe. But I'd have a hard time getting anyone out." He shook his head. "I just don't think it's possible."

"You're pathetic," Dee said. "Broussard, how many people on that base?"

Broussard thought it over. "Well. There's the command staff. The ships' crews... support staff, Marines, and civilians. Eh. Maybe fifty?

"That isn't *that* many," said Dee.

"That's a *lot*," Sky Ranger retorted. "You forget. They have guns, armor, and vehicles. And they'd see us coming a hundred thousand miles away. We'd be destroyed by their ships before we even got to the planet. And that's assuming we could even get a ship to begin with!"

Dee's good mood was evaporating quickly. "But we can't just abandon them. We can't! Sky Ranger, come on," she pleaded. "We have to do something."

Sky Ranger and Broussard exchanged glances.

"There may be a way," Broussard said slowly. "But we'd need to get very, very lucky for it to work."

Dee grinned fiercely. "I can do luck! What's the plan?"

The ancient hopper appeared as a speck low down on the horizon. Dee pointed and clapped her hands. "There he is! I can see him!"

Sky Ranger squinted. Definitely a flying craft of some kind, heading their way.

"I can't see him yet," said Broussard. "But I'll take your word. He's right on schedule. He's a good kid."

"Should be here in a couple of minutes," said Sky Ranger. "He's expecting us, right?"

Broussard nodded. "Got your gear together?"

Dee hefted her pack. "Yup!"

"We have some ration bars left," said Sky Ranger. "I'm bringing them."

"Good idea," said Broussard. "I'm tired to death of that moss!"

They watched as the hopper grew larger, then banked and began its descent. Soon, the chunky, durable craft had settled onto the sands next to Broussard's place with a whine and a massive cloud of dust and exhaust. Broussard, Sky Ranger and Dee walked out to meet it.

The door opened, and a gangly young man of maybe seventeen tromped down the gangway. "Mr. Broussard!" he cried. "Good to see you, old man!"

"Felipe!" Broussard beamed, grabbing the young man in a bear hug. "It's been too long!"

"And who are these, then?" Felipe asked. "Your people you found in the desert?"

Broussard was about to say something when Dee pushed forward. "Hi! I'm Dee. Nice to meet you, Felipe!" She smiled her widest, toothiest smile at him, causing the young man to laugh.

"Uh. Yes, I found both Dee here and... him... lost out there," said Broussard, pointing at Sky Ranger.

"No name?" asked Felipe.

"Uh. You can call me Ted," said Sky Ranger, trying desperately to come up with something. Dee rolled her eyes.

Felipe laughed. "Okay, Ted! Well, you got anything to bring on board? If not, we can get going back."

"Sounds good," Broussard said, heading for the gangplank. "Let's go."

Sky Ranger trotted over to him. "You're coming?"

Broussard nodded, a rare sharpness in his eyes. "I am."

"You're sure?" Sky Ranger asked. "You'd give this up?"

Broussard looked back at his cave home. "You could use the help," he said. "And like I said, it's time."

Who was Sky Ranger to tell him no?

They walked up the gangway and into the hopper. Seats lined the cargo area, and Sky Ranger and Dee strapped themselves in. Broussard took the co-pilot's seat next to Felipe.

"All aboard?" Felipe asked. "Got all your stuff? House secure?"

"No," said Broussard. "But it isn't like I need to worry about the neighbors."

Felipe laughed again, eyes bright. "Well, all right then! Let's get going." He brought the powerful engines of the hopper to life, and wrenched the short, squat craft off the ground with a stomach-turning jolt. "Back to civilization we go!" he called as the hopper made a wide, banking turn and, with a groan and a shudder, shot off into the early morning sky.

The trip took less time than Sky Ranger had expected. Because Seera Terron had no other air traffic, and no cities below to worry about sonic booms, Felipe could push the creaky hopper to its speed limit, and take the most direct route. In all, nearly eleven thousand kilometers vanished in only about three hours. They passed through morning into night, and back into evening and afternoon.

Broussard chatted with Felipe for a while in the front of the hopper while Dee pretended to nap. But as soon as Broussard retired to the back to talk with Sky Ranger, she bolted out of her seat and took the co-pilot's chair. Soon, she and the young man were having an animated conversation about some point of recent pop culture that Sky Ranger couldn't penetrate.

Broussard chuckled. "Anywhere else, they'd never talk. Too far apart in age. But Felipe never sees other kids, so he likes talking to them. Everyone else in the settlement is old enough to be his mother or father. And your girl looks very happy."

She did, in fact. "There weren't any other children at the camp," said Sky Ranger. "I think she was lonely. And I wouldn't call her 'my girl,' either."

"No?" said Broussard. "Still, it must be hard for her. No parents, no family or friends. You'd never know it to look at her."

Sky Ranger had to agree. "She's strong. Everyone has limits, but she hasn't found hers yet."

The featureless desert gave way to wind-rounded hills and rocky mountains, then more desert. "Aren't there any forests or grasslands on this planet?" Sky Ranger wondered, watching the ground speed by below.

"No," said Broussard. "Only desert and mountains, and the somewhat nicer lands around the lake. They're sort of half desert, half bush. Sort of. It's like scrub. You'll see. But it isn't what you'd call lush." He leaned back in his chair. "Now I remember Earth, from when I was a boy. We lived in the mountains of France, near the border with Switzerland. I remember green, and snow, and high jagged mountains everywhere. And I remember a yellow sun in a deep blue sky. But it seems so long ago, that even the memory is alien to me. As if the sky and the ground couldn't have really been that color. They must have been blue-white and gray, and I'm just forgetting."

Sky Ranger looked out the window. "All I really know is New York," he said. "That's where I grew up, in the Tower. I spent my entire life there."

"Did it rain much?"

"All the time," said Sky Ranger. "And it snowed every year. We had hot summers and cold winters."

"Do you miss it?"

"Sometimes. But I try not to think about it." He looked out the window at the landscape below. "I wish I had seen more of Earth. I mostly just saw one small patch of North America, and another piece of Australia. When I was on the run, I actually flew through a lot more of the world, but I didn't have time to pay attention. I wish I could go back and see it again."

"Maybe things will change," said Broussard.

Sky Ranger shook his head, and a heavy, maudlin sadness settled on him. "No, they won't. Not until a little boy grows up, somewhere."

Broussard gave him an odd look.

"It's... it's something someone I once knew said. That there was a little boy who would fix everything when he grew up... if he grew up in the right place."

"And how did your friend know that?" asked Broussard.

"He was like me," said Sky Ranger softly. "He had a different power, he knew the future sometimes. But I believe he saw the truth."

"And is the boy growing up? In the right place?"

Sky Ranger smiled a fierce little smile at the memory. One time, long ago, he'd done the right thing. "Yes, I think so."

"So long... that does mean you can't go back to Earth, if it's true."

"No. I can't. I'll probably never see it again." He sighed, his smile sagging into a frown.

"Do you think *they* ever will?" Broussard waved a hand at Dee and Felipe laughing in the front of the hopper.

"I hope so," said Sky Ranger. "If I can just do one thing right, it'll be that she grows up to see the end of the Reformists."

"You seem to care very much about her. Did you know her, before?"

"No, I didn't," Sky Ranger said. "I barely know her now. But she's one of my people. So yes, I do care. I think my people may be all I've ever cared about."

The hopper sped onward across the face of an empty world, drawing ever nearer to the one tiny speck of human civilization that clung to it.

Mountains gave way to gray, windswept desert plains again, and then, wonder of wonders, to *water*. Sky Ranger couldn't help staring. He hadn't seen so much water in one place since leaving Earth; he'd given up on ever finding it here on Seera Terron.

"The Lakes of Judas," Broussard said. "There are twelve, all different sizes. That one, I think, is Lake Seven. They're salty, undrinkable. Ha! That's Terron's little joke. But if you look around the edges, you'll see plants living there, and there are some fish living in the lakes themselves. Not many, but some." He smiled grimly. "Saltiest fish you'll ever have. And I expect we'll all have some. Not much else to eat in Hauptstadt."

The hopper began its long, slow descent towards the surface. Sky Ranger strained his eyes searching for signs of human habitation—a farm, a boat on the lake, a building. He found nothing.

Then, almost without warning, the ground was next to him as the hopper settled into the middle of a gray, sandy field. Off in the distance, Sky Ranger spied a cluster of buildings standing lonely against the flat horizon. Hauptstadt, the capital and only town.

"Well, this is it," Broussard sighed. "Back home again."

"Hey, we're here!" Felipe said, shutting the engines down. He stood, but gracefully swept an arm out in front of him, bowing to Dee. "After you."

Dee blushed and hurried forward. The ramp lowered, and the heat of the day blasted them. Sky Ranger wilted.

"Eh, it's colder here," Broussard said as he stepped out into the sunlight. "I'd forgotten."

"I don't know how you don't melt in the heat out there, old man!" Felipe laughed. "You must have fire in the veins."

"Where's the town?" asked Dee impatiently. "I don't see anything!" Felipe pointed to the cluster of faraway structures, and her face fell visibly.

"Well," Sky Ranger said. "We're here. What do we do now?"

"Scrap yard," Broussard said. "Time to go scavenging for something that'll get us off this rock."

"What?" Felipe said. "You're leaving?"

Broussard's eyes narrowed. "Could be."

"Hey," Felipe said. "What's the plan? Come on, let me in on it. You never told me who these folks are, or where they came from!"

"Maybe later," Broussard muttered. "First, we're headed to the scrap yard. Is Tony still there?"

Felipe shook his head. "Nah. Tony left for Earth last year. His ma was sick; he had to go home and see her."

"Oh." Broussard's face fell even further. "Well. Who's running the place?"

"Max is," Felipe said. "He's the guy Tony hired as a helper. He used to be part of the Fleet on Trikon, but left."

"Max? You mean Max, the guy who used to fly the supply ships?" Broussard's face took on a thoughtful expression. "Huh. All right, let's go see him. Felipe, thanks for the lift."

"Sure, no problem," Felipe said. "Hey, come by my place later. Saltfish for dinner!"

Broussard shuddered visibly. "I despise those fish," he said. "But we'll be by."

"See you there?" Felipe asked Dee. She giggled and nodded.

Felipe ran off with a laugh and a wave.

◀▷▶ ◀◁▷

Hauptstadt was less a town than a loosely associated, widely spaced accumulation of buildings. Everything was far from everything else.

"Where are all the people?" Dee wanted to know. Sky Ranger had been silently asking himself the same question.

Broussard shrugged in his Gallic way. "Mines, some of them, or out fishing. Not many folks come out during the day anyway. Too hot, they say." He snorted his opinion of people who thought the current searing weather was anything more than balmy.

After another half hour of marching in sweaty silence, they reached the scrap yard's gate. A tiny shop stood next to the massive, locked entrance. Broussard poked his head into the shop.

"Max? It's Émile Broussard! Max, are you there?"

Shuffling, clanking, and swearing came from the back room. A short, squat man emerged.

"Broussard," he stated.

"Hello, Max. How are you?"

Max spat on the floor. The gesture seemed less rudeness than foul habit. "What'cha want?"

"To go in!" Broussard waved at the gate. "What do you think? We want to look and see if you have any working ships in there. And do you?"

Max grunted. "Got lots of stuff. Maybe something you could fix up. Go in and see." He pressed a button, and the huge gates outside began to rasp, clank, and scream open. "But I got video. Don't steal nothin'."

"We won't, Max," Broussard promised as they left.

"He didn't seem nice," Dee said. "What's his problem?"

"He's a donkey," Broussard said cheerfully as they marched through the gate.

◄►► ◄◄►

Ships, machines, and other broken metal husks sat scattered on the ground for as far as Sky Ranger could see.

"Some scrap yard," he remarked to Broussard, who shrugged again.

"Machines break down easy here, and we have lots of space to put them," he said. "Let's go and see."

They wandered among the silent hulks, pausing here and there while Broussard inspected the outer hulls, or took a look at some arcane piece of machinery within.

"How long is this going to take?" Dee asked while Broussard immersed himself in the study of yet another wreck. "I'm starving."

"I have no idea," Sky Ranger said. "Do you want a ration bar?"

Dee made a face. "I guess."

Broussard came back out of the ship. "No, this one's no good," he said. "There's a big hole in the side, and half the engine is gone. Plus, I think there's mice. Come on." He strode gamely forward, towards the remains of yet another massive, ruined cargo ship.

"This plan is nuts," Dee said angrily. "None of these ships will ever fly again." She sighed and took a bite of the ration bar Sky Ranger had given her. "Yuck, it's warm. Where did you have it, your pocket?"

"Everything is warm," Sky Ranger said, exasperated. "It's the desert."

"Oh, right, it's the desert! I'd forgotten. And seriously, this is the best he could come up with?"

"I don't think there are many other options," Sky Ranger said. "From what he told me, the only other ship that comes here is a Confederation Fleet supply ship. There aren't enough people on the planet for a regular run by passenger ships."

"Great," Dee said. She sighed, looked around, and then

perked up, like a cat spotting a bug on the wall.

"Dee?" Sky Ranger asked.

"Shut up," she said, and walked determinedly off towards a ship that had all but collapsed in on itself.

"Dee, that ship looks dangerous," Sky Ranger said, breaking into a run. Immediately, his leg muscles started to whine in agony. He hated running. He never ran. He always flew. But he couldn't take the risk, not if Max might see him. "Dee!" he puffed as she receded into the distance. "Slow down!"

She shot him a quick, contemptuous look and disappeared into the ship. He looked around, and, seeing no one watching, levitated a few inches off the ground and shot forward with a burst of speed. He arrived at the ship within a few seconds, and settled back to the ground. "Dee?"

"In here," she called, the sound muffled by the interior walls of the ship. He followed her voice down a dark and musty corridor, and into an open space. Light seeped in through several holes in the ceiling.

"Look," she said, pointing.

There, in the middle of the bay, sat a shiny, new four-person shuttlecraft.

Sky Ranger ran his hand appreciatively over the hull, pretending to know something about space vessels. He'd never cared much about flying vehicles, though. Why would he? "It's nice," he said. "I wonder what it's doing here?"

"I bet it belongs to that Max guy," Dee said.

Sky Ranger looked around. "This is a good hiding place, if so. No one would think of looking here. Except you." He regarded her. "That's a useful power you have."

"Thanks!" she said, beaming.

◂▸▸ ◂◂▸

Broussard let out a low whistle when he laid his eyes on the shuttle. "Now that's a nice ship," he said. "Looks almost new. But why is it here?"

"Dee thinks it belongs to Max," Sky Ranger said. "Makes sense, right?"

"Yes," said Broussard. "He was always paranoid, so I wouldn't have trouble believing he'd have a ship ready to go, should he need one. And it's well-hidden. How did you find it?"

"*I* found it," Dee said smugly. "I got lucky."

Sky Ranger exchanged glances with Broussard, but neither said anything.

"So," Dee said. "Now what do we do? Can we buy it?"

"With what?" Sky Ranger said.

Broussard waved his hand dismissively. "I have money, don't worry. I have plenty. But he might not want to sell it. In fact, I know he won't." He looked around. "Let's go," he said. "We can talk more later."

They marched back outside. Broussard leaned in and whispered to Sky Ranger, "Max has cameras everywhere. He's probably watching us now." Then, louder, he said, "Let's go look at some more ships." Dee groaned.

When they made it back to the little shop, exhausted, Max was waiting for them with a scowl on his face. "Well?" he asked. "See anything?"

"That shuttle in the ruined hanger," blurted Dee before anyone could stop her, "Is it yours? Can we buy it?"

Max didn't seem surprised by the question, which confirmed what Broussard had said. "Not for sale."

"You have a lot of junk out there," Broussard said. "Nothing that will fly."

"Why do you want a ship?" Max said, fixing them with a beady-eyed, suspicious glare. "Where do you want to go? And who are these people you brought with you? I haven't seen them before."

"I just want to buy a ship, so I can leave this planet like everybody else," Broussard said haughtily. "What do you think?"

Max laughed unpleasantly. "You? Leave? I don't believe it. No, don't tell me; you didn't find God out in the desert after all, so you're going to go look on another planet? Right?"

Broussard said nothing, but a dark look crossed his face.

"So tell me," Max said sharply, "Where did you get the little girl? And what about the man who can *fly*?"

Sky Ranger felt his blood turn to ice.

Max snickered. "Maybe you should go while you can. Before I let Trikon know what's happening here."

Abruptly, Broussard spun on his heels and strode from the shop. Sky Ranger and Dee followed quickly, Max's laughter ringing in their ears.

◀▶▶ ◀◀▶

"I had forgotten how angry he makes me," Broussard said, shaking visibly. "Oh! I wish I had punched him in the nose."

"You don't think he was serious about telling Trikon about us?" Sky Ranger asked, worried despite himself. *When did I become so afraid?*

Broussard shook his head. "No, I don't think so. He hates the people on Trikon even more than he hates the people who live here."

"You're sure?" Sky Ranger pressed.

"Yes," Broussard said testily. "Don't worry about it."

"So what do we do now?" Sky Ranger asked, trying not to worry about it.

"Why are you asking me? You're the man of action," Broussard said. "And this was all I had thought to do!"

"Well, I say we go eat dinner with Felipe," Dee said. "I'm hungry, it's getting dark, and we need to come up with a real plan for how we're going to get to Trikon and free our friends."

Sky Ranger and Broussard both deflated. "All right," Sky Ranger said. "Where is it?"

Broussard pointed. "Not far. Over this way, toward the shore."

"What was that thing Max said?" Sky Ranger asked Broussard as they walked, "About you finding God in the desert?"

Broussard's brows creased. "That's my business," he snapped.

◄►► ◄►►

Felipe lived next to the lake in a tiny tumbledown shack that looked as if it had been cobbled together from the remains of older, larger shacks. Still, he had the lights on and white, spongy saltfish set on four plates for them at his neat, clean table.

"The chairs don't match," he said apologetically. "But the plates and cups are a set from my mom. So go ahead, sit and eat! Caught fresh yesterday."

Broussard wrinkled his nose. "Haven't had saltfish in a decade," he grumbled. "And it's too soon, I say."

"Oh, go on and take a bite!" Felipe said, cheer undimmed. "It'll bring back all the old days, right?"

Dee sat and poked at the fish experimentally. She took a bite and burst into a surprised grin. "It's good!" she said, diving into the rest. Sky Ranger sat in the remaining rickety chair and bit into the fish.

He immediately reached for the water. He'd never had fish this salty. Worse, once you got past the salt, the fish tasted gamy and had a tough, rubbery texture. It was like eating a tire made of salt, with a hint of rotten squid.

"Well?" Felipe asked eagerly. "What do you think?"

"Great!" said Dee, mouth full of fish.

"Very tasty," Sky Ranger managed politely.

"Peh," Broussard spat, stabbing the fish with his fork. "Misery on a plate. I don't suppose you have any moss to get the taste out of my mouth?"

Felipe laughed. "You and that moss! I can't stand to eat it! I don't know how you stay alive, old man!" But the laughter didn't quite reach his eyes.

"Well," Sky Ranger said, popping as much of the fish as he could stand in his mouth and chewing hastily. "I think it's very good. Thank you, Felipe."

Dee put her fork down with a clang. Felipe winced. "Have any more?" she asked.

Felipe shook his head. "Sorry, all there was."

Dee's face fell. "Aww."

"Take mine," Broussard said, sliding it off his plate onto hers. She dug in with gusto.

"You live here alone?" Sky Ranger asked.

"He does," Broussard said, gesturing with his fork. "You can't tell from the mess? A bachelor, this one."

Felipe nodded. "Yah. It's mine. Been ever since my dad left for Earth."

"Wow," exclaimed Dee in between bites. "Your own place! When did your dad leave?"

"When I was eight," Felipe said.

Sky Ranger couldn't think of anything to say. Dee looked shocked. Broussard spoke into the lengthening silence. "His dad was a drifter. He came here looking for work with Felipe and his wife. Then the wife died, and the father decided to go back to Earth without him. A couple of the pilots took Felipe in, made sure he had food. I made sure he had some money."

Felipe nodded. "Mr. Broussard gave me the money to buy my hopper," he said. "But I think he just wanted me to come visit him in the desert!"

Sky Ranger wondered how an old hermit had had enough money to buy an aircraft, but said nothing. Broussard was full of mystery.

"Ha," Broussard snorted, but he was smiling. "And you never do! Ingrate."

"Old crank!" Felipe retorted playfully.

"You see?" Broussard said, laughing. "You see how he treats me! After all I've done? Saltfish and insults."

"So Broussard and the pilots were like your family?" Dee asked.

Felipe nodded. "Sure, but most of them are gone now, too. Back to Earth, or to another colony world. So it's just me anymore. Town's getting smaller."

"Which is how it is here," Broussard said. "I told you so. People don't want to stay. Felipe, I've told you that you should go, too."

"I like it here," said Felipe. "And you stay."

Broussard shrugged the same shrug he always gave. "I'm me. You're a young man. You should go see the Confederation! Go to Earth, see France. It's very nice there."

"Only when you come with me," Felipe said.

"Or when I'm dead and gone," Broussard replied.

After the meal, they sat at the table—other than Felipe's bed, it was the only place in the shack they could sit—and told Felipe what had happened at the scrap yard.

"So," Felipe said. "Max has a shuttle. I'm not surprised. I knew he was hiding something in there, with all the video he has put up. Who would bother stealing scrap? There's nowhere to sell it but the scrap yard!"

"Max gave us a hard time," Broussard said. "But he's a fool!"

Felipe's smile sagged. "Hey, don't mess with him too much," he warned. "He's the Party guy, you know."

Broussard's eyebrows flew upwards. "What? What do you mean? The Reform Party?"

Felipe nodded, glancing nervously around. "He's the head of the Reform Party on the planet."

"*Here?*" Sky Ranger asked, shocked.

"Yeah, believe it. A couple of the guys from the mines joined, so it's a real organization. He's got a direct line to Trikon, and he and the others report on what people get up to in town. Sometimes Trikon people come and take them away. So I wouldn't piss him off."

"But Max hated the military!" Broussard said. "He hated the government!"

Felipe shook his head. "He hated the *old* government. He hated the military as it *used* to be under the UNP. But he thinks the Reformists are great."

Broussard glanced at Sky Ranger. "That could be bad for us."

"He probably reported me," Sky Ranger said. "A ship from Seera Trikon could be on its way."

Felipe's smile disappeared entirely. "What do you mean? Why would Trikon be looking for you, Ted?"

Sky Ranger sighed. "My name's Sky Ranger," he said. Broussard opened his mouth, but closed it again, shaking his head in frustration. "Sorry, Broussard. I'm not used to hiding. Felipe, I'm an extrahuman. Do you know what those are?"

Felipe rolled his eyes. "Yeah, we do get the news out here. I thought I recognized your face. You have some sort of power, right?"

Sky Ranger lifted off the ground and hovered above the table. His head brushed the corrugated metal ceiling of the shack. "I fly."

"Gotcha," Felipe said. "Wild! Wish I could do that." He

thought a moment. "Wait. You're a Reformist."

"I was," Sky Ranger admitted. Did he have to keep going through this? "But I'm not anymore."

"I thought he was full of it when he said that, too," Dee added helpfully. Sky Ranger shot her a look. She grinned back, fish bits stuck in her teeth.

Felipe recovered quickly. "So what, why would they be after you?"

"I did some damage to government property, among other things, after the Reformists killed all my people," said Sky Ranger.

"Well, damn," Felipe said, letting out a low whistle. "So tell me, is that why you needed a ship? To get off planet and out of the system?"

"No," Dee said. "We're going to save our friends on Trikon."

Felipe's eyes bugged. "You're nuts!" he said. "No way you can do that."

"I'm strong, and I can fly," Sky Ranger said. "And Dee—" She turned white and shook her head frantically. "Uh. Dee will help."

"But still! Just two of you against the whole base up there! That's still nuts. Nuts!" Felipe exclaimed. "How are you even gonna get there? Max is the only game in town for ships!"

"I was thinking," Broussard said. "Max's shuttle has plenty of room in it."

"Agreed," said Sky Ranger. "Tonight."

"That's insane," said Felipe, but his now-familiar grin spread back across his face.

"What?" asked Dee. "What are we doing?"

[CHAPTER 10]

RENNA PACED; FIRST ONE SIDE OF THE CELL, then the other.

"Stop it," Allison said for the fifth time. "You make me nervous. Sit the hell down and take a nap or something."

Renna ignored her. She hadn't gotten to know Allison very well back on the planet—she always seemed to be off with Anna and Luci, apart from everyone else. They'd done a lot of the moss-gathering and fire-tending—or at least they said they had. But Allison and her friends had never been particularly open, and Renna hadn't felt like approaching them. It was impossible to strike up a friendship now, of course.

She sighed and leaned up against the cold metal grating that separated them from the corridor. She missed the desert heat, so like home in Arizona. This cold was too much like Toronto; she shivered and shook, trying to get warm. The Fleet guys had given each of them a ratty old blanket to wrap around their shoulders, but not much else, and they seemed to have forgotten to leave the heat on in the prison wing.

A uniformed man walked softly down the hallway. He looked in on the men, and then met Renna's eyes.

"You're UNP" he asked in a low voice. Not accusatory. Questioning?

Renna's heart pounded. *This could be something.*

"Yes," she whispered. "Most of us are. Were."

He nodded. She couldn't really see his face very well through the dense grating. "Twenty-three hundred thirty hours," he whispered. "Tonight. Be ready."

She opened her mouth, a million questions ready to leap out, but he marched off briskly down the corridor.

She looked back at the group. No one seemed to have noticed her conversation. She staggered over to where Marsha sat.

"I think we have something," was all she could think of to say.

"Huh?" Marsha had been dozing. "What?"

"Look," she said quietly, motioning for those near to gather round. "That guard said something to me. He said—he asked if I was UNP. I said yes. And he told me to be ready for 23:30 tonight."

"Ready? For what?" Willow asked.

Renna shook her head. "I have no idea. What time is it now?"

Marsha sighed and pointed. The nearby wall clock read "17:23."

"Oh," said Renna. "Sorry. I think I need to sleep."

"You have some time," said Marsha. "Sleep now. Be ready."

Renna nodded. "I better tell the others first." She stood and crossed the room. Allison greeted her with a suspicious glare.

"Hey," she said nervously. "Look. Uh." She motioned for them to move in closer. They didn't. "Come in closer, I need to tell you something."

"Like what?" bellowed Allison. "Come on, out with it!"

"Not so loud!" Renna said. "Shh! Look. That guard I was speaking to—"

"What guard?" Allison asked.

"I was just speaking with a guard a minute ago," Renna said, exasperated. "He told me to 'be ready' at 23:30 for something. He asked if we were UNP."

"So, ready for what?" Allison asked, voice not lowered one

bit.

"Shh! I don't know," Renna whispered.

"It could be some sort of trick," Anna said doubtfully. "Don't trust so easy."

"I'm not!" Renna protested. "I'm just passing it along."

Allison scrunched her eyes up. She could, Renna reflected, be thinking.

"You know," Allison said slowly and, mercifully, softly. "There are plenty of people in the Fleet who were here before the Reformists took over. Some of them have to be unhappy with how things turned out. Divided loyalties, you know?"

Renna nodded. "That's what I'm assuming," she said.

"And this here is about the worst posting in the entire Confederation," Allison continued. "No better place to stash the undesirables."

"So what do you think?" Renna asked.

Allison flashed her scary, toothy grin. "Could be an interesting night. You should catch some sleep before it all goes down. I'm gonna."

Renna nodded, and shuffled off.

"I still think it's a trap," Anna said sourly.

"Sure, but so what?" Allison said. "Something's always better than nothing."

Sneaking into Max's scrap yard was the easy part. In the dead of night, Sky Ranger approached the high walls surrounding the yard; Broussard and Dee in tow along with Felipe, who had insisted on not being left behind. No sounds broke the still air, and he couldn't see any motion in Max's shack.

"How are we going to get in?" Felipe asked.

Dee made a face. "He can *fly*, remember?" she said.

Sky Ranger eyeballed the fence, thinking. "I'd rather we did this in one go," he said. "Broussard, on my back. Felipe and Dee, you're lighter, I'll carry you."

"Are you sure?" said Broussard doubtfully. "That's a lot of weight."

"I've carried more," Sky Ranger said. "Now let's go."

Broussard tentatively put his arms around Sky Ranger's neck. "This is not going to work," he said.

"Try not to choke me," Sky Ranger gurgled.

"Oh. Sorry." Broussard relaxed his grip.

"You'll want to wrap your legs around mine when we get aloft," Sky Ranger instructed. "Felipe, Dee?"

He put an arm around each of them. His hand on Dee's side brushed against something small, round, and hard. Dee squeaked.

"That's my nipple," she gasped.

"Oh! S-sorry," he stammered, moving his hand to her waist. Felipe laughed nervously.

"You sure about this?" he asked.

Sky Ranger nodded, tightening his grip. "Ready?"

"No," all three passengers said.

"Here we go!" Sky Ranger bent his knees and *willed* himself into the air. Broussard's grip tightened around his neck. He veered a little, but righted himself as the old man's legs tightened around his knees.

"Ow! Ow! Ow!" Dee yelped in pain at being jerked up so violently. "Ow! That hurts!"

"Sorry!" Sky Ranger strained to say. They were up over the fence. Now where was the ship hiding the shuttlecraft?

"Sky Ranger," Broussard gasped. "I can't hold on much longer!"

"Okay," he said, looking frantically around. He wanted to get close. Who knew how many motion sensors were around?

There!

He banked sharply to the west and screeched in for a landing. His feet touched the ground, and he let go of Dee and Felipe. Broussard gratefully slid off his back.

"If I never do that again..." Broussard muttered. "My back!"

"Your back? What about my *ribs*?" Dee complained. "I thought he was going to crush me! It was a lot more fun *last* time."

"At least you wouldn't fall," Broussard said. "I didn't know how much longer I could hold on! I'm an old man, I shouldn't have to do things like that."

"That was great!" Felipe said. "Man, I wish I could fly like you." He grinned at Sky Ranger, who smiled tightly back.

"Okay," Sky Ranger said. "There's the ship. Let's go. We have to be quick."

They ran up the gangway and into the belly of the ruined vessel.

"Which way?" Felipe asked.

"Follow me," Dee said, taking off down a corridor. "I remember where it was."

They jogged after her, footsteps echoing dully off the rusty metal flooring. A light shone up ahead. Sky Ranger had a sudden sense of danger.

"Dee," he called, but it was too late. They rounded a corner and stumbled into a room full of light. In the middle sat the shuttlecraft—and Max, holding a very large, sinister-looking weapon.

"Thought you might come back for it," he said, raising the gun. "Flying man."

◄►► ◄◄►

The hours crawled by. Marsha, with some doing, had managed to let the men know what was going on, first by knocking on the wall to get their attention, then speaking softly with a hand cupped against it. The wall was thin enough that the man on the other side—Mick, as it turned out—could hear her words.

Renna managed to get a few hours of fitful sleep. The teenage guards brought food and water, and shouted abuse at them when the mood struck. Renna squinted through the metal grid, but couldn't be certain that any of them were the guard she'd talked to earlier.

23:00, the clock read. She started pacing again. Allison grabbed her, and forced her to sit, claiming she was getting seasick from watching Renna go back and forth. Renna sat, but fidgeted.

23:20. Renna felt like she might be sick. She looked around, feeling the sweat beading under her arms and on her forehead. She started feeling too warm, despite the cold. Everyone else seemed equally nervous, except for Allison. Allison looked like she might doze off.

23:28. There was a burst of shouting from the men's cell, which just as suddenly cut off. Renna found herself on her feet. Willow actually screamed. Renna stood stock-still, listening.

23:29. Renna looked at everybody, communicating the same silent message.

Ready?

Ready.

The clock ticked and read 23:30.

Nothing happened.

"Well," Allison said. "That was a big nothing."

Renna was about to say something, when a crackling spark and sizzle came from the hallway. The lights dimmed, and then the door slid soundlessly open.

They stared at it for a moment.

"Go!" Renna said.

Everyone sprang to their feet and scrambled for the exit. Allison hiked up her pants and sprinted out at a dead run. Renna raced at the end, herding Willow in front of her. The corridor was full of refugees, men and women both.

Renna looked around frantically. The security cameras on each side of the hall sparked, clearly dead. At their end of the hallway was the door Renna had taken to the interior of the compound. On the other end... the exit? Suddenly, the heavy door on the far end slid open with a creak and a moan. Easy decision—if it wasn't a trap. One way to find out.

"That way!" she called, pointing at the open door on the far end. Everyone sprinted to the exit.

Ahead, a limping Mick whooped with glee. Renna raced to the front, and found herself grinning like an idiot. They were in an *armory*. Weapons stood on racks everywhere.

"Everyone grab a gun!" she called. "Now!" She picked up a slender pulse rifle, found the on switch, and rocketed to the door on the far side of the room. "They'll be coming soon!" she said. "Come on!" She glanced out the window, and sucked in a breath of air. Night. *Outside.* Freedom.

"All armed!" someone called.

"Let's go! At a run!" Renna called, and shoved the door open. Renna picked a direction and sprinted as fast as she could. She glanced behind. Someone was helping Mick. Good.

She spotted the fence almost immediately, and saw the gate a second after. A small guardhouse sat next to it. She flicked what she assumed was the safety of her weapon off. The fact that she hadn't actually *shot* a rifle since she was a kid flashed through her mind.

A man carrying a rifle ran out of the guardhouse and shouted something incomprehensible at them. He tripped a little over his feet, as if he was drunk. He raised his rifle.

A short, loud, sharp retort rang out behind Renna. The guard crumpled and fell.

"Nice shot!" Allison called.

Renna's mind reeled. They'd killed someone. Who had fired the shot?

Her brain scrambled to concentrate on something—any-thing—besides the corpse lying a few feet from her. She trotted up to the gate. "How do we get this open?" Renna said, glancing nervously back at the prison building. No activity there yet.

Allison, huffing and puffing, lifted her gun and shot the lock off. *That's one way to do it,* Renna thought. Allison pushed the gate open, and the refugees streamed out of the base into the night. Behind them, an alarm finally started to howl and wail.

Blood blossomed beneath the dead man, staining the white snow a deep wine red. Renna forced herself to look away.

"Deep into the woods!" Allison ordered. "Let's go!"

Max hit the "send" button on his communicator. "That ought to do it," he said. "I took the liberty of recording a mes-sage for the captain ahead of time. That message will reach Trikon in a minute, then they'll send a ship for you. And I'll get a nice, fat reward for leading them right to the famous Sky Rang-er. Treasonous scum."

"If you like," Sky Ranger said calmly, advancing on Max. "But you are aware," he said, a patronizing tone entering his voice, "that I'm also impervious to weapons fire." He lifted off the ground and flew forward. "So I think I'll take that gun now."

"Stop there," Max said, pointing the gun at Broussard. "Or I shoot someone who isn't 'impervious' to my gun."

Sky Ranger jerked to a halt, and raised his hands in the air. "Don't be a fool, Max."

"That's a silly thing to say, coming from someone who

doesn't have a pulse rifle," Max said. "Now come down."

Sky Ranger floated down to the ground. A million thoughts chased each other through his head. He could fly fast. But fast enough? Would he get there before Max pulled the trigger? Should he evade, fly up, hope to distract him? What if Broussard got hurt? What if *Dee* got hurt?

He tensed his muscles. He couldn't just stand here. He had to do something.

At that moment, he glanced over at Dee.

◂▸▸ ◂◂▸

Dee was studying the ground. A small lizard was crawling across the floor of the hanger. A lizard? Lizards lived on this planet? She hadn't ever seen one.

It was kind of gross.

Kick the lizard, her body willed. A little sing-song tune ran through her head. *Go on. Kick it at Max.*

◂▸▸ ◂◂▸

Sky Ranger watched, transfixed, as she lifted the lizard up onto the toe of her shoe, and more *flicked* it than kicked it towards Max. It landed on his arm.

"Aaa!" he screeched, and shook it off, taking a step backward.

Behind him was a small pile of debris, maybe from the collapsed roof. He tripped with a yowl and fell on his back with a sickening crunch.

Sky Ranger was on him in an instant, and wrestled the gun out of his hands. He gave him a solid punch to the head for good measure. Max groaned and passed out.

"Wow!" Felipe said. "That was *lucky!*"

"You're telling me," Broussard said, exhaling. "That gun was aimed at my head! I thought he'd kill me for sure."

Dee smiled proudly.

"See?" Sky Ranger said quietly, so only she could hear. "Pretty useful, huh?" She nodded, eyes bright.

"Now," Felipe said, "Let's get this thing working! I bet I can have it flying in a few minutes."

"Yup, they're gone," the soldier said. "Too bad the cameras on the base malfunctioned right then, otherwise we'd have had an idea of where they went. Damn unlucky!"

Captain Veselinovich fought down the urge to strangle the private. "Yes. That, I imagine, was the idea," he said stiffly. He already had several of his more sober and loyal men sifting through evidence, trying to find the saboteur. The worst part was that Veselinovich wasn't even surprised that one of his soldiers had turned out to be a traitor. Whoever it was had probably done it for laughs, such was the high quality of the men under his command.

"Should we go after them?" asked Lieutenant Gannett, a sandy-haired young man who was the most competent soldier the captain had. "Shouldn't be hard to track. They'll be the warmest things out there."

Veselinovich shook his head. "Not at night. Too cold and too risky—one of our men might get hurt. We'll get them back in the morning, when we can see better." *And when our men are less drunk and violent.* "They aren't going anywhere. There's no way off planet."

"Yes, sir," Gannett said. "I'll start organizing a search team for the morning. We'll get them."

"You do that," Veselinovich said tightly, trying not to panic.

The ConFedMilPol ship was due in less than a day. But he'd have them back by then. He *had* to. Gannett was one of his best men. He could do it. Right?

He leaned up against the wall, struggling to control his emotions. This had been an awful evening. He could only hope he had everything under control before ConFedMilPol got here. Maybe, if he bribed them, his men would keep quiet about the fact that there was a traitor in their midst. Maybe they'd even tell him who it was. Maybe...

He needed a drink. The flask in his desk beckoned.

"Captain," a soldier said, running up to him. Veselinovich mentally cursed him. "Sir! A message from Terron, sir; it's Max Hladic. He says there's a man there in the town who can fly, that he has him captured! He said you'd want to know."

Veselinovich remained outwardly calm, but inside an ember of hope stirred to life. "Thank you, Corporal," he said stiffly. "Please send a copy of the message to my desk."

The corporal nodded and, mission accomplished, wandered lackadaisically off. Veselinovich doubted he'd be back at his post anytime soon.

He thumbed his communicator. "Sergeant Lyushenko," he called. A moment later, Lyushenko responded.

"Sir?"

"Get a ship ready," he ordered. "Bound for Terron. At *once*."

"Right," Lyushenko said, clearly annoyed, and cut the signal.

This could be my ticket off this planet, Veselinovich thought. *Sky Ranger, gift-wrapped for ConFedMilPol. The rest won't matter, the saboteur won't matter, if I can just deliver him.* Visions of better planets than this danced through his head. Civilization! Warmth! Competent soldiers! Women...

Oh, please please please. He jogged down to the hangar, shouting out to anyone who was nearby to follow.

◆>►◄◄►

Felipe pushed a button, and the engine of the shuttlecraft roared to life. "Hey hey!" Felipe called. "That's more like it!"

"Good work," Sky Ranger said. "Thank you! You can head out of here if you want. You'd better be gone before the Fleet ship gets here."

"What?" Felipe's face fell. "No way! I'm coming with you!"

"Oh, Lord," Broussard said. "Look. Felipe. You have a life here. You can't risk it. I'm an old man, and they're fugitives. What do we have to lose? But you could lose everything. You need to stay behind."

Felipe shook his head, and for once he looked absolutely serious. "No chance. What good's my life if I don't ever get off this dustball? And I want to help you do what's right. Think of this as my way of getting back at the Confederation for abandoning my homeworld, and letting it turn into sand. Or something!" He grinned. "And, of course, for saddling me with jerks like Max. Besides, you need a pilot."

"We do need a pilot," Sky Ranger admitted.

"Yeah!" Dee seconded enthusiastically.

Sky Ranger gave up. "Fine, you can come. But let's go now."

They strapped themselves in while Felipe fiddled with the controls. "Okay, I think I've got it," he said. "Everyone ready?"

"Ready," they said.

"Okay! Next stop, Trikon!"

The shuttle heaved off the ground and blasted up into the atmosphere, bound for space.

[CHAPTER 11]

THEY RAN FOR WHAT FELT LIKE MILES, until finally they collapsed from exhaustion.

They huddled together in a tight circle, in a small clearing in the dense woods. The trees were short but grew thick on the ground, creating more of a vast expanse of head-high bushes than what Renna thought of as a real forest. They had to huddle down on the ground to have any hope of escaping the bitter, howling winds that blew above the treetops.

"I'm so cold," Willow said, teeth chattering. She pulled her blanket around her bony shoulders. "I haven't ever been so cold."

"Well, now what?" Marsha asked, kneeling in the snow. "I'm soaked, freezing and tired. We can't be more than a few miles from the base! What happens now?"

Renna listened to her own breath wheeze in and out. "I have no idea," she admitted after a moment. "I'm sorry. When the chance came, we took it. I took it. But I don't know what to do next."

"They're going to come for us," Raul said grimly.

"We have guns," another man said. "We can fight them."

"We got away too easy," Allison said distractedly. "Only one damn guard. This has to be the worst-run base in the whole Confederation! How the hell did we do this? I don't get it."

"Who killed that guard?" Mick asked. "I didn't see who fired the shot."

A few people glanced at Willow, who had begun to shake visibly.

"Willow?" Renna asked softly.

Willow looked up at her. There was something wild in her eyes that Renna didn't like. "He—he was in the way," she said. It sounded like she had something caught in her throat. "I had to."

"Yes, you did," Mick soothed. "You did the right thing. You did good."

"Damn right," Allison said admiringly. "That was a great shot. Right in the head!" She mimed taking the shot. "Kapow! Splat!"

Willow turned green, and hastily scrambled out of the clearing. They could hear her being sick behind the bushes.

"Good one, Allison," Marsha muttered, loud enough for Allison to hear. "You dumb cow."

"Hey, you damn—" Allison snarled. Renna, without thinking, clamped a hand on her arm.

"Not now!" she ordered, in as commanding a voice as she could muster. "Keep cool!" Belatedly, she realized that Allison was twice her size, and a lot stronger.

"I'm damn cool *enough*, thank you," Allison snapped, wrenching her arm away. "This planet rots. I'd rather be back in the desert."

"Me, too," Raul seconded. "At least I was warm."

"I didn't know Willow had that in her," Tricia said. "Wow. I don't think I could have done that."

They listened to Willow retching. "Well, it's out of her now," Allison commented with a laugh.

"We need to find food," Renna said after everyone glared at Allison. Being a busybody was keeping her warm and awake, at least. "Then shelter, and fire."

"This is a plasma rifle," Raul said, holding his weapon up.

"We can use it to light a fire."

"Don't be stupid," Allison said. "They'll be able to see a fire from miles away."

"They have infrared sensors," Mick said. "They can see us anyway. It's amazing they haven't come for us already."

"Maybe they're waiting 'til morning," Tricia suggested.

"They haven't come, and that's good enough for me. So let's try to get warm and take a rest before we move out," Renna said. "Can someone go gather some dead wood? We can try to light a fire."

"What about food?" someone asked.

"Look around," Renna said helplessly. "I don't know what's good to eat here. Maybe you'll see an animal we can roast or something."

"That's a big help," Allison said snidely.

Renna locked glares with the other woman. Allison was a lot less fun when she was needling Renna instead of Karl. "You have a better idea? Why don't you tell us?" she snarled. Allison kept her mouth shut, for once, and folded her arms over her chest.

Renna seethed. "Go find food. I don't care what it is or how you find it."

A few of the refugees trudged off. Renna leaned against a rock that was jutting up at the edge of the clearing, and glanced around at the people remaining in their makeshift camp. They looked tired and miserable. First the flight on board a cramped refugee ship, then the crash, then the desert, then this. How much could people take?

Willow sat apart from the rest of the group, cradling her rifle in her hands. Renna hesitantly moved close to her. "Willow?" she asked softly. "How are you?"

"Fine," Willow said stiffly.

"Seriously, Willow—"

"I'm *fine*," Willow snapped. "Go away."

"Whatever you want," said Renna. Let her be alone if that was what she needed. Dimly, she realized from staring at Willow's gun that they needed to post a sentry of some sort. She picked four of the men and sent them off in different directions. Maybe she should have sent more. She had no idea. She didn't know anything about military strategy.

She didn't know what to do now. They couldn't survive like this. The ConFedFleet soldiers would come for them. They'd either die or be recaptured, since what chance did they really stand against trained soldiers?

Except that Willow had killed one of them. *Willow* had killed one of them.

Renna's mind reeled. It was too much. She fought it down, and started to pace around the camp, tired but unable to stop moving. She couldn't think of anything else to do. This was impossible. There was no way out. They were still in prison, just a bigger, colder one.

The sun began to rise.

Light from blue-white, remorseless Seera illuminated the inside of the cramped cockpit as the shuttle flew on towards Trikon.

Sky Ranger felt his guts ascending through his esophagus. He hated being on ships with artificial gravity, but this one had no gravity at all. He couldn't decide if he hated it more or less.

"Well," Felipe said after a moment. "Seera Trikon, coming up. We should be there..." he checked his instruments. "Uh. We should be there in... in... Broussard?"

Broussard tapped at his console. "An hour."

"Yeah. Um, an hour. Not too long."

"You *sure* you know how to fly this thing?" Dee said, only half-joking.

"Yeah, we're fine," Felipe muttered nervously, glancing around at the bewildering array of control panels. Sky Ranger suppressed a groan.

Dee ran a hand through her hair. "Hey!" she said. "My hair sticks up! No gravity! Anyone have a pencil or something we can float?"

"No!" Sky Ranger and Felipe shouted at once.

"Sor-ry," groaned Dee, taken aback.

"It'll mess up my concentration," Felipe explained. "I didn't mean to yell. I'm sorry."

"Oh, it's okay," Dee said, a little too sincerely. "I'm sorry I suggested it!" They proceeded to go around in circles for another minute or so about how sorry they were.

Please shut up, Sky Ranger willed, shutting his eyes tightly. He couldn't feel gravity, or, worse, he could only feel a fraction of what he was used to feeling. His body tried without any luck to exert influence on something that barely existed. It made him nauseous.

Broussard turned around. "You all right, Sky Ranger?"

"Yes," Sky Ranger said between clenched teeth. "I just don't like being—weightless."

Broussard shot him an amused little smile. "Well, don't throw up in here. It'll float around."

"Eww!" Dee said, staring at Sky Ranger. "You're not going to, are you?"

Sky Ranger just glared at them both and tried to calm his churning stomach.

Felipe jabbed experimentally at the controls. "This shuttle is weird. Nothing's where it should be!"

"That," Broussard explained, pointing slowly and deliberately, "is thrust. You move it to go fast."

Felipe waved his hand away. "I know that, I know! I'm just looking for sensor controls, and—"

Broussard started pointing out some of the shuttle's features. Dee squirmed in the seat next to Sky Ranger.

"I feel strange," she said softly to him. "I mean, I never used my power before and *knew* without hesitation that I was *using* a power. Does that make sense?"

Sky Ranger nodded, grateful for the distracting conversation. "Yes," he said. "I remember the first time I flew and meant to fly. It's like you said: strange. But wonderful, too."

"Yeah," she agreed enthusiastically. "Like, I *knew* when I saw that lizard that I had to kick it up onto Max's arm. I didn't know what was going to happen, but I knew it would be good if I did that with the lizard. And I wonder where the lizard came from? I never even saw any lizards around before this."

"That's the way it is," he said. "I knew another woman who was lucky like you. She said it was like that for her, too."

"How does it actually work? Do you know?"

"No," he said. "Not really. There are lots of theories as to why prescients and others can do what they do, but none of them explain everything."

"It's like magic," she said.

"It isn't, though," Sky Ranger said. "It's just who we are." He glanced out the porthole, remembering. "There was a man back at the Union. We called him Watcher, or sometimes the Watching Man. He could see the future so clearly... but only a few hours ahead of time. That was the extent of his power, but within those hours he was very strong. We would often take him out into the field with us, on LED missions, because he was so good at seeing what was coming, and what we were facing. He would tell us in advance where traps were set, or where enemies were hiding."

"That would be nice, to see that," Dee said.

"I envied him, too, you know," Sky Ranger said, hastily adding, "Sometimes. We came to rely very strongly on him, and he... well, he became very... convinced of his own importance. He and I would fight, when he disagreed with what I wanted to do. After a while, he simply refused to help us anymore."

Dee's eyes widened. "What did you do then?"

"Nothing," Sky Ranger said. "What could I do? He left the LED, but it wasn't as if I could punish him for it. After, he would rarely leave the floor he lived on. His friend Longview, who was also a prescient, would bring him meals and stay with him. But other than that he was alone." Sky Ranger paused, remembering. "I think it drove him mad. He started to believe he could do other things. He came to believe that he could fly, like me. So one day he jumped out the window, intending to fly away from the Union. He fell fifteen floors."

Dee blanched, clearly disturbed.

"So it isn't magic, you see," Sky Ranger said gently. Somewhere in the back of his mind, he remembered the Sky Ranger before him giving a young Little Hawk the same speech. "Watcher thought it was, after a while. He thought he could do anything, just because he willed it. But it isn't magic; it's science. Science has limits, when magic doesn't. It's specific, and your abilities are just a part of who you are. Just like flying and being strong are part of me, but I have limits."

"Okay," Dee whispered. "I promise I won't jump out of a window. Even though I wish I could fly."

Sky Ranger sat back, satisfied. He hadn't listened back then to the old Sky Ranger, but it had turned out okay in the end. For a while.

"Do you miss all of them?" Dee said suddenly. "The people in the Union?"

The question struck Sky Ranger like a bag of bricks. He leaned back in his restraints, nausea returning. "Yes. Every day.

Every minute. All the time. Dee, do you miss your parents?"

Dee looked away. "Yeah," she said in a small voice. "I do. But I try not to think about it."

"It's the same for me. The Union was my family." He considered for a few moments what to say next. He desperately wanted to keep this conversation going, to pass something of the Union on to Dee. "I never really knew my real mother and father, understand. We were all taken away when we were little, so the other Union members were all the family any of us ever had." He shook his head. "It was such a limited life. You were right about that. We couldn't marry; it was forbidden. We all took drugs that sterilized us, so we couldn't have children. We all lived alone, each in his or her own apartment in the Tower. We almost never left. "

"It sounds awful," Dee said.

"But we were all very close," Sky Ranger added quickly. "When Watcher died we all felt the loss. Even though he was so hard to live with... we all still loved him. And we missed him when he died. So... now that they're all gone... I do miss them. All of them. Every second." He looked Dee straight in the eye. A tear rolled down her cheek. "It never stops hurting. I can't not think about it, though I try."

Crim's voice came floating back to him. *Plus, it was your fault we all got killed, Sky. Don't forget to tell her THAT.* He winced.

Dee thought for a moment, wiping away her tears. "I don't really have a family anymore," she said at last, her voice barely a whisper. "They're all dead or back on Earth. But...but."

She reached into her pack and pulled a beaten-up bag out of it. She handed the bag to Sky Ranger.

"This is Renna's pack," he said, surprised.

"Take it," Dee insisted. "I found it at the camp. I want you to give it back to her. Okay? You have to. We have to get her back. She's my friend. She's all I've got."

Sky Ranger started to say something about their chances and being realistic, but stopped himself. "Okay," he said, nodding. "I promise."

"Hey, I think I've got it!" Felipe called joyously from the front. Dee and Sky Ranger started. "So! Let's take a look around with the sensors." He jabbed a few buttons on the flat panel in front of him. A diagram appeared, with a small blinking light. "Uh. So what's that?"

Broussard cursed. "We're being scanned from Trikon."

"A ship approaching," said Sergeant Lyushenko. "It's Max's shuttlecraft."

"Oh," Captain Veselinovich said. "I thought he was going to wait for us there. Well. It doesn't matter. Send him a landing clearance."

"Yes, sir."

It was, Veselinovich thought, a good thing that they hadn't been able to find enough reasonably sober men to form a crew for their ship. Besides, Lieutenant Gannett had requested the ship for his search anyway, although Veselinovich didn't really understand why. That, of course, was why he had Gannett.

Felipe blinked at the message that appeared on his screen. "We're getting a landing clearance," he said in wonder. "Wow. That's nice of them."

"They think we're Max," Broussard said. "I'm sending an acknowledgment." He keyed in a message and sent it off. "Lucky. We're lucky today. Are we too far out to scan the planet? We need to find a place to land. And we need a plan, yes?"

Sky Ranger straightened. "Where on the base would they be kept?" he asked.

"Don't know," said Broussard. "We can find a few things out with the sensors. They'll tell us how many humans are down there, and where they are. We might be able to see the most likely places for them to be by finding where there are a lot of people clumped together. There are, what, two dozen?"

"Yes. I'm thinking we won't have much time to get in and out," said Sky Ranger. "And we're going to be pretty cramped in this shuttle."

"You thinking this was a bad idea?" Felipe said. "Because I'm thinking that."

"Hmm," Broussard murmured, half in agreement. "We might be able to land, pick them up quickly, and get out before... but then we're still stuck in this system."

"We'll be fine," Dee said firmly, but they ignored her.

"We might be able to sneak in and steal their hyperspace-capable transport," Sky Ranger said dubiously. "Maybe."

Felipe poked at the sensors. "Hey. Woah. Broussard, what's that?" he asked. "It just appeared."

Broussard paled. "That's another ship. Beacon says... *merde.* Confederation Military Police. CFMP *Architect.*"

ConFedMilPol. The secret police.

"What are they doing here?" Dee said frantically. "We ran from them! Why are they here?"

"If I had to guess," Broussard said, "They're here for *him.*" He nodded towards Sky Ranger, who was looking greener. "But it's pretty far out. We'll get to the planet well in advance of them."

Felipe, seemingly unconcerned, tapped at his console. "Okay. Let me see. I'm getting the hang of this—this should be the life signs sensor. I'm telling it to scan the planet."

Sky Ranger craned his head to peer out the window. The

ConFedMilPol ship lurked out there in the darkness somewhere, gaining on them.

"Okay. Okay! Take a look," Felipe said. A schematic appeared in the air in front of Felipe and Broussard. "There. That's the area around the base. It's the only part with any human life signs, except—"

"Look over there," Broussard said. "About twenty or so, out away from the base."

"That's them!" Dee exclaimed. "They escaped!"

"We don't know that," Broussard cautioned. "That may be a prison facility."

"No," Felipe said, examining data. "Scans say it's a clearing in the forest. But I'm seeing some other life signs closing in on them pretty fast." He pointed at seven dots moving rapidly towards the big cluster in the forest. "See? I think that might be a big aircraft."

"We need to get there fast," Sky Ranger said.

"I know! But they're going to beat us. I'm at full speed," Felipe said. "I'll try to make us go a little faster, but they'll still beat us there."

Sky Ranger lapsed into silence, as they watched the aircraft close on the refugees.

"There's nothing we can do," Broussard said.

Renna jerked awake and grabbed for her weapon at the sound of someone crashing through the woods. A moment later, one of the men she had put out on sentry duty broke through into the camp.

"Big ship!" he gasped. "Coming fast!"

[CHAPTER 12]

LIEUTENANT BRIAN GANNETT GENTLY LOWERED
the ship onto the forest floor. He checked the scans: All of the
refugees had moved back to the clearing, and were setting up
a clumsy perimeter. Well, good. That would make things a little
easier.

He flipped on the sound in the cargo hold.

*"Gannett, you traitorous bastard! I will eat your guts for
breakfast and hang you with your intestines! Are you hearing me,
Gannett?! I will come for you! I will come for you!"*

Sergeant Sanchez was not happy with his confinement, it
seemed. Gannett turned off the sound. They had no idea how
to get out. That was the thing with these young foot soldiers
of the New Reformist Confederation, the hope of humanity's
future: They weren't all that bright.

Brian Gannett slung his rifle over his shoulder, just in case,
and headed out to meet the refugees.

◂▸▸ ◂◂▸

Renna pointed her weapon out into the forest. A dark shape
moved beyond the low trees, but she couldn't be sure.

"Hold fire," she called. "Wait until you're sure of your shot!"

That sounded good, right? Wasn't that what commanders told their troops: Wait to shoot until you see the "whites of their eyes"? Did that even make sense anymore? She found she couldn't steady her aim. How many were out there?

"Refugees!" a voice came from beyond the trees. "Listen to me!"

Renna almost shrieked in alarm. A few of the others did. God, here it came. Here it came.

"I can get you off this planet! I can get you to Reilis! But you have to trust me!"

That wasn't what she'd been expecting.

Renna straightened and looked around. People all over the camp were looking at her in confusion.

"A trick!" called Allison. "Come and fight, cowards!"

"Allison!" Renna snapped.

"They know we're here," Allison retorted. "I want to get this over with, damnit!"

"It's no trick," the voice said. "I'm the one who let you out of your cells. I have a ship. We can get away together! But you have to trust me!"

"How do we know that? How can we trust you?" someone shouted at the distant voice.

"I asked one of you if you were UNP, and told you to wait until 23:30! Do you remember? Look, I'm alone. It's only me. I'm not a threat!"

That checked out, but it was still probably a trap. "Then come into the camp," Renna dared. "Come forward so we can see you!"

"We don't have time!" the voice shouted. "There's a Con-FedMilPol ship heading for the planet—we need to go now if we're going to get away!"

"A trap," said Allison confidently.

"No deal, then!" said Renna. She raised her rifle, scanning

the dark forest for movement. She used to be a crack shot. She could probably take him out if he showed himself.

The voice seemed to consider. "All right. I'm coming. But then we have to go as soon as possible. I'm coming now."

The bushes rustled and shook. Renna tried to steady her weapon. "Don't shoot him unless he looks like he's going to open fire," Renna ordered the other refugees. They didn't look like they were in any shape to obey, but they held their fire.

A young, sandy-haired white man in a black Confederation Fleet uniform broke through into the clearing. He raised his hands above his head.

"See?" he said. "I'm harmless. Please, we need to go."

Allison instantly raised her weapon. "I could shoot him," she offered to Renna.

"What?" Renna was shocked. "No! What if he's telling the truth?"

"If he is, then we can take his ship and get out of here," Allison said. "If not, he's dead and it doesn't matter."

The man leveled his remarkable, penetrating gaze at her. "You'd be killing your only chance to get out of here," he said steadily. "You can't start the ship without my biometric scan."

They looked at each other. Mick nodded shakily. "That's standard for most Fleet ships."

Renna, still on the edge of pure panic, gritted her teeth and tightened her sweaty-palmed grip on her gun. "I don't see why we should trust you. You're a Fleet officer!"

"Yes. I am. But why do you think I'm posted here? I don't get along with the people in charge these days. This is a different Fleet from the one I joined."

"So why didn't *they* just shoot you?" Allison said, keeping her rifle trained on the man's head.

"They probably will soon," the lieutenant said evenly. "I was a UNP supporter before, and pretty open about it. But I haven't done anything outwardly rebellious or subversive—until now—so they just shuttled me off to a lousy posting. I've had enough. I want out."

"That sounds like it could be bullshit," Allison observed.

"So I know it isn't easy," the man continued as if he hadn't heard her, looking around at all of them. His gaze settled on each of them for an instant as he spoke. "But I have to ask you—trust me. I can get us off this planet. I can get us to Reilis, where we'll be safe. But you have to let me do it."

Renna found herself briefly under the spell of his words. They were all quivering wrecks, while he was calm and self-assured. It was entrancing. She tried to shake it off. "And what happens if we don't?"

The man glanced up at the sky. "That ConFedMilPol ship is coming. They'll be here, soon. I imagine they're coming for Sky Ranger, but they won't mind taking you, too."

Renna sucked in her breath. *Sky Ranger.* "Do you know where Sky Ranger is?"

He shook his head. "We think on Terron, but no one knows for sure. Please," he repeated, looking a little worried for the first time. "There's no time."

Renna glanced around at her fellow refugees. What alternative did they have? Stay in the woods and get shot? They were tired, cold, and hungry. If this was a trap, then so be it.

"All right," she said. "All right. We'll follow you. But we're keeping our weapons."

"Renna, no!" Allison said. "This—"

"If it's a trap, so what?" Renna sighed, letting her exhaustion show. "I don't have a better idea right now. It's this or get captured by ConFedMilPol."

The group seemed to accept that. Allison scowled but lowered her gun.

He nodded. "Okay. Fine. Let's go. The ship is this way." He

took off into the woods. Renna motioned everyone to follow.

"This is stupid," Allison complained as she lumbered past. "We should have shot him. Believe me, girl, you're going to regret letting him live."

◄►►◄◄►

They trudged as quickly as their tired, frozen legs would carry them, through a kilometer or so of dense forest and scrubland, to where the ship lay. The exhausted refugee party moved slowly, despite the lieutenant's exhortations and warnings about the coming ship.

Renna marched near the end of the line, helping stragglers keep up. Willow struggled along behind everyone else, and Renna had to grab her and force her to keep moving forward. Willow said nothing throughout the march, and her eyes were cold and distant.

They finally reached the ship after about half an hour. The lieutenant waited at the door for Renna and Willow to arrive.

"Okay," he said. "I'm going to open the ship up, and you need to get aboard as quickly as possible. The sooner we get into the sky, the better." He searched for and found Renna. "All right?" he asked her.

She nodded. "Fine. Go ahead."

He smiled. "I'm Brian Gannett, by the way."

"Renna Fernández Silva," she responded tiredly, but managed a small smile. A tiny piece of her mind noted that he had very pretty hazel eyes.

"Okay, let's go!" he called, and opened up the hatch.

At that moment, a terrible whine and roar of engines came from above. A shuttlecraft was descending rapidly towards them.

"It's the ConFedMilPol ship!" someone cried, and they bolted for the door. But as Renna watched, the hatch of the shuttle snapped open and a man *flew* out.

"Stop!" Sky Ranger cried dramatically. "And let those people go!"

◂▸▸ ◂◂▸

It took a few embarrassing minutes to get everything sorted out. Renna called and waved, and eventually Sky Ranger settled warily onto the ground. The shuttle, confused, circled around a bit before landing next to the Fleet transport. Dee bounced out of the shuttle and ran to Renna.

"Hey!" she shouted. "Good to see everyone! What's going on?"

Renna was explaining things to Sky Ranger while Gannett looked on when they heard another roar in the sky. Gannett cursed.

Everyone looked up. A massive black troop transport was descending rapidly. This one was for real.

"It's the other ship!" A boy Renna didn't know called out from the shuttle Sky Ranger had come from.

"Everyone inside!" Gannett ordered. Refugees who had just crept out of the transport now rocketed back for the door. The other two occupants of the shuttle, the boy and an old man, obviously figuring they were safer in a bigger tin can, abandoned their tiny ship and ran for Gannett's.

"Stay where you are," a voice demanded over a speaker. "Move and we will open fire!"

To prove the point, a bolt of white-hot energy sizzled past and slammed into Max's shuttle, where the boy and the old man had been just a moment before. The shuttle burst into flames.

Holy hell, Renna thought. This was it. This was finally, definitely it.

◄►►◄◄►

Dee, terrified, felt a sudden heat rising in her veins, and she clenched her fists. Fire danced in front of her—*inside* her.

Everyone else froze.

"Drop your weapons at once," the ship blared as it settled down onto the forest floor.

"Fuck off!" Allison called, and raised her rifle.

"Allison, no!" Renna shouted, but it was too late. Another blast of energy shot from the ConFedMilPol shuttle. Allison burst into flames. She screeched and crumpled, a smoldering corpse, to the ground.

Renna, pale as a ghost, threw her rifle away from her. Everyone else did the same.

Dee felt the fire rising higher. That sing-song tune ran through her head again, and she raised her arms.

◄►►◄◄►

ConFedMilPol agents, clad in their unsettling and unmistakable gray uniforms, streamed from the belly of the shuttle, fanning out around the refugees. A woman wearing a blood-red beret, a complex facial tattoo and major's tags emerged last, surveying the scene with a cool and practiced eye. Renna watched how the soldiers moved, the sheer power radiating out from their every action, and knew she wasn't dealing with teenage rejects anymore. ConFedMilPol had the best of the best.

"You are all under arrest," she pronounced in clipped tones. "You are traitors to the Confederation."

Gannett stepped forward. "Major, I'm Lieutenant Gannett," he said. "I was taking these prisoners back to the base. I can continue if you like."

The ConFedMilPol major smiled coldly back at him. "We

monitored your actions here," she said. "And we detected five Marines confined in your hold. You're helping these traitors escape, which makes you a traitor yourself." She fixed her gaze on him. "It must run in the family. You remind me of your brother."

Gannett turned white. "Wh-what do you know of him?" he asked shakily.

She ignored him. "Retake that ship," she said to her soldiers. "And bring all of them into custody."

"Wait!" Sky Ranger hovered in the air. "Wait, please. I'm Sky Ranger. It's me you want. Take me, but let the rest go."

She laughed. It wasn't a pleasant sound. "Why would I do that, when I can take all of you with no trouble?"

He balled his hands into fists. "I'll fight you," he said.

She stepped forward, near to where he hovered. "And what good would that do? You're strong, but not, I think, able to withstand the weapons I have on this shuttle. So go ahead, resist. Then you'd be dead, I'd still have them, and how many would have died in the fight? Better to live, I think. Now. Come down and surrender."

Sky Ranger settled back onto the ground, hands in the air, defeated.

"Hands on your heads," the major ordered. Several of the dozen or so ConFedMilPol agents ran into the ship as the refugees complied. The rest formed up in a circle around them.

"I'm sorry," Gannett said to Renna.

She smiled sadly back at him. "You were right, we should have trusted you right away."

"Not your fault," he said. "I was asking a lot."

The formerly captive Marines emerged from the ship. They scowled triumphantly at Gannett as they passed.

"Now you're dead meat," Sergeant Sanchez crowed, and spat in Gannett's face. "Always wanted to do that. Lieutenant!"

"Move along, soldier," a ConFedMilPol agent said, prodding

him in the back. Sanchez started to say something nasty, but something in the ConFedMilPol man's expression seemed to make him think twice. He moved along.

The others emerged. "All clear," said one.

"Good," said the major. "We'll take the Fleet men back to their base, and the prisoners to our ship."

The ConFedMilPol agents moved away from the refugees, intending to herd them into the transport.

◄►►◄►

Hey, said a little voice inside Dee's head. *You should set them on fire.*

What? Dee's thoughts replied, shocked. *But I can't do that.*

Sure you can, you can, sang the voice—and what a persuasive little voice it was. *You know, just like Grandma. Remember the burglars she surprised?*

Dee remembered.

So it's just like that. You can do it!

I never have before.

First time for everything, said the voice. Funny how the voice always sounded a little like her grandma...

And suddenly it seemed possible. Fire, fire.... *fire* raced through her veins. All she had to do was call it forth. The air around the ConFedMilPol agents shimmered. The energy was there, she could make the molecules rub together, make them combust. *But I can't—I don't want to kill them—*

All right, said Dee's luck. *So how about this?* A plan formed in Dee's mind. *Now is a good time. No other chance but this!*

Dee whirled around and *threw* her energy at the air around the agents.

"Keep moving," a ConFedMilPol agent said, training his weapon on her. He opened his mouth to say something else when a solid wall of fire roared up in front of him. He shrieked in surprise and backed off.

Dee advanced on the soldiers. "Drop the guns or I set you all on fire!" she snarled, heat and rage in her voice.

◄►► ◄◄►

Renna shrank back. It seemed that Dee was made of white-hot energy. The air around her *glowed*.

Where had *that* come from?

Sky Ranger's mouth fell open in shock. She was a firestarter, and she was *strong*.

The major, hidden behind a massive wall of flames, held her weapon aloft. "I see we have another freak in the bunch," she said. Very well. Drop your weapons, all."

Weapons clattered to the ground.

"Of course," said the major conversationally, "We have a very large ship in orbit. And there are gunners in our own shuttle who are even now training their weapons on you. Plus, you're starting to look tired."

Dee grimaced. The effort was clearly draining her rapidly.

"So maybe we should make a deal, yes? Here's what I suggest. We really don't care that much about the others. A few refugees more or less, what's the difference? We can say they were all killed, when in reality they'll be safe on Reilis. It doesn't matter to us. But we want Sky Ranger. And now we want *you*. Both of you come with us, and we'll let the others go in that transport. Deal?"

"I don't trust you!" Dee screamed. The flames were getting hotter.

"I tell you what," the major said. "If I go back on my word, you can incinerate me."

"No, Dee!" cried Renna.

The flames danced for a moment, then blinked out. Dee staggered back, barely keeping her footing. "Deal," she gasped.

The major nodded. "Both of you come here first."

Sky Ranger helped Dee over to where the major waited.

"Dee!" Renna called again. "You don't have to do this!"

Dee didn't respond.

"Let the rest go," said the major. "I'm nothing if not an honorable solider."

Gannett leaped into action. "Everybody aboard, now!" he called. The remaining refugees bolted into the ship. Renna was the last. She cast one final look at Dee and Sky Ranger, standing like statues alongside the major, before the door closed and the ship rumbled to life.

The transport lifted off, and powered its way up into the atmosphere. Exhausted, Dee watched as the major nodded to one of her agents, who withdrew a small remote control.

Sky Ranger began to yell something, but Dee's instincts grabbed her.

A little heat there, said her luck.

She complied, and the box burst into flames. The agent shrieked and fell back. The box burned to a cinder while they watched.

"What was that?" Sky Ranger demanded angrily.

"A hyperspace inhibitor," the major said. "Once they entered hyperspace, it would have caused them a world of trouble. Their ship *should* have been ripped to shreds." She smiled coldly. "We had to try."

"You gave your word," he said.

"You aren't worthy of my word, traitor," she snapped. "Get them aboard. You're both headed for Calvasna now." She glared at Dee. "Sedate her."

Dee barely had time to react before someone stuck a needle in her arm, and she fell into a deep sleep.

◄►► ◄◄►

Seera Trikon dropped away rapidly behind them.

"They aren't pursuing," Felipe said from the pilot's seat. "They're just sitting there."

"Remarkable," Broussard said, shaking his head. "I had no idea she could do that. I didn't know she was like him."

"Neither did I," Renna said. "No one knew."

"She had some secrets, it seems," Brian Gannett said.

"Hyperspace engines ready," Felipe said. "This ship is great! Course set for Reilis."

"Go," said Gannett and Renna at the same time. They glanced at one another, and then, after holding one another's gaze for a few long seconds, looked away again. *He does have nice eyes,* Renna thought.

"I hope they'll be okay back there," Renna said.

"I have my doubts," said Broussard sadly.

"Okay," said Felipe. "Okay... yes! Here we go!"

The ship shuddered and accelerated. Then, with a bang and a jolt, they left the Seera system behind.

"Be safe," Renna breathed.

[PART TWO]

[CHAPTER 13]

RENNA DREAMED OF FIRE.

At night, she felt the blue heat of Seera pouring down on her shoulders in shimmering waves as the world around her baked, cracked and burned. The gray desert sands shifted and blew in the endless, moaning wind.

She saw Allison raise her rifle, and shriek that horrible, wailing shriek as fire consumed her from the inside out.

She felt the refugee ship pitch, lurch, and burst into flame all around her. *Amy. Amy!*

And, at the center of everything, Dee laughed and danced as the white-hot flames roared all around her. Above it all, Sky Ranger hovered, impassive.

She started awake in a cold sweat, panting and delirious. A few moments passed before she remembered she was safe on Reilis. Dee was far, far away on Calvasna, and more than a month had passed since they'd escaped from the Seera system.

Brian Gannett stirred in the bed next to her. "All right?" he asked sleepily, his sandy hair an unkempt mess.

"Yeah," she said. "Sorry. Go back to sleep."

"Same dream?" he asked, that sharp incisiveness returning for a moment.

"Yeah. I'm... I'm going to get up for a while. But you go back to sleep."

He mumbled an agreement, rolled over and started snoring softly again.

She smiled fondly down at him. Their relationship had taken off right after they'd made it to Reilis. Brian seemed lost without the Fleet; meanwhile, the other refugees, unsure of how to feel about him, gave him a wide berth. He'd saved them, and they repaid him by treating him like something they scraped off the bottom of their shoes. It made Renna want to scream.

They'd done the same to Sky Ranger, of course. Sometimes she wished he were here. She missed talking to him.

And yet, she had sought Brian out once they'd landed. When she was alone, she missed his crazy spark, his strange and steady charisma, and his quiet strength. When they discovered themselves in his bed together night after night, she decided it only made sense to put off going back to her lonely room alone permanently.

He was no Sky Ranger in bed, but he was kind, sincere, and above all else, determined. He made up for his lack of skill with a mad enthusiasm she found endearing. She discovered the patch of hair on his well-muscled chest, the way he groaned and arched, the taste of his lips.

He filled an empty place in her heart. It was, for now, enough.

She took a shower and fixed herself a cup of something the Rätons called *ilynisilili*, but that humans had shortened to "hot silly." The Rätons, who were completely unaffected by caffeine and found the drink's sweet taste mildly off-putting, had no idea why humans had developed such a passion for the stuff, but didn't mind selling it by the truckload to them. It was, Renna reflected, cheaper than smuggling coffee across the border.

She sat by the window and watched the city of Arheligon drift past thirty stories below. Rätons didn't keep to diurnal cycles, preferring to sleep in short bursts like cats, rather than all at once like humans, so the city was nearly as lively as it would have been during full sunlight.

Reilis was a beautiful, ancient world, and Arheligon lay at its heart. Majestic peaks rose high off in the distance, while ocean waves lapped the city's shores just a few kilometers away. All of the plants were a vivid, verdant green or orange, the sky was deep blue, and the air smelled clear and crisp. It could have been Earth but for the teeming mass of lithe, greenish Rätons.

The exile community on Reilis had plenty of money and provided well for the steady trickle of refugees who found their way across the border. Renna suspected that the Räton government was behind a lot of the money that seemed to flow endlessly from the top exiles. Maybe they were hoping that the exiles' leaders, most of whom were former UNP members who had held positions of power under the old government, would eventually get their act together enough to go back and force the Reformists out of power. So far, all they'd done was sit around in the city, accumulating wealth and influence.

Renna sipped her hot silly gingerly, and thought of Dee. Where was she now? How was she doing? Was Sky Ranger with her? Was she even still alive? They had no word. No one knew anything about what had happened to the two extrahumans, except that they'd been taken to Calvasna. People didn't come back from the Confederation's capital world.

She shivered. Cold thoughts, and the hot drink provided little comfort.

A warm arm slipped around her shoulders. She leaned back into Brian's embrace and sighed.

"Rough night?" he asked.

"Yeah," she mumbled. "Sorry."

"Don't be." He kissed the top of her head. "Are you up now?"

"Yeah. You?"

"Might as well be." He slid into the seat across from her. "You shouldn't drink so much of that stuff," he said, pointing at the hot silly. "The Rats say it's bad for you." "Rat" was a not-particu-larly-nice way to refer to a Räton.

She shrugged. "So what?"

"So it's bad for you." He smiled wanly.

"Lots of stuff is bad for me," she said. "Not sleeping. Wor-rying." *You.*

The silence stretched between them.

"I think we need to get out of here," she said at last. "Go do something."

"Like what?" he said, not bothering to muster any interest.

" Something," she said. "Anything."

"I don't know," he said, voice flat.

"We could try looking for work with the Refugee Council again," she offered. "Maybe they'll have something for you today."

"I'd have to get in line with about a hundred other guys," he said. "And they don't like me much anyway."

"Well..." she considered. "We could head out to the moun-tains. Or to the shore."

"Mm," he said, eyes blank. "Maybe."

This was a familiar impasse. He was restless, he wanted to do something, but never wanted to do any of the things she suggested and had no ideas of his own. So he'd sit around all day and fume or be depressed, and *she'd* be annoyed and bored out of her skull.

"Fine," she said. "Do what you like. *I'm* going out for a while. Maybe I'll go catch up with Marsha, see if she's seen Willow."

"Okay," he said. "Want me to come with you?"

"No," she snapped. She threw her coat on. "I'll see you later."

◄≽►◄≼►

She left the dull human quarter and walked down through the foggy morning cold to the shore. She passed Rätons walking together in groups of three, four, and five. They always seemed to be in groups. She almost never saw a solitary Räton, or even a pair. Different psychology, she mused. By comparison, even the most social humans would seem like loners.

She had no intention of going to see Marsha, who had become an insufferable martyr during the last month. Willow, on the other hand, had disappeared entirely. Renna hadn't seen her since just after they landed on Reilis. Raul claimed to have seen her hanging around in the city center, but Renna had never been able to find any sign of her there or anywhere else.

Some other people, though, were a lot easier to find. She sat on a bench on the beach and waited. Sure enough here came Broussard and Felipe, right on schedule, dragging their home-made metal detector/excavator behind them. They'd apparently made the device out of other stuff they found on the beach. The whole situation was oddly circular. Renna waved. They both broke into grins and headed in her direction.

"Hey, stranger!" said Felipe, upbeat as always. "How's life with the soldier-man treating you?" "

"Fine, I guess," Renna replied. "How are you two doing? Find anything good?"

Broussard shook his head. "No, not today. But it's still early—the sun hasn't even come up yet." He and Felipe had gravitated to the shore instantly, and spent most of their time strolling along, looking for things that they could sell. They had been able to scrape out a pretty good living from it. Broussard insisted that people from Seera Terron were just naturally resourceful, and Renna believed it. Of all the people who had arrived on Reilis with her, only the two of them had taken no money or shelter from the exile leaders.

They claimed to have fallen in love with the ocean. Renna figured they just liked places where there was sand.

"Have either of you seen Willow?" she asked.

"No," Broussard said. "And I doubt we will. She's in hiding, poor thing."

"Yeah," Felipe said. "I tried talking to her back on the ship..."

More like flirting shamelessly, Renna thought. Felipe wasn't good at being subtle.

"...But she never even looked at me," he finished. "It was like she was a million light-years away. I guess killing that guy really got to her."

"She was always fragile," Renna said. "And what happened back there... it hit her hard. But I'd hoped she'd have come out of it by now."

Broussard shrugged in his way. "Eh. She either will or she won't. If she's hiding and doesn't want to be found, there's little enough we can do about it." He sighed and stared at the foggy sky. "I think it's going to be cloudy."

"No, it'll be sunny," said Felipe. "Remember that this keeps happening, it's foggy in the morning and then sunny later on?"

"Oh," Broussard said. "That's true." He smiled gamely at Renna. "I don't know much about clouds. There's so much water here! France was like this when I was a boy. I like it."

"It's easy to get used to," Felipe agreed. "I like it, too. Did I tell you, Renna, that I went sailing the other day? We went out on a boat! We used to do that sometimes on the lakes on Terron, but the water here is so huge, it has all these big waves!"

Broussard turned a little green. "Of that, I don't wish to be reminded."

"It was a lot of fun," Felipe said. "I threw up only twice. I think I'd be a lot better at it if I went again! See, the lakes on Terron are flat, they don't move at all. That's what I'm used to."

"Sounds like you two are having fun, at least," she said.

"So no work?" Broussard asked.

She shook her head. "Nothing. Brian is going stir-crazy."

"Well, they're not going to give a job to a guy who was in the Fleet only a few months ago," Broussard said. "They don't trust him."

"He only saved us all," Renna said irritably.

"Your group doesn't trust easily," said Broussard. "I suppose I don't blame them."

"I haven't been able to find work, either," Renna said, changing the subject back. "There's just nothing out there for us."

"Did you have a job back on Earth?" Felipe asked.

"Sure," Renna said. "I did a lot of things. But there's nothing here for me to do."

"So then. What are you up to today?" Broussard said.

"I don't know," said Renna heavily. "Nothing. I just needed to get out for a while. See if there's anything going on."

"There probably isn't," Felipe said.

"Never is much," said Broussard.

Silence drifted in like the fog. Felipe and Broussard exchanged glances. Renna got the sense that they wanted to get going.

"Okay," she said. "Hey. Will you let me know if you hear anything about Willow?"

"I'll keep an ear out," said Broussard.

"Thanks," Renna said. "I hope you find some good stuff today."

Felipe grinned again. "You bet we will." With a wave, they set off, hauling their strange machine behind them.

Renna exhaled, and listened to the sound of the waves crashing against the shore. She could feel her body start to relax. Her mind drifted. She thought of hot deserts, and cold cities huddled against northern lakes. She thought of Amy, of Sky Ranger, and of Brian.

She wondered how her mother was. Maybe by now she'd have forgiven her. Probably not.

She wasn't sure how much time passed after that. The sun rose, and the fog burned off. After a while, she became aware of someone sitting next to her on the bench; a slight human woman with long silver hair.

"Renna Fernández Silva," she said without preamble. "My name is Penny Silverwing. We need to talk."

[CHAPTER 14]

PAINFULLY BRILLIANT ORANGE-RED LIGHT streamed in from the viewports as Calvasna's ancient sun set over the brown, blue, and white ball below. Sky Ranger could see the lights of Confederation City radiating out from the dark circle of Crescent Bay like a starry spider crouching on the surface of the planet. Calvasna had no other real cities beyond the Confederation's burgeoning new capital.

The nameless prison ship floated silently above the rapidly darkening surface, completing yet another cycle around the planet. It was the strangest of the few ships Sky Ranger had been on; there was almost no engine noise and the artificial gravity was surprisingly low, but oddly stable.

Soon the orbiting Peltan Station would slide into view, and Sky Ranger would strain his eyes to see the short bursts and flares of shuttles ascending and descending.

In the beginning, he'd hoped that one of those shuttles might be coming for him, or that it might carry Dee back. But in the weeks since, that hope had gradually ebbed away.

"Hey," a woman called from the doorway. "Sky Ranger!"

He waved from the chair. "Over here, Jill," he said. She perked up and half-walked, half-flew across to where he was sitting. She seemed to skip over the ground like a flat stone over the water.

He'd seen her do that the first day, and his heart had leaped with wonder. In the next seconds, he'd recognized her.

"You must really like the view," she said, settling into a chair next to him.

"It's peaceful," he said. "And it's a nice view."

"I guess," she said, bored. "Hey. Doug's here. Thought you ought to know."

Sky Ranger lifted an eyebrow. "I didn't see his shuttle come in," he said.

"He's been here for a couple of hours. Why do you care when he comes and goes, anyway?"

Sky Ranger smiled. "I just do," he said. "I'm sure he'll come find me sooner or later. He always does."

"Well, whatever. He's here. I'm off." Jill skip-flew out of the room.

"Thanks," he said to her retreating back.

Jill. He leaned back, eyes closed in thought. She was one of five others who lived aboard this ship. Every one of them had been here almost three years.

And every single one of them was an extrahuman.

Sky Ranger and Dee had suffered a two-week trip on board the ConFedMilPol ship, during which Dee was almost always kept sedated. The guards in gray clearly feared her powers, and with good reason. If she had been able to regain consciousness and focus, she could have crippled the ship with a thought. Once they arrived in orbit around Calvasna, they had immediately hustled Dee into a shuttle to the surface. This time, Sky Ranger had been the one sedated. When he'd woken up, he was on board a shuttle docked with this ship.

They'd shoved him through the airlock and left him to his own devices. The ship had no guards or other Confederation personnel. Why would they bother with guards? There was no escape. He floated through the corridors, adjusting to the ship's surprisingly steady gravity, and entered the common room.

Jill was sitting at the table, gnawing on a fingernail. She had screamed and flattened herself against the ceiling. In a few moments, four others raced into the room.

"My God," said someone. "Sky Ranger."

Sky Ranger could only gape at them. He realized after a moment that he was grinning like an idiot.

"Well, well," a short, balding man said, his voice like nails across metal. "Look who's been caught. Hey, Sky Ranger. Welcome to the second coming of Union Tower."

It was astonishing to find so many other extrahumans here, three years after he'd been sure they'd all died. Even more astonishing, they all knew their original names. For reasons he didn't quite understand, the Confederation had given them back those crucial missing pieces.

Sweet, compassionate Emily, formerly Whitelight, was a limited flyer and strong healer. James, who Sky Ranger remembered as a boy called Blue Blur who used to run to the kitchen for him, had grown into a prickly, nervous young man with incredible speed. Anthony was a sad and lonely old man with the rare ability to manipulate matter and generate force barriers; someone had stuck him with the unoriginal name of Forcefield. And then there was Jill, who was a young woman with a variety of low-level powers, including flight, healing, and strength. She claimed to have a little prescience and firestarting, too, though she never actually seemed to be able to manage either. Her name had been the Sampler, which she openly despised.

Then there was Roger, a prescient of limited ability who liked calling himself Longview. Roger had walked up to the front door of Union Tower one day early in Sky Ranger's tenure as leader, demanding to be allowed to join. It was, Sky Ranger recalled, the only time he knew of that *anyone* had joined the Union voluntarily.

Roger, not content to sit on the sidelines, had also begged for a position in the LED. When his powers proved too inconsistent, he befriended the Watcher and commenced making himself as obnoxious as possible. After the Watcher jumped to his death, Roger got much worse. He had become so critical of every move Sky Ranger made that eventually Sky Ranger had him banned from the top floors of the Tower.

Roger told the story of how they'd all survived that evening as they gathered together in the common room.

"I woke up that morning and everything felt wrong," he explained, clearly relishing the chance to tell the story to someone who hadn't heard it a million times before. "But I didn't pay it any mind at first. Then, as it got worse and worse, I knew I had to do something. So I grabbed as many people as I could find and all but shoved them out the door! James helped me with his speed; he got Emily's cats."

James grumbled.

Roger smiled, arms folded over his chest. "It was the strangest thing. There was no one guarding the gate in the fence. The ConFedMilPol people who were usually there had left. So we just ran out and across the street. A minute later, we heard the first explosions. I got everyone across the street, and yelled for anyone left to come out. I wanted to run back in there, but there was no point."

Jill snorted. "You were crying like a little girl the whole time."

Roger glared at her.

"We got lucky," Anthony said, absently flicking his force-field on and off. It cast a dull yellowish aura around him. "What can I say?"

"When the Tower came down, I thought for sure we'd be killed," said Roger grandly. "But we weren't. It was by luck and my quick thinking that we got out at all."

"Anthony saved us at the last minute," Emily said quietly. She held a purring cat on her chest. She smiled down at it. "I had my cats with me, I grabbed them when Roger said to go. When we got across the street, Anthony put up a forcefield. We were saved from any debris."

Sky Ranger glanced at Anthony, who shrugged and looked away.

"In any case," Roger said. "I think that was the clearest indication yet of the possibilities of my powers."

"I... I can see that," said Sky Ranger. "But how did you end up here?"

"Well, there's not much to tell there," said Roger with a dismissive gesture. "We had nowhere to go, so we all stayed together to see if we could help find any survivors. Then the Black Bands took us into custody, and turned us over to ConFed-MilPol. Oh, I was furious about it all in the beginning. How dare they keep us like pets when we'd done nothing wrong! But as time has gone on, I've become accustomed to it."

He glanced at Sky Ranger, his narrow eyes fixing on him like a hawk eyeing prey. "I've always wondered. Where were *you* that day?"

Sky Ranger shook his head. How could he explain? "It's a long story," he said evasively.

"We have plenty of time," Roger said, leaning back in his chair. He seemed to be delighting in Sky Ranger's discomfort. "Let me guess. Off playing with your black-clad pals?"

"In a manner of speaking," said Sky Ranger. "Yes. I was with the government in Australia. But...but when I found out that they were behind the destruction of the Tower, I turned against them. I spent years fighting them before I had to run. That's when they caught up to me."

"The *government* did it?" Emily breathed.

"You ever thought otherwise? Poor, innocent Emily, did you actually believe that nonsense about terrorists?" Roger asked snidely. "You can be so marvelously dense sometimes."

Emily seemed to shrink into herself. She petted her cat and looked away from everyone.

"And that's it?" he asked Sky Ranger. "You just turned on them and that was that?"

"There's more to it," said Sky Ranger. "But that's essentially what happened."

"Well then," said Roger. "It seems that you were a big hero after all!" He smirked. "Who could have guessed?"

Now, four weeks later, Sky Ranger sat in the lounge and waited for Doug Palma to come find him. At length, he would.

Once Sky Ranger was aboard, Doug hadn't wasted any time; he'd summoned him to his windowless interior office right away. The place was brightly lit and furnished with a little table, two chairs, and a couch.

Doug was the kind of man anyone could look at and not see. He wasn't special or unique in any way; the eye just slid right over him. Yet he had a kind of magnetism when he actually spoke that seemed to draw everyone to him. He came to visit and talk with the extrahumans aboard the prison ship. Apparently, he had been doing this for a long time. "I'm not sure what you think you're going to get out of me," he said. "I don't know too much beyond what I've already told the ConFedMilPol guys."

Doug's expression didn't shift a micron from that irritatingly bland smile. "You make the mistake of thinking this is an interrogation! Let me assure you it isn't."

"So why are you here?"

"To help, at least today."

Sky Ranger gave him a sour look. "Come on. Do better. Why are you here?"

"It's the truth, I'm here to be of assistance. Specifically, I'm here today to help you adjust to the ship, and to give you a little information about what we're all doing here."

"The only information *I* want," said Sky Ranger, trying his best to be menacing, "is what you're holding all of us for, and where you've taken Dee."

"Oh, that second one's easy," said Doug. "She's been taken to Military Command."

It figured. "What for? And why only her?"

"I don't pretend to know why they do what they do," said Doug. "But I'm led to believe that it's because she's been deemed to be more unstable than the rest of you. From what you told ConFedMilPol, she's just coming in to her powers now, correct?"

"Yes," said Sky Ranger. "I told them that. She was lucky before, but she didn't display firestarting until Seera Trikon."

Doug nodded, a strange glint in his eye. "Yes. Fires. More powerful than Jill's fires, what few she has... well. They want to supervise her, and make sure she doesn't hurt anyone. That's hard to do if she's confined here with you." Sky Ranger made a disbelieving grunt. "I have to assume you'd try to force her to find a way to escape."

"And that would be bad."

"Yes. We're in space, Sky Ranger! Fire aboard a spaceship is a dangerous business! It's a lot safer for her to be on the planet."

"So why am I not on the planet?"

"It's safe to hold you here. And they have no interest in you right now," said Doug evenly.

Sky Ranger winced. After all he'd done, they didn't even have an interest in him?

"So why did they come after me on Seera Trikon?" he asked, pride smarting. "Come on. They came out that far to catch me, not her! They didn't even know about her."

"You're just a run-of-the-mill traitor, if a high-profile one. Oh, don't get me wrong, they wanted you. But Dee turned out to be a lot more interesting, apparently," Doug said. "They're like that sometimes. They don't have a long attention span over there."

"And what are you doing with us, now that you have us?" Sky Ranger asked.

"Our purpose here is twofold," he said. "Our first is scientific. We're observing how your powers work and how you use them. That's the sort of research that's been done since the very beginning, as I'm sure you're well aware, and we think we're getting closer to isolating the cause of extrahuman mutation."

"Okay," Sky Ranger said. A lot of people had tried that one. No one had ever succeeded. "Good luck with that. And the second?"

"Second," said Doug, "And I feel most importantly, we're preserving and *protecting* a type of human that has been almost entirely eradicated.

Sky Ranger fingers twitched. He had to restrain himself from leaping out of his chair and ripping the man in half. "*You* destroyed us! It was *you* who brought the Tower down!" he accused Doug.

Doug shook his head. "No. Sky Ranger, listen to me. Please!" Sky Ranger forced himself to sit still, thoroughly enjoying the sudden look of fear in Doug's eyes. Maybe he was remembering that Sky Ranger had, in fact, once ripped a man in half with his bare hands. *Not so run-of-the-mill after all, am I?* "I know you've been out of circulation, so you have no reason to know. But it wasn't the government that brought the Tower down. It was a rogue element within the Reform Party and ConFedMilPol who wanted to see all extrahumans destroyed."

"You expect me to swallow that?" said Sky Ranger. "I was *there*. I saw what happened for myself."

"I'm afraid it's the truth," said Doug. " ConFedMilPol caught up with the rest of them after you, er, took care of their leader." *The thin man,* thought Sky Ranger. He had never known his name. *Security,* he had said. *We must be safe.*

The man he had ripped in half.

"Okay!" cried the thin man. "All right, we did! We had to! It was for the good of the world that extrahumans not exist! Please, you must understand, we did what we had to do! What if one of you went rogue? Look at your own power! You can't be trusted, not forever, so you had to be destroyed!"

"Extrahumans are dangerous?" asked Sky Ranger, voice suddenly calm.

"Yes," confirmed the thin man.

"They should be eliminated."

"Yes," said the thin man, breathing again. "I'm glad you finally understand."

"You're an extrahuman, too," said Sky Ranger calmly. He held the thin man by the shoulders and, with a quick, neat motion, ripped him in half. The thin man's final shriek echoed through the room.

◆▷▶◀◁◆

"We executed or imprisoned them for their crimes," Doug was saying. "They did not represent official policy in any way. Sky Ranger, we are very, deeply sorry for what happened."

"Amazing," Sky Ranger said, laughing. "You can't seriously expect that I'm going to think it was all a big *misunderstanding,* can you?"

"That's an interesting word to use," said Doug. "'Misunderstanding.' Hm. Trust me, if you can, though; I am telling you the truth."

"Why should I believe you?"

Doug looked deadly serious, and leaned forward. "You're all still alive," he said. "If we wanted you dead, why didn't we just kill you? You're a little harder to kill than most, granted, but there are many things even you can't survive. We could have just irradiated Seera Trikon, or tossed you out an airlock on the way back to Calvasna."

There was that. Sky Ranger fell back for a moment. Doug smiled his maddening smile again.

"There are a lot of people who hate you for so publicly turning against the state," Doug said. "Sometimes we try to rehabilitate traitors. In your case I don't know if they'll expend the energy. Well." He shifted gears. "I should tell you about the ship. There are two distinct sections—one here in the aft, and the other forward for crew and controls. The sections are completely separated by a solid steel wall. They run on different systems, with different power supplies and air circulation. No vents, no common circuitry, nothing. There's no way to get through, unless you think you can punch through twenty centimeters of steel."

"Nice prison," said Sky Ranger icily.

"We have much worse," said Doug cheerily.

◄►►◄◄►

Sky Ranger walked the corridors endlessly those first weeks, trying to find something, anything, that he could use to escape. There had to be a way off this ship. Every prison had ways in and out. But what?

He found nothing. He waited at the airlock, but they wouldn't cycle it unless he was in a completely different room. They would detach the shuttle if he tried waiting them out, and they always knew where he was. The walls were thick. There was next to no engine noise, so he couldn't tell where the engines even were.

There was, he slowly came to realize, no way he could think of to get off the ship.

Still. There had to be something he could do. He'd just have to watch for it.

◆►◄◆

Their next meeting, which happened a few days after their first, went a little better.

"Settling in?" Doug asked.

"Oh, I'm fine," said Sky Ranger. "No troubles here. Except for being a prisoner on board a spaceship above Calvasna."

"Glad to hear it," said Doug. He held up a syringe. "I know they took some samples from you before, but I've been ordered to get another. Can you hold still a minute?" Sky Ranger nodded. Doug jammed the needle in Sky Ranger's forearm, pulled up about a milliliter of fluid, and withdrew it. Sky Ranger winced. Everyone needed a lot more force to get through his tough skin. "So I'm guessing you've got questions," he said, capping the needle and slipping it into a case.

Sky Ranger did, in fact, have dozens.

The only thing he trusted himself to ask, though, was the same question he had led off with last time. "Where's Dee?"

"You already asked that," said Doug. "And I told you. She's down on the planet."

"I want to see her," said Sky Ranger.

Doug shook his head. "I'm sorry. It's just not possible. Not right now. But maybe soon."

"That's not good enough for me," said Sky Ranger.

Doug made a note on his datapad. "I tell you what. I'm going to put in a request. Maybe we can get some communications time. She can call up here. You can see her, talk to her. I can't let you leave the ship, and I know they don't want her coming up here, so that's the best I can do. Okay?"

It wasn't okay. But Sky Ranger desperately wanted to see that she was alive and unhurt. "Fine," he said. "When?"

"No telling," said Doug. "All I can do is request. So. What else is on your mind? Have you tried to escape, yet?"

Sky Ranger's knuckles ached at the mention of it. "No," he replied.

"Yes, you have. You don't think we monitor what's happening here?" Doug said. "Trust me, punching the wall won't help at all. It's pretty thick. I did say that, didn't I?"

"Right," said Sky Ranger.

"But you can keep trying," said Doug. "Try all along the wall. Take James with you. He used to kick the walls. Put a little dent in one, but that's all. He broke that leg, I think; he's lucky he heals fast."

"Blue Blur," said Sky Ranger. "That's what he was back at the Tower."

"Yes," said Doug. "The old names. We gave everyone else back theirs. Do you want yours? We can look it up for you, you know."

Sky Ranger shook his head. "No. I don't need it. Sky Ranger is who I am."

"You're sure?"

"I'm sure," said Sky Ranger. They moved quickly on to other things. The food. The temperature. His problems with the gravity, which he still couldn't get used to.

And then he was left on his own.

Names again. Crimson Cadet had told him about names, and everyone here was just as attached to their original ones. He had tried to call Jill "Sampler" only one time before she had icily informed him that she was *Jill* now, thank you very much, and that she'd kick him if he dared say that name again. Anthony and James had reacted the same way. Roger had been the worst. He had ambushed Sky Ranger after his run-in with Jill.

"Seriously, why did you name her the Sampler?" Roger had scoffed, glaring at Sky Ranger. "How demeaning! She sounds like she's on the menu."

"We were running low on names," Sky Ranger deadpanned.

Roger didn't laugh. "But can you imagine going through your entire life named that? Can you imagine the humiliation? Why not use our real names? We were born with them. Why invent stupid fake names? Why steal what was ours originally? Answer me that."

Sky Ranger shrugged. "Tradition," he said. And truly, that was part of the reason, but he didn't feel like going into the rest with Roger.

Roger seethed. "One good thing about the Reformists," he said. "They gave us our names back. Names *you* stole. So why should I follow you instead of them?"

"Names are important," Sky Ranger II said in his quiet baritone.

"You have to hold them with special regard, SC"—he called his new Sky Cadet "SC." He had called the old one simply "Cadet"—"They matter to us in ways that they don't for other people."

"Why don't we have normal names?" Sky Cadet, so recently Little Hawk, had asked. He was still not used to his own newly granted one.

"It's complicated," said the old Sky Ranger. "Do you know what a superhero is?" Sky Cadet shook his head. "Well. Long before we ever existed, there were lots of stories about people like us."

Sky Ranger waited for Sky Cadet to ask the obvious question. When he didn't, Sky Ranger cleared his throat and continued. "These stories came from people's imaginations. They didn't know that people would be born one day who could actually fly, or actually see into the future, but they imagined stories about them. They were very popular for a long time. These people in the stories were called 'superheroes,' and they all had names that were something like ours. Captain this, Wonder that, and so on. When the first extrahumans realized their powers, they decided to give themselves those sorts of names. The first Sky Ranger did that, you know. That's where our title comes from. It was part of that tradition. Do you understand?"

Sky Cadet didn't, not really, but he nodded anyway.

"Good. Some extrahumans kept their own names, back then. That was before the Union, of course. At some point, after the Union came into existence... it became more of a requirement than a choice."

He stared pointedly at Sky Cadet. "Uh. Why?" Sky Cadet finally asked.

Sky Ranger II furrowed his lined brow, clearly annoyed that his new protégé wasn't as quick on the uptake as the old one. "I don't know. But I have some ideas. It could be that the original Sky Ranger preferred it that way, although I think I knew him well enough to say that that wasn't the case. Another possibility is that because we aren't allowed to have families of our own, the names and naming make us feel more like a family. But the real reason, I think, is that it cemented our differences from other people. It became harder to be normal. We were separated from our own human origins. And that... made the Confederation happy."

A shadow passed over Sky Ranger II's face. "We exist," he said gloomily, "Because they allow it. So we make them as happy as we can. There's no other way to survive."

"Tradition," Sky Ranger III said helplessly. "That's why."

"That's stupid," said Roger, and stalked off.

What could Sky Ranger say to that? He knew his old name. He remembered a kind woman calling him "Robbie," once. But what did that matter? The Union had given him his name. The Union had been his family, not some half-forgotten mother or father.

He didn't understand why the others didn't see it that way.

Sky Ranger still wandered the corridors, but he found himself drawn to the observation lounge, too. It reminded him a little of his old office at the top of the Tower.

He hid there. His interactions with the others had started off well enough, but he found that everyone here tended to just drift to their own spaces. There wasn't a lot of conversation to be part of. He tried engaging them, at times, but most of them just slipped away. The exceptions were Jill and, annoyingly, Roger. Sometimes they got together and needled one another about the old times, and everything Sky Ranger had ever done wrong.

For now he sat in the observation lounge, waiting for Doug.

He fiddled idly with the clasp on Renna's pack. Someday, he promised himself, he would give this back to her.

On cue, the door opened and a familiar voice said, "Hey, Sky Ranger. Mind if I join you?"

"Go ahead," said Sky Ranger, although he did mind.

"I have some good news for you," Doug said.

"Sure you do," said Sky Ranger.

Doug smiled beatifically. "I've arranged a communication with Dee."

Sky Ranger levitated out of his seat. "When?"

"Tomorrow," said Doug. "I wanted to let you know as soon as I found out."

Sky Ranger settled onto the floor. "Thank you," he said to Doug, actually meaning it.

Doug's smile broadened. "You're welcome."

[CHAPTER 15]

HYLAR **G**ORDON **B**RIETS HAD ONCE BEEN THE United Nations Party chairman for the city of Melbourne, and because of that, he was one of the highest authorities among the refugees on Reilis. He was short and squat, with a dark mustache that quivered when he became agitated.

It was quivering now. "You can't seriously—! Of all the insane—! Do you—?" He paced around his luxurious office. "No. Flat out. No."

Renna felt like kicking him. "Please! You can't just leave them! Um. If we do this it would be a great propaganda coup," she said, hoping that wasn't as pathetic as it sounded. He fixed her with a porcine scowl.

"And who would see it? We can't transmit into Confederation space. The media is controlled by the Reformists, and would they tell everyone what had happened? I think not."

"But they helped save us," said Renna. "You have to admit that we owe them."

Briets's expression darkened, mustache twitching. "They saved *you*. *We* have no obligation to them. Besides, why would we save someone like *Sky Ranger*? He's a traitorous Reformist Black Bander, just like the rest! I can't imagine *he* needs much rescuing."

"He was a refugee, like us," snapped Renna, seething with

fury. "He had turned against them. He *fought* them. It's why they wanted him back so badly! Don't you get that? And if not for him, what about *Dee*? It's wrong to abandon her there. She's just a thirteen-year-old girl!"

Briets's expression softened and he stopped pacing. "Look. I have a daughter that age, so... I do sympathize." The edge came back into his voice. "But understand, miss, we can't go after them. We don't have the resources to spare. Do you know that 2110 is right around the corner? You know what that means."

Renna stared at him blankly. This year was 2110. What was he talking about?

"The election!" he sputtered. "The election for the new Senate, and the presidential race! Don't tell me you've forgotten."

In truth, Renna *had* forgotten. The UNP and almost all other opposition parties had been outlawed. The Senate was filled with either Reformists or with members from regional parties closely tied to the Reformists. Yes, elections were held every five years, but Renna had never thought for a moment that the Reformists would allow anyone but themselves or their allies to run.

"You're kidding," was all she could say.

"Not at all," he said smoothly. "The election must happen. That's the law, and we are ready for it." He held up a hand as Renna started to object. "Yes, the UNP can't openly compete, due to their illegal banning of our party. But we can support *an* opposition candidate. *That's* where our efforts will go. Besides, it would be suicide to send someone to Calvasna after two extrahumans," he continued, voice dripping with disgust as he pronounced *extrahumans*. "Especially with the elections coming up. We'd lose men for no good reason, and our backers would wonder why we were wasting their money and supplies."

"You don't have to send in your own men," Renna said, mortified to hear the pleading tone in her voice. "You can just help us to go. Get us a ship. Better, let us have the ship *we* brought you."

"It's too dangerous," said Briets. "Anyway, that ship is already being retrofitted for other uses." *Like what?* Renna wondered. *Space yachting?*

Briets continued, "Listen. It is my *duty* to think of the Party and the general fate of all humankind! If everyone came to us asking to help them get their loved ones out of wherever the Reformists have them stashed, we'd be doing nothing but that. Let me be perfectly frank, *miss.* We are sorry for your loss, but we can't do anything to help you. And that's final. ...Is there anything else I can do for you?"

She stood up. "I think that's fine, thanks," she said coldly. "I'll see myself out, then."

Brian met her at a small café outside the luxurious hotel where the UNP bosses of the refugees made their headquarters. He immediately frowned as soon as he saw her murderous expression.

"It went badly," he guessed.

She sat down and slammed her hand down on the table with such force that the hot silly Brian had waiting for her sloshed out of the cup. "I knew it wouldn't go well— Penny said they wouldn't be likely to go for it—but I was hoping he'd at least have a damn *heart* about the fact that the Reformists have a *little girl* trapped there having *God knows what* done to her!" She took a breath. "Gah! I'm so pissed off, I'm actually shaking."

He awkwardly placed a hand on her shoulder. "Well, you tried. But Penny was right. We're going to have to find a way to do this ourselves."

Renna looked around. "Speaking of Penny... where is she?"

"Back home. She said she didn't want to be seen if she could help it."

"Oh." Renna leaned into his arm. He smelled nice. He'd showered. Progress! "Thanks," she said.

"For what?" he asked, surprised.

"For being here."

He was silent for a moment. "I... I'm sorry I couldn't come in with you," he said.

"That's okay. They probably would have just thrown you out." His first meeting with the UNP big shots had ended that way. They despised him because he had been in the Fleet, despite the fact that he had risked everything to bring refugees here. That summed up the United Nations Party in exile perfectly.

Renna sipped her drink, deflating.

"...So now what?" she asked. "I'm not sure where to go from here."

"Obviously, we need to go to Calvasna," said Brian.

"Do we?" Renna found herself asking. "Maybe Briets was right. It could be suicide, going there. I'm a refugee, and you're a traitor." He grimaced. "Sorry! But you know that's what they think."

"I know," he admitted. "You're right. It's what I am. But..." He trailed off, and stared out the window.

"Sorry," said Renna, meaning it though she still had no clue what had upset him. She put a hand over his. "Really, forget it. I'm sorry I said that."

"You do have a point, though," he said slowly. "It would be dangerous, to say the least. But...it's better than sitting here for the rest of our lives. Like those guys in there." He jerked a thumb at the building across the street."

"So why are we still sitting here, then?" Renna said, egging him on. Brian almost never said this much in a single sitting anymore, and she thrilled to see the passion building in his eyes as he spoke. "Are we cowards?"

"No, we're refugees and traitors," he said, grinning. "But unlike them, we're going to make the most of it. ...I think I have a plan. We should go see Penny." He got up.

"My hot silly," Renna reminded him, not actually caring.

"We've got lots at home. Come on." He strode off briskly. Renna had to run after him to keep up, elated and unbelievably turned on. Later. Later!

Penny sat on the couch and stared at the wall, bored out of her mind. She hated being inside all the time, and she desperately missed flying.

She was tempted to try anyway, except that Prelate Celeste had extracted a promise from her *not* to fly while off-planet.

"And don't think we won't find out," Celeste had said, fixing her with a glare that would have made the devil wither. "If you do and get in trouble, don't expect us to come to your aid."

She wasn't taking it well. Three years of flying couldn't make up for over a decade of being grounded. Stupid Celeste.

Arheligon reminded her a little of New York. She found herself looking at the forest of gracefully tall buildings and expecting to find Union Tower among them, or Sky Ranger flitting in and out of the canyons, high above the street. But of course, Union Tower was gone and Sky Ranger...

Well, only the Temple seemed to know anything about *him*.

Whoever was running intelligence at West Arve Temple had received information that Sky Ranger was alive through their military sources. He was, they reported, a prisoner of ConFed-MilPol and assumed to be somewhere on Calvasna. But possibly of more interest was the rumor that they'd captured a young woman who could start fires with a word. Intrigued by both possibilities, the Temple had sent for Penny.

Prelate Celeste was short and slight, but always commanded the attention of everyone in whatever room she happened to be in. Her voice was high and clipped, and she wore a permanently stern look. She had aged quite a bit since Penny had seen her last. The lines around her eyes and mouth had deepened, and she had lost weight.

She offered a chair to Penny. "You're finally here," she said, clearly miffed. "Good. Sit." She studied Penny. "It's been a while, hasn't it? I don't believe I've seen you since I sent you and the boy off into the hills."

The boy. Ian, the baby they had rescued from Earth. Michael Forward, and others, had seen a future in which he had grown up to lead a revolution against the Confederation.

"I understand you regained your powers of flight," Celeste said.

"Yes," said Penny, wondering where this was going.

"A most wonderful miracle," Celeste said. "You should be glad."

"I am," Penny said honestly.

Celeste regarded her shrewdly for a moment further. Then she said, "So. I have information for you about Sky Ranger."

Penny leaned forward. Finally.

"Before I say anything further, let me tell you that we're planning to move the boy you knew as Ian and his adoptive father off-planet. It's become more difficult lately for us to protect them from the Confederation government. To put it bluntly, they know he's here on Valen and they want him. They currently are unaware of exactly where he is or what name he now goes by, but we believe it's only a matter of time before they find out."

"If they can find him here," Penny said, "then there's nowhere safe."

"No, not in human space," said Celeste with a tight smile. "So. We want to take him to *Räton* space. We have lined up several unobtrusive transports that will carry him to Reilis. From there, he will be taken by their government to a safe location deep within Räton space."

"Huh," said Penny. *What did this have to do with Sky Ranger?*

"I imagine you're wondering why I'm bothering to tell you this," continued Celeste in her high, clear voice. "I have not, as you can guess, told Monica, nor shall I. It's vital that this secret be kept, at least until the boy is safely out of the Confederation's reach."

"So why tell me?"

"We have evidence that Sky Ranger is alive," she said. "I know how much he meant to you. Monica explained it to me." Penny began to say something, but Celeste held up her hand. "Originally, we just had evidence that Sky Ranger's transport went down somewhere in the Seera system. However, our intelligence sources are now saying that there was a fight between the Confederation Military Police and a group of refugees on Seera Trikon very recently."

Penny idly wondered how it was that a religious organization had come to possess an intelligence network to rival Con-FedMilPol's.

"The sources say that a man who could fly and another, a girl who could start fires, may have been captured." Celeste continued. "I have to ask you, do you know who that girl might be?"

Penny shook her head, truly bewildered. Firestarters were extremely rare. "I don't remember knowing anyone like that."

"Then the story may well be false. But it's all we have at the moment."

"How is this connected with Ian?" asked Penny.

"Well," said Celeste. "Those two were the only ones captured. The rest of the refugees were allowed to escape, and presumably went to Reilis. Refugees end up there; the Rätons have a whole system in place there to keep them busy." She leaned forward intently. "I want you to accompany the boy and his adoptive father to Reilis. From there, you can find the refugees from Seera Trikon, and find out more about what happened to Sky Ranger."

Penny didn't hesitate. "Fine," she said. "But how am I going to get to him once I find out where he is?"

Celeste settled back into her chair. "In that, you're on your own. My primary concern is to make certain the boy is safe."

"...And you think I can do that."

"You have extraordinary capabilities, Penny," said Celeste. "And I don't dare expand the circle of people who know about him."

Penny frowned, feeling used. "You don't care if I find Sky Ranger."

Celeste shrugged. It was a tiny, almost imperceptible motion. "I do care, in fact. I have standing instructions to bring as many extrahumans to Valen as possible."

"Why?"

"Many reasons," Celeste said, expression unchanging.

Penny studied Celeste like one wolf might study another she wasn't entirely sure of, trying to figure her out before she took the wrong step.

"This has something to do with Val Altrera, doesn't it?" Penny asked shrewdly.

Celeste eyes shone, and her lips relaxed into a wistful smile—a genuine, almost beautiful sight. *Ah ha.* "Yes," she said.

"You knew him."

"I did." Her features darkened again, although the smile remained. "I was at his side when he died."

"And do you think he was...a saint?" Penny asked, trying to

keep the disbelief out of her voice.

Celeste nodded slowly, her eyes faraway. "I'll tell you this. I was born and raised a Catholic, but I never saw anything in that old Church that compared to the light that came pouring off of Val. He was incredible. The most amazing and infuriating man I've ever met. He gave me the orders to bring extrahumans here." She looked away, and rearranged the papers on her desk. The moment for speaking of Val Altrera was clearly fading fast.

"I see," said Penny. "I'll do whatever I can, then."

"Right," said Celeste, as if there had never been any question. "Be aware that the Temple can't provide you with much beyond a little money and the very limited intelligence we already have. You'll have to rely on your own resourcefulness to get more information, get to Calvasna or wherever they're keeping him, retrieve him and the girl, and return safely to Valen."

"Oh, that's all?" snapped Penny.

"I have full faith in you," said Celeste, and the interview came to an end.

Penny scowled as she left Celeste's office. It was impossible.

Still. Maybe she'd get lucky. Maybe it would actually work out.

Why not? She'd done impossible things before.

But once she was stuck aboard a tiny cargo ship with the boy formerly known to her as Ian, now improbably named Bann Delarian, and his gruff foster father, Ced, she began to have second thoughts.

How would she find out any more information? How could she get back into Confederation space once they left it? Could she break Sky Ranger out of a prison cell and escape to safety?

Penny had enjoyed seeing the now much larger, walking

and talking Bann, who she still thought of as Ian. The boy had obviously taken to life with his adoptive parent well, and each seemed quite pleased with the other. It gave her a little burst of pride to see them together and think, *I did this.*

Her good mood vanished as soon as she tried striking up a conversation with Bann's adoptive father, though.

"So," she began. "You remember me, right?"

Ced Delarian's face remained a stone mask. "Yes."

"How...how is he? Is he doing okay?" Bann was happily playing with some small tools he'd found lying around. He clanked them together, trying to make them into more than the sum of their parts.

"He is fine," Ced declared. He spoke with an accent she couldn't place.

"Oh, good. Ah," she said, and waited. He didn't elaborate.

"The Temple... how much did they tell you about him?" she ventured hesitantly.

"All," he rumbled.

"Really?" She was surprised. "And? ...What do you think of all of it?"

"We do as God and St. Val command," he replied instantly. A glint of some strong emotion registered in his eyes for a brief, startling moment. "But we do not speak of it."

"I wish he remembered me," she said. "But he was so young. He was a good kid, even though he cried a lot and pooped everywhere. Ha! I don't miss that. Still... We cared a lot about him. He—"

Ced held up a hand, stopping her. "I don't want to know," he said. "This is my son. His life began when he entered my home." His expression grew incrementally stormier. Penny had a sudden desire to be across the room. "And that is that."

"I see," she said.

"I would ask you not to talk with him."

"Why?" she cried.

"Respect my wishes," he said, mouth turning down at the corners. "He isn't to know. Not any of it. And he is *my son*. Do you understand?"

"Fine," she said, feeling her heart crack a little. "Whatever you say. You're the boss."

She stood and found a place to sit and meditate, far away from them both. The days stretched out ahead of them, interminable and dull.

There were times when she'd wake up on the cold floor and think for a horrifying moment that she was back in New York, living as Broken the bag lady on the streets. She'd look up expecting to see one of the alleyways she slept in, only to remember with relief that she was aboard a cargo ship deep in space, bound for an alien world... and that her name was Penny now. Broken was still a piece of her, but Penny found she could go long stretches without thinking of the decade she'd spent on the streets of New York before Michael Forward found her.

But she still thought of Sky Ranger. She found herself wondering where he was, if he was all right. She sometimes tried to be angry with him for all that he had done, but no matter how hard she tried, she couldn't stay mad for very long. She wanted to see him again.

The closer they drew to Reilis, though, the more difficult her task seemed.

She caught Bann once when his father was napping.

"Tell me," she whispered. "Do you remember me at all?"

His dark eyes were serious and large. He shook his head no.

"I'm Penny. I helped you when you were a little kid. And I'm taking care of you now, too." She smiled. He didn't smile back. Children always confused her.

"Okay," he whispered.

"Do you remember anything about before? The city, the cold...any of it?"

Again, he shook his head no.

"Well. All right." She kissed the top of his head. He smelled like warm hair and dust. "You're a great kid. You really are. I'm glad I knew you...and I think it was all worth it. Hey. Do me a favor, okay?"

He waited.

"Stay safe."

◄►►◄►►

The trip took more than a month in space. When they finally reached Reilis, Bann and his father had disappeared into the custody of uniformed Räton officials almost immediately, before she had even a moment to say farewell. Ced Delarian was infuriating.

As she watched them go, though, Bann turned for a moment and waved goodbye.

Penny broke into a smile and waved as hard as she could. Then Ced turned him around with a sharp word, and they were gone.

Penny quietly slipped through customs and out of the alien starport. No one was waiting for her, but no one bothered her either. She emerged into the rain, smelling the sharp, strange scents and hearing the unfamiliar sounds of an alien city. She trudged off in search of answers.

Penny suspected she'd never see Bann/Ian again, unless he

really did manage to save the human race from the Confederation someday like Michael Forward had believed.

She found herself hoping he enjoyed a quiet, uneventful life. Let the future take care of itself.

◆►◄◆

That had been a little over a week ago. Now she waited, bored, for whatever plan her hosts had cooked up involving the useless UNP exiles gathered in this city to fail. She didn't have to wait long.

The door opened, and Renna and Brian walked in. Renna looked irritated and exhausted; Brian just looked mad.

"I told you," Penny said with her usual lack of grace.

"Yes, thanks," growled Renna. "You don't have to rub it in."

Brian sat down. "That's that. So. How do you two feel about stealing a ship?"

Renna gasped. "What? Oh, God, Brian. You're kidding."

Penny shrugged. "It wouldn't be the first time for me," she drawled lazily.

"Good." He glanced up at Renna. "You wanted a plan," he reminded her.

"Stealing a ship?" Renna asked, agog. "What ship are we going to steal?"

"You remember the ship we arrived on," he said. "That pig Briets thinks it's his, of course, because we were kind enough to not demand it as our own and let the bosses take possession of it. Well." A small smile crept across his face. "I still remember the codes I created to override all the systems on that ship."

"I hate to tell you this, Outer Space Fleet Boy," Renna interjected, "but I know for a fact that whenever a ship changes hands, they usually wipe all codes out and start fresh."

"Not *these* codes," insisted Brian. "I put them in so deep

that they could survive a pretty thorough wiping. Wipes and re-installs of C-and-C software and codes every few months are SOP in the Fleet, not that we ever actually did them on Trikon. The idea is to prevent the kind of tampering I did, except I buried what I wanted to do so deep that they couldn't be touched. They should still be there."

Penny nodded approvingly. This guy was full of fun surprises. "Nice," she said. "Really good."

"So how do we *get* there?" Renna asked, clearly headed for a rolling boil. "How do we actually steal this thing out from under Briets's nose? How do we do this and not land in *jail* for it?"

"Never fear," Brian said grandly, dismissing her concerns with a wave. "We have a little time to figure something out."

"We're going to need a crew," said Penny.

Renna made some truly glorious faces, but seemed to give in. "I bet I know some people who'd be willing to help out," she said, with some effort.

Penny found she was grinning from ear to ear. Brian caught the expression and returned it. *Now this is more like it,* she thought, and she could tell he was thinking the same.

◆►◄◆

God help all of us, Renna thought, fighting down panic. Not for the first time, she devoutly wished she could just set people on fire like Dee could. That would be useful right about now.

But which one to set on fire first? She glanced in the kitchen, where Penny and Brian talked strategy. Apparently Penny had done enough pseudo-police work in one of her previous lives that she had some grasp of tactics. It figured. Brian, naturally, knew everything about everything, so they were getting along famously. They were both convinced that nothing could possibly go wrong with their great plan.

Right.

She'd just have to find a way to make it all work, for the sake of Sky Ranger and Dee.

Keep them both safe... for just a little while longer.

[CHAPTER 16]

DEE STRAINED TO FOCUS ON SOMETHING, *anything*, as she faded in and out of consciousness. Dimly, she realized that this was the effect of the drugs they had been pumping her full of ever since they left Seera Trikon.

She'd never been so cold. It felt like they'd stuck her in a freezer.

Her eyelids were glued together with gunk. With some effort, she managed to get them open, blinking to clear the goop from her vision. A painfully bright light shone down on her from overhead. She couldn't move her arms or legs; something restrained her. All she could do was shiver.

She sank down towards the black pit of unconsciousness again, and moaned softly as she tried to fight it.

Two shapes hovered nearby. Their voices came and went.

"...levels of the serum were a little too... other testing... done..." said one.

"I don't agree with... isn't there? If... extrahuman physiology has these... right?" said the other. One voice was higher than the other. A woman and a man, Dee thought. She clung to that thought. *A woman and a man. A woman and a man. A woman and a man.*

The voices started again. "...a few more weeks... communication... Sky Ranger..."

Sky Ranger. The name burned through the fog smothering

her mind.

She grimaced, and heat began to build within her. She was a prisoner. She had to escape. *Sky Ranger, help me burn this place to a cinder.*

"Skk—" she moaned. "Skkkk!" The fire in her veins started to pulse and dance. She warmed up, ever so slightly.

The shapes hovered over her. Dee's vision cleared enough to make out their faces. *I will burn you,* she thought fiercely.

"She's coming out of it. I wondered if she'd hear me," said the woman.

"The name again. She just happened to hear it," said the man. "That luck of hers is incredibly powerful."

"I wouldn't have agreed a few weeks ago," the woman said, raising a syringe to Dee's left eye. "But this has happened consistently. This is going to be an interesting report. Freeze the eye open."

The man did something with a spray, and Dee found she couldn't move her eyelid. The needle descended down towards her eye, and plunged inside. A second later, as the needle withdrew, intense pain shot through Dee's entire body. She shrieked.

"Such a screamer," observed the man dryly.

"She's not setting anything on fire this time," said the woman. "That's progress."

Beyond the pain lurked the black pit. Dee embraced it gratefully, and passed out again.

Dee pulled her eyelids apart with difficulty, and blinked to clear her vision. She couldn't move, and she was freezing cold.

A face swept into her view. The woman? "You're awake. Good. We're going to try something. Do you understand me?"

"Buh," said Dee. Her tongue felt ten times bigger than normal.

"Good. Okay." She set a small piece of wood in front of her. "Set this on fire."

Dee felt herself start to slip away. She heard a sigh, and felt a prick in her arm. "No you don't. Stay with me, kid. Now look at the wood. Set it on fire. If you do, we'll let you stay awake for a while. Okay?"

Dee concentrated on the wood. She felt around for the fire inside her. She remembered it being a white-hot surge of flame, bursting to be set free. But now all she could find was a dull ember. What had happened to the rest?

It took all her strength to hurl the ember at the wood. It smoked and blackened, but no flames appeared. Exhausted, she gave up, shivering.

"Excellent," said the woman. "You may stay awake for a while." She sat down in front of her.

"That worked well," said the male voice.

"Yes," agreed the woman. "I was monitoring her readings. She was putting the same amount of effort in as the time she almost set the entire lab on fire. It works."

"Does it affect her luck as well?"

"It should, but I wouldn't be surprised if it didn't. We don't know exactly how luck works."

"Chaos field," said the man.

"You keep saying that," sighed the woman.

They looked at her.

"She stinks," said the man. "We should have the nurses give her a bath or something."

"Mmm," said the woman. "Not a bad idea. I'm getting a little tired of being near her."

"We should have the full data by now," said the man. "Should we put her back under? I know you said she could stay up."

"Yeah." The woman looked back at her. "I said she could stay up if she set the block on fire. She didn't."

"Suuuh," Dee tried to scream. "Beeehhh!"

"Put her under," the man said. The eye spray came back out.

◀▷▶ ◀◁▷

The next time she awoke, it was completely dark. She shivered uncontrollably, worried that her sight had disappeared entirely. Her mind was still clouded, and she couldn't concentrate on anything for long. But her tongue seemed smaller, and she could talk.

"Hlp," she spat into the darkness. "Hellllp!"

Cold overtook her. She couldn't feel her fingers or toes. She felt for fire, but found none.

Images swam in front of her. Endless gray sands shifted and blew. Her parents' faces shimmered in front of her.

Her grandmother held her hand. *No fox will get you, my little chicken-Dee. Hold on for me.*

The visions vanished, replaced by the darkness of the room. Cold tears slipped down her cheeks.

She had no idea how long she remained like that until the lights switched on and the man and the woman entered.

"She said she didn't want to think about it," said the woman. "And I can't blame her. Joey's a handful even as it is. He'll be a monster when he's a teenager."

"Mmm," said the man. "One reason I'm glad I don't have kids."

"Same here," said the woman. "Not that I'd ever see them anyway, I'm always here." They both grunted a humorless laugh. Dee watched as they hung their gray uniform jackets on a nearby peg. Was this the same room she had been in before?

What was that shape under a sheet on the far side of the room? The man and woman walked over to it and checked a few readouts attached to the wall.

"He's doing better," said the woman.

"Yes, but not as well as he should be," said the man. "It's almost as bad as Jiankowski. I hate to say it—"

"Don't say it, then," snapped the woman. They worked for a moment, checking readouts and priming syringes. They pulled the sheet back a little. A man lay underneath. He didn't seem to be moving at all, and his body was covered in strange blackened patches.

The woman cursed. "This should be working."

"Maybe..." said the man, turning around to look at Dee. "Maybe we need to move him to another room."

"What do you mean?" The woman turned and looked at Dee again. "Oh. You don't really think..."

"Why not? I told you. Chaos that works in her interest somehow."

"Hmm." The woman thought for a moment. "Fine. Let's move him. ...Hey, is she awake?"

"Brh," said Dee quietly.

"Christ, when did *that* happen?" said the woman, exasperated. "Would you go put her under again? We don't need her today."

"Fine," said the man. He came over to stare at Dee. "I hope you haven't been awake long." He prepped the needle. Dee's eye started to ache. Her whole body ached and throbbed, and she tried to thrash and scream. It was no use.

◄►▸ ◄◄►

Something tugged insistently at her spine, and a dull ache throbbed through her upper back. She became aware of the fact that she was lying on her stomach, face pressed through a hole in the headrest. There was a bucket beneath her head, filled with what might have been her own drool. She slowly became aware that she was only covered by a thin sheet from the waist down, and nothing else. She felt colder than she could ever remember.

She tried to move, and pain lanced her spine. They had stuck something into her back, into her *spine*, and whenever she moved, it caused agony. She tried to stay as still as possible, trying not to shiver in the cold.

She stayed that way for a long time, trying desperately to distract herself or think of something that wasn't this place and the cold. Seera Terron...she dimly remembered heat and sand all around. A man who could fly...was there a fight? Where were her parents—no, maybe better not to think about that. Where was she? What was happening to her?

She couldn't focus, and her thoughts drifted lazily from one memory to another.

...Gramma told her to put her boots on, to be careful of the cold. Cold was the enemy, Gramma said with a strange look on her face...

...Mom was making dinner, and Dad laughed at something in the living room. The cat was doing something silly...

...I am an extrahuman, Dee said to Sky Ranger. Gramma nodded sagely. ...

...Fire arced across the divide. The soldier burst into flames with a terrible screech...

...Felipe floated above her, dressed like Sky Ranger. He grabbed her, and she squeaked in protest. Or was it protest...?

...Two faces hovered in front of her. Put the needle in her eye. Put it in her eye. Stick it into her brain...

...Little Fred Tabors was pulling her hair. Ow! he cried. Your hair is hot! She giggled and looked around for Gramma, but she wasn't there...

...Felipe smiled that brilliant, beautiful smile at her...

...She sat in class, bored. Who needed algebra anyway? She doodled in her notebook, writing "Fred" in big loopy letters and drawing a heart around it. He sat in front of her. He turned around, and it was Sky Ranger instead. 'Did you get an A on the test?' Sky Ranger asked. She smiled smugly at him. She always got an A...

...Great red creatures moved across a plain she had never seen. They were waiting for her...

...She found the space and packed herself in. People were screaming outside. There was a terrible crash and a jolt, and Dee blacked out. When she came to, she opened the door and saw...

Mom? Dad?

Drip. She realized she was crying. Another tear fell from her cheek and splashed into the bucket below. As sobs wracked her body, the needle jabbed into her back shifted and tore her. She cried out in pain, praying someone would come to save her. But no one came for hours.

◆▷ ▸ ◂◁▶

"The sedative isn't working as well as it used to, Dr. Rivers," said the man. "I think we've been using it too much. She's resisting it."

"Doesn't matter," said the woman (Dr. Rivers? Dee hadn't

heard her name before). "If this is working right, we should be able to keep her awake for longer periods of time." She eyed Dee, who stared blankly back at her. "She's calmer. She isn't fighting us anymore."

"I worry about that sedative," said the man. "There was a study that suggested long-term effects like brain damage and memory loss."

"What choice do we have?" said the woman, clearly irritated. "Look. I'll sedate her, then you give her some more of the serum. In a couple of days, we can start testing her awake. The danger period should be gone by then. Besides, now that Thunder is up and running... she's less vital."

"True," said the man. The woman held the syringe in her hand.

Dee waited for the needle and the pain, and both came... then nothing.

She dreamed of a warm blue-white sun, and an endless shimmering hot expanse of gray sand stretching out beyond a deep, blue pool.

◀▷►◀◁▷

"Hi, Sky Ranger!" chirped Dee. "How are you? I hear they put you on a ship."

Sky Ranger leaned forward, flush with relief. She looked fine. She looked *fine*. "Dee! It's great to see you again. How are they treating you? Okay?"

She nodded. "I'm fine, don't worry about me. How are *you* doing?"

"I've been better, but I'm unharmed." He felt his tension level ebb and flow. "It's so good to see you. I was afraid that—I was afraid. But you're all right."

She nodded. "Yeah. I can't go outside, but otherwise I can

pretty much do what I want." She made a strange face. "The rooms I stay in are fireproof."

"What do they have you doing?"

There was a slight pause.

"Weird stuff," she said. "Tests, mostly. They want to know how powerful I am."

"...And?"

"I'm powerful," she said with a very Dee-like smile. "And what do they have you doing?"

"A whole lot of nothing," he said. "I can't really fly much. There isn't room. A man sometimes comes in and asks me questions, but that's it."

Another pause. Sky Ranger's heart skipped a beat.

"Oh," she said. "That sounds boring."

"It is," he admitted. "Don't let them hurt you," he said. "Stay safe if you can."

"I won't," she said. "...I should go. They want me back at the lab."

"All right," Sky Ranger said. "Take care of yourself. Come and visit me."

"I will!" she said. "If I can. I'd like to see you again. ...Goodbye."

"Bye," he said.

The screen blinked off.

"She seems in good spirits today," Doug said from the chair next to his. "I think she'd been looking forward to this for a while."

Sky Ranger nodded. "Thank you, Doug. I appreciate it. Believe me."

"No problem. Glad I could help!" He stood. "I have to go, too. But I'll be back tomorrow. I think I can bring up some interesting food you might like. Native Calvasnan beef and greens. Sound good?"

Sky Ranger managed to smile. "Sure."

"Okay, then. So long." Doug picked up his things and left the room. After a few moments, Sky Ranger floated out of his chair and into the corridor. The smile he had fixed on his face dropped.

A terrible worry gripped him, making him almost dizzy. He settled down against a wall and listened to himself breathe.

He hadn't been speaking to Dee at all. The facial expressions, the inflections... It had seemed like Dee, but also not like her at the same time, like a bad copy. Something had been off. A simulation; he was certain of it.

Which led to the question: where *was* Dee? Why couldn't he talk to her? She had to be in serious trouble...if she was even still alive.

Sky Ranger tried to push that dark thought from his mind, but it returned, relentless. She could be very badly hurt, in serious danger, or even dead.

He made his way back to the observation deck and watched Calvasna slip by below, desperately wanting to smash the windows and fly to the planet.

He had to get down there.

Somehow.

[CHAPTER 17]

BROUSSARD AND FELIPE LIVED A LITTLE TO the south of the city proper, in a tent on the beach. Renna found Felipe watching the waves crash on the shore.

"Hey," she said. He waved, without turning around. She sat next to him. "What's happening today?"

He smiled at her. "Same as every day. We found some nice junk this morning, and Broussard sold it this afternoon. I ate this strange stew today, made from seven different types of grasses. Grass stew! Have you ever had anything like that?"

Renna shook her head. "Never. What did it taste like?"

He made a face. "Grass soaked in water, what else? It was worse than the stuff we made from moss back on Terron. But the Rätons seem to like it, so that's what there was."

They watched the waves for a while.

"It's really beautiful here," said Renna. She'd always wanted to live by the ocean. Tuscon hadn't been near one, and Lake Ontario wasn't the same thing.

"I know, isn't it? The Rätons don't like it, though. They don't like the wide-open spaces, one of them told me. They'd rather be in a house or a city, or in a valley surrounded by mountains. I guess they have a hard time when they go to sea."

"I bet they wouldn't like Seera Terron," said Renna, thinking of the wide, sandy plains.

"Oh, no! When they were there a long time ago, I guess they

really hated it." Renna thought about the heavily reinforced
outpost they'd found in the desert. "They also hated the hot
weather."

"To be fair, most humans hate that, too."

"Not me," said Felipe. "I miss it! I get cold here, even during the day." He shivered. "I wonder if I'll ever see the desert
again?"

"Regrets?" asked Renna softly.

The smile reappeared, seemingly genuine. "No. This is an
amazing adventure! I mean, look at all the water!" He spread
his arms out toward the rippling, undulating ocean. "I never
thought there could be so much! And the mountains and val-
leys are so full of plants and animals, and the city...this city is
amazing!" He chuckled ruefully. "Life here isn't so bad. And who
knows where we might go next!"

"That's why I'm here, actually," she said carefully. "Brian
thinks..." she looked around. "Uh. Is anyone out here likely to
overhear us? And is Broussard around?"

"Broussard's over there," Felipe said, thumbing at a fire off
in the distance. "He goes to hang around with the old Räton
bums at night. But here we're alone; they don't come near the
tent."

Renna nodded. "Okay. Here's what's going on. Brian thinks he
can get the ship back. The one we came here on."

Felipe's eyes widened.

"He thinks he can take it," Renna continued. "And once we
do, we can go after Dee and Sky Ranger on Calvasna."

"So you want to go," Felipe said. "And you want us to come
with you."

Smart kid, Renna thought.

"Got it in one," she said. "What do you think?"

"Calvasna..." said Felipe, whistling through the small gap
between his front teeth. "I don't know. How do we even land

there?"

"I have no idea," Renna said, trying not to let her worry show. "Brian thinks he can do it."

"And you think he can?" Felipe, expression completely serious for once, fixed his gaze on her.

She shrugged. "I have no idea. Maybe."

Felipe said nothing. Then: "I guess he'd know about Calvasna. He was Fleet."

"Yeah," said Renna. "He was."

They heard the soft footfalls of someone approaching. Renna looked up, and saw Broussard ambling towards them.

"Renna," he said gruffly by way of greeting. "Thought I heard a woman's voice over here!"

"You're back, old man," said Felipe.

"Hey, kid," Broussard said, his face cracking into a smile. "So how come the two of you are sitting on the beach at night? Something Brian ought to know about? Are you making Felipe here forget all about that girl he left behind?"

Renna blushed, but Felipe just laughed. "What girl? There weren't any girls on Terron even close to my age!" It occurred to Renna just what a strange childhood Felipe must have had. That he remained so cheerful despite it all was a minor miracle.

Broussard sat on the sand next to them with a creaking sigh and a groan. "Ah, my poor back! Oh, this is going to be a hard night for me."

"I can bring you some painkillers from the city," Renna offered, but he waved her away.

"Pain is good," he insisted. "If I don't feel it, I go too far, and then I regret it when the medicine runs out. Damn this cold weather anyway. So. Why have you come to see us?"

"She wants us to go to Calvasna with her and Brian to rescue Dee and Sky Ranger," Felipe said before Renna could respond.

"Oh," he said. "Ah. Is that Hylar Breits man from the city

backing you?"

"No. He won't stick his neck out," Renna said, biting back a snarl.

"Well, that's something," said Broussard. "What's the plan, then? How do we get there?"

"Brian thinks he can steal the ship back, and get us to Calvasna."

"Heh," said Broussard. "And then what? We go where? The military's headquarters? Some prison?" He shook his head. "There's no good way to get them out of there. We were damned lucky back on Trikon."

"He's right," said Felipe. "We shouldn't push our luck so much."

"Brian says he has a plan," said Renna, realizing how pathetic that sounded. "And...and I trust him."

"So do I," said Broussard. "But sometimes his plans aren't all that good. He didn't think of how to deal with that ConFedMil-Pol ship. He only figures things out so far."

"I know," said Renna, fighting down the panic again. "I know all of that. Look. I have to tell you, Broussard, I have no idea what we're going to do once we get to Calvasna. I think even if we get down to the surface without getting caught, it'll be impossible to get out again—especially if we manage to free them. Which I don't think we can. The whole Confederation military will be against us."

"So why go?" asked Broussard.

She shook her head. "What else can we do? We have to try. And if I didn't go...he would just go without me."

"Why does he care so much?" Felipe said. "He wasn't even there."

"I don't know," said Renna. "It all means something to him, but I don't know what."

Felipe and Broussard sat for a while without saying anything. Renna watched the waves break and recede, dancing endlessly with the shore. It was true. She had no idea why Brian cared so much about Dee and Sky Ranger. She knew why *she* cared, and she had a good idea of why Penny cared, but Brian?

She knew people who liked to set stuff on fire just to watch it burn. Maybe he was like that. Maybe he was bitter and angry and wanted to get back at the Confederation. Or maybe it was just part of Brian's nature to save people. She was disturbed to realize that she couldn't really say, not for sure. He remained a stubborn mystery, even now. *What*, she wondered for the millionth time, *have I gotten myself into?*

"Well," Broussard said, groaning as he stood. "I see only one thing to do. We'll go ask the *zirhini* what they think."

"The what?" Renna asked, scrambling to her feet. "Who are they?"

He pointed to the distant fire, where a group of Rätons huddled together. "Them over there. The bums. The *rhi*-less Rätons. Come on." He hobbled off, Felipe in tow.

"Wait!" called Renna, running to catch up. "Hey, wait. Hang on. You've got to be kidding! Why are we talking to *them*? We can't trust them not to tell Breits or the government what we're planning! Broussard!"

"No," he said, "It's fine. They won't betray us." He stopped for a moment. "I've learned a lot about the Rätons. They have a certain loyalty, but only to their family groups. To no one else. Their *rhi*. You know what those are, yes?"

Renna knew. Rätons formed big family groups, with many adults bonded to one another in something that resembled, in a vague way, a polygamous marriage. It had a lot to do with professions, social status, and even governing. The Reformists back home had vilified the Rätons for their strange and unique families, labeling them as perverse and corrupt.

Renna knew how they must have felt.

"Well," Broussard continued. "These ones, they don't be-

long to a *rhi*, and they're too old or too disgraced to join or form
a new one. So they live together down here, away from everyone else. They form their own *rhi*, but without a house or children or any kind of status. They aren't loyal to anyone but their
friends."

"And you're their friend," said Renna.

"In a manner of speaking," said Broussard. "They think I'm
okay. I'm not Räton, which is hard for them to accept. But I'm interesting to talk to. They know a lot of things worth knowing."

"I didn't know you spoke Räton," said Renna.

"I don't, not really," said Broussard. "There are a lot of them
there who speak English, though. You'll see why. Come on." He
hobbled off. Renna followed.

Two dozen Rätons sat around the fire, smoking something
vile-smelling and drinking various teas. They wore a motley as-
sortment of blankets, robes, and jewelry, all of which was caked
with dust and sand. They were nothing like the elegant, well-
dressed Rätons Renna found in most of the rest of the city.

There was a low murmur of conversation, which ceased as
soon as Broussard, flanked by Renna and Felipe, entered the circle.

"Brou," one, a white-haired and wrinkled man, said. "We
know the boy. But not the other."

"Ahara," said Broussard. "I apologize, this is Renna. She
came with me from Seera Trikon."

"Ah," said the old man, Ahara.

"She is going to go to Calvasna to rescue two friends," said
Broussard. "I'm asking for your advice."

Advice?

Renna stood there, fidgeting, while Ahara and the others
considered. One, an elderly woman who had to be over a cen-
tury old, stood. Even stooped and bent with age, her lithe frame
towered over tall Renna.

"I wo—I wass—I was in embassy on Earth," she said. "Many

friends, all *rhin*, all die there. Calvasna, much worse. No, you should not go."

Another stood and spoke in a rapid, flowing language. Ahara translated. "He says he lived in Patharga, on Mantillies. It was our city, before it became a human city. He and his *rhin* stayed on the planet after it was given to the humans. Then they started to kill them. So he left. But all of his *rhin* were killed." Ahara's expression was unreadable as he looked at Renna. "He says they're insane, the humans."

The others around the fire murmured. *Ilyos. Ilyos yumana.* Crazy humans. Renna suddenly felt less than safe.

"Renna and the others are refugees," said Broussard quietly. "Like us. They worked or lived in the Confederation, and when things went bad, they escaped here. But they don't have any family or friends here, so no one wants them."

Ahara cleared his throat. "You," he said, fixing his large, strange purple eyes on her. "Why return?"

Renna stepped within the circle, in front of the fire. She thought of a million things to say to try and explain. It was right to go. She couldn't let innocent people suffer for nothing. She'd be striking a blow against the hated Reformists. But all that came out of her mouth was, "They're like my family. I don't have anyone left but the people I was with on Seera Terron. My real family back home hates me, and I have no one else. Plus, the two of them saved my butt back on Seera Trikon. How can I not go?"

She looked around at the Rätons assembled there, and was shocked to read understanding in their huge, glassy alien eyes.

Ahara nodded. "*Rhin*," he said sadly. The others repeated the word. *Rhin, rhin.* Family.

"She's right," said Felipe, who had been silent so far. "It's like that, sorta."

"This is true," admitted Broussard sadly. He and Felipe exchanged glances. "*Rhin.*"

The word hung in the air for a moment as Renna nodded her thanks at both Felipe and Broussard, though she was a little confused. The old man and the kid hadn't been with them in the oasis, so why did they care? But, somehow, they did.

"How will you go from here?" asked Ahara. "Will the human leaders in the city help you?"

Renna shook her head. "No, they won't help."

"How, then?"

"They want to steal a ship," said Broussard. Renna winced. "The one we came in, originally."

Some of the Rätons spoke quickly in their own language for a moment.

"I will help you," said a Räton woman. "I know a traffic controllers' *rhi*. Possible to bribe. Let your ship escape? No one follows."

A man spoke. Ahara translated again. "He knows a trading *rhi*. He can get you some money. They owe him a favor."

"Thank you," Renna said. "You don't have to do that!"

Ahara's eyes seemed to glow. "We will help. I will also help you. When you go to Calvasna, go to see the family Lorraine. They know me, and will help you. Use my name."

Renna was in shock, trying to figure out what this meant. "Thank you," she said. "I can't... I don't know what to... Why?"

Ahara held up a four-fingered, green hand. "You remind us of what we no longer have, and of what we do. For *rhi*. " The other Rätons sighed at the word, and huddled closer together. "*Rhi* is important," Ahara finished. "It's worth everything."

He inclined his narrow head to her in salute. "Be lucky, and come back some day," he said.

<>► ◄<>

Felipe and Broussard stopped to say farewell as they reached the tent.

"I'll come," said Broussard to her as they embraced. "You're right. It's about family, in a strange way. I haven't had one in a long time. ...Eh. Even if not, I can't stand the thought of Dee and Sky Ranger locked up and myself free and doing nothing to help them."

"Thank you," she said. "Really. You're a wonderful man."

She turned to Felipe. He was looking out at the sea, and wouldn't meet her eyes.

"I'd like to see the rest of the Räton planets someday," he said softly. "And I like the ocean. But..."

He sighed, and it was the most mournful sound she'd ever heard him make.

"Nothing lasts forever. And I'm glad I got to come here and live this life."

"Boy," growled Broussard. "I can go, because I'm an old man. But you can stay here and live your life. Yes? We don't need you to come."

"Sure you do," said Felipe. "I can fly anything, and I'm all right in a fight. Besides," and now he attempted to smile again, "What would I do without you, old man? I'd be lonely. So I'm coming."

"You don't have to," said Renna. "Really."

"But I will," said Felipe firmly. And that was that.

◀▷▶ ◀◁▷

Penny flew through the metal and brick canyons of Arheligon, softly, silently, flitting from rooftop to building side to overhang, not daring more than a few moments of sustained flight at a time. The cool air rushed through her long, silver hair, spreading it out like a fan behind her whenever she leapt into the breeze. Rätons walked in pairs or large groups on the streets below, but none looked up and none saw her pass by overhead. She knew she probably shouldn't have, but what Celeste didn't know wouldn't hurt her. Right?

There, an open space. She was coming to the edge of the city, where open fields began. There was a sharp cutoff between city and country; there were no suburbs at all. It was disorienting, but at least there was less chance of someone looking up and seeing an alien streaking by above. She stayed low and in the shadows until she felt reasonably secure, then, with a burst of power, rocketed up into the clouds. There was little air traffic out here, and any ground sensors would likely just register her as one of the huge birds that lived on this planet.

An icy chill surrounded her as the air grew cold and thin. The wind rushed, freezing and sharp, in her face, but she paid it no mind. She liked the freezing air. It made her mind focus on nothing but speed.

Now. Faster. *Faster. As fast as I can!*

Penny closed her eyes and let the air rush around her, speeding faster and faster, wind clawing at her hair, her clothes, her face. One more moment—!

She pulled back, opening her eyes and righting herself. She drifted down to a slightly warmer altitude, and looked back. The city lay far, far behind her, only a dim halo of light on the horizon. Below lay dark fields and a single illuminated ribbon of road.

She scanned the sky. Nothing was coming after her, at least not yet. Her breath came fast, in visible puffs in front of her face. Her heart was racing; her entire body seemed to tingle. She drifted slowly downwards, allowing her exhilaration to fade.

Renna and Brian probably knew she was gone from the open window she'd left behind. They'd worry.

Let them worry. There was time. It had been several days since Renna had returned from meeting the Rätons on the beach, and their plans had started rolling quicker and quicker. Brian had been out all day today, making deals and getting supplies.

They were all meeting tomorrow for the final stage, but it wasn't tomorrow yet. She settled down near the ground and hovered just above the surface of the road. There was an entire world to explore; she could stay out a little longer.

She shifted back into the horizontal flight position and flew lazily above the road, out of sight of any vehicles that might come along, mimicking the road's many twists and turns. Where would she be by morning?

She flew on, deeper into the night.

◄►►◄◄►

Renna, Brian, and Penny left the city early in the morning. Penny seemed worn and tired, but calmer than Renna could remember seeing her. Renna didn't ask, or mention the open window she'd found. Whatever Penny needed to do to clear her mind was fine. It hardly mattered now in any case.

They drove out into the hills, along a winding road that took them far from the city. At last, they reached their destination— a grassy hillside in the middle of nowhere.

Felipe and Broussard were waiting—alone—on the hill when they pulled up in their rented car.

"So you're it, huh?" Renna asked, trying to hide her disappointment. She'd had hope that Felipe and Broussard would have been able to talk Marsha or one of the other women into coming along, or that Mick, with his technical expertise, would have volunteered. So much for the rest of the *rhi*.

"Afraid so," Broussard said. "And it isn't like we didn't try, eh Felipe?"

"It's true," said Felipe. "But they kept talking about Allison... I think her getting shot spooked them."

"Mmm," agreed Broussard. "They know it's *possible* to get shot now. But here. They took up a collection." He pressed a wad of cash into Renna's hands. With it was a note, signed by Mick. *Good luck,* it read. *Bring them back safe! We'll be here.*

Well, it was better than nothing. She smiled fondly.

"So it'll be five of us," said Brian. "That's fine. More than enough to crew the ship." He didn't sound entirely convinced, though.

Broussard handed him a small bag. "Money," he said. "The beachfront *rhin* send their regards, and you will be clear to fly."

"I wish I could thank them," Brian said. "And what was the last part? A family to look for on Calvasna?"

"The Lorraines," said Broussard. "I've heard the name. One of the big-time families there."

"Right," said Brian. "I know about them."

"Hey," said Felipe, intent on something in the woods near-by. "Who's that there?" He pointed.

A young woman crouched next to a nearby bush. Her eyes widened as they turned to stare at her, but she didn't move.

"Oh my God," said Renna softly. "Willow." She slowly walked over to her. "Willow? Sweetie? Is that you?"

"R-Renna," Willow said. She looked gaunt, her eyes were sunken, and she was filthy. Bits of dirt and plants were stuck to her clothing, and in her hair.

"Have you been living out here?"

"S-Sort of," Willow said. She shivered violently. "Renna. Please let me come with you."

Renna knelt in front of her. "What? Why do you want to come with us?"

"You're going after S-Sky Ranger and Dee," she said. "Dee saved us all. I would have been k-killed for what I did." She started to shake. "And I don't want to stay here anymore. N-No one will talk to me. Please." She stared into Renna's eyes, pleading.

"*Please.*"

"Willow, you look terrible," Brian said, standing over her. "Are you sure about coming with us?"

"Yes," she said. "If Renna is okay."

Why is this my decision? Renna wondered. Willow didn't look like the picture of mental and physical health. They'd have to constantly watch her and keep her out of trouble. She'd almost certainly disintegrate in a fight.

Brian smiled. "Sure, Renna's fine. The more the merrier. Right?"

This is a terrible idea, Renna thought. *I am the opposite of fine. Willow can't handle anything right now, so how will she be able to cope with this?* But she painted a smile on. "...Yeah, I'm fine," she said.

Brian clearly needed more kicking.

"Come on, I'll help you up," she said, extending a hand and hauling Willow to her feet.

She glanced over at the others and found, to her surprise, that Penny was staring at Willow with a strangely fascinated look on her face.

The ceaseless wind blew hard and cold on the hillside as Renna, Penny, Broussard, Felipe, and Willow assembled in a semicircle around Brian.

"So!" said Felipe. "We going to go get that ship? I'm ready."

"No," said Brian. "We're not."

"What?" cried Renna, disappointment and relief warring within her. Were they not going after all? What decision had Brian made without telling her? "You've got to be kidding me!"

"No," said Brian. "It's too dangerous to try and sneak into their refit facility. They'd probably catch us." He smiled. "But we *are* going to Calvasna today. Right now, in fact." He withdrew a small remote control. "I'm sorry I didn't explain anything earlier, but I couldn't be sure we wouldn't be overheard."

He pressed a button on the control, and examined the output. "Good. It's on the way."

"Wait," said Renna. "Did you...?"

"This control overrode the new systems they put in place. I had the ship close all doors once it was empty, lift off, and head to this hill."

Renna shoved him. He lurched back in surprise, almost tipping over.

"You—You! *This* was your plan? You *ass*. How *dare* you not tell me about it!"

He held up a hand, eyes wide. "I couldn't risk it!"

"You have *got to be kidding me!*" Renna screeched. She advanced on Brian, who nervously held his ground.

"Renna, it's okay," Felipe said nervously. "Really."

"Sure it is," she said, and shoved a finger in Brian's face. He flinched. *Heh. Got him.* "You. Tell me next time. Got it?"

He flashed his brilliant smile. "Can't promise a thing."

She shoved him again, not really meaning it, and then stalked off, shaking her head.

A low whine off in the distance rapidly turned into a deep, loud roar as the transport ship sped towards the hillside.

"Here it comes!" Broussard said.

Brian and Felipe sped into action, grabbing bags from the car. Penny, Broussard, and Renna moved out of the landing area, which was almost certainly the huge clear space before them. Willow lurked at the edge of the forest. Renna worried that she might bolt again, and watched her carefully.

The ship hovered overhead for a moment, heat blasting out of its thrusters, before settling on the ground with a groan and a hissing sigh.

"All right," called Brian. "Everyone on board! Run! Briets may send someone after it!"

Renna ran to Willow and helped her up.

"Come on," she said. "It's all right. It's not like last time."

"I know," said Willow softly. "I know it. I'm coming."

Brian thumbed the remote again, and the hatch opened. He and Felipe threw their bags inside, then ran back to the car for a second load. Broussard ambled aboard, followed by Penny. Renna and Willow were next, followed closely by Brian and Felipe.

"All right," said Brian, "We're gone." He hit the remote a third time, and the airlock closed tight behind them. The ship lurched and shook as it heaved itself off the waving, windswept grass of the hillside.

◆►◄◆

Brian ran to the stairs and hurtled up towards the control room. Renna couldn't keep up with him, and arrived to find him firmly settled in the captain's seat.

"Okay," he said. "Everything's online. We're all set. They didn't even bother putting in rudimentary security precautions! Nothing's wiped or blocked; we have access to everything. Amateurs! Ha!" His eyes had that manic glint. He keyed in a sequence and the ship started climbing up towards space.

The rest of their crew arrived in the control room. "Hey," said Felipe. "Where's the pilot's seat?"

"Right here next to me," said Brian. Felipe slid in and took control. "Hang on, transmission coming." He tapped a control on his console.

"—*Alin ai viliulinnu Iyiuai Reilisi virun sval? Mirui iuni i e suir!*"

"Reilis space traffic control," explained Brian. "They want to know what we're doing. Broussard?"

Broussard spoke a phrase in halting Räton into the speaker. The traffic controller responded with a rapid stream of alien words.

Broussard seemed to be started to sweat. "...*Bara a.*"

There was a pause.

"*Sa na. Vi si a yi!*" said the voice, sounding considerably more friendly. The comm cut off.

"What happened?"

Broussard bent over in relief. "I said the words they wanted to hear. The Rätons on the beach taught me to say that, so they'd know who we were. They're letting us through, so it looks like the bribe worked. God bless this planet for being so corrupt."

"So that is *that*," said Brian with a fierce joy. "We should be in the clear while they get things sorted out down there—if they ever do. Ha! I Can you imagine Briets's face right now? Serves him right!"

"He can't do a thing about it," said Broussard. "This isn't his planet. The Rätons can ignore anything they like. Felipe, get us out of here."

Felipe punched in another sequence, and the ship started to accelerate. The hyperdrive began to come online. He pumped his fist in fierce joy. Renna hadn't seen him this happy since they escaped from Trikon. "Even if he can ever persuade the Rätons to listen to him, we'll be long gone," said Brian.

Renna folded her arms, trying to feel more hopeful. They were on their way to Calvasna. It was insane, but there was no stopping them now. *This had better work*, she thought. *I hope we can keep it together long enough.*

The transport ship slipped past the orbital defenses out into interplanetary space. Then, after a few minutes, a flash and a ripple in space were all that remained to mark the ship's passage. They had entered hyperspace, bound for the Confederation.

[CHAPTER 18]

"No," said Emily. "No, no, no. I'm not helping you."

"Why not?"

"Because! It's dangerous," she said, lowering her voice. "And we'd have no way to live once we got there."

"I've mentioned what's at stake," said Sky Ranger.

"Yes," Emily said, scooping up her fat, slow cat, Linda, and hugging her. The other cat, skinny Diana, was lurking under Sky Ranger's chair. Sky Ranger absently tried to scratch her ears, but she shied away from his touch. Cats. "You have. But I don't know what you think *we* can do about it!"

Sky Ranger felt like putting a cat through the wall. James and Anthony had given him the same responses. *We can't do anything. We're just people. We're prisoners here. It's too dangerous anyway. Leave it alone.*

"We're extrahumans," he said patiently. "We can do all kinds of things that they can't. You can fly!"

"Not very well," she said.

"Plus, you can heal other people. That's a useful talent! Not many I knew had it. I don't know why you didn't decide to try out for the LED. We could have used you."

She shuddered. "I would have hated that. Volunteering in the medical center was bad enough."

"Why?" he pressed. "What was so bad about helping people?"

She looked at him as if he had grown another head. "I had to *touch* them," she said with a shudder.

There were lots of different comebacks to that, but Sky Ranger wisely decided to move on. *Try tact for a change, Sky.* "Tell me. Emily. Do you really want to stay here for the rest of your life? You have to know they'll never let us go."

"And then what?" Emily said, panic in her voice. "What would happen to us? Where would we live? What would we do? Where would we get our food! Who would give us a place to sleep? Where would my *cats* live?"

"We'd find something," Sky Ranger said soothingly. "Trust me."

Emily looked away. "I want to. Really. But I—I just don't think this is a good idea. I'm sorry. Please go."

And that was that. Sky Ranger let himself out of her room. The door slid shut behind him, and he sighed, leaning against the bulkhead.

"Didn't go so well, huh?" said a familiar, snide voice.

Roger was waiting for him in the hallway.

"I'm not in the mood, Roger," Sky Ranger said, turning his back and floating briskly off.

Roger fell in step beside him. "She didn't like the idea, did she? I know what you're planning; the others have all come to tell *me*. I bet Emily will, too. She'll stop by later tonight, and she'll *tell on you*. She'll probably tell Doug, too. And do you want to know why?"

"Why?" asked Sky Ranger, resigned to yet another long explanation of why it was his fault somehow.

"Think about it. Back in the Tower—"

Here it comes, thought Sky Ranger.

"—Would she have given a second thought to coming to tell you if someone she knew was planning an escape?"

"No," Sky Ranger said. "She would have said."

"Exactly."

"But that was in the Tower," Sky Ranger said. "And that was with me. That was different."

"Was it?" Roger asked. "Are you sure?"

"Listen," Sky Ranger said. "You can keep making the point that this prison and life in Union Tower were the same thing all you want, but there were *important* differences."

"And I'm sure if the little hamster in your head runs around in his wheel enough times, one will occur to you," Roger said, waving a hand dismissively. "The point is that Emily and all the others are conditioned to respond to *authority*, no matter where it's coming from. They have been since birth. All of you have. It's why you were so willing to help out the Reformists—they were the ones in charge. They had authority, and you listened to it."

"Whatever," said Sky Ranger.

"I, of course, am immune," said Roger. "I joined the Union of my own free will, as an adult. So I see things you don't. You really should listen to me on this one, Sky Ranger. I know what I'm talking about. Maybe I can even help."

In response, Sky Ranger turned a corner and floated away faster than Roger could follow.

Crimson Cadet trailed after him. "Don't walk away from me, Sky!" he demanded. "You have to listen!"

Sky Ranger neatly stepped out of the window, and flew high up atop the tower. Here, in the gorgeous glass office with the old Sky Ranger's things still lining the walls, he could be alone.

Sky Ranger sat gloomily on the observation deck and stared

out at the planet spinning below, thinking about how much he hated Roger, when the voice he least wanted to hear said, "I thought I'd find you here. Always retreating to your sanctuary when things get rough. You never change."

"Go away," said Sky Ranger.

Roger took the seat next to him. "You can't ban me from *this* room. Listen. Have you thought about what I said? I bet you're going to go see Jill next, am I right?"

"No," said Sky Ranger, even though that *had* been his plan.

"Sure you are. Because you always follow through on a plan even though it doesn't have a prayer of working. Same old Sky Ranger."

"You're a twit," said Sky Ranger, his frustration giving way to anger. "You were nothing but a leech! Your suggestions were terrible."

"No," said Roger. "They weren't. But that doesn't really matter now, does it?"

"Shut up," Sky Ranger snapped. And, wonder of wonders, Roger did. For about a minute. Sky Ranger considered getting up and leaving, but stubbornly stayed put. Why should he be chased out of his favorite spot by Roger, of all people?

"As I was saying," Roger said eventually, picking up on their earlier conversation. "None of the people aboard this ship are willing to make that bolt for freedom because—and let's be honest here—they've never actually known it. They've been taken care of all their lives. I don't know how you miss such obvious stuff, Sky Ranger. Maybe it's because you led a life that was very different from everyone else's. You could actually go out and do things. The rest of us were constrained by all the rules. We had to stay on the Tower grounds at all times except when we were allowed to go out, together, as a group. I have to tell you, it was like being five years old again."

"Uh-huh," said Sky Ranger, not really paying attention. He'd heard this complaint from Roger time and again.

Roger stared thoughtfully at Sky Ranger for a moment. "Listen. They don't know how to take that first step. They can't even fathom it, trust me on that. When we fled, the first sign I had that something was wrong was that there were no guards at the gate. I'd never seen that before. But what did they want to do? They sat there and waited for the police. They could have run into the city. But they didn't."

Sky Ranger thought about that for a moment. Had his people really been such sheep?

Roger changed the subject again. "So. Tell me—what was your plan for getting us off this ship? Bearing in mind that the cameras are always recording each and every one of us, all the time. Everywhere on board."

Sky Ranger said nothing, still lost in thought.

"I thought so. You had no idea." Roger grinned smugly at him and tapped the side of his head. "I can see the future, sometimes, and I know that for a fact."

"You can't see anything," Sky Ranger said bitterly. "Your power barely exists."

"You'd be surprised," Roger said thoughtfully. "It saved our lives at the Tower. Here's my point. You can go ask Jill, but what will she do? No one here is going to follow you, especially if you have no plan. You'll have to give them a very hard shove if you want them to make a run for their freedom."

"You know nothing about these people," Sky Ranger protested, quietly despairing. "You don't know what they're capable of."

"Apparently," said Roger, "neither do you. Come find me when you've had a chance to think. And I mean *really* think. About this ship, about everything." He got up, stomped the ground once, and walked out of the room.

What a jerk. Sky Ranger stood, intending to pace moodily in

front of the windows, when he saw a piece of paper on the chair where Roger had been sitting. He picked it up. Some writing was scribbled on it:

GRAVITY
WINDOWS

That was odd. He turned the paper over.

Sky Ranger, you are an idiot.
-R

He crumpled the paper in his fist, and glanced out the windows. Calvasna turned slowly beneath them. Nothing made any sense.

He muttered something unflattering about Roger's parentage under his breath, but stowed the paper in his pocket.

Later, as he lay on his bed, he pulled the note out again. Bypassing the "you're an idiot" side, he stared at the two words written on the reverse. What about gravity? What about the windows? Was this another one of Roger's always-wrong premonitions? Why did Roger think he an idiot *this* time?

He floated off his bed. The gravity was still wonky, and he still was having trouble with it. Nothing more. He looked out the tiny portal in his room. Stars shone through it. If he tilted his head, he could see the planet below. He tapped on the warm glass. Just a window.

Maybe Roger was the idiot this time. Sky Ranger sighed and settled back down on the bed.

Escape seemed farther away than ever.

◆▶▸◀◆

Sky Ranger floated down the hall near Jill's room. Should he bother talking to her? The stubborn streak in him wanted to see this through to the end, to the final rejection.

But...what would the point be? As much as he hated to admit it, Roger was right. He turned around, then turned back. Would it hurt to ask? What would she say? Dee...he couldn't get that false image of Dee out of his mind.

Maybe he should just go. It was late. She was probably asleep.

Then again, she slept at odd hours. Maybe...

The door slid open, and Jill bounced out into the hallway. She saw Sky Ranger and broke into a grin.

"Hey, stranger," she said, voice low. "I haven't seen you for a while."

"Um, hi," he said, her presence making up his mind for him. "...Do you have a minute? I need to talk to you."

Her wicked smile got bigger. "Sure. Come on in."

◆▶▸◀◆

Sky Ranger jolted awake and was suddenly, acutely aware of Jill sleeping next to him.

Oh, he thought. *Right. Sky Ranger, you are an idiot.*

Jill hadn't been subtle. He'd gone into her room intending to give her the same sales pitch for his idea of escaping and making for the planet, but about three sentences in, he noticed that she was unbuttoning her shirt and fixing a very intent look on him. Things had progressed from there.

It was, he thought groggily, the nicest time he'd had in months. There was a bed and everything; this was much better than scratchy desert sex.

He listened to her steady, contented breathing. She'd taken control in ways Renna had never dared, but she hadn't seemed quite as fixed on him, either. Just a whim, then? Jill seemed to exist on her whims.

For some reason, his mind kept returning to Roger.

Gravity. Windows. Damn that irritating, insufferable—What could those two words possibly mean? What ridiculous puzzle had Roger concocted for him?

Gravity...

...he thought of Silverwyng beneath him as they fell endlessly together high above New York.

Gravity. He had been master of it. Sil had slipped, but steadied herself. She'd lost her flight entirely later, but not yet. Not yet. Why hadn't he thought of this before? It was such a pleasant memory. He remembered being barely conscious of the workings of gravity around him... Earth's atmosphere had been like water to a fish for him. Not like Seera Terron or that damn spaceship with its strange artificial—

Wait.

He slipped an arm out from under Jill, and rose a few feet into the air.

Jill murmured and opened her eyes. "Oh, right," she said groggily. "It's you. Why are you up there?"

"I think," Sky Ranger said in wonderment, "that I've just figured something out."

"Huh?"

Sky Ranger stretched out, testing his new idea. Maybe. Maybe it was something. He settled back down onto the bed. "I should go."

Jill snaked her arm around his. "Oh yeah? You sure? Didn't you come here to tell me something? We have lots of time, nowhere to go."

He gently withdrew his arm and floated out of bed—*Incred-*

ible! Why didn't I notice this before?—to the floor. He turned on the light and hurriedly found his clothes.

"Sky?" she asked. "You're leaving? Just like *that*? Uh. You, uh..." She sounded like she might be on the verge of either crying or ripping him to shreds.

"I'm sorry," he said, all but ignoring her. "Thank you...I had a great time. And I'm not leaving because of you. But...but I've figured something out and I have to go right now. It's important."

"Oh? Sure. What is it?" Jill's voice shook a little.

Sky Ranger opened his mouth, but stopped himself. Were there recording devices in here, too? If he was right, he needed to be careful. At least for a little while. "I...I can't tell you about it now. I'm sorry. But I promise, I will."

And with that, he fled, lost in furious thought.

◀▷▶ ◀◁▷▶

Jill collapsed back on the bed. "Aw, crap," she said.

After a little while James stuck his head in. "Hey, are you coming?" he asked. "Sky Ranger said he has something important to show us."

"I don't care," said Jill, still pissed off. "He can shove it out his ass."

James was at her side in less than an instant. "What is it? What happened?"

Jill arched an eyebrow at him, a wicked look in her eye. James suddenly turned red.

"You didn't," he said, and let out a low moan when she said nothing. "Oh, for the love of—! Why? Why *him*?"

Jill shrugged, looking pleased with herself.

James threw his hands up in the air. "Goddamn it! I guess at least it wasn't Roger."

Anthony shuffled by outside. "Come on, you two. Sky Ranger wants us. And like dogs called by the master, we go whether we want to or not."

◄►► ◄◄►

The observation lounge was piled high with sacks of food and other gear. "What is this for?" James asked, doing a double-take. "What's going on here?"

"You'll see," said Sky Ranger. He looked at Jill, who glared at him. *Oh*, Sky Ranger realized belatedly. *Uh. Oops.* He shoved the problem out of his mind. Later. There'd be time to sort it all out once they got out of here.

"Well," he said. "We're all here."

"Get on with it," said Roger, who was looking a lot more smug than usual. "No reason to hold up the show now."

Sky Ranger sorted through the junk he'd strewn around the observation deck, and picked up a bookend he'd lifted from Emily's little library. Emily gasped a little, recognizing it.

"That—" she stuttered. "That—!"

"Don't worry," said Sky Ranger. *I hope.*

He hefted the bookend—the heaviest thing he'd been able to find on board.

"Now," he said. "Get ready."

"Get ready for what?" said James, bored.

"Are you—? What are you doing with that?" asked Emily nervously, brushing cat hair off her shirt.

Jill and Anthony said nothing. Roger smirked.

"After all of this, I hope you're actually right," said Roger.

"Me?" Sky Ranger blurted, shooting him a panicked glare. "This was your idea!"

Roger waved him away, still smirking. "Just do it already."

Sky Ranger exhaled—and hurled the bookend as hard as he could at the window.

The glass shattered.

Emily screamed, James fell back open-mouthed, and Jill moaned, bracing for the deadly rush of violent decompression.

It never came.

"I'm breathing," said James after a moment. "What? The air's staying in."

They peered fearfully out into the dark sky, and gasped as it flickered, then turned to gray. Sky Ranger walked to the window.

"We were never in space!" he said triumphantly. "The gravity was all wrong—but like a different *planet's*, not like artificial gravity! That's why I couldn't get used to it! Roger tipped me off, but once I got the idea, it all made sense."

Roger took a shaky bow. Sky Ranger had detected the expression of profound relief on his face.

Oh, God, thought Sky Ranger. *He really didn't know for sure. It was just a hunch. It was one of his premonitions! I'm going to kill him.*

Meanwhile, Roger had regained his composure, and was busy taking credit. "Thank you, thank you. I admit, it was a stroke of genius. A perfect demonstration of my prescience in action. However," he held up a finger, "the people who run the show here—wherever *here* actually is—surely must know what's happening. We should escape. Now."

"Grab some gear!" ordered Sky Ranger. "Whatever you can carry. Now!" They sprang into action. *Good. Give them no time to think about it.*

He glanced out of the now-shattered window, and saw that they were in a massive, gray room. The hologram had to have been linked in with the window somehow.

Wonder of wonders, orange sunlight filtered in from above. There. A skylight! He felt the planet's strange gravity all around him. He gathered himself and leapt upwards, powering his way up to the skylight. It was just a short distance through the air outside their prison to where orange-red sunlight beckoned. The skylight was made of glass.

He shattered it with a well-aimed kick, dodging falling shards to make his way back to the "ship," which, he noted, was nothing more than a derelict sitting in a hangar.

Why had the Confederation done this? Why go to all the trouble? What sort of trick could this be?

Maybe, he thought, the illusion of being in space was a way of making sure they'd stay put.

No time for that now. He burst back through the window to find chaos.

"I can't go! I can't!" Emily wailed. "What about my *cats?*"

"What do you care more for, your cats or your freedom?" Roger said, shaking her. "Come on! You can fly! We need you! Can you get to the window up there?"

"I can carry two or three," said Sky Ranger.

"I can take myself," said Jill. "But no more." A hard, determined look had crept into her eyes. "I want to go *now.*" She took off, shakily but firmly.

"Wait! We go together," barked Sky Ranger. Jill shrank back a little and thumped to the floor, but held her ground.

"I have to go get them," Emily said, mind still on her cats. She raced off. "I can't leave them!" she called.

"No!" shouted Sky Ranger, but it was too late. She'd already gone.

"We don't have time!" James called. "They know what we've done! Emily!"

"Leave her," said Roger. "Her and her stupid cats!"

"Come on," said Sky Ranger. "We have to go now. I'll come back for her. Roger, James, Anthony, you'll have to grab on to me."

They managed to secure themselves awkwardly to Sky Ranger, who hesitated, struggled, then lifted off. "Go, Jill, now!

I'll follow."

She ran to the window and jumped. At first, it seemed like she might falter and plummet to the ground, but she caught herself and sped unsteadily up to the skylight. Sky Ranger followed after her, grunting under the strain of three extra bodies.

"There!" came from below. Sky Ranger picked up speed, as did Jill in front of him.

Shots cracked. Instantly, Sky Ranger saw a yellow blur around his vision, and felt something bounce off his leg. Anthony's forcefield!

"Fly faster," Anthony grunted, "I can't keep this up forever."

Jill was almost at the window. *Come on, Jill,* Sky Ranger willed. She'd never been a strong flyer. *Don't lose power.* There! She was through!

He burst through seconds after, and into the dazzling sunlight. They were on the roof of a building. Forests stretched away in all directions. Sky Ranger touched down beside her.

"Keep going!" he said. "To the forest!" He pointed to the faraway reds and greens. Jill nodded, eyes bright, and jumped over the edge of the building.

He glanced through the skylight. No sign of Emily. The men with rifles were aiming up at the hole.

He couldn't wait. He turned to go, and heard a scream behind him. He looked back.

Emily, two terrified, howling cats cradled in her arms, flew slowly and shakily towards the window. She was a perfect target.

The men below fired.

Blood spurted from Emily's side. She yelped and started to lose altitude.

Sky Ranger dove into the window and sped down to where Emily was falling.

Her legs dangled out in front of him. The floor careened closer.

He snatched for her legs, and caught hold—! She lurched and shrieked. The sudden jerk of weight threatened to overwhelm him. He pulled as hard as he could, straining against gravity, praying his strength would hold.

He rose, picking up speed, clutching Emily's legs tightly. Shots cracked around him.

He closed his eyes—

And burst through into the sun again.

"You have her!" Roger cried, with clear relief. Sky Ranger settled her gently onto the roof. She was bleeding from her leg, but was conscious and lucid.

Somehow, she still held two very agitated cats in her arms.

"Whitelight," he said, using her old Union name. "Can you still fly?"

Emily nodded numbly. "I...I think so," she said.

"Good. Wait here a moment. James, I'll take you to the ground. Run. Follow Jill."

"Yes," James said. "I will."

"I'll give us what protection I can with my forcefield," Anthony said to Sky Ranger.

"And what can I do?" said Roger.

Sky Ranger plucked a wiggling cat out of Emily arms. "Hold her. Don't drop her." He took a split second's satisfaction in the sour look on his face. "James, come on." James hopped aboard Sky Ranger's back. They sped to the ground outside the compound's fence. Sky Ranger returned a moment later.

"Emily, keep up as best you can."

"I—I can't fly very far," she said.

"That's all right. We'll stop often. But we'll fly fast, okay?"

She nodded.

"Try not to think about the pain," he said. "We'll fix you up once we're safe."

She shook her head. "O-okay. But it's healing a little already.

I can heal myself. I should be fine."

"Let's go. Roger, can you help her up?" Roger nodded and picked Emily up with his free hand. She rose above the rooftop.

"Sky Ranger?" Emily said.

He turned to look at her.

"Thank you." She shivered. "I always wondered what it would be like—to really *use* my powers."

Sky Ranger smiled back. Below, the shouts intensified. The guards would be getting vehicles, soon. "Now you know," he said. "Let's go!"

Roger and Anthony grabbed hold of Sky Ranger, and he jumped up into the sky.

[PART THREE]

[CHAPTER 19]

"We will create the perfect metropolis, one that embodies our principles of Virtue, Honor, Loyalty, and Strength."
—Damien Peltan,
upon the official founding of his new capital, Confederation
City, 2107

"What a place. No life, just endless sprawl and misery. Confederation City was a slave camp with a downtown."
—Writer Antoine D'Avilare,
upon his forced arrival in Confederation City in 2110

A NONDESCRIPT, LIGHT-BROWN-HAIRED YOUNG woman walked quietly through the empty streets of Confederation City's Centre District. The orange sun hung low in the sky, and the inhabitants of the sprawling, sterile government office parks had all retired to the self-contained worlds of their gleaming new apartment towers for the night.

The Ministry of Defense building loomed nearby, an imposing granite edifice festooned with statues and carvings of warriors from every era. President Peltan's face beamed happily down from a massive holographic poster hung above the entrance. His eyes seemed to follow the woman as she walked.

The real military power, however, lay in the massive Confederation Military Command complex just outside the city. She knew this, yet it was still possible that what she sought was here. She didn't dare stop and examine the building, though. She couldn't afford to attract attention.

She wore the deep purple and gold uniform of the Ministry of Education, and carried a small tote bag. Inside the bag were a few notebooks and a digital notepad, upon which was saved absolutely nothing of interest or value. It was the sort of thing a Ministry of Education employee might carry, and in fact, she'd managed to pass several impromptu inspections by authorities in various parts of the city. Even her ID card and retinal implants seemed to function properly. And why not? They'd paid enough for them.

She glanced around. Almost no one else was out on the streets, save for a few other uniformed employees of various ministries who looked to be on their way home. She turned down Great Calvasna Avenue and entered vast, paved Confederation Square, home to the ornate, columned Senate building and the even fancier Presidential Palace. The Palace sat on a square of grass, cut off from the square by high fences and a platoon of guards. She briefly wondered if Damien Peltan was sitting inside that building right now. Doing what? Poring over reports of political detainees? Planning out more ways to indoctrinate the young? Eating dinner? Who could say?

Maybe he was somewhere else. It hardly mattered.

Fountains and light erupted from all parts of the square, creating a dazzling spectacle. The massive open area had been created to be a crossroads, a meeting place for all of the inhabitants of the Confederation's new capital. However, only a few people loitered here and there. Police and military personnel stood watch over the square, outnumbering citizens by far. From every conceivable surface, animated portraits of Damien Peltan stared down, or holograms illustrated happy families with slogans whirling around them. A great black-and-white flag fluttered from a pole at the square's exact center.

She hurriedly walked around the edge of the square, not quite daring to cross through its exposed heart. She kept her eyes down like a good bureaucrat, only glancing up to make certain she wasn't about to crash into anything.

She rounded the corner onto Australia Avenue, and glanced up just in time to avoid running into a tall man in a lime green uniform—Energy? Environment? She didn't know. "Excuse me," she said hastily.

"Sorry," he said.

She caught a whiff of his scent, and something made her stop dead. She turned back to face him. He was staring at her.

"You," she said softly. "Sky Ranger."

"Renna?" said Sky Ranger.

She grabbed him, squeezing him tight for a brief second.

"You!" she said into his shoulder. "I've been looking for you!"

She pulled away and he grinned. "Ha!" he said fondly. "What did you do to your hair?"

She punched him in the arm. It felt like hitting a steel girder. "I come halfway across the galaxy to look for *you* and the first thing you can say is about my *hair?*"

He just kept grinning.

Somewhere, shouts rang out. Renna glanced around nervously. This was a bad place to linger.

"Is she with you?" Renna whispered.

Dee. Sky Ranger shook his head. "No. I wish. We've been looking, but..."

Renna's heart sank. "Damn."

Was it her imagination, or were those guards near the fountains looking at them? Time to go.

Renna took the initiative. "Sir, it's excellent to see you again. Would you like to come to my apartment? We can have some tea."

"That would be lovely," Sky Ranger said with relief. She linked her arm into his and led him down the gray avenues, towards their safe house.

Confederation City had once been the sleepy little town of Crescent Bay, capital of the colony of Calvasna. Before Damian Peltan had moved his capital here from Terra City, Australia, the city had been home to about 10,000 people. Now, after only three short years, its ranks had been swelled by more than a million people, with more on the way. All of this was part of Damian Peltan's plan to make his capital the largest, most impressive city in the known galaxy.

Renna led Sky Ranger down several more broad, straight avenues. Young, dying trees imported from Earth lined the empty sidewalks. The light here was wrong for them.

They didn't speak. He simply followed her lead as she moved from the great avenue to a small, drab side street. Temporary wooden housing stood here among scattered concrete and stone structures, leftovers from swiftly vanishing Crescent Bay.

"Here," she said, stopping at a wooden house. She stepped up to the door and knocked three times, then waited a beat, and knocked again. The door opened, and Brian's face peered out.

"Renna?" he began, then noticed Sky Ranger standing behind her. "Oh!"

"I found one of them," said Renna, breaking into a sunny smile. "Can we come in?"

Everyone chattered excitedly as Sky Ranger sat in the middle of the unfurnished room. They peppered him with questions, many of them about his escape, and Dee's possible where-abouts.

"Did you actually talk to her?" Felipe wanted to know. "Did you see her?"

"How did you ever get away?" Broussard asked. "It seems impossible!"

"I'd be curious about that myself," Brian admitted. "Confederation Military Command is a fortress."

"What did they want with you?" asked Renna.

Willow alone remained silent.

Sky Ranger, clearly pleased to be the center of attention, held up a hand. "Please, one at a time! I'll start off by saying that we've been looking for Dee as well, but with no luck."

"Who's 'we'?" asked Brian.

"Just what I'd like to know," came a voice. Penny Silverwing strode into the room. "Sky Ranger."

His mouth fell open. "Sil," he breathed. "Oh my God."

"Hey, stranger," she said, and burst into a radiant smile. "Been a while."

"Sil!" He leapt to his feet, and astonished everyone by gathering the normally impassive Penny into his arms, swinging her around, and kissing her full on the mouth, cutting off her yelp of surprise and unrestrained delight.

Renna's eyebrows went through the roof.

"Damn!" Penny cried, coming up for air. She pushed herself away lightly, unable to contain her grin. "I could get used to that."

"I thought I'd never see you again!" Sky Ranger said. "What are you doing *here*?"

She shrugged, trying to look nonchalant. Renna noticed she was gripping Sky Ranger's hand tight. "Came to find you, like I said. What else?"

He started bobbing back and forth, like a little kid with a

great secret. "Sil. You'll never believe what's here, what I found. What they had. It's amazing!"

She narrowed her eyes. "What?"

"We're not alone." He shook his head, laughing. "There are others alive! There were others from the Union imprisoned with me!"

Penny gasped. "You're joking!"

"No! They're back at the house now! Whitelight, Longview, Blue Blur," he said, reciting their Union names, "Sampler and Forcefield."

"What?" Penny looked like she'd been run over by a truck. "You're kidding. Really?"

"Really. They all go by their original names, now, though, so it's Emily, Roger, James, Jill, and Anthony. But they're all alive, and free!"

"Oh," said Penny, who looked as if she were about to cry. "Oh, Sky..."

To Renna's shock, she threw her arms around Sky Ranger and kissed him again. "I can't believe it!" she exclaimed after she detached with a little *pop*.

"Believe it," he said, satisfied.

Renna laced her fingers into Brian's fingers, wondering how she was supposed to feel about all this. She settled on worried.

"Are they the only others...?" asked Penny, smile flagging a little.

He nodded soberly. "As far as I know. But that's five more than we thought. Plus there's you, and there's me...and there's Dee, too."

"Best news I've had in years!" Penny declared. "All right!" She looked around. Everyone was staring at them, open-mouthed. "What?" she demanded.

◄►►◄◄►

Sky Ranger spent the next half hour telling them of his imprisonment and escape, skipping over the parts where Roger had been right, and Sky Ranger wrong.

He told them about the ship, and his reunion with the other extrahumans. He told them about Doug, and Roger's story of escaping the Tower. He told them about the false Dee, and then about how he had discovered their true location (leaving out Roger's part in it) and their subsequent escape.

"That," he finished, "was two months ago."

"What have you been doing since?" Renna asked, a little too sharply.

"We searched for Dee. We still do. We have *no* leads... so mostly right now we're working for a living," said Sky Ranger with a short laugh. "Believe it or not. We found a place to live, and we're working on the construction projects out at the edge of the city. We figured out pretty quickly that we were being tracked, and we ditched the tracking implants they'd given us. Sil, you know all about that."

Penny, who had once sawed her own arm off to get rid of one, nodded.

"Now people assume we're just City Plan workers, same as everyone else. No one asks questions."

"City Plan?" asked Renna.

"The government forces workers to come here to build the city," said Brian quietly. "And once they're here, they can't ever leave."

"Oh," said Renna. *I should have known that. Everyone else seems to.*

"There are lots of restrictions on where we can go. However, being able to fly helps a lot in getting around them."

"I imagine," said Renna dryly.

"I've tried everything short of busting into Military Command itself to find Dee...and no luck," he said, frowning, suddenly looking very tired. "It's all we can do to survive for now. But I know she's still out there... somewhere."

"Somewhere," agreed Renna, fighting that sinking feeling again. If Sky Ranger hadn't been able to save her, how would they?

"And what about you?" he asked at last. "How did you get here?"

The plan had gone well enough. They'd piloted their stolen ship across the border without incident, thanks to a couple of smuggling tricks Brian knew of from his Fleet training—one of which involved impersonating a piece of interstellar debris for a few very long days—and parked it near Mantillies. There, they sold it to a Mantillian junk dealer for the price of six tourist tickets to Calvasna and a bag full of fake IDs. They'd also managed to meet quietly with some of the beach *rhin*'s families and friends, assuring them they were all right and exchanging information, before leaving for the capital world.

Renna almost went out of her mind waiting for the officials at the Mantillies starport to pass them through. Every awful scenario played itself out in her mind. Finally, the uniformed men took a few cursory scans of Renna's ID and tickets, and waved her through, waved each of them through in turn.

Keep going, she thought to herself. *Keep pressing on.* It was all she could do.

Three weeks had passed in a toxic mix of boredom and panic as they made their way across the Confederation. They talked, and they worried. They planned, and they fought. Brian and

Renna stopped speaking to one another, then made up again. Willow tried to befriend Penny, who pushed her away. Felipe and Broussard played checkers.

They'd stopped briefly at Earth to take on passengers. While there, the six of them stayed in the stateroom they'd booked, not daring to show their faces. What if Confederation Fleet Marines came aboard? Earth was dangerous.

That night, though, Willow had disappeared. Renna hesitantly left the room to go searching for her, and found her next to a big window, staring longingly out at the blue and white sphere below.

"I used to live there," she whispered.

"I know," said Renna. "Me too."

"I can't ever go back, can I?"

Renna put her arms around Willow, who flinched. Renna let her go. "No. Not yet. I'm sorry, love. Not for a long, long time."

Below, she could make out the lights of Toronto hugging the shore of Lake Ontario, and there, far away, the ribbons of light along the highways in the Arizona desert. For a moment she wondered, *What if...*

But no.

"Come on," she said, steering Willow back down below. "We have a job to do. We'll get back there someday."

They'd arrived on Calvasna with the rest of the tourist group, but managed to slip away. They'd dropped Ahara's name with someone who knew the Lorraine family, and were promptly given the address of a safe house in the city. They'd been there for three days, now, waiting for the wealthy, powerful Lorraines to get around to them.

Renna had spent her time pacing around the city in a uniform she'd bought from a shady street vendor, looking for anything that might be useful: a direction, maybe...maybe not. Apparently, to get by in the city, a uniform of some type was pretty much necessary. Otherwise, the police would figure you for someone who didn't belong and pounce.

It was pure luck, Renna reflected, that the uniform had fit her, and only her. Otherwise she'd have been cooped up with the rest of them.

◆►◄◆

"I don't want to leave," Sky Ranger said after Renna and Brian had filled him in, casting an eye at the door. "But I need to get back."

"I'll come with you," said Penny immediately, an arm curled protectively around his.

He shook his head, gently removing her. "Sorry. I need to fly to get there, and I need to go fast. Sil..."

She broke into another astonishing smile. "Oh, I know. But *guess* what."

She spread her arms and tilted her head back. She floated off the ground, and reached a hand up to brush it along the ceiling, shooting him a smug, triumphant look.

"You....you fly again?" he exclaimed, eyes wide. "When did *that* happen?"

She grinned happily.

"Come on, then," he said decisively. He rose up to where she was. "Let's go. You can meet the others." He glanced around. "Then we can plan. I'll come back tomorrow. We'll figure this out, I promise. We'll find Dee."

They hovered in midair while the others looked on, unable to tear their eyes away. And then, as one, they darted towards the street.

"Sky—" Renna started to say, but the two of them had already disappeared out the door.

Brian squeezed her hand, a little bit too hard. She bit her lip. Okay. Objective one down. But now what?

◆►◄◆

They darted from building to building, from roof to overhang, from shadow to light and back to shadow, chasing and looping after one another, hearts beating together in exhilaration.

This is what it's supposed to be like, thought Sky Ranger, as Penny surged beside him.

At first, they were careful, hesitant, not daring to be seen. They flew close to the ground, and hid in the shadows together. But Penny drove Sky Ranger on, taunting him by flying higher, staying out in the open for longer. He strained to keep up with her effortless flight, trying to catch the silver mane of hair spreading out behind her.

Memory flooded him. The city below could be New York. It could be fifteen years earlier. How he had missed this!

They raced faster, heedless of where they were or who saw. They dove and rose, twirling around one another, in and out of loops, back and forth.

Then Penny shot straight up into the sky. Gathering his strength, Sky Ranger burst after her, trying desperately not to lose sight of the silver speck receding into the distance. She was so, so fast. He'd forgotten that. She could fly rings around him, back when they were young.

He caught her at last—she was waiting for him up in the clouds, high above Calvasna City. She had tied her clothing securely around her waist—all of it. She looked like a terrible, beautiful storm goddess, silver hair whipping in the jet stream.

He flew up to her, desperate longing consuming him. "... Aren't you cold?" he murmured, but the wind tore his breath away.

In response, she reached for him, pressing her lips to his.

The freezing wind raged and howled around them. They began to race and plummet, diving and rising, moving together.

"There," said the tech. "That's it."

"You've traced it?" asked the lieutenant.

The tech nodded. "Whatever it was, it was down in the noise of the city, where we couldn't see it for a while. Then it shot straight up, and now it's looping and weaving."

"Birds?"

"Could be," said the tech. "Big ones, though."

The lieutenant thought it over. "Keep an eye on it. Probably nothing, but send the info along anyway."

"Yes, sir."

[CHAPTER 20]

DEE PICKED AT HER FOOD, TRYING NOT TO shiver. She couldn't remember ever being so cold. The paper-thin hospital gown didn't help.

Across the table, a huge man with a bandaged, swollen face stared at his soup, his eyes distant and lost. She didn't know his name, though she had often seen him in the lab.

"Don't..." she said, working hard to form each word. Her tongue felt like lead. "Don't... you like your... soup?"

"Mmm," he replied. "Cold."

"I... used to... be able to warm... things up," said Dee slowly, carefully.

He narrowed his eyes, and Dee felt a sudden flash of warmth from the table. Steam rose from the soup.

"Better," he said.

The female doctor stood behind him. "Very nice," she said. "Can you make it even hotter?"

He looked back at the soup and concentrated. The metal bowl glowed an angry red, and the soup sizzled and popped. Dee stood and backed away, her rail-thin frame swaying unsteadily.

"Very good," said the woman. He smiled beatifically up at her; she glanced at Dee. "Don't you think? Isn't he doing well?"

Dee shivered. She found she couldn't say a word.

"Lunch is over," said the woman. "It's back to your room

for you," she said to the scarred man. He nodded and stood. His arms, Dee noticed, bulged with muscles. Had he always been that way? He lifted a few inches off the floor and floated off, down the hallway.

Dee stared back at the soup. She felt warmer all of a sudden. She could *see* the molecules if she looked hard enough. Now all she had to do… was make them dance.

The bowl exploded in a shower of superheated soup and plastic. Someone screamed. Dee sighed as the scalding water hit her flesh, sinking in, almost bringing her to life. Warmth!

The woman turned to Dee. "And as for you… you clearly need another injection."

"No!" Dee shouted, reaching for her fire, but it was too late, and she was too cold. The orderlies restrained her.

"I know it hurts," said the woman, a cruel glint in her eye. "But really, isn't that the point?"

◄►►◄◄►

Roger hated digging ditches. And yet, that was what he was stuck doing, nine times out of ten.

"Nothing personal," the foreman drawled. "It's just you aren't any good at anything else."

Roger seethed. He was a smart guy. Why couldn't he weld? Or hammer things? Or, for the love of God, cart a damn wheelbarrow? No, always the ditches. He looked down at the rust-red dirt piled at his feet. Just a few more to do. Didn't they have machines for this kind of stuff? Or were machines out of fashion on this awful planet?

The worst part of it was that they were doing work at all. They hadn't figured out a way to get Dee, they were stuck on Calvasna, and right now, a cool, dry prison ship was looking pretty good.

He picked up his shovel and started digging again. Damn, but it was hot today. It hadn't been hot all week. Why now?

"Hey, Rog! Straight line, buddy!" called one of the other workers. A few others laughed. Roger glared at the man, hoping to glimpse a vision of his terrible, imminent death from a falling crate of bricks or something. But nothing came. No visions, accurate or otherwise, had come to him in weeks. He told himself it was because he was tired—which he was.

Down dove the shovel, sticking itself in the dirt. He grunted and pulled up, tearing away the soil from the ground and heaving it to the side. Then again, and again. Same thing, over and over. It was driving him nuts.

Where the hell was Sky Ranger? Wasn't this supposed to be his job today? The foreman hadn't looked all that worried about his absence—guys wandered off all the time. He'd come back, the foreman assumed, when he got hungry or desperate enough. There was precious little else to do in the Dig, the massive construction zones of Confederation City.

Roger glanced toward the rising towers of Calvasna Centre off in the distance. Sky Ranger had flown off to the walled-in downtown last night, and hadn't come home. Roger had terrible thoughts of him being held by ConFedMilPol somewhere, unable to escape and in awful danger. The others wouldn't have any reason to be nice to him, now, and sooner or later, their cover would be blown.

He shoveled more dirt into the pile. Some of it was running back down into the hole.

"Damn it!" he cursed, doubling his efforts to get the hole cleared again.

"Hey, Roger," said a woman's voice. He looked up. Emily. "Time for lunch. Coming?"

He wiped his forehead clean with the back of his sleeve. "Yeah, sure," he said, throwing the shovel to the ground. "I had

---

no idea it was so late."

They marched tiredly over to the canteen. Some sort of soup today. Great, hot food. That was the last thing he needed.

He got his bowl of steaming hot hell and a slice of bread and headed for an empty table. Emily sat next to him. James joined them a minute later.

"We're putting up the walls on the place," he said, gesturing to a new apartment block under construction. "We ought to be done tomorrow, then we move out somewhere else."

James had been a singular success at construction work. He was managing a small team of workers, specializing in walls and windows. James enjoyed the work tremendously, and was happier than they'd ever seen him. This annoyed Roger to no end.

"What's next?" Roger sneered, dipping his bread into his soup. "Off to work at the Palace? Putting up drywall for Peltan himself? Glad to see you've found your true calling."

"Fuck off, Rog," said James cheerily. "It's not bad work, actually. Maybe once we get out of here..." He visibly bit the end of that sentence off. They had no way off the planet, and even if they found one, where would they go? It was an old discussion, and clearly no one wanted to have it again.

Roger cleared his throat. "We still have a problem," he said quietly. "Sky."

Emily leaned in, lowering her voice. "He's still not back. I checked with Jill a few minutes ago." Today was Jill's day off, and she was loafing around back at the apartment. Anthony was there, too, nursing what he said was his bad back.

"This is very bad," said Roger.

"No shit," replied James, a little too loudly. Roger shot him a glare, and he lowered his voice. "I don't know. You think they got him?"

Roger shrugged. "No clue. Maybe."

"What do we do?" Emily whispered, voice high and tight

with panic. "That's two of them gone! He was our best chance to get—!" she cut herself off, trying not to say too much. Who knew which of the surrounding workers worked for the government here? Roger suspected that at least one man out of every twenty was a spy.

"I know," said Roger, trying to keep his voice even. "He's been taking a lot of risks lately. I wouldn't be surprised if he's caught. We should move on."

James caught Roger's meaning. "Why? I've got a base here, I can earn some decent money—I may not get the same breaks somewhere else."

"You could get caught again if we stay," whispered Roger. "Can't earn money from prison, can you?" James grimaced.

"We might have to, James," Emily said. "I don't like it, either, but..."

James banged his soup bowl down. "Fuck it. I'm going back to work, I'll see you at home tonight." He stormed off.

"What's with him?" asked Emily.

"He likes it here," said Roger. "Little idiot. He thinks it's a normal place, where he can get a job and work hard and he'll be treated just like everyone else."

"Can't he? I mean, no one's bugging us now."

"They will, eventually," said Roger. "One slip, and it all comes out. We have a choice: we hide, or we take a ton of crap from people. Plus, we're just as much prisoners here as we were back on the ship."

Emily nodded absently as she watched James head off towards his site.

This is very bad, Roger thought. *Worse than I thought. They're forgetting about why we escaped in the first place.*

"Emily," he said, on impulse, leaning close to her. She jumped, startled out of her reverie.

"Wh—what?"

Roger lowered his voice to the barest whisper. "Don't you want to fly again? I mean, *really* fly. Wherever you wanted. No limits. Anytime."

"I—there—yes," she whispered. "Of course, I'd love that... but I can't do that *anywhere*."

"You can," he insisted. "Stay with us. I promise. We'll get off this rock and go somewhere you can fly as much as you want, use your powers whenever you like. Okay? That's what we're after. For me, for you, for that kid Dee, too, if we can find her. Okay?"

She nodded, eyes wide. Roger rolled his eyes. Had he crossed that line between intense and creepy again? Probably.

"Good," he said, withdrawing rapidly from her personal space. She relaxed a little.

Shit, but this gets harder every day, he thought glumly. *We need a break.*

Jill sat on the couch, watching someone on the apartment's built-in holographic display. News, movies, news, dull political documentaries about how great the Reform Party was, some show about pretty celebrities losing their clothes in a game, footage of cops beating up on traitors somewhere, something else... she sighed. They'd had the same shows on board the ship. Some change.

Too bad Sky Ranger wasn't here. She'd been irritated with him for a while for running out on her, but now she figured she understood what had happened. He'd realized how to get them out of the ship, probably because of something clever she'd done or said. She could forgive him for that. Besides, he annoyed James, and annoying James was a ton of fun.

She lay back, dreaming. A warm breeze wafted in through

the window. She lifted herself off the couch, levitating a little, then plopped back down. She wished her powers of flight were stronger. Then she could go fly with Sky Ranger, wherever he went. She wouldn't be afraid like Emily.

A little scrape came against the window. The heck? She groaned, and got up to investigate.

"Hey!" came a sharp, familiar whisper.

"Sky Ranger?" She looked out the window.

"Up here!"

She opened the window and stuck her head out. Peering over the lip of the roof was Sky Ranger's head.

"Hey!" she yelled, waving. "What's up? Besides you."

"Shhh!" He put a finger to his lips. "Shut up! I don't want anyone seeing me up here."

"So come down," said Jill. "You *fly*, right?"

He turned red. "Uh. Could you find me... uh."

"What?"

"I need my pants," he said at last.

Jill burst out laughing.

He shook his head, eyes big and desperate. "Please? ... Oh, and can you find... a shirt, too? A long one."

A low female voice said something. Jill couldn't see where it was coming from. "Who's that?" she asked, annoyed. Had Sky Ranger been out all night getting some? Jerk.

"Jill, please," pleaded Sky Ranger. "I promise, I'll explain when I get down there. But—for now—pants? And a shirt?"

"Fine," she snapped, then yelled, "Asshole!" at the top of her lungs. People in the street below turned to look. Jill snickered to herself and withdrew.

◄►►◄◄►

A few minutes later, Sky Ranger, bare except for his pants,

sat on the couch with a satisfied-looking silver-haired woman, who had both pants and Jill's borrowed shirt.

"Lucky I managed to hang on to mine mid-flight," she was saying in a sweet, smug voice to Sky Ranger.

"So you've been saying," he grumbled.

Anthony had emerged, and his characteristic grimace had been replaced by an amused scowl. "What's happening out here? Sky Ranger, who's your new friend?"

"Where's everyone else?" Sky Ranger asked.

"Work!" exclaimed Jill. "Where do you think? It's after noon!"

"Oh," said Sky Ranger. "Uh. Really? I thought it was morning."

"The sun, dear," said the new woman mildly. She seemed to be enjoying Sky Ranger's discomfort as much as the other two.

"Right," said Sky Ranger. "Sure."

She leaned forward, suddenly excited. "Sky, are these...?"

He nodded. "Oh! Yes, they are! Anthony, Jill, this is Silverwyng. Do you remember her?"

Jill didn't know a Silverwyng, but Anthony jumped up, an indescribable expression on his face. "Silverwyng! I knew it! I knew the hair! You're still alive!"

"Hey, Force," she said with a smile. "I remember you. How's things?"

"I...you...we worked out together sometimes," he said. "When you were a little girl. Do you remember, truly?"

She burst into a happy grin. "I do!" She stood, and hugged him. He leaned into her, a blissful expression on his face "It's so good to see you again. I thought everyone was gone!"

"Were... you're an extrahuman?" said Jill. "Do I know you?"

Penny nodded. "My name is Penny, actually," she said. "Not Silverwyng anymore."

"Oh," said Jill. "I didn't know there were any other extrahumans alive!"

"Believe it or not. There's me and one other woman I knew back on Earth," said Penny. "Janeane. I have no idea where she is now."

"Who?" asked Sky Ranger. Penny ignored him.

"You were in the Union?" asked Jill.

"For a while," said Penny evenly. "Then I left."

"What?" asked Jill, incredulous. "You could *leave?* When? How?"

"About fifteen years ago, now..." Penny said. "A long time ago. I decided I didn't want to be in it anymore. I had my reasons."

"But the implant..." began Jill.

"I'm a healer," explained Penny matter-of-factly. "I cut off the arm with the implant in it, and threw it over the fence."

Everybody winced.

"Yeah, we had to gouge ours out," Anthony muttered. "Only Emily healed right up. I think I have a scar."

"I grew a new arm after that!" Penny said cheerily, waving it for effect. "Didn't take too long at all. After that, I was free."

"Oh," said Jill. "Wow. I mean... I have a little healing and flight... but... nothing like that."

"You always were amazing," said Anthony. "Really. I always heard about you being on the LED, doing good work."

Penny blushed. "Thank you," she said shyly. "You weren't too shabby yourself."

"And here you are now," Jill said with cutting sweetness, "Naked on the roof with Sky Ranger."

A thick, awkward silence descended. Sky Ranger cleared his throat. "We... we were happy to see one another."

Jill couldn't help herself. She burst out laughing. Even Anthony cracked a smile again.

◄►►◄◄►

Jill called Emily, who filled Roger and James in on every-thing. That night, they sat at the tiny kitchen table in the apart-ment, sharing their joy at another survivor of Union Tower in their midst.

Penny soaked it all in greedily. It was extraordinary. Yester-day, she'd thought she, Sky Ranger, Dee, and Janeane were the only ones left of her kind, but here sat *five* more extrahumans.

It was weirdly like coming home.

"We may be the only extrahumans alive," speculated James. "Right here in the room. The whole race of us."

"Except for Dee and Janeane," said Penny.

"Right, true," said James. "But just the nine of us. That could be it, in all the universe."

Sky Ranger shook his head. "I refuse to accept that. You're here. Maybe others got out."

"No," said Roger. "Not from the Tower. It was just us. Trust me there."

"There were plenty of others who never went into the Tow-er," Penny reminded them. "Like Michael."

Michael Forward had seen the future more clearly than Rog-er could have ever hoped. Penny still wondered, sometimes, how much more he could have told her if he'd wanted to. Or if they'd had the time.

"Penny?" asked Sky Ranger, breaking into her thoughts. "Did... did you complete your mission?"

She nodded. "Oh, yes. I did. ... And that's when I flew again, just like Michael said I would."

A hush fell over the table. "You weren't able to fly?" asked Emily.

"No," said Penny, looking away. "Not for ten years. It... I was physically unable to fly. I tried so hard. But I couldn't. It's why I threw myself out that window. I felt useless."

"That happens, I've heard," said Emily. "I knew a few people whose powers came and went. What did you do?"

Penny's lips stretched into a taut line. "I lived on the streets for ten years."

"You two were *lovers!*" Anthony said, jabbing an accusing finger at Sky Ranger. "Why didn't you go find her?"

Sky Ranger spread his hands. "I tried. But she didn't want to be found."

"That's stupid," said Jill. "You should have looked harder."

"I did!" said Sky Ranger, glancing over at Penny. "I really did look. I promise you. I did."

She shook her head. "I'm sure you did," she said, voice betraying nothing. She'd been there for him to find if he'd really wanted to. Still, it was grimly satisfying to see the others take him to task for it. Served him right.

"But then you flew again?" asked Emily, changing the subject.

Penny nodded. "Yes. I did. I... I don't know why. I don't even know why I stopped being able to fly in the first place. But when... when I completed my mission on Valen, I felt..." She trailed off. How could she describe it? It had been like being filled with radiance. The light had carried her up off the ground, and her wings had come back to her. "It was incredible," was all she could say.

Emily said something soft, a little whisper.

"Please," Roger, who had heard, sniffed. "There's no such thing as God."

Emily glared at him. "Like you'd know," she snapped back.

"It doesn't matter," interjected Penny, who had no idea what to believe. Celeste had said it was a miracle. Was it? Who was Penny to say? "What happened, happened. A few years later I was sent here, to find Sky Ranger. And so now I have."

"Someone sent you? Who?" asked Sky Ranger. "I don't know anyone on Valen, I don't think."

"The Temple," she said simply. "Val Altrera's Temple, in Arve."

A dark look crossed Sky Ranger's face.

"Look," said Penny, all business. "We need to get it together and find Dee."

"We're working on it," said Sky Ranger.

"I'm here with others," Penny continued.

"Oh?" said Roger, barely interested.

"And...we think we may have a way to get to Dee," said Penny.

Utter silence. She had their attention at last.

"You do?" Sky Ranger said. "You didn't say that before."

"I'm saying it now," she replied archly, and quickly explained the Lorraine family to them. "They may be able to help us. They have connections here. But we may need your help, too. Can I count on you?"

"Sure," said Jill and James together.

"You can always count on me, Silverwyng," said Anthony.

Emily smiled, nodding slightly.

"Whatever," said Roger. "Fine."

And so that was that.

Doug looked at the images and the sensor data being displayed on the screen. "Yes, that's definitely him," he told the ConFedMilPol major with the complicated tattoo on her face. How non-regulation. "I recognize the energy output. Very distinctive. But the other one... No. I don't know."

"One of the others who escaped with him?" asked the major.

"Maybe," said Doug, scratching his chin. "But I don't think so. None of them could fly like this, not for so long. ...And besides, I know what their energy patterns look like. None of them are so...bright."

"Hm," said the major. "So someone new."

"It would seem so," said Doug. "Or someone old, come back. It's possible. ... I assume the track is clear?"

"Yes," she said. "We know where they are right now. An apartment complex in the West Dig."

"Excellent," said Doug. "This will be a good test for Torres."

The major frowned a little. "I could have my men take them. No problems."

"You *could*," said Doug. "But why expose them to the risk? Extrahumans can be dangerous, and besides, Thunder is far more efficient. We won't have many other field test opportunities."

The major considered. "Very well," she said, clearly unhappy. "But he's your responsibility. If something goes wrong—"

"I know," said Doug. He thumbed his console. "Dr. Rivers?"

A cold female face appeared on the screen.

"Yes?"

"Wake Torres up. We're sending him out."

She shook her head. "No. He isn't ready yet."

"I don't care," said Doug. "*Get* him ready."

[CHAPTER 21]

PENNY TOOK THE LONG WAY BACK, FLYING ONLY when she had to clear a barrier, and where no one could possibly see. Last night... maybe that had been a mistake. This was Confederation City, not Valen or Arheligon. They weren't safe here.

She arrived at the safe house as afternoon started falling down towards dusk. Penny knocked—three, then four times. The door opened.

"You're back!" said Willow, who seemed genuinely happy to see her.

"Hey," said Penny. She stepped into the safe house, shutting the door behind her. Suddenly, the place seemed a whole lot roomier. She frowned. "Where is everyone?"

"Lorraine family came," said Willow excitedly. "About ten minutes ago. I was told to tell you where they'd be if you wanted to catch up." She withdrew a piece of paper. "This is the address they're going to."

"You aren't coming?"

Willow's face fell. "Brian said I should stay here. I'd be safer. And I'd stay out of the way. That's what *Renna* said."

"Mm," said Penny noncommittally. It was true enough. She glanced at the address. Easy to find. She pulled up the map on a screen and checked it. Fine. "You take care, then—better to stay safe," she said.

Willow caught her arm. "Please don't leave me alone. Please?"

Penny shrugged her off. "We'll all be back soon." She didn't like Willow. The girl reminded her too much of who she used to be. "Just stay put."

With that, she sped out the door.

◄►►◄◄►

Brian's face was an unreadable granite mask. He stared straight ahead as the car maneuvered slowly through Confederation City's wide, empty streets. Broussard looked thoughtful. Felipe seemed more relaxed than any of the others, but not by much. Compared to his usual self, he was a nervous wreck.

Renna couldn't blame any of them. She wasn't thrilled by this adventure, either. But what choice did she have? Trust the Lorraine family, or go up against the Confederation Military alone. Those had been the choices.

"The Lorraines are powerful," Brian had said. "They're one of the sixteen original families. You know what those are, right?"

Renna had barely been paying attention. "Hmm? What?"

"They were the original colonists," Brian continued. "The first people from Earth to settle on another world. They came to Calvasna in 2055."

"Oh!" said Renna. "I remember. There weren't any laws about who could have what land, so they just divided up the whole world sixteen ways. Great story."

"Right," said Brian. "No court could stop them. No laws were in place! So they got to keep it...and that's what led to the Colonization Authority being created, to parcel out land to colonists. Meanwhile, families like the Lorraines get rich from selling their land back to the government or to other people, one little piece at a time."

That's who they were heading to see: the head of one of

those insanely rich colonial families. What would he be like? They'd originally gained access just by dropping Ahara's name, but what then? Would the Lorraines help them?

And for what price?

The car turned north, driving along the west bank of the grandly named Calvasna River, which was barely more than a trickle of water here. The houses in this neighborhood were huge, almost palaces. Renna's mind boggled. She'd never seen wealth like this before.

"This is Lorraine territory," Brian murmured. "All these homes belong to members of the family."

Renna stared. They passed soldiers, but they wore a dark blue uniform with a stylized cross logo instead of police or other Confederation uniforms.

"Private soldiers," remarked Broussard. "I wondered if they still were allowed to keep them. I suppose they are."

"They can do what they like," said Brian quietly, glancing up at the Lorraine driver. He seemed to take no notice of his passengers' conversation. "No one stops them."

They pulled into a long driveway, and drove up a treeless hill. Renna looked to her left, and saw the entire city spread out before her.

"Wow," she said. "Nice view." She could see all the way to the mirrorlike shimmer of Crescent Bay, far off to the south.

They pulled up at a gate. Renna tried not to panic.

"All out," said the driver gruffly.

They scrambled out of the car, and two of the blue-clad soldiers stepped up to them with scanning devices. They frowned at their machines for a moment, then nodded.

"Clean," said one. "No weapons."

"Right," said the driver.

"Hey," called the other soldier to someone they couldn't quite see. "They're here!"

Penny appeared from around a corner.

"Where did—?" Renna began.

"Sorry I'm late," she said, grinning.

"Walked up to the gate," said the soldier, giving them a hard look. "Said she was with you. Is she?"

"Yes," said Brian. "She's one of us."

"Okay. All back in the car. We're going up to the main house," said the driver.

◂▸ ▸ ◂▸

Somewhere north and west of the city, a huge, well-muscled man with a fresh, strangely blackened scar on his chin and neck emerged from a well-concealed hole in the ground.

"Capture the new one. Kill the others," said the voice in his ear.

He shielded his colorless eyes against the red-orange glow of the setting sun, and leapt into the air, streaking south towards the Dig.

◂▸ ▸ ◂▸

Sky Ranger sipped a glass of water, feet up on the battered couch. He sighed.

"Poor boy," said Roger. "I think he's in love!"

"She's still very striking," Anthony said admiringly. "She was back then, too."

"She lived for years as a *bag lady*," sniffed Jill.

"So what?" said Anthony. "She isn't one now."

The cat on Emily's lap pricked up its ears and stared, wide-eyed, out the window.

"What is it, sweetie?" Emily asked lazily.

The cat jumped off her lap, and darted away.

"What's with her?" James asked.

"Oh, just being a cat," Emily replied, but she was frowning. "Huh. Did you hear something?"

"Like what?" Sky Ranger started to say.

He glanced up in time to see a car come crashing through the wall.

Wood, plaster, and glass sprayed everywhere. The jolt threw him off the couch, and he was cast, arms flailing, across the room—hitting the wall with a sickening crunch. All he could hear were screams as he struggled to stay conscious.

He leapt to his feet, the world swaying dangerously around him. "Hey!" he slurred. "Where is everyone?"

"Here," said Roger, struggling to his feet. "Emily's here, too."

"James!" Jill stood against the far wall. "Where's James?"

"Oh, I..." whispered Emily. Her face was white, and blood trickled out of her nose. "Where..."

"Jill, go help heal her. Where's James?" Sky Ranger looked around. James lay prone on the floor, near where the front end of the car still stuck in the wall. *What the hell happened?* Sky Ranger wondered. They were on the third floor.

"James," he said, speeding over to where he lay. "James! Are you all right?"

James opened his eyes and moaned. He was covered in blood.

"Help over here!" Sky Ranger called. "Jill and Emily, James is hurt!" They were the two with healing powers. They could help him. Emily, already looking steadier thanks to Jill, moved as fast as she dared to his side.

"Why is there a car in the wall?" asked Jill, who seemed absolutely drained. "We're not on the street!"

"I don't know," said Sky Ranger. "Focus! James needs help."

"Where's Anthony?" said Roger.

"Here," came the reply. Anthony was sitting against a wall.

"I'm fine, just got the wind knocked out of me. I'll be fine."

Sky Ranger grimaced. This could have been worse, but still. Emily knelt next to James, pressing her hand against his forehead. "Hey," she said softly. "I'm here. I'm here. You'll be okay."

Sky Ranger looked intently down at him. "How is he?"

"Not great," said Emily. "But he'll heal." She looked up at Sky Ranger. "Here." She laid a hand on his head. Some of the fog lifted from his brain, and he stood up a bit straighter. Emily sagged a little.

"Are you okay?" he asked quietly.

She nodded sharply. "I'm going to be very hungry later. But I'm fine for now." She grabbed Jill's hand and squeezed. Jill perked up a little, too.

He zipped over to the car, and hesitantly looked out the window nearest it. How *had* a car managed to get up here? Had it dropped out of the sky? Were they in any other danger?

"We can't stay here," said Roger. "We need to get out. Building could collapse."

"Yeah," said Anthony, getting up. "Come on! Let's go."

Sky Ranger looked outside. There was no one down on the street, save for a single black-clad, bulky man. A soldier? Here? Were the police coming?

That could be bad. "Yeah," he said. "We need to get out of here. Emily, can James move?"

"Soon," said Emily, voice deeper and heavy with fatigue. She pressed her hands against James's temples. He moaned. "Give me a minute."

Sky Ranger glanced back out at the street. The black-clad man walked over to another car—and casually picked it up, holding it over his head.

Oh shit.

He'd *thrown* a car at them. "Everyone against the far wall!" Sky Ranger cried. "*Incoming!*"

They scattered. Sky Ranger reached the wall and ducked down just as the second car impacted against the wall. The building shook, and Jill screamed. The first car fell out of the wall, dropping with a terrifying crash back onto the street three stories below.

Emily held James, her muscles bulging against the strain. She'd picked him up and *flown* across the room, just in time.

"What's happening?" she cried, eyes wide.

"Someone's attacking us," said Sky Ranger. "He's throwing cars."

"Oh, God," said Jill. They all got it at once. Someone strong enough to do that... another extrahuman?

One who really didn't like them.

"We need to go," said Roger. "Now. While we still can."

"Right," said Sky Ranger, in rare agreement with Roger. "Everyone out. Now!"

They struggled down the stairs. Other residents forced their way past, demanding to know what was going on. Sky Ranger feigned ignorance, and the rest did the same.

Another car hit their apartment. The entire building shook and heaved, creaking and groaning from the strain. The whole place could come down. Sky Ranger's eyes narrowed. He need-ed to stop this guy—but first, he had to get his people to safety.

"The cats!" wailed Emily.

"They'll be fine," said Sky Ranger, not giving her room to turn around. "You left the door open. They'll get out. Don't wor-ry. Keep going."

They streamed out of the lobby and into the dying sunlight. The man was still staring up at the building. He'd run out of cars, and now was lazily lifting himself off the ground.

"He can fly!" said Roger. "Who *is* he? Do you recognize him?"

"No idea," said Sky Ranger. "And I don't care. He's the one who attacked us." He turned to the other extrahumans. "Get out of here. Get far away. I'll stop him."

"Wait," began Roger.

"No, Roger, go. You can't help," said Sky Ranger. "I'm the only one strong enough."

With that, he turned to the black-clad man, who had only just now noticed them. Sky Ranger took to the air while the others ran.

◄►►◄◄►

"The thing is," said Lois Lorraine, "I'm glad to hear that Ahara is doing well. Believe me, I am. He was a constant companion when I was a girl. But...I don't know why I should help you in this matter otherwise."

Penny paced back and forth. Brian sat, clenching his fists. Renna put a hand on his shoulder.

"Well," she said. "It's a noble cause. And there may be something we can do for you."

"Extrahumans, yes," Lois sighed. She was not the head of the household, but one of the younger daughters. She had apparently been delegated to deal with them. Renna wondered if they should be insulted. She was a little pipsqueak of a woman, too, tiny and squat. She looked rather like a baked potato. "I don't know. My father was never all that fond of them. And to get into Military Command and break this one out... that's a tall order. It isn't impossible, of course. But it's difficult. I'd need something specific."

"Madam," said Brian, remaining respectful only through visible effort. "Maybe there is a deal we can offer. This would be a strike against the government, and would weaken their power here on Calvasna. Surely that interests you."

"Oh?" asked Lois Lorraine lightly. "And why would I be interested in that?"

Brian faltered. "I assumed your family would rather be in control."

Lois smiled indulgently. "That's a very blunt way to put things. But no. The status quo is profitable."

"Ma'am, if I may," said an aide, who was standing near Lois's shoulder. "The head of the Special Division... if you recall..."

Lois sat up straight. "Ah! You're right. And they would definitely have her. Yes, that *is* interesting. Much more so than I thought. Hm." She looked back at Brian. "I don't care what the government does, frankly. For now we work with them. Peltan will die someday, and all this will crumble. Calvasna is a permanent thing though, it *will* remain, and so will the great families. That's what we care about." She nodded towards her aide. "As Kenneth has reminded me, your girl would be held by the Special Division at Military Command. That division is headed by someone from the Vasna family."

Brian understood at once. "Ah. And if we succeed..."

"Vasna is hurt. Perhaps fatally!" Lois smiled sunnily. "They've been on the way down for a while. They identified very strongly with the UNP government, so the new government doesn't trust them. This could be the final nail in their coffin!" She clapped her hands together. "Yes, I like it! I like it very much." She nodded to her aide again. "Inform Father of this. I'll meet him tonight to discuss it."

"The other extrahumans," said Brian carefully. "We can bring them here if you like, but it may be best not to compromise their position."

Lois was about to respond, but something made her jerk up and listen. She held a finger to her ear. *Cochlear implant,* thought Renna.

"Ah," she said, and held up a finger. "It may be too late for that."

"What do you mean?" asked Renna, feeling a sudden dread.

"I'm getting a report of fighting between two flying men in the West Dig."

"What?" asked Penny sharply.

"One of them, it seems..." said Lois, listening. "One of them wears black. A uniform, perhaps. Is one of your—"

"I have to go!" said Penny. She ran from the room.

"Sky Ranger," said Renna. "One has to be him."

"But who's the *other*?" asked Brian, bewildered. "One of the other escapees? Why would they fight one another?"

Renna shook her head. This was getting complicated. "Black. A government uniform. Someone new?"

Lois nodded towards the window. They could see Penny streaking through the skies, bound for the West Dig. "Maybe she'll tell us. If she ever returns."

◆►◄◆

"Who are you?" called Sky Ranger, dodging another piece of debris. The stranger seemed to love throwing things at him. "I mean you no harm! Please!" He wondered if the others had managed to get away. The man threw a chunk of fallen wall at Sky Ranger. "Stop it! We can talk!"

The huge, scarred man didn't respond. He had a twisting, black scar on his chin and neck and hard, colorless eyes. He lunged at Sky Ranger, gnarled hands closing on air.

"We don't have to fight!" said Sky Ranger from just out of his reach. "We're both extrahumans. Right? We should be friends!"

The man leered, then flew high and darted towards Sky Ranger. He held a long, thin gun in his hand. Where had *that* come from?

Sky Ranger pushed himself *up*, and out of the field of fire. Shots glanced off the pavement below.

"Okay," said Sky Ranger. "I gave you a chance." He gained

altitude, then pitched sharply downward in a murderous, inescapable dive.

The huge man only had time to glance up before Sky Ranger smashed into him.

It was like hitting a ton of bricks. Sky Ranger carried him forward a little ways, knocking the man back off his feet and onto the ground. Sky Ranger flipped and landed neatly on his feet, his LED training automatically kicking in. He spun woozily around to face the man, who was still getting up.

"Please tell me! Who are you?" he demanded. "Where did you come from?"

The man's lips stretched into a terrible, leering grin, and advanced. Sky Ranger lifted off again, the stranger following.

I need to get off this street, Sky Ranger thought. People had gathered to gawk.

He glanced over at his damaged building, which groaned and dropped debris. *Perfect.* He bolted through the air, and touched down on the roof. "Come on, follow," he said under his breath. The big man hung unsteadily in the air, then lifted his arms over his head.

The air around Sky Ranger shimmered. He inhaled sharply—

The firestarter screeched and railed, lifting up his arms. "Careful!" cried Crim. The air shimmered. Then flames erupted everywhere.

He gathered his strength and leaped high into the air. Behind him, he could feel the awful heat of the flames. He glanced back—the roof of the building was a forest of fire, which then vanished as suddenly as it had appeared.

A firestarter, too! What can't this guy do?

This time, Sky Ranger realized with a shock, he might actually be outclassed.

Sky Ranger looped around. He needed to find a weapon. Something! He landed on another nearby roof. *I can wear him down, maybe.* They'd done that before.

The scarred man followed. The air shimmered again, and again Sky Ranger burst away in the nick of time.

"Have to do better than that!" he called.

"Enemy!" cried the man. "Traitor!"

"So you can talk!" Sky Ranger said. "Listen! I don't mean you any harm! I'm not your enemy!"

Sky Ranger dodged as the scarred man picked up another car, and hurled it at him. It smashed harmlessly into the empty street below.

"Kill you!" the man snarled. Well, that didn't work.

Sky Ranger had an idea. No one would be out at the ring of construction sites now that the workday was done. Maybe, just maybe, there would be something there he could use against this guy. He streaked off towards the west, into the setting sun. He glanced back—good. Scarface was following.

"Catch me!" he called. "Come on, faster!"

To his shock, the scarred man picked up significant speed. Sky Ranger could clearly see the leering grin on his face, twisting the blackened tissue. His lips moved—*Kill you.*

◄►►◄◄►

They hid in an incomplete building, invisible from the air, watching. Emily paled as Sky Ranger sped off towards the construction sites.

"He's heading away," she said.

James whimpered. She took a deep breath and put her hands on him again—good. He was stable; she could feel his vital signs getting stronger under her touch. He wasn't awake, but he would survive intact. She sighed as the energy flowed out of her body.

There was nothing more she could do for him right now. Jill had a little healing power—she could keep him going. In the meantime, there were other things she could do.

Jill and Anthony huddled against the wall, their eyes wide. "Jill, Anthony," Emily heard herself whisper. "If he comes back, can you move James?"

Jill stared. "I guess. Why?"

"I'm going after Sky Ranger. He might need me."

"What?" Jill shrieked.

"Don't be an idiot," said Roger, nearby. "You could get killed!"

"That other guy—he's strong!" said Jill. "He was picking up *cars*, for God's sake! He'll turn you into a pancake. Stay here!"

Emily shivered. She didn't want to face the other man. But Sky Ranger... he'd bought them time. What if he was out there bleeding right now? She had to go find him.

"I'll be back," she said. "Move if you have to, we'll find you."

With that, she vaulted out the window and flew slowly, haltingly off towards the construction sites.

There! Sky Ranger dodged and weaved through and around the half-finished buildings, leading the man deeper into the Dig. He touched down, hitting the ground at a dead run. He glanced over his shoulder, and saw the man stumble and fall hard. *Not trained for this, then.*

But he picked himself up quickly and sprinted after Sky Ranger.

His speed was incredible! He ran nearly as fast as James. Sky Ranger kicked off into the air to gain ground.

He grabbed a board on the way by and hurled it at his pur-

suer with all his might. Instead of dodging, the strange extrahu-
man let it smash into him. A yellow field snapped up around him.
A forcefield! Sky Ranger thought with dismay. *All of our powers.
Like Jill, but so much more.*

He staggered a little, then kept coming. That terrible grin
was still plastered to his face.

This guy doesn't stop, thought Sky Ranger, panicking.

The scarred man withdrew his long, thin weapon again and
fired. Sky Ranger leapt into the air. The bullets whizzed harmlessly beneath him. Bullets wouldn't hurt him in any case.

He ducked into a darkened building, and flew up to the second floor.

"You can't hide!" called the man as he followed. "Traitor!"

Come on, come get me, thought Sky Ranger as he crouched
down behind a door, a length of pipe in his hand.

For a few breathless seconds, Sky Ranger heard no sound.
Of course, he wouldn't be walking, thought Sky Ranger. *He's
floating up the stairs.*

A shadow appeared on the floor. Sky Ranger waited until he
was sure the man was right next to the door, and burst out at
full speed, catching him in the chest.

A bang sounded, and Sky Ranger felt something pull at his
side. He ignored it; his skin was tough enough to protect him
from guns. *Damn, his reflexes aren't supposed to be that fast!*

He reached for the gun, grabbing and twisting it free. He
tried to raise it, to turn and fire, but the leering man drew back
his fist and brought it home in Sky Ranger's gut.

Sky Ranger exploded through the window behind him, and
sailed through the air. He tried to fly, tried to gain height, but fell
end over end. He smacked into the ground at sickening speed.

Pain shot through his body. He gasped, wind gone, as the
scarred man loomed over him. He had a huge chunk of concrete
in his hands.

"Kill you!" he announced.

Sky Ranger tried to get out of the way, to at least roll over, but he had no time.

This is it—

The man raised the concrete—

Then, suddenly, a silver-and-blue flash slammed into the man, knocking him back. The concrete fell from his hands, toppling onto the ground in front of Sky Ranger.

Penny!

She darted back, eyes wild, a silver-haired ball of seething fury.

"You bastard!" she screamed at the scarred man. "Come on! Take me on!"

"The new one!" said the man. "Capture the new one!"

Oh, no, you don't, thought Sky Ranger. While the man was distracted, and hopefully forgetting to put his field up, he raised the gun and fired once, then twice. His aim was shaky, but one of his shots hit the man square in the gut. He reeled back, howling, spurting blood.

Penny threw herself at him again, driving him into the wall. He bounced off, sending her flying back.

She readied herself to fly at him again, but he sailed high up into the air. He was bleeding more heavily now. He screamed something unintelligible at them, then disappeared off over the horizon in a burst of speed.

"He's moving away. Is he hurt? His vitals don't look good," said the major.

"Yes," said Doug, voice tight with anger and frustration. "He's coming back. Get a medical team ready, he looks like he's losing blood."

The major smiled, adjusting her red beret. "Seems he wasn't ready."

Doug shot her a ferocious look. The major retreated.

"Sorry," she said.

"You can send your men in, now," said Doug darkly.

Sky Ranger looked down—blood spread underneath his shirt. He had been shot. How had *that* happened? He wasn't supposed to get shot.

"Sil," he called.

"Damn, you're hurt!" She landed and ran over to him. "How did...? Oh, God. They shot you! How?"

"Don't know," said Sky Ranger. *They must have designed the gun for me...* Unconsciousness spread around the edges of his vision. *No, stay awake, stay awake...*

Penny looked up and spotted someone flying in graceful, arcing hops from one building to the next. "Whitelight!" she called, waving. "*Emily!*"

Emily turned and made for them as fast as she could, hopping and sputtering as she pushed her flying powers to their limits.

"He's hurt," Penny said. "Please. I can only heal myself, I can't help him."

"Right," said Emily. She looked wiped out from her trip, but she put her shaking hands on Sky Ranger's head. "Hey," she said softly, as he tried to focus on her. "How are you?"

"Been better," he said weakly. "Ooohh..."

Emily seemed to lose her balance. "What..." she began, steadying herself. "What happened? Where's that man...?"

"Gone," said Penny. "Sky shot him with his own gun. I helped a little." She grinned fiercely. "Just like old times."

"I was never in the LED," said Emily. She gasped, and Sky

Ranger moaned a little. "Uh. I never qualified. Not strong enough." She exhaled, and they both relaxed. Sky Ranger's chest had begun to knit up. "... Never brave enough, either."

"You're here," said Sky Ranger. "That... I thought I told you to stay out of sight."

Penny chuckled. "Braver than you thought, maybe."

Emily removed her hands. "There. Can you get up? The wound isn't bleeding anymore, but it's fragile. Whatever they shot you with, it went right through you."

Penny suddenly looked up, straining to hear something.

"We can go back to the hiding place," Emily said. "Can you move?"

"Maybe," Sky Ranger said. "I can try."

"Shh!" said Penny.

They listened for a minute. Off in the distance, they could hear the rumble of engines. Penny gazed up into the southern sky—a dozen or so tiny black shapes were approaching.

"Military," she said. "We need to go, right now! Emily, help me grab him!"

Emily put her arms under Sky Ranger's left shoulder, while Penny took the other side. They lifted.

"Fly!" said Penny. "I'll do as much of the work as I can! But we need to fly now!"

Emily nodded. She looked utterly exhausted. "I'll try!" she called back as they lifted off the ground.

"Sky, we need you to help if you can," said Penny. She powered forward, the heavy load dragging her back. "Come on! Faster!"

They gained altitude and speed. Penny looked over her shoulder—of course the military ships were gaining. Extrahumans were no match for machines.

◄►►◄◄►

"Your friends are having some trouble," said Lois Lorraine, who had been following the fight on her terminal. "But fortunately, I think we can help them out."

"How?" demanded Renna. "What can they do? The military—"

Lois smiled cockily. "Watch."

She keyed in a sequence. A green light flashed—and then her sensor data disappeared.

Penny swerved one way, then another. They were still behind her. Emily's strength was ebbing quickly, and Penny had to strain to keep up their speed.

Sky Ranger remained inert between them. At this rate, they'd be caught within the next couple of minutes. She reached down to find what strength and speed she had remaining.

A sudden vertigo stunned her senses for a moment. What? She shook it off, and made another wide turn.

To her shock, the military ships didn't follow. Instead, they continued straight, although three broke off in what seemed like looping search patterns.

No time to argue with good luck. She exhaled and pushed ahead, carrying them faster and faster towards the distant hills. The military ships disappeared behind them, and they were free.

Doug was furious. "What happened?" he demanded.

"Sensors are offline," said the ConFedMilPol major, suddenly paler. "I... it may have been a solar flare."

"*Again?* Didn't we put precautions into place about that?" He scowled. "No, this seems deliberate. Tell your men to start searching—we need to find that new one!"

"Right away," stammered the major.

"It's the sort of electromagnetic pulse that is common around here," Lois explained coolly. "We get lots of solar flares on Calvasna. This pulse is designed to act like one of those—except more reliably."

"And you just happened to have that ready, did you?" Brian asked, suspicious.

Lois smiled tightly. "We have many tools at our disposal. We had thought to use them against the Vasnas, or maybe the Scotts. But this will do. It's a good test of the equipment in any case." She leaned closer to Brian. "I don't like this extrahuman that the government has at their disposal. It wouldn't do for them to become too powerful... especially considering that a Vasna is heading up this operation. Any doubts I had about this plan are gone." She glanced at her aide, who inclined his head a fraction in return. "And I am told that my father agrees."

"So you'll help us get Dee back?" Renna asked. Her heart was pounding.

Lois nodded. "Yes. On one condition—that the other extrahuman is found and destroyed."

Broussard opened his mouth, then thought better of it.

"Sky Ranger won't like it," said Felipe.

"It isn't his call," said Brian.

Renna knew the stubborn look on Brian Gannett's face. She nodded.

"He's right," said Renna. "We have no choice."

Felipe looked away. Broussard sighed, but nodded his agreement as well.

"Deal," said Brian, and shook Lois Lorraine's outstretched hand.

[CHAPTER 22]

EMILY, SKY RANGER, AND PENNY SAT, EXHAUSTED, on a hillside deep in the Calvasnan countryside. They had flown as far as they could manage while still supporting Sky Ranger between them. Emily had done what healing she could once they landed, and Sky Ranger was now able to sit up and converse.

Emily, however, had taken a turn for the worse. Like Penny, she became ravenously hungry after healing. Unlike Penny, she wasn't a very strong self-healer, and was in serious danger if she didn't get enough to eat, so Penny had flown to the nearest town to buy some food—a loaf of bread, some drinks, several slices of roast beef. She had returned to watch, bemused, as Emily devoured more than half of it.

I must be like that, she thought, fascinated.

She had turned her attention back to Sky Ranger after eating, though both he and Penny cautioned her against going too far. They'd still need to return to the city, after all.

"Who *was* that guy?" Emily wanted to know between bites. "Did you find out?"

Sky Ranger still felt stiff and clumsy, despite the healing Emily had been doing. He must have been in worse shape than he had thought. He groaned and lay back. "I don't know," he admitted. "I kept asking him. But he didn't seem like he could talk very well."

"You didn't recognize him, then," Penny said.

"No. He wasn't at the Tower. I've never seen him before."

"A new extrahuman," said Emily weakly.

"So it would seem," said Sky Ranger.

They digested that for a moment to the sound of Emily wolfing down the rest of the food.

"He was wearing what looked like a military uniform," said Penny. "He works for the government."

"Agreed," said Sky Ranger. He glanced up at her. "When you arrived, he said 'capture the new one.' I assume he meant you. He just wanted to kill the rest of us."

"Mm," agreed Penny, thinking. "Why would he want to capture me, though?"

"I don't know," said Sky Ranger. "Maybe because we were already captured, and they'd learned all they could about us." He frowned for a moment. "His powers... He had so many of them—I've never seen that, except in Jill."

He could fly," said Penny. "And he was strong. Very like you."

"Right," said Sky Ranger. "But he had a forcefield—he just didn't seem to be able to use it very well. And he could run fast."

"Like Blue Blur."

"James," corrected Emily.

"Right," Penny said. "James. I need to learn these names. Names are important." She flashed a quick grin at Emily.

"And he was a firestarter..." continued Sky Ranger.

"...Like Dee," finished Emily.

They looked at one another.

"It's an odd coincidence," Sky Ranger said slowly. "But... maybe he just has all our powers available to him."

"Except one," said Penny. "Mine. He didn't heal himself. He was still bleeding when he flew off."

"That's why he wanted to capture you!" said Emily. "I think I get it now. It's why they had all of us. Do you remember? They took tissue samples from us. We always wondered why. Well, now we know!"

"Oh, how awful," said Penny. "They *made* him, and gave him all of our powers."

"Including Dee's," said Sky Ranger. He shook his head. "Although... he doesn't seem to be all that lucky. If he had been, a building would have fallen on my head, or you would have missed him by a millimeter, or something."

"True," said Penny. "But maybe he doesn't know how to use it. Lucky Jane used to say she had to think about it a little."

Sky Ranger smiled sadly. "I remember her saying that."

"Yeah," said Penny, looking at the ground, an unreadable expression on her face.

"This is awful," said Emily. "Is there anything can we do against him?"

"We beat him once," said Sky Ranger.

"Barely," said Penny.

"Still," said Sky Ranger. "We *did* it, and we can do it again."

"Sure," said Penny. "Except he has all the tools to beat *us*. He just has to learn to use them. We got lucky. So what can we do when we're not?"

No one really had an answer.

They sat in silence as night fell over the wooded hillside. The trees here on Calvasna were shorter, squatter and denser than the trees Penny was used to, even on Valen. Their long, finger-like leaves swayed and danced in the breeze.

"Back when I was in the Union," said Emily dreamily, staring up at the stars. "I used to go up to the top floors and stare out at the sky at night. But I could never see anything. The lights of the city were too bright."

"We went on trips to the countryside," said Penny. "I re-member we'd go out to this lake in Pennsylvania every year. Do you remember that?"

Sky Ranger laughed. "I do! The old Sky Ranger loved those trips. I used to go flying over the mountains with him."

"I was only allowed to fly within sight of the lake," said Pen-ny wistfully. "I almost wish I'd just flown away."

"We were ready if that happened," said Sky Ranger seri-ously. He exhaled, deflating. His shoulders sagged. "... Sil, I'm so sorry."

"For what?"

Sky Ranger shook his head. His body ached more than he could ever remember. "I don't know. Everything. For keeping all of you prisoner in the Tower. I... the old Sky Ranger knew. He *un-derstood*. It tore him up inside, to see his people trapped back there. He never went on LED missions to track down renegades. He couldn't bear it."

He sighed heavily. "He looked forward to the trip out to the lake all year. He loved the mountains. But he never got to go visit them, except for that one time per year. He had to stay in the city, unless he had permission to leave. That was the law."

"I almost never thought of it like that," Emily said. "It was Roger who showed us how bad things really had been. But be-fore... I think I was happy living in the Tower. I had my life and my cats." She started. "Oh! I hope they're okay."

"I bet they are," said Penny. "Cats survive all kinds of things. They're probably hanging out in the alleys right now, looking for food."

"I hope you're right," said Emily, obviously not convinced.

"Sky," said Penny, looking back at him. "I didn't see it as prison, either. Not for a long time. Crim really had a lot to say about it, though... and I listened to him. That's one of the rea-sons I didn't come back."

"I don't really remember him," said Emily. "Crimson Cadet. He was dashing, and I'd see him around, but he didn't really talk to me."

"He was such a good man," said Penny. "Smart. He really saw what was happening."

"I miss him," said Sky Ranger, voice unexpectedly tight. "He was my best friend. He kept me even. After he died... I think I let my worse impulses take over. I turned blind." He stared up at the sky, the stars blurring through his tears. "I wish he had survived. He made me a better leader... though I hated him for it sometimes. He drove me insane!"

He laughed, a short, sharp chuckle. "But it was good for me. If he hadn't died... maybe I would have been a better leader for the Union. Maybe I wouldn't have failed us."

Emily put a hand on his shoulder. "You didn't fail. You did what you thought was best. Don't listen to what Roger says; you did what you had to do. The law was the law."

"The law was wrong," said Sky Ranger. "Crim knew that."

"And what could we have done?" asked Penny. "I've thought about it. What if we all had just... left? They wouldn't have allowed it. We'd have been hunted down like animals. The whole Army would have been after us. Everyone would have had to live just like we're living now... and it couldn't have lasted."

"She's right," said Emily. "Roger can talk all he wants about heroic stands and whatever, but we would have been killed or captured again."

"We escaped today, didn't we?" said Sky Ranger. "And before. We could have survived." He sighed. "We could have followed Val Altrera to Valen. We didn't."

Penny perked up at his mention of the name. "What about Val Altrera?"

"The old Sky Ranger told me," he said. "Val Altrera was an extrahuman, like us. His power was seeing the future. Like Michael Forward. They never dared capture him and put him in the Tower, though, because he lived such a public life. He had so many followers that they couldn't touch him—they were afraid of what might happen. His fame was his shield. So they cut a deal with him. He had to take his followers and leave Earth, and they'd leave them all alone. He did."

Sky Ranger shook his head. "The tragedy is that the old Sky Ranger was offered the same choice. But he was young, and he didn't like Val. So he said no."

Emily shivered, eyes wide. Penny inhaled sharply. "You're kidding."

"I wish I was," said Sky Ranger sadly. "It drove him mad, later on. We could have gone to Valen. We could have lived free there. But he said no."

"I wish he had said yes," said Emily in a small voice.

"Me, too," said Sky Ranger. "Then we'd still be..."

He didn't have to finish the sentence. They were all thinking the same thing. Hundreds of extrahumans, living tranquilly on another world... It had nearly happened, but for the whim of one man almost forty years ago.

"We can still go there," said Penny quietly. "We have to get Dee, and then we can go to Valen. That's where I've been. We can live there in peace. The Temple, Val's Temple, will protect us from the Reformists. They're powerful, and they would welcome us."

"Really?" asked Emily.

"Yes," said Penny simply. "So they tell me. And I have no reason to doubt them."

"Then we need to do that," said Emily firmly. "If there's a home for extrahumans waiting out there, we need to find Dee, free her, and take her there."

"It sounds too good to be true," said Sky Ranger.

"I've been there," Penny reminded him. "It's true. The prelate of the Temple in West Arve said to bring you all back." They were gathering extrahumans together on Valen. Maybe this was why.

"We should go back now," said Sky Ranger. "We should go to the city and meet up with the others."

"Hang on," said Emily, yawning. "I don't think I can fly again for a while... we should try to rest first. And you need to heal a little more."

"She's right. Plus, we need an actual plan," counseled Penny. "We can't go into this blind, guns blazing." She looked away. "Trust me. It doesn't work."

Emily slept. Fortunately, the night was warm. Penny and Sky Ranger sat together, watching the stars. The Calvasnan day and night were longer than Earth's; it would be a while before the orange sun rose. Off in the southern sky, they could see the dull, white-yellow glow of Confederation City.

"So you've really been working construction?" asked Penny. "Seriously? I can't believe it."

Sky Ranger ducked his head, grinning. "I'm actually not bad at some parts of it. Like digging, or picking stuff up."

Penny laughed. She was lovely when she laughed.

"James has some real talent, though," Sky Ranger continued. "He's the leader of a window team. He goes to something like three or four different sites per day, putting up windows. He's the boss of maybe five people."

"Wow," said Penny. "That's impressive. I didn't really know him all that well. He was just a kid when I left."

"I can't say I know him well either," said Sky Ranger. "He wasn't on the LED, though his speed would have qualified him."

"I bet his powers are useful when putting up windows," said Penny. "He could get them up faster than anyone."

"He told me he doesn't use them," Sky Ranger said. "Heck, I try not to use mine too much. It would attract attention." He sighed. "I guess that's over now. I hope James is okay. He was hurt pretty badly."

"He was? I didn't know!" Concern spread across her face.

Sky Ranger nodded. "Emily had him stabilized before she left. Jill has a little bit of healing power—she can hopefully do enough to keep him getting better. I wonder where they are..." He trailed off.

"How are you feeling?" Penny asked.

"Not bad," Sky Ranger admitted. "Emily's very good. Better than I realized."

"You never know what people can do until you test them," said Penny.

"True." He smiled at her. "Look how much you did, back on Earth."

She shrugged, looking away, "I was just along for the ride. It was Michael who did all the work."

"You did more than you realize," Sky Ranger said. She made a small noise acknowledging what he'd said, but nothing more.

They let a few minutes pass in silence. She rested her head on his shoulder.

"Hey," she said. "About last night."

He snorted softly. "Here we go."

"Let's not make it into a big thing."

His eyebrows rose. "Okay," he said.

She smiled softly. "It was nice. Better than nice! I was so happy to see you. But..."

"You don't have to explain," he said. "I understand."

He did, too. She knew it. She nestled into his shoulder. He put an arm around her.

"Just so we're clear," she said.

"We're clear," he responded.

They sat together for a while.

"I want you to know," he said, although he suspected she

had fallen asleep, "I did look for you. I should have looked more. But I went through the streets, looking. I looked through records. I never found you."

He tilted his head back to look at the stars. "I gave up too easily. I was stupid, back then. I should have looked harder for you. I missed you. But I wouldn't let myself admit it." He glanced down at the top of her head. Her straight silver hair, parted in the middle, ruffled a little in the wind. She breathed softly. Why was her hair silver? Not gray, not white, but actually silver...so unique. He'd never known anyone like her.

"I was stupid until you snapped me out of it," he continued. "I just wish I'd found you sooner. I wish I'd been smarter. I wish I'd listened. Crim was right, you know. I need someone to kick me in the ass, pretty much every day."

"And that's just for a start," she murmured.

"Heh." He squeezed her closer for a moment. "You should catch some sleep."

"You know," she said, "I don't sleep much."

"Yeah," he said. "Me neither."

She looked up at him, and their eyes met. He held her gaze for a moment, until she looked away.

"Hey Sky," she said sleepily.

"Yeah, Sil?"

"...Tell me...what if I couldn't fly again?"

He frowned. "What about it? Are you having problems again?"

She shook her head. "No! Far from it. I'm doing great, better than ever. But...you know." She seemed to struggle to find words. "I couldn't fly...before. You know. ...Right?"

"What do you mean?"

She sighed in frustration. "I'm not saying this right. Forget it."

"No, go on."

She looked up at him, her face a mask of heartbreak. "When

I couldn't fly before. You weren't interested in me. And..."

"Oh," he said. "What? I was interested! I just... I had a lot on my mind."

She gave him a look.

"Come on, Sil," he pleaded, caught. "It was a long time ago."

"So what would happen now?" she asked. "Would I still be interesting to you?"

"I'm not the same as I was," he said deliberately. "And I thought you didn't want this to be a big thing."

"I...I don't."

"So what are you worried about? That I'll never talk to you again if you can't fly?"

"Seems like that's what happened last time," she said, hurt plain in her voice.

"Last time is last time," he said. "That was what... fifteen years ago now?"

"Something like."

"We were both young. Stupid." He chuckled. "Me especially. I don't know, Sil... all I can say is that I'm glad you're here with me now. And that has nothing to do with whether you can fly."

She gave him a hug. "Okay." She stood.

"Where are you going?"

"Have to take a leak."

"Ah."

She tromped off into the woods. He sighed. *Damn, but I'm bad at relationships.* He could almost hear Crimson Cadet laughing at him.

◄►►◄►

"Sky, you're the biggest idiot I've ever seen. That girl's head over heels for you." They weren't talking about Silverwyng, but another LED member. Astarte, maybe? This was when Sky Ranger

was still new in his job.

"So?" said Sky Ranger haughtily. "What does that matter?"

"So say something to her! Even if it's just to let her down."

"Why?"

"Why?! Because then she won't get pissed off and leave the LED. She won't spend the next year writing bad poetry about what a jerk you are. You want her to be happy, so maybe find her someone else to fixate on."

"Like who?"

"I don't know. How about Hammer?"

"Hammer's a tool."

Crim laughed, and punched Sky Ranger in the arm. That had been their joke for years. "Look, though! You need to get serious about her. You really don't get it, do you?"

"No," admitted Sky Ranger. "But that's why I have you! You're like my social secretary."

"Oh, great. See if I ever give you advice again! It's like trying to tell a rock how to dress up and dance!" said Crim, but he was laughing. They traded insults for a while, then went flying.

Penny returned and sat, a little ways away from him.

"Hey," he said. "You okay?"

She nodded. "Yeah."

"I meant what I said," he said. "I don't care if you can fly. You're still you, no matter what. Sil—Penny. Sorry. I can't get used to you not being Silverwyng. The others weren't so bad, but it still took me a couple of days with them."

"It's all right," she said.

"Listen," he said. "I think about all the things you've been through, out on the streets and then with Michael... I don't know if I could have stood it as well as you did."

"I didn't stand it well at all," she said. "I cracked up. I went nuts. I don't really remember half of my life on the streets."

"But you came out of it."

"People can change," she said simply.

"Yeah," he said. "They can."

They sat together for a while. Penny moved over and nestled back into him; he wrapped an arm around her.

"...Look, I don't care if you can fly," he said. "You're amazing enough here on the ground. And if you can't fly, I can carry you."

She smiled up at him. "Thanks," she said, then laughed quietly. "You're corny as a cob these days! What happened to the thick-skulled, oblivious doofus I fell for all those years ago?"

"Oh, he's still here," said Sky Ranger, amused. "He comes out all the time. It's nice—I can forget all the things I regret when I'm him."

"Ha! You? Having regrets?"

"A lifetime's worth," he said.

"Well, get over it," she said after a moment's silence. "We have lots of living left. We have to make a home for our people on Valen."

"Always Valen," said Sky Ranger.

"I know," said Penny. "I think you'll like it there. I know I do."

"Is it a nice world? Lots of flowers and trees? There aren't any deserts, are there? I don't think I can deal with more deserts."

"I don't know if there are deserts. What's wrong with them?"

"I spent six weeks stranded on a desert planet," he reminded her.

"Right," she said. "Renna said. Sounds like fun."

"I'll tell you all about it sometime."

"I'm looking forward to it." She considered. "Most of Valen seems to be pretty nice. I haven't seen a lot of it, understand.

But where I was, it was mountains and woods and streams. Real nice. Sort of like the lake."

"That sounds great," he said, stifling a yawn. He stretched out on the ground. "You know... I think maybe I should sleep after all."

"Maybe you should," said Penny. "You're still hurt."

"I know. Keep watch... " he said, trailing off into sleep.

Hours passed. Penny watched the sky. It might be cold, but she had no real idea. She didn't feel heat and cold so much. She wondered which tiny speck of light was the Terran solar system, and which was Valen's star.

Ian, Bann Delarian, whoever he was now, was way out there in Räton space somewhere. She wondered how he was doing. Did he get sick? Did he fuss and refuse to eat his food? Did he still cry a lot? Did he still smell the same?

Would he grow up to be a boring businessman, a restless drifter, a misunderstood artist, or humanity's savior? It didn't matter too much right now. It was too far away.

Monica was on whichever one was Valen, walking from village to village as a sort of itinerant priest of the Temple. How strange. It seemed to make Monica happy, though.

Michael Forward was dead. She wondered if he'd ever seen what was happening to her now, though. Somehow, he seemed like he was still a part of her present in some ways.

"Hey, Michael," she said, just in case. "Keep going. We did all right."

She looked down towards the glow of Confederation City, off to the south. She could see the tiny, blinking lights of aircraft high over the city.

One seemed to separate itself from the pack. Was it heading

their way?

Penny stood, watching intently. The speck of light rapidly expanded, and now she could hear the whine of a hopper engine.

"Crap!" she said. "Sky! Wake up, hopper's coming!"

He roused himself and staggered to his feet. Penny was already shaking Emily awake.

"Huh? Wha...?"

"Hopper's coming. We need to hide," said Penny. "Come on, get up!"

"Scatter!" ordered Sky Ranger.

◆►◄◆►

The small aircraft touched down gently on the hillside, and the hatch opened. A tall, brown-haired woman ambled out.

"Hey!" she called. "Penny! Are you here?"

The bushes rustled. Penny emerged. "Renna?"

"Hey, there you are! Thought so." Renna waved, jumping down to the ground. "Is Sky Ranger with you?"

Sky Ranger strode into the light cast by the hopper, shielding his face. "I'm here. Emily, it's all right!"

"Okay!" called Emily, struggling forward out of the woods where she'd been hiding.

"This is Emily," Sky Ranger said.

"I got that," Renna said, amused.

"Renna, how did you find us?" asked Penny. "And whose hopper is this?"

"This belongs to the Lorraines," said Renna. "And they found you." She tugged on Penny's blue shirt. "I think they put a tag on you. Clever, huh?"

"Oh," said Penny. Damn. She hadn't even thought of that when they'd patted her down at the Lorraine house. "Huh."

"Sneaky, huh? You may want to change your shirt at some

point."

"Right," said Penny, feeling a little embarrassed. "Okay."

"Is this all of you?" Renna asked. "I thought there were more."

"Back in the Dig," said Sky Ranger. "We split up."

"Are you all okay?" Renna asked, frowning. "Sky, there's blood all over you!"

"Most of it's mine," admitted Sky Ranger. "But Emily's a healer. She fixed me up."

"Oh," said Renna. "I see."

Someone inside the hopper said something. Renna turned to listen, then said to the others, "Okay, get your butts inside, we're leaving. We'll drop by the Dig first to collect everyone else."

"Then what?" said Sky Ranger.

"Believe it or not," said Renna, "we have a plan. We're going to grab Dee from Military Command and get out of here."

Sky Ranger's jaw dropped. "You're not serious."

Renna smirked the smirk of the just, while Penny shot Sky Ranger a triumphant look. "Aren't you glad you waited?"

[CHAPTER 23]

JILL KNELT OVER JAMES, RELEASING WHAT little energy she had into his system. He was better, if not actually well, but she was fading fast.

"Come on," she said quietly. They'd relocated to the basement of the half-finished apartment building after Emily had taken off, and they hadn't left it since.

Roger paced back and forth, restless and mumbling to himself. Anthony slept fitfully over in the corner, alternating between snoring and twitching. Jill examined James closely, watching for any sign that he might be coming around.

"James," she whispered. "Please. Come on." She felt a little more energy inside herself and gave it to him. She felt something inside him respond, but it made little overall difference. It was like dropping a teaspoon of water into a wide, deep lake. He still felt cold, and he had not awakened.

I wish I was Emily, she found herself thinking. Emily could fly reasonably well and had strong healing powers. Jill, on the other hand, had just a little bit of everything—flight, speed, strength, and healing—but not enough to make any kind of difference. She thought she might have a little prescience—she had odd dreams about things that might happen—and she was convinced that she could warm up a cup of coffee if she really concentrated, but she couldn't help James. She certainly couldn't have flown off to help Sky Ranger like Emily had.

She felt like pounding her fists against the wall and screaming. Being the Sampler, with a small, almost useless bit of all kinds of powers, was infuriatingly frustrating. She was hardly an extrahuman at all. Better to be someone else. Anyone else.

Roger stopped pacing and looked at James. "Well? Are you actually doing him any good?"

"Yes, thanks," she snapped, glaring at him. "He's not any worse."

"We really need to take him to a hospital," said Roger.

"When Emily gets back..." Jill began, then trailed off. She and Roger looked at one another.

"She's coming back," Jill insisted quietly.

"I hope you're right," was all he said.

Jill sat as still as she could, drenched in her own misery, watching James's chest rise and fall. They'd been lovers on and off for most of the three years since Union Tower fell. They didn't have a lot in common. She didn't even like him that much. They'd been together mainly because they were the same age and both willing. He was prickly, hyperactive, quick to take offense, and could sometimes be cruel.

And yet, now that he was busy with construction work, he seemed calmer. His job at the Dig made him happier than she'd ever seen him. He even seemed to get along with Roger and Sky Ranger, which was amazing.

In fact, she'd been starting a lot of their arguments these days. They'd be talking, and she'd suddenly have an overwhelming, irresistible urge to needle him. She wished she knew why.

She let a little more energy flow into him. He sighed and murmured.

He's kind of sweet like this, she thought. *Not talking.*

Roger was saying something to Anthony, she couldn't hear what. She concentrated on James instead.

He was fine. He wasn't going to change. She stood up, legs

aching and sore from sitting for hours.

Emily popped back into her mind. She had been so brave, to go off alone. She knew she'd be back. She had to come back.

She gasped. "Emily's cats!"

"What about them?" Roger said wearily.

"They were left in the apartment! They're probably starving right now."

"So?" Roger shrugged. He had never liked Emily's cats. "They're cats. They'll be fine."

"No!" Jill insisted. "They lived on the ship for most of their lives, and the Tower before that. They won't know what to do!"

"We can't do anything about that now," said Roger testily. "We have to *wait*."

She hesitated, then decided. "I'm going to go find them, and bring them back here."

"What?" Anthony almost got to his feet. Roger arched an eyebrow at her.

"That would be amazingly stupid," Roger said.

"I don't care," Jill said. "I can't sit here anymore. I have to go do *something!*"

"Jill, be reasonable," Anthony began. "It's dark out, and we don't know if that…man…is still out there. Go when it's light, at least."

"Dark is better," said Jill. "He won't be able to see me, either." She hoped. "I can handle it," she insisted. "I can fly a little, and I'm stronger than most regular humans."

"Not by much," said Roger, crossing his arms in front of him. "Emily at least could fly reasonably well. You can barely get off the ground! You're staying here. Period."

Jill snapped. "Fuck off, Roger! Who do you think you are, Sky Ranger? I don't care what you think. I never liked you anyway!"

Roger stepped back, as if struck. Jill leaned forward, years of frustration spilling out of her. "Fucking meddling busybody, think you know *everything*. Well, to hell with you! I'm going no matter what you tell me! As if you even *knew*! We got out of the Tower because we were *lucky*, not because of anything *you* did. So I'll go where I like!"

"Jill," said Roger after a moment, but it was too late. She had spun on her heel and gone.

◄►► ◄◄►

Willow sat quietly, fully awake. She hadn't moved from her chair opposite the door for hours. Dawn would come soon. It had to. Then maybe the others would come back.

She breathed in, then out. She listened intently, trying to discern if there were any other sounds out there she should worry about.

She wished she had a gun. Why hadn't she insisted on taking one with her? Maybe she could have stolen one from a cop or something. Maybe, maybe.

Ryan had taught her to shoot. She'd just been a kid from the city when they'd met, but he'd showed her how to handle a gun. *Just in case*, he'd said. *Because you never know.*

When the Black Bands had come for him, he'd grabbed his rifle right away. He'd never fired it, though. They ran for the back alleys and the underground instead, joining the endless, faceless parade of refugees and fugitives moving across North America, searching for a way off Earth. Somewhere up in Canada, they'd been lucky enough to find Jackie Nabors and her ship, just waiting to take them to Reilis if they could pay for it. They'd had to do some pretty awful things to raise the money (Willow shivered when she thought of that), but they'd managed to put it together before the ship left.

Now Ryan was dead, and Willow was a killer. What had it all been for? The life they'd hoped for, planned for, had gone down the drain when he'd posted his anti-government tracts, and died for good with him on Seera Terron.

Was that a creak? Footsteps? Willow stopped breathing, straining to hear. She wished she had a gun. She should have insisted.

Yes, definitely someone outside. She stood nervously. Probably the others. Where was the knock? ... Although, she reminded herself, Renna had taken the key. They wouldn't need to knock.

A heavy thud echoed off the door. Willow squeaked in alarm, putting the chair between herself and the door.

Another thud. Then, with a terrible crash, the door splintered and caved in. Black-uniformed troops rushed in.

Willow backed up against the wall as they surrounded her. "Wh—wh—what?" she stammered as troopers raced through the house, calling and searching.

"You are under arrest," said a man in what looked like a ConFedMilPol uniform. "Do not resist; your safety cannot be guaranteed. Put out your wrists."

Willow meekly obeyed. Someone slapped a pair of handcuffs on her. They led her out into the street, where the glare of bright lights from police and ConFedMilPol vehicles blinded her.

Somewhere nearby, a vehicle fired off a flare into the sky. It exploded with bone-jarring force, directly overhead. Willow screamed in terror as they slipped a cover over her head.

The signal. Willow knew it so well from her days in Reformist Houston.

Celebrate, citizens! it cried. *Another Enemy of the People has been captured! Rejoice, and be glad that the blast doesn't sound for you.*

◆▷▸ ◂◁◆

Jill jumped as the dull boom echoed across the city. They heard those sometimes. Where had it come from? What did it mean?

The sound faded. She put herself back together and scanned the street ahead. The apartment building was up ahead. The police had sealed the building, but maybe she could get in. She could fly straight up about twenty feet, maybe a bit more. That might be enough to reach the apartment. How far had it been from the prison ship windows to the roof? She couldn't remember.

She looked around as she approached the building. No one was out. The sun would be up in a few hours, but for now Confederation City and the endless reaches of the Dig slept.

This is exciting! she thought. Adrenaline pumped through her. *And kind of fun, too.*

She stood next to the old building and looked up at where their apartment had been. A black hole gaped in the side, and part of the roof had caved in. The cars and other debris had been cleared away, but the damage to the building remained.

The cats might still be up there. She gathered herself and pushed straight up.

She gained altitude, and then suddenly felt herself running short of energy. She stalled out and started falling.

"Crap!" she yelled, flailing. She grabbed for the wall and held on. By some miracle, she found herself hanging precariously from a second-floor window ledge. She cast around, trying to pull more energy together for another try. What the hell? She should have been able to do that.

Of course. James. She'd put so much energy into him, she had almost none left for herself.

She hung for a moment, feet scraping against the wall, and then felt the air steady beneath her. Okay. She let go and pushed again. The window sped by, and the gaping blackness of the hole appeared. She dove wildly for it, grabbing on to the crumbling walls. Her left hand came away with some loose material, but her right hand clutched something solid. She gave herself a boost with the last remnants of her flying energy, and hurtled into the dark room with a thunk.

She had done it. But now what?

The cats, right. She held herself still for a moment, letting her eyes adjust to the darkness in the room. Above her, the broken roof creaked and groaned. She'd have to be quick.

"Hey, kitties," said Jill softly. "If you're here, come on out. I have some nice tuna for you... or something like it." She padded softly over to the kitchen, taking out a bag of dry cat food. She shook it once, twice. Usually that was enough to bring them running, but not this time.

She made her way, feeling through the dark, into the room she shared with Emily. No cats on the bed. Maybe she should have brought a flashlight. She made little clucking sounds, like Emily often did, hoping they'd hear and come running.

No luck. "Stupid cats," she said to the darkness.

She left the room, looking left and right. The door to their apartment was open. Maybe they'd left it that way?

But if they had, the cats had likely managed to get out. She sighed. All that for nothing. They probably weren't here.

She made a cursory pass around the apartment, and satisfied herself that the cats were indeed somewhere else. She considered flying down, but thoughts of her less-than-successful flight up caused her to take the stairs instead.

Her footsteps echoed loudly in the ruined concrete stairway. She cursed and stepped as quietly as she could—then stopped herself. No one was in the building, of course. Why worry? She skipped down the stairs as fast as she could.

The doors were shut, but not sealed. She looked around, and saw two cats huddled together next to the doors.

"Hey!" she said. "Hey, you two." She held out a hand. One of the cats—Linda? Diana? Who could tell?—came over to her and butted its head against her hand.

"Mrow," she insisted.

"Oh!" she said. She was still holding the bag of cat food. "Here. I bet you're hungry." She opened up the bag and poured food into a neat pile on the floor. The cats dove for it—clearly, they'd been stuck in the building all night with next to nothing to eat.

She knelt down to pet them as they greedily devoured the food. How was she going to get them back? They'd really hated being carried from the ship to the Dig, and that had been when Emily had done it. She'd probably end up being clawed. It figured.

She decided to take a quick look outside. She opened the door a crack, and peered outside.

What were all those black shapes?

Suddenly, a painfully bright light blinded her. Someone was opened the door, and grabbing her hands.

"Hey!" she said, struggling.

Someone dove on her, knocking her to the ground. "Stay still!" a male voice shouted in her ear. Don't move! Your safety cannot be guaranteed!"

At that moment, something like a pillowcase was roughly slipped over her head, blacking out her field of vision. It smelled a little strange... she inhaled, coughed, and passed out.

A deafening boom, directly overhead, was the last thing she heard as oblivion raced up to meet her.

[CHAPTER 24]

"**Willow's missing, too,**" said Broussard grimly. "I knew leaving her alone was a bad idea."

"To be fair, boss," said Felipe, who had gone with him. "That place looked like elephants attacked it. No way even all of us could have resisted, right?"

"Hm," grunted Broussard. "Should have brought her with us."

"Right," said Renna heavily. First, the hopper crew had been unable to find Jill, even after they'd found the others. They'd checked the apartment building, cleared out whatever stuff there was to take. They'd found no trace of Jill except a few hushed stories of an arrest in the night. Discouraged and worried, they'd headed back to the Lorraines', only to find that now Willow was gone, too.

"That's two gone," said Sky Ranger. He looked worried. Brian sat next to him in a conference room deep in the complex of homes and offices that made up one of the Lorraines' main estates.

"Based on my information," said Lois Lorraine, "they've both been taken by ConFedMilPol. Your extrahuman friend is likely being held by the same people who have Dee. I don't know about the other woman. I have no information beyond that,

but I believe, based on my sources, that they were able to track someone's flight back to both of them." She eyed Sky Ranger and Penny. "No more flying. Understand? We were lucky they didn't come for *us* because of you the other day."

Abashed, Penny murmured an apology. Sky Ranger turned red.

"That's under the bridge now," said Brian, clearing his throat. "We have to concentrate on how to get into Military Command, get all three of our friends, and get out." He stood to face Lois. "You've talked about your sources, and your information. We need access to at least some of that if we're to do what we need to do, and get out in one piece."

"You will have good information," Lois assured him.

"Excellent," said Brian. He turned to the display. "Call up the diagrams you showed me."

Lois raised an eyebrow at Brian's commanding tone, but did as he asked. A three-dimensional schematic of a building flickered to life. "This is Confederation Military Command. Or, at least, part of it. These schematics are from its construction four years ago." She pointed to a highlighted location on a sub-level. "This is where I suspect your friends are. Special Projects. That's Doug Vasna's unit."

"Doug who?" Sky Ranger frowned. "Surely not the same man..."

"Oh?" Lois tilted her head to one side, interested. "You knew him?"

"We knew someone named Doug *Palma*, who was part of the Ministry of Scientific... something. I forget."

"Scientific Advancement, I'm guessing," said Lois. She entered a few more commands, and a picture of a man in a severe black military uniform appeared.

"That's him," said Sky Ranger.

"I see. Well. Special Projects is part of the military, but there's a civilian arm as well. Doug Vasna heads both units. I imagine he didn't want to trip any alarm bells in your head with his real name."

Roger laughed. "Vasna! Of course. Nothing at all was real there! Why am I not surprised?"

"He's a very powerful man. His uncle is head of the Vasnas and Governor of Calvasna. He's been having...trouble lately." Lois Lorraine looked like she'd just eaten something delicious. "If we can make this happen, House Vasna is going to be in very serious trouble indeed. It could cause chaos all across the city. They might even fall from power." She smiled wolfishly. "My father is very much in favor of this, as you know."

"So who becomes the big shot, then?" Sky Ranger wanted to know. "You?"

"No, not us," said Lois. "We're too small. No, I'm guessing it'll be the Allgotts. That's our candidate, anyway, and the choice of many of the others. Father has been talking with other House heads. There's a lot of support for getting rid of the Vasnas."

"Why?" Renna wanted to know.

Lois waved a hand. "Oh, many reasons. One being that their lands will become forfeit. We have a claim on several very large and expensive tracts. If the family is out of favor, and the All-gotts assume leadership, we've been promised those lands in exchange for our loyalty. It works out very neatly."

"It doesn't matter to us," said Brian, trying to reassert control of the situation. "Bring up the schematic again."

Lois obliged with a flick of her wrist.

"We will have to get from here," Brian pointed to the entrance, "down three levels and across half the installation, in order to get to where they are." He pointed at Special Projects. "The Lorraines have been providing us with good information about how to get into the base, and how to get to where Dee, and now presumably Jill, are being held. Willow may be there as well—we don't know. The Lorraines say they can get us there. However, getting out will be more difficult."

He pointed to another part of the base. "We won't be able

to get out the front door. However, the Lorraines have assured me that there will be a ship waiting for us."

"That's not *too* far," said Renna.

"No, but it's far enough," said Brian. "That's why we're going in armed."

"Brian, you've got to be kidding," said Renna. "We're not commandos. We aren't trained to break into the Confederation's most secure military facility."

"Breaking in won't be hard," said Lois. "We've created identities for you, you'll have high-level access to most of the building, and we have a special guide for you. You should be able to get around without a problem. Getting out, however, will be more of a challenge, as Brian said. At that stage, they will almost certainly have figured out that you're not who you say, and try to stop you. We will have as many of our people posted in the area as possible, but the actions they can take will be... limited."

"Right," said Renna dubiously. This was sounding worse and worse all the time.

"Sky Ranger," said Lois. "I'd like to discuss another objective with you."

"All right," said Sky Ranger, frowning.

"I want to be present for that," said Brian.

"Very well," agreed Lois gravely.

"We will be working on a detailed plan of action tonight," said Brian to everyone else. "We *will* make the attempt tomorrow morning. It can't be any later than that."

Renna exhaled and looked around the room. Sky Ranger and Penny stood together. Emily sat next to James, who was sitting up and looking around, if not talking much yet. She'd been healing him for most of the night. Broussard and Felipe sat next to one another, Felipe seeming at ease and Broussard looking as troubled as ever. Anthony sat a bit apart from the rest, and Roger leaned against the back wall, scowling. Neither looked particularly happy. Renna stood next to Brian, and Lois sat at her console, overseeing it all.

"This...isn't going to be easy," said Brian, looking the group over. Clearly he was seeing the same things Renna saw. "We'll need as many of you to come as are willing, but it has to be your choice."

Sky Ranger and Penny immediately stepped forward. "We'll go," Penny said. She grabbed Sky Ranger's hand. "You can count on us."

Brian acknowledged them with an appreciative nod.

"I'm absolutely going," added Renna. "I don't care how dangerous and stupid it is." Brian smiled at her. She didn't smile back, fighting the urge to smack him again.

"Felipe and Broussard," Brian said. "Can we count on you to get to the ship, and be ready for a quick takeoff?"

"It won't be *too* difficult," said Lois. "We can get you in there very easily."

"Fine," said Felipe. "Can't beat that! Sorry to miss the action, though."

"And of course I'll go," said Broussard with characteristic fatalism. "Why not?"

Brian looked over at Anthony and Roger. Anthony shook his head. "I'll just get in your way," he said. "Battle's no place for an old man like me."

"I'm going," muttered Broussard to Felipe. Felipe made a gesture with his hand, and Broussard laughed. Anthony flushed.

"Stop it," Brian snapped. "We can't turn on one another. Anthony's choice is his own, and he has the right to make it. To put it another way, I don't want anyone on the team who doesn't want to be there. Understood?"

Silence. Broussard shrugged. "Eh," he said. "Sorry, then."

Anthony nodded, a little shaken.

Roger sighed. "I think, on the other hand, that I can be a

little bit useful. I'll go."

"I'll be glad to have you along," said Sky Ranger with perfect sincerity.

Roger looked at him, astonished. "Ha!" he said. "We'll see."

"Thank you, Roger," said Brian. "James, obviously, can't
go..." His gaze settled on Emily.

Emily studied her hands. "I'm afraid," she said quietly. "I
flew after Sky Ranger, but it was the most frightening thing I've
ever done. But..." She looked up. "You may need me."

"Yes," said Brian simply. "We will."

"Then I'll come."

"Thank you, Emily," he said.

Penny touched her hand. "I'll be right with you the whole
way," she said.

"Thanks," Emily said.

"You can back out if you want," Brian said. "Any of you
can." He looked around. "But please let me know before the
hour is up—we need to finalize who is going, and who's staying
behind."

No one said anything. "All right," said Brian. "Sky Ranger
and I will meet with Ms. Lorraine." He nodded at Lois. "Then
we'll want to speak with Felipe and Broussard. After that, we'll
brief again in a few hours. Get some sleep if you can."

Penny found Emily in the lavish room the Lorraines had assigned to her. The place looked as if it had been decked out
for an 18th-century French princess. The wallpaper, the carpet,
the bedspread, and even the ceiling had various combinations
of pink and white shapes and patterns. Emily sat on the huge,
canopied bed, surrounded by frilly cushions and pillows, looking
entirely lost.

"This room isn't really me," she said as Penny marveled at the décor.

"No, but it sure is fancy," said Penny. "Wow! Is that gold?" She touched a decoration on the wall. "I bet it is."

Emily hugged one of the pillows to her chest. "They said the cats are in some sort of kennel downstairs," she said. "They can't come into this room. They'd get cat hair everywhere, and the housekeeper forbade it."

"Too bad," said Penny.

"I miss them," said Emily. "I usually sleep with them. I hope they don't get lonely." She looked like she was about to cry.

"Hey, it's okay," said Penny, her heart going out to the young woman. "I'm sure they're happy. The Lorraines look like they take good care of people and whatever else."

"Yeah..." said Emily. She seemed to look past Penny, out into space.

"You all right?" asked Penny. "I know what's coming isn't going to be easy...and I know it's scary."

"It is," said Emily. "But I'll be fine." She smiled, though it didn't reach her eyes. "I'll be okay. Really."

"Nothing to worry about," said Penny with a confidence she didn't really feel. "We'll be fine. Sky Ranger will be there. He's been in this sort of situation dozens of times. I have, too, you know."

"Yeah..."

Penny studied her for a moment, realizing how little she really knew Emily. She had only the barest memory of the little girl, Whitelight, Emily had once been.

Right now, Emily looked terrified. She'd probably never faced anything like this before.

Penny sat on the bed. "Let me tell you a story...a long time ago, when I was in the LED, we had a horrible mission to go on. We had to go and take down a guy who had been building up a supply of weapons and traps in this cabin up in the mountains of western Massachusetts. Worse, he was strong, could fly even better than I could, and he had a little prescience, so he had an idea of what we were going to do, and when. We had to go take him out anyway. He had started raiding the nearby town, see."

"Oh," said Emily. "I don't remember this one."

"It was a long time ago," said Penny. "Before your time, I think. I was just eighteen. This guy we were after thought he was the biggest, baddest thing around. He wanted the attention. He wanted to try to take us out."

Emily shivered.

"The night before we went out," Penny continued, voice low, "I was scared to death."

"Really? Of what?"

Penny closed her eyes. "Of pain. I was so afraid of pain."

"But you'd heal!"

"Yes...but you'll heal eventually, too, if you break your arm. It doesn't make it any less unpleasant to break it. And back then...I'd never really been hurt. There were a couple of times, but I'd never experienced anything like what I've gone through since then. So I was afraid."

"I can understand that," Emily said.

"The night before, I was sitting in my room, thinking of all the awful things that could happen, or everything that could go wrong with the plan. It was nerve-wracking. I wasn't with Sky Ranger then, and I didn't have many friends, so I was alone. Then Crimson Cadet stopped by. You remember him?"

"Of course," said Emily. "He was wonderful."

"Wasn't he? Well, he stopped by to see how I was doing. He saw how scared I was, and he said to me—I'll never forget this—he said, 'Sil, I know you're scared. I'm scared, too.' Imagine that, him being scared of anything. It just about blew me away. But he went on. He said, 'Don't be afraid. Tomorrow I'll be like your brother, and you'll be my sister. We'll stick together,

and look out for one another. And we'll come through it. Okay?'
So of course I said okay. ...It made me feel a lot better, knowing
I was going into the fight with a buddy."

"Did it help?"

"Yes." Penny pursed her lips, eyes far away. "Oh, that fight...
it was terrible. He threw everything he had at us. We were lucky
not to lose anyone...but so many of us were hurt. Even Sky
Ranger was wounded. But Crim and I, we stuck together. We
watched out for one another. And we came through just fine."

Emily smiled shakily. "I'm glad."

"Emily." Penny met and held her gaze. "I know you're scared.
I'm scared, too." She smiled at her. "But tomorrow, we'll be
okay. I'll be your sister, and you'll be mine. We'll stick together,
we'll watch out for each other. And we'll come through it just
fine. Okay?"

Emily nodded gratefully, tears in her eyes.

"Okay," said Penny, not sure what to say next. "Uh. ...Want
me to stick around? I don't have anything better to do. I can
tell you all sorts of embarrassing stories about Sky Ranger from
when we were kids."

"That would be great," said Emily, making room on the bed.
Penny sat down.

"This is pretty soft!" she said. "Wow. I mean, I hope my
room is this nice."

"I bet it is."

"Anyway... Oh, here's a good one. One time Sky Ranger,
who was Little Hawk back then, was sitting on the big couches
in the lounge on the fifth floor..."

◆❯▸ ◂❮◆

"I think we need to get a few things cleared up," said Brian. Lois Lorraine and Sky Ranger regarded him warily. "First, it

needs to be clear who is actually in command of this mission. The three of us can't be running around undercutting one another if this is going to work."

"Agreed," said Lois. "I will remain here as an operational commander. Only I will be able to see the mission's parts as it proceeds, so I submit that both of you should report to me."

Sky Ranger and Brian exchanged glances.

"You? I don't know about that," said Sky Ranger slowly. "I have far more field experience than either of you. Brian, you have more of a military background, but this sort of mission is similar to what I've done in the past."

"Right," said Lois. "However, we have a special objective for you."

"Oh?" asked Sky Ranger.

"Let's settle the command issue first," said Brian dryly. "Ms. Lorraine, I understand what you're saying..."

"Let me remind you whose venture this is," Lois cut him off sternly. "And who has the most to lose, should you fail."

"I rather thought *we* would," Brian said dryly. "Seeing as we'd be dead or imprisoned."

"This mission puts my entire family at risk," said Lois soberly. "This is a very, very dangerous game we're playing. We have an enormous stake in seeing that it goes well." She made a little *hmph* noise. "I am the commander of the Family Regiment, and we *have* trained for this kind of mission. I do know what I'm doing. Lieutenant Gannett, you will command in the field. Sky Ranger, you will have a separate, equally important mission. However, I will be in charge of the mission overall."

Brian and Lois held one another's gaze for a long minute. "Very well," Brian said at last. "But I don't want you to interfere unless it's vital. Understood?"

"Naturally," said Lois. "As long as you'll follow the orders I'm giving."

"...Agreed."

"If we're done with this," sighed Sky Ranger. "What's this mission you have for me?"

"Ah," said Lois. "That would involve the other extrahuman." She turned to Brian expectantly. "Please explain our arrangement."

Brian did his best to look Sky Ranger in the eye. "Sky Ranger...as part of the agreement with the Lorraines, your mission will be to find the other extrahuman...and kill him."

"What?" Sky Ranger's eyebrows flew up.

"Now, listen," Brian held out a cautioning hand. "I know he's one of your people. And Renna said you wouldn't like it. But this is the agreement we've made. If we want to rescue Dee and the others..."

"I have to *kill* one of the last extrahumans in existence," Sky Ranger finished, clearly disgusted. "No. I refuse."

"We can't have him alive and working for the government," said Lois. "It's simply not feasible. He represents a serious threat to Calvasna's stability that we must address. We enjoy good relations with the Confederation because we have enough money and power to balance them out, so in the main, they leave us alone. If they had him, or if they had *more* of him, this could change."

"So you think he is manufactured," Sky Ranger said.

"Yes," she said. "Based on the information you've given us about his movements, his apparent lack of experience, and our own intelligence reports, we believe he is a normal human with extrahuman abilities grafted onto him somehow."

"They could make more of him, then," said Sky Ranger. "Killing one won't solve anything."

"It'll send a message," said Lois. "We won't tolerate this. Besides, once Doug Vasna is no longer in charge of Special Projects, I would expect the program to shut down. Special Projects is very personal."

"If he's manufactured...he isn't *really* one of you," Brian said hesitantly.

"Isn't he?" Sky Ranger said, wheeling on him. "Isn't he? He can fly, like me. He's a firestarter, like Dee! He's fast and strong, like James! Where did they get the genetic material? Where did his powers come from, if not from us? Don't tell me he's not one of us. He's *all* of us. I *will not* do this."

"Then our deal is off," said Lois sadly.

"No!" said Brian. "Sky Ranger, if you won't do it, I will. For the sake of everyone else."

"You won't be able to," said Sky Ranger arrogantly.

"I have to try," said Brian. "We have to get our people out of there."

"I don't think so," said Lois. "You would fail, Brian. He would wipe the floor with you. Sky Ranger has to make the attempt, he's the only one who can possibly succeed."

"I won't kill him," insisted Sky Ranger, with quiet determination. Lois opened her mouth, but Sky Ranger held up a hand. "No. I will not kill another extrahuman for you. But...I could capture him. I'll take him with us to wherever we're going, as my prisoner. He'll be separated from the government. He won't work for them anymore, and he won't be on Calvasna. That solves your problem."

Lois regarded him coolly. "I would rather see him dead," she said simply.

"Sky Ranger does have a point, though," said Brian gratefully. "We don't have to kill him to neutralize him."

"And what if he escapes, to return here?" Lois asked. "Don't tell me it isn't possible. I've seen what he can do."

"He won't," said Sky Ranger. "Trust me. We can confine him."

Lois eyed him thoughtfully. "I don't trust you, I'm afraid. I know you quite well, Sky Ranger. You're a man of no certain loyalty. You were quick enough to join, and then turn on, the

Reformists. How do I know you won't turn him loose at the first opportunity?"

"They betrayed me!" said Sky Ranger, horrified.

"Mmm. Or so it would seem. But I still can't know you won't go back on your promise to me."

"I'll vouch for him," said Brian. "I wouldn't do that for just anyone."

"And how do I know *that?*" Lois asked. "I'm not trying to upset you or catch you, there's simply not enough here to make me comfortable with anything less than what I've asked for."

"The death of a man, you mean," said Sky Ranger. "An extrahuman death."

"Yes," stated Lois. "I won't flinch from it."

"I won't kill for you," Sky Ranger said flatly. "If I don't agree, then he'll still be out there, the Vasnas will still be in charge, and you'll be nowhere."

"But your friends will almost certainly die," said Lois softly.

"Have a heart," pleaded Brian. "Please."

Lois suddenly looked up, listening intently to the voice coming over her earpiece. "I'll...have to consult with my father," she said after a moment. "But if you can remove him from Calvasna, with a guarantee that he won't return...then I believe the deal can be saved."

"Yes, of course," said Sky Ranger.

"Right," said Brian.

Lois nodded and quickly left the room. A few minutes later, she returned.

"He wants to see you," she said. "Upstairs. Second door to the left." She stopped Brian as both men made to leave the room. "Not you. Only Sky Ranger."

Puzzled, Brian remained behind.

◄►► ◄◄►

Sky Ranger knocked on the door. The second floor was so quiet compared to the bustle of the first. It felt like a tomb up here. "Enter," said a voice. Sky Ranger eased the door open, and slipped inside. An old, wizened man sat in a floating chair, his frail body hooked up to the tubes, wires, and sensors of a major life support system. A little boy sat next to him, flipping through something.

"You're Sky Ranger," he said.

"Yes, sir," said Sky Ranger, deference automatically snapping into place.

"I'm Georges Lorraine. I am the lord of this place." It was a strange thing to say, but from this powerful man, on this insane planet, it seemed to make a certain amount of sense.

"A pleasure to meet you, sir," said Sky Ranger.

"No," said Georges Lorraine. "The pleasure is mine. Ah. Duncan. Say hello to our guest."

The little boy said something that could have been "hello." Sky Ranger tried to smile back at him, but the boy just gave him a blank look.

"Thank you, Duncan. You may return to your playroom," the elder Lorraine said, mock-seriously. The little boy wordlessly trotted off. "Ah, such a quiet little boy. The only son of my eldest daughter, did you know? I have many children. So." He looked over Sky Ranger with a thoroughly appraising eye. "I have always wanted to meet a Sky Ranger. I'm old enough to remember the first, you know. Not that I met him. But I remember him when he was alive."

"I never knew him," said Sky Ranger. "Well before my time, sadly."

"Yes," said Georges. "You are a very young Sky Ranger, compared to the two who came before you. I remember them both primarily as older men. But you were a young Sky Cadet, were you not? Something happened to the first one."

"He died in a fall," said Sky Ranger.

"A flying man? How strange."

Sky Ranger grimaced. It wasn't a pleasant memory. "I wasn't there. But apparently he fell from a height, and simply failed to fly. I don't know what happened, exactly. But his Sky Ranger was in mourning for a very long time."

"You never took a Sky Cadet."

"I didn't feel the need," said Sky Ranger defensively. Who would he have taken, in any case? There was no one.

"I see," said Georges. "And yet, here you are. The last of your kind. Who will be Sky Ranger after you are gone?"

"No one," said Sky Ranger. "There's no more Extrahuman Union to be Sky Ranger of."

"Yet..." Georges said slyly. "You keep the title. You could be Little Hawk again. Or, I suppose, Big Hawk now."

Sky Ranger shook his head. "It wouldn't feel right. Sky Ranger is who I am."

"I see." Georges coughed. An indicator attached to his chair flashed for a moment, then settled down. "No need for alarm," he said, noticing Sky Ranger's worried expression. "I assure you, I'm not in any immediate danger." He paused thoughtfully. "I am the last original Lorraine. It was my family who came here in 2055. I personally arrived with my father on that first colony ship. I was a young man at the time—I think I was twenty-six. I served in the Last War, you know. There aren't many survivors of that war remaining."

"No," said Sky Ranger, a little awed. "It's my honor, then." He idly wondered which side the elder Lorraine had fought for.

"I studied your people for a long time. I was fascinated by you! As a boy, I had posters of the first Sky Ranger on my wall. He was truly incredible. He was right to keep his people out of the Last War, though the American government denounced him as a traitor for it." He sighed a long, wheezing sigh. "It's very sad for me, to see your people here at the end." He gazed at Sky Ranger through his rheumy eyes. "My young daughter Lois is a good girl, but there's a lot she doesn't understand yet. I agreed with her, at first, that the new extrahuman must die. However... now I think I like your way better. You *can* take him away from Calvasna? For good?"

"Yes," said Sky Ranger at once. "You have my word. We'll take him to...wherever we're going. There are people there who I believe can contain him."

"Where *are* you going? I would like to know."

Sky Ranger hesitated. "Valen," he admitted.

"Ah," Georges breathed. "Ah. Altrera's world. I see."

Sky Ranger waited while the old man considered.

Georges Lorraine exhaled after a few moments. "Then you have my blessing." He extended a frail, bony hand to Sky Ranger. Sky Ranger took it gently. "I've done a lot of terrible things during my life, you know, in pursuit of greed. But I also have done some very grand things to protect my family, and to make Calvasna a better place. If I can help save your people, even if just for a little while, I'll feel a little better about facing St. Peter when the time comes."

Sky Ranger didn't know what to say. "I won't let you down. I promise."

"Good," said Georges, withdrawing his hand. "I warn you... my vengeance is quite awful for those who do." He winked cannily at Sky Ranger. "Just so you don't think I'm nothing but an old pushover." He withdrew a metal case, which held a single syringe. "Inject this into him. He'll pass right out. It'll tranquilize an elephant, so it should do for him. I suspect you'll need all your strength to get it through his skin."

"Thank you," said Sky Ranger.

Georges Lorraine nodded briskly, a surprisingly sharp look in his eye. "Now do your job," he said.

◄►►◄◄►

Broussard and Felipe played cards together, as they often did.

"So then, tomorrow," said Broussard.

"Right," said Felipe, throwing a small amount of change on to the pile. "Fifteen."

"Oh? You must have something pitiful for such a little bet."

"The joke's on you if you believe it," said Felipe. "I'm out of money."

Broussard snorted. "Fine, then, we'll see. I'll see your fifteen and raise you another fifteen."

They sat for a moment.

"Tomorrow could be it," said Felipe.

Broussard shrugged his characteristic shrug. "I've come to terms with it. I never really expected to leave Calvasna alive, you see."

"But we have a chance," said Felipe. "If we do it right, we can get away to Valen."

"I have my doubts," said Broussard. "But we'll see what God wills."

"Is that why you're here?" Felipe asked. "God's will and all that?"

"Heh," said Broussard. "No, boy. I stopped trying to figure that out long ago."

Felipe shuffled his cards around in his hand.

"I wonder if Valen has any deserts?" mused Broussard.

"Don't tell me you miss the gray sea?" Felipe joked. "Moss for dinner, catching water, living in a big rock? You miss that?"

"Eh. Maybe a little. It was nice and quiet there."

"Hm," said Felipe. "I bet there are quiet places on Valen, too."

They sat in silence for a few moments, studying their cards.

"The next desert we go to will have better food," vowed Felipe.

"Amen to that," said Broussard. "So, bet or call."

Felipe thought a moment. "Oh, I fold," he said. "I had nothing."

"I knew it!" cackled Broussard, claiming the pile of change. "Ha, your every emotion is plain as day on your face!"

"Someday, old man," Felipe said with a cocky smile. "You'll never see it coming."

◂▸▸ ◂◂▸

Anthony sat in Roger's room, looking miserable. "It isn't that I don't want to go," he said. "I just can't. I'd be in the way. I know how useless I am."

"You can make a forcefield, you idiot," said Roger. He'd been fed up with Anthony's sniveling cowardice for some time. "You're practically invulnerable!"

"It never works right," said Anthony. "I have trouble getting it to work at all! And even when I do, it isn't very strong."

"Excuses," said Roger. "I saw it work when we escaped the ship."

"I can't go back there," Anthony said, his face haunted. "I can't! I don't want to be a prisoner again."

"Now *there's* the admission of fear," said Roger. "Was that so hard?"

"But everyone else is going," said Anthony nervously. "I'm not good at this. They'd capture me, just like they took Jill! And she was young and strong." His dull yellow forcefield flicked on and off, taking some of the paint on the wall behind him with it. "They'd vivisect me. They'd chop me up. Or maybe they'd just shoot me."

"All true," said Roger, who really didn't want Anthony coming along anyway. "So stay here."

"But they'll think I'm a coward!"

"Don't worry, they think that already."

Anthony looked up at Roger, his lip trembling. "Y—you don't like me very much, do you, Roger?"

"No," said Roger thoughtfully. "But I don't like anyone very much."

"You like Sky Ranger."

What an odd thing to say. "Sky Ranger is a lot more interesting than you are," Roger said acidly. "He betrayed his people and caused the deaths of hundreds. What have *you* done?"

"Maybe I will go after all," said Anthony. "I can help."

"No, you can't," Roger said, becoming alarmed. "Stay here with James, or do whatever it is you're going to do."

"But *you're* going, and you can't do *anything*!"

Roger glared at him. "That's because I'm not the kind of man who cries into his beer about what a loser he is."

Anthony looked like he was about to start crying again.

"Oh, for the love of Christ, *have* the room," spat Roger, and left.

◄►► ◄►►

Renna was pacing the halls, worried and alone. She happened to glance out at one of the many balconies in the vast, empty home, and saw a tall figure standing there.

She joined him. "Sky Ranger," she said, putting a hand on his shoulder.

He tensed, then relaxed and smiled when he saw who it was. "Renna! It's good to see you."

"And you, too. You gave us a scare today."

"Tomorrow will be worse," he said, trying to make it into a joke and failing.

She wanted to take his arm, but she didn't dare. Not this time. "So," she said. "You and Penny. I had no idea."

"It was a long time ago," he said with a smile. "At least, the first time."

"You two seem good together," she said.

"As do you and Brian."

She considered. The lights of Calvasna winked far away.

"We were never a thing, were we?" she asked.

"We couldn't be," he said. "Though that doesn't mean I didn't..."

"Oh, I know," she said. "Same. It was nice while it lasted. You were good company, back there in the desert."

He snapped his fingers. "Speaking of... I have something for you. Wait here." He took to the air and zipped off. A few minutes later, he returned, clutching a worn leather bag.

"Oh!" Renna breathed. "My pack!"

He handed it to her. "Dee found it. I kept it for you."

Her heart skipped a beat. "Did, um... did you look inside?"

He nodded.

"It's mine," she said. "All of what's in there."

He kissed her forehead. He was so wonderfully tall. "I know."

A tear slipped down her cheek. "And?"

"And nothing." He smiled.

She hugged him impulsively. "I should go," she said after a moment. "I should find Brian."

"Go ahead, then," he said. "And I'll see you tomorrow."

◄►►◄►

Brian and Renna's lips separated reluctantly. "This isn't exactly what I had in mind," Brian said.

"So?" She smiled, pulling him towards the bed. She was feeling inspired for some reason tonight, and she was determined not to waste the moment. "You need to relax. And I want you to know... you've been absolutely brilliant. I'd follow you to the ends of the universe." In that moment, that night, it was true. Renna knew she would, and that she'd prove it to him for many years to come.

"Good to know," he said hungrily, and kissed her again.

Give him my strength, Renna thought over and over as they made love. *Give him my courage. Give him my clear mind. Give us victory.*

◄►►◄◄►

"Thanks, everyone, for coming," said a far more relaxed Brian to the motley group of refugees and extrahumans who had gathered for the briefing. He looked around, and was surprised to see Anthony sitting nervously in a chair. "Anthony...?"

"I do want to come," said Anthony. "Don't leave me behind."

"We weren't planning on it," said Brian. "But if you want to... you can help get James to the ship."

"I'm feeling better," said a groggy-looking James. "I'd come with the main team if I could."

Emily smiled and squeezed his hand. She'd been working on healing him again, and he looked much better.

"I'll do it," said Anthony, though he suddenly looked like he was going to be sick. "I will."

"Okay," Brian said, bringing up the schematic of Confederation Military Command. "We're ready."

[CHAPTER 25]

"Hello, Jill," said the pinch-faced woman in white. She peered sternly down at her. "I'm Dr. Rivers. You don't know me, but I know you very well. I watched you for years, *years*, as you did absolutely nothing at all on board your fake spaceship. I can tell you, it was just as fun as it sounds."

Jill made a little gurgling sound.

"Ah. That's the paralytic. It's taking effect. We're testing out a new serum—it knocks you out and keeps you from manifesting your powers temporarily. Isn't that useful? Of course, in your case, you'll hardly be able to tell." She laughed, a short, unpleasant sound. "'The Sampler.' How surprisingly accurate. Do you know your name isn't actually Jill? We don't know who you really are, so we made something up. The Union found you in some sort of shelter. Your parents left you there! I suppose a DNA trace would find out for sure, but no one really wanted to bother."

Jill moaned through clenched teeth.

"I'm sure you want to know where your friend is. Yes, your friend Willow. We've caught her. The lady next door turned her in! Isn't that wonderful? She was a block captain for the local Party; she'll probably get some sort of medal or whatever it is they give people. She thought they were being suspicious, so she snooped! That's why this form of government works so well, you know."

Dr. Rivers smiled devilishly. *Who the hell is Willow? Did she mean Sky Ranger?* Jill wondered through the sea of pain.

"Everyone spies on one another," Dr. Rivers continued, "So we catch all the bad guys before they even have a chance to do anything. Well, Willow is nearby, though we don't have anything to test on her. That is, unless we come up with something. Which we probably will. Ah. The serum is ready."

She paused with the needle. "We'll test this a few times, just to see if it works well. Then? I don't know. Maybe we'll take you out back and shoot you. Unlike your friend Dee, you probably won't turn everyone into a pillar of fire if you're threatened. Maybe you'll fly a few centimeters, or heal a paper cut."

A tear trickled out of Jill's eye.

"Oh, crying? Well, not for long." She sprayed Jill's eye. Jill suddenly found she couldn't close it. "I'm guessing you'll dry up pretty quickly."

Dee watched from a distance as Dr. Rivers administered the serum to Jill. She winced, but there was nothing she could do.

Another extrahuman? Was…did she say a woman named *Willow* was here? She remembered Willow as a refugee. She'd escaped, hadn't she? Dee stifled a moan…if Willow had been recaptured, the others must have been as well. All for nothing. She had saved them all for nothing. Her heart felt like it was sinking into a deep, dark trench, far beneath the ocean.

A group of five smartly uniformed Confederation Fleet soldiers marched up to the massive, imposing entrance of Confederation Military Command. The building was nothing but a great windowless block, seemingly carved from a massive lump of obsidian. The edifice loomed over them, a demon of Calvasna threatening to swallow them whole.

They'd been let out of their car at the required distance, and had covered the ground briskly. They showed their identification at the entrance, and calmly performed the required scans. They were, the computer said, precisely who they claimed to be. Entrance to the main hallway was granted.

Renna, Sky Ranger, Emily, Penny, and Brian walked softly into the hall. The identities the Lorraines had set up for them had worked, for now. Brian plucked absently at his uniform. It was strange to see him in it again.

"The desk," Renna said softly. A dark-skinned woman with only a day's growth of hair on her head sat at the desk, waiting patiently.

They were supposed to go up to the desk and introduce themselves, using their real names. That's what Lois had said. She hadn't elaborated, at least not to Brian's satisfaction. It seemed impossibly risky. They had decided in the car to see what the situation looked like, first.

It didn't look great. Heavily armed guards ringed the entrance hall, and one stood on either side of each of the four doors leading into the main building.

Emily paled. Penny put a hand on her back, trying to steady her. "I'm here," she murmured. "Sister, I've got you."

Emily gulped and nodded. They advanced on the desk. Renna started to look around nervously. The guards were watching them closely. Brian was about to give the signal to bypass it, and try for one of the doors, when Penny broke into a rare, wide grin.

"I'll be damned," she said, hurrying forward. "Janeane!"

The elegant, ebony-skinned woman at the desk stood and smiled broadly.

"Well, well," said Janeane. "Look who it is. Welcome to Military Command, Penny." The two women embraced over the desk. "You look well," Janeane smiled.

"You look exactly the same," said Penny. She shook her head in amazement. "I can't believe it's you, after all this time."

"Uh," said Renna, completely lost. "You know her?" She looked around again. The guards were all smiling, relaxed, expressions of peace on their faces. She had the sudden sense of having fallen through the rabbit hole. What was going on?

"Renna, this is Janeane," said Penny, grinning. "She helped us back on Earth. She's...uh." She, too, looked around at the guards.

"It's all right," said Janeane. "They aren't really hearing you."

"You have that effect," Penny said. "I remember. Calm."

"They're at the sea," said Janeane simply. "Penny, please introduce me to your friends."

"This is Renna," said Penny. "And Brian Gannett. They're in charge. This here is Emily, she's like me. She flies, and she can heal others."

"You flew again," said Janeane. Penny nodded happily. "I knew you would." Penny blushed. Renna's eyes bugged out.

"And this," she said, "is Sky Ranger."

"Ah," murmured Janeane. "I have you to thank for helping my dear Broken escape." Penny straightened up at the sound of her old name.

"Yes," said Sky Ranger, frowning in thought. "Have... have we met?"

"It could be," said Janeane mischievously.

"Janeane is one of our people," explained Penny excitedly. "Like I told you. She saved us. When we were stuck at the CA, a long time ago. She knew Michael and Monica, too."

"I helped Michael as best I could," said Janeane. "I only wish he could have survived. It wasn't to be."

"I hate to break up this reunion," said Brian nervously. "But we have... we need to get moving."

"Yes. I'm guessing Lois Lorraine didn't explain things very well. She's like that. We're just going to walk into those doors there, and head for Special Projects." Janeane turned to the guards. "I'll be back in a few minutes. One of you can cover for me."

One of the guards obediently came to sit in her chair.

"Thank you, Jeremy," she said, her melodious voice filling the room. Everyone seemed to sigh. "I'll return soon." She nodded at each man. "All right, follow me."

She walked to one of the doors, and the guards on either side swung it open for her. "Thank you, Javi and Yuri," she said. "My wonderful protectors." They smiled, eyes fixed on something far away.

They followed her into the massive military complex.

They walked, dreamlike, through the beating heart of the most powerful force in human space.

"We need to go about halfway across the base, and down two levels," Janeane said evenly as they strode down a hallway lined with troops. "All of your people are there. Even Willow is there."

Renna breathed a sigh of relief. Officers and other soldiers in the black uniform of either the Army or the Fleet flowed around them. A few were in the gray of the Confederation Military Police. All of them nodded and smiled as Janeane and her escort passed.

"Won't... won't they see you on camera?" Renna asked. She felt like jumping out her skin. This was the most nerve-wracking thing she'd ever done.

"No," said Janeane. "All they'll see is what they think should be there. They'll be calm, and they won't see anything bad at all."

"How do you... I don't understand," said Brian.

She didn't respond, that small smile fixed on her face.

Sky Ranger gasped. Doug Vasna had appeared, rounding a corner. There was nowhere to hide! Doug looked him up and down... then smiled and walked past, completely calm.

"What?" Sky Ranger said, shaken. "That was... that was Doug!"

"I saw," Emily said, clearly terrified. "Why didn't he raise the alarm? Is he doing that now?"

"No, be calm," said Janeane. "He didn't see a thing. Or, to be a little more accurate, he did see you. He just didn't care. His mind was on other things."

"This doesn't make sense. What is your power?" Sky Ranger demanded. "Are you actually an extrahuman? I've never even heard of a power like yours. It isn't cataloged anywhere."

"Everyone has their different thing," she said warmly. In his mind, Sky Ranger saw a beautiful blue sea, and waves crashed on the shore. He smelled the salt air, and could taste the ocean. He exhaled.

"There, you see?" Janeane said. "That's what I do. Nothing more."

"It's... incredibly powerful," said Sky Ranger, impressed.

"I think you're better than you used to be," said Penny.

"I think so, too," agreed Janeane. "Turn here. We're about halfway there."

They passed more people on official business, and more heavily armed guards at various posts. They all smiled and nodded as Janeane led them deeper into the base. They descended a flight of stairs, then another, emerging in a dingier underground hallway.

"The ship is easy to find," said Janeane. "Just keep following the hall we're on."

"Okay," said Brian.

"I can't come with you," Janeane said regretfully. "I have to go back once you reach Special Projects. I have things I need to do back there."

"You should come with us!" Penny urged. "We're going to Valen. You should come with us. You could be safe there!"

"I don't remember wanting to be safe," said Janeane. "And this is a good position. The Lorraines are interesting employers, and I'm happy on Calvasna. For now."

"Will you come eventually?" asked Penny.

"For you?" Janeane said slowly.

"...Yes. But also for Monica. I know she'd like to see you again."

"Ah, Monica, my *rhin*," Janeane's lips parted in remembrance. "I'd like to see her again, too. Well. For all of you, then, I may come to Valen. I know of a place there called Clearfield. It's next to the sea. Why don't we meet there?"

"It's a deal," said Penny.

Janeane stopped. "The door to Special Projects is up ahead. Are you prepared for what lies beyond that door? I am calm, but beyond that door is chaos. Be ready." They nodded, fingering the sidearms they'd brought.

"I have to leave you here, and return," she continued. "What I've done lasts a while, but not forever, so I need to be back in position. Once you have them, you may face a difficult fight to get to the ship. Troops loyal to our employer will do their best to help you, as will I, but I can't guarantee anything."

"We'll be all right," said Brian.

"Thank you for your help," said Penny.

"The two of you make an interesting couple," said Janeane. It was unclear whether she was talking to Penny and Sky Ranger or Brian and Renna. "I can see history spooling around you, wrapping you tight. Be careful." She turned to Emily. "I don't know you, but you have a kind heart. Try not to lose it today."

Emily nodded numbly.

"Penny, farewell. I'll see you again some other day."

They hugged again, and parted. She pointed to Sky Ranger. "What you're looking for isn't there," she said. "It's the next door down. Be careful, and stay clean if you can."

"I will," he said.

"Then goodbye, last Sky Ranger," Janeane said. "And good luck."

With that, she was gone, receding quickly and quietly down the deserted corridor. They could feel the sense of ease and dreamlike peace evaporate as she went.

"Ready?" asked Brian, suddenly sharp again.

"Ready," said Renna.

Sky Ranger nodded curtly, and set off on his mission. Penny, Renna, and Emily lined up behind Brian.

He opened the door.

The ship had been easy to capture, easier than Felipe had dared hope. Three helpful soldiers, loyal to the Lorraines, had escorted Felipe, Broussard, Roger, Anthony, and a hobbled James from their landing position to the ship, which waited in a hanger underground. They were warned that the ship was checked every hour or so. They'd try to delay any inspection... but it might be next to impossible if enough time passed.

"We'll just have to hope they work quickly," said Felipe, with a joviality he didn't feel.

They got settled, and began the long, tense wait.

◄►►◄◄►

Another hallway. At the end of it, a guard waited. Brian strode up to him, and presented his identification.

"Your business?" asked the guard.

"We've been ordered to report for testing to this office," said Brian. He had memorized his lines perfectly. "Major Fusco's command." He handed a datapad to the guard, who gave it a cursory glance.

"Okay, go ahead," he said.

The door opened. Brian tried to keep the relief from showing on his face. He wondered how he'd get past the guard on the way out.

They emerged into a well-lit area, apparently empty of any people. Strange-looking machines were strewn haphazardly around the room.

"We need to find them *now*," said Brian. "Back room first. Let's go!"

They were on the clock. They had to move quickly, to squeeze as much time out of their cover as possible. Without Janeane's calming influence, they might not have long.

Sky Ranger quietly entered the room. A man lay prone on a bed, a guard standing next to him.

"Hey!" said the guard, raising his weapon—but too late. Sky Ranger streaked to his side, and knocked his head against the wall. The guard slumped, unconscious, to the floor.

"So there you are," murmured Sky Ranger. The scarred, blackened man breathed deeply, in and out, and his eyes were closed. He wore an Army uniform, with the name TORRES on the front. He was a sergeant, according to his rank pins,

"Sergeant Torres," said Sky Ranger. "Just a soldier." He bent over the man. How badly was he hurt? He didn't see any bandages. He felt for the syringe in his jacket.

Torres's eyes snapped open. Sky Ranger started back.

The scarred extrahuman leered his awful grin at Sky Ranger. "Sky Ranger. Kill you," he whispered.

"Here!" Emily called. There was a little room at the very back with three beds. In each lay an inert person.

"Here they are," said Renna, feeling a rush of relief wash over her. Maybe, maybe... "Come on, help me get them up."

"I don't like this," said Brian. "We haven't seen anyone since that guard. Where are they all?"

"I don't know," said Renna. "But let's be quick."

"This could be a trap," said Penny, but she was trying to rouse Willow. "Hey!" she said. "Willow, it's Penny. Come on, we need you to wake up *now*."

Emily stroked Jill's hair. Jill opened her eyes. Emily gasped— her right eye was bloodshot and sick-looking.

"Em," croaked Jill.

"We're here for you. We're getting out of here," said Emily.

"Dee?" Renna knelt next to the girl. She barely recognized her; she looked terribly thin and pale, her hair was a wild tangle, and she smelled awful. They hadn't been taking care of her. Rage burned in Renna. She would make them pay for this.

"Help me," she said to Brian.

Dee opened her eyes.

"R—Renna?" she rasped.

"Hey, Dee!" Renna said. "Hey, sweetie! We came for you, we're here with Sky Ranger. We're getting you out. Can you get up?"

Dee struggled to sit. Brian knelt and picked her up. "She weighs next to nothing," he said, shocked.

Renna heard a small sound behind them.

◂▸ ◂▸

Sky Ranger found himself backed up against the wall, Torres's hand clamped around his throat. His head smacked against the concrete wall, and sparks flew in front of his eyes. He shook himself. Torres loomed in front of him with his sideways grin.

"Torres! Sergeant!" said Sky Ranger. He pitched his legs up and kicked. Torres went flying across the room. Sky Ranger darted over to a far corner. "Listen, you don't have to fight me. You're one of *us* now. You're an extrahuman, like me! Do you understand? Sergeant, do you remember what they did to you?"

Torres grimaced and roared.

"No! No!"

He launched himself at Sky Ranger, who, finally ready for his opponent's speed, dodged away just in time. Torres crashed off the wall, and bounced back onto the bed. Sky Ranger flew at him, intending to knock him out if he could, but Torres deftly maneuvered out of the way.

"You can come with us," Sky Ranger said. "Come with us to a place where you can be free! You don't have to serve the Confederation."

"Serve!" said Torres. "Honor. Loyalty. I *serve*."

"You don't have to," said Sky Ranger, thinking quickly. "Look at what they did to you! They could have killed you! You never asked for it."

Torres laughed as they circled one another. "I did ask!" he said. "Volunteered! Now, I am *strong*." He darted at Sky Ranger again. Sky Ranger couldn't move fast enough to avoid him, and Torres drove Sky Ranger into the wall. Blackness threatened to overtake him. He fought it off.

"I'm not here to kill you," said Sky Ranger, struggling against Torres's vise of a grip.

"Ha! I knew," said Torres. "I knew!"

"What...?" said Sky Ranger, aiming a punch at Torres's midsection. Torres grunted and backed off.

"Knew you'd come," he said.

Sky Ranger didn't respond.

"Knew your *friends* would come," he snarled.

"What do you know about them?" Sky Ranger snapped, diving for him. They grappled together in the air above the bed, muscles straining.

Torres leaned in and whispered something, so softly Sky Ranger almost couldn't make the word out.

"Trap," whispered Torres. A manic grin appeared on his face. "Trap!"

<>►◄<>

"Hey," Renna said, turning around. "What's—"

Her words died in her throat.

Two dozen ConFedForce troops stared her in the face, weapons ready. Each had the distinctive triangle badge of Special Projects on his shoulder. Doug Vasna and Dr. Rivers stood at their head.

"Go ahead," said Doug. "Finish. We can wait."

[CHAPTER 26]

SKY RANGER SWUNG WILDLY IN PANIC AND rage, and missed. Torres cackled and kicked him hard in the belly. Sky Ranger spiraled down to the floor.

<◆>►◄<◆>

"How did you..." Brian said, backing up. Doug advanced. Penny put herself between the government troops and her friends.

"We knew you'd come eventually," said Doug. "And here you are. The guard at the door recognized your faces. I have to say, I'm impressed. I don't know how you managed to get all the way in here without being caught! I'm guessing you had some help from my friends, the Lorraines. Or was it the Allgotts? It doesn't matter, of course. We'll find the traitors. But we had to scramble once he saw you. I had to run down two flights of stairs!"

"She sold us out," said Renna darkly.

"No," said Penny without looking back. "She wouldn't."

"Ah!" said Doug, suddenly focusing on Penny. "I know you now. 'Broken,' wasn't it? I should have guessed."

Penny bristled. Doug stepped up to Penny and took out a portable scanner, and waved it near her. "Yes. You're incredibly strong! Did you know that? Your energy readings are very interesting."

Penny scowled at him.

"I'm hoping," he said quietly, "that you can tell me where the boy you stole from us is. He still matters a great deal to us. There are a lot of people on Calvasna who would love to have him back."

Penny said nothing. The boy was safe. He was beyond their reach. Right?

"Well," said Doug. "No matter. You'll tell me eventually."

"I doubt it," said Penny. She hadn't come this far to fail Michael Forward now. She glared at him and steeled herself.

He smiled coldly. "Everyone always says that at first."

Penny's heart skipped a beat, but Doug's attention was already elsewhere.

He indicated the woman next to him. "This is Dr. Rivers. She's been watching all of you. Well, you, Emily. I don't know the rest of you as well as I'd like."

"Too bad," said Penny.

"Your friends were in good hands here," said Doug. "Dr. Rivers will take good care of you."

"Like you took care of Dee?" said Brian. He clutched her tightly. Emily had grabbed her hand. Dee's eyes tracked from Dr. Rivers to Doug and back. At least she had stopped shivering. "She's in awful shape."

"She was very useful," said Dr. Rivers. "She helped us to refine the serum that suppresses extrahuman abilities."

"What?" said Emily, eyes wide, squeezing Dee's hand.

"Think about it," said Dr. Rivers, a small glimmer of enthusiasm in her normally cold eyes. She held a little vial of liquid. "You could lead normal, *legal* lives with this. We have certain assurances from the government—you'd be free, and we would leave you alone, as long as you took the serum."

"Yes, because why would they want to actually have the abilities they were born with?" said Brian sarcastically.

"You must be Lieutenant Gannett!" exclaimed Doug. "A traitor from the Fleet. It's a real shame about you. We were going to hand you over to the military for trial. However, we have special dispensation to take you out to the Yard and shoot you pretty much right away. How does that sound? It'll save you a lot of worry and bother."

"You're nuts," said Renna.

"Oh?" He examined her. "I don't know you. One of the refugees, I imagine. You really should have stayed on Reilis, or wherever it was you'd escaped to."

Renna seethed. "Go to hell."

"All right," said Doug, clearly bored. "Enough chatting. Take them."

◄►►◄◄►

Sky Ranger smashed his fist into Torres's nose; blood spattered the wall. Torres howled, an unearthly, disconcerting sound. Sky Ranger tensed. Torres flew back, then righted himself. With a terrible roar, he flew at Sky Ranger.

This time, Sky Ranger was ready for him. He neatly blocked Torres's charge, deflecting him into the wall. He landed with a sickening crunch, but sprang back onto his feet.

"Not hurt," he said.

"Sure you aren't," said Sky Ranger. "Maybe you're strong. But you don't heal, not on your own." He shoved Torres back. "You're not indestructible."

"Neither—" cried Torres, "—are you!" He delivered a vicious kick to Sky Ranger's side. The leader of the Extrahuman Union fell, gasping for breath, to the cold concrete floor.

◄►►◄◄►

In the ship, Felipe and Broussard nervously scanned the datastream from the camera mounted near the door. No one was coming down the hall. Where *were* they?

"What's that?" Felipe said. Two Fleet techs had appeared, and were looking up at the ship. One held what looked like a scanner. They were gesturing at the ship with it, and speaking in low tones to one another.

"This could be bad," observed Broussard.

"What is it?" Roger said. He appeared, Anthony in tow.

"Fleet guys," said Felipe. "I'm guessing that's the inspection. They're early! Figures, huh?"

"What do we do?" said Roger.

"I don't know," said Broussard. "We should think about hiding."

"That's a life-sign scanner, among other things," said Roger, pointing. "They'd find us no problem. They probably see us now. Besides, how would we hide all of us?"

"I have no idea," said Broussard. "But what do you suggest we do? Go fight them?"

"No," said Roger. "Give me a second. I'll think of something."

"Hey," said Felipe. "Where's Anthony?"

They looked around, startled. He had gone.

"Coward!" spat Roger.

◆►◄◆►

Dee blinked the sleep out of her eyes. She ached everywhere. She felt like she hadn't been warm in months.

She stared around. Men with guns... she remembered facing something like this, long ago. She was too cold to do it again. She had so little left, just this little ember inside her...

Emily's hand felt warm. As she held on to it, the warmth

seemed to spread up her arm and into the rest of her body. She squeezed harder, and Emily inhaled sharply, shivering violently.

She looked over at a still-groggy Willow. She remembered Willow. She liked her.

"Willow," she croaked. Willow's head swiveled her way. She seemed alert, at least.

"Hey, Dee," said Willow, a strange edge in her voice. She looked wildly around.

A man was giving some kind of order. "Take them," he was saying.

Dee lay back in Brian's arms and sighed, a familiar warmth spreading through her veins.

◆>▸ ◂<◆

Willow looked away from Dee, who seemed to be passing out.

In front of her, she noticed Renna's holster had come undone.

Renna backed up as the troops advanced. *They couldn't see her.* She suddenly made a grab for the weapon, slipping it out of the holster. Doug was so close—

"Stop!" Willow cried, whipping the weapon up and pointing it directly at Doug's head. "Any closer, and I'll shoot him!"

They halted for a crucial moment.

◆>▸ ◂<◆

Torres brought down his boot—it stamped into the floor right where Sky Ranger's face had been. He rolled away, and righted himself. The room spun. This wasn't going well. Time for a different tactic.

He gained altitude and waited. Torres, his nose still leaking blood, stared up at him.

"You forgot I can fly," Torres said, that merciless leer still plastered on his face. He streaked up to where Sky Ranger was. Sky Ranger spun in midair—and kicked. His boots caught Torres in the side of the head, and he spiraled, howling, to a heavy impact on the ground.

He sprang up, and a spray of fire arced toward Sky Ranger. But once again, Sky Ranger was ready. He whirled around as fast as he could, and the flame spread out across the room. Torres cried in frustration. He gathered himself and leapt—

This time, Sky Ranger avoided him altogether. Torres smashed into the wall—and fell to the ground, knocked out. Sky Ranger fumbled for the drugs Georges Lorraine had given him. Thankfully, the syringe was still intact. He plunged the needle into the man's thick, tough skin, and delivered the sedative.

Torres's breathing steadied. Sky Ranger sat on his chest until he was sure the other extrahuman had truly passed out.

"I *will* save you," he said to the unconscious Torres, breathing hard. "But we have some work to do, first. We have time."

Dee was feeling warmer by the moment. She clutched Emily's hand tighter as the woman's healing power flowed into her. She gazed at the scene before her. Dr. Rivers was standing, open-mouthed, as Willow pointed a pistol at Doug. Dee didn't like Dr. Rivers.

It was well past time for her shot. They hadn't given it to her today. She wondered if they knew. Maybe they'd stopped caring.

"Oh, please," Doug said to Willow. "You won't shoot. Look at you. Just a little girl."

"You have no idea," said Willow, trembling.

"I bet you have no idea how to use that," Doug said. "Shoot

her," he instructed the soldiers.

"Stop," said Willow calmly, tightening her finger on the trigger. "I am not kidding around. I will kill him. I've killed before."

They hesitated.

"Oh, have you!" mocked Doug. "Wonderful! You're a talented kid! Wow."

"Willow," said Renna softly. "We can't win here. Put it down."

"Listen to her, kid," said Dr. Rivers. "This isn't a situation you can win."

"Besides," Doug said with a sneer. "I don't think you have the guts."

"Willow, don't," said Penny.

"This is too much!" said Doug. "For the love of God, someone shoot her! There are what, twenty of you?"

"Angle's bad," muttered one of the soldiers.

"Oh, bull," said Doug.

"Only five in front," said another. "Small room."

"You're in danger," said yet another.

"I am in *no* danger," insisted Doug.

"Willow, if you shoot, we all die," said Renna.

"We're all going to die anyway," said Willow. "They won't let us live. I heard what they said to Jill."

Jill glared at Dr. Rivers. "She wants to shoot me," she said. "Probably kill all of us."

"Maybe so," said Doug. "But that's Dr. Rivers. We can work something out, I'm sure."

Dee stirred in Brian's arms. She felt... stronger. Warmer.

"You're lying," said Brian to Doug.

"And so what if I am? Go on." He walked up to Willow. "Shoot me. You're a killer. You've murdered before. Shoot. Kill me."

Willow whimpered.

"Or you can drop the gun," said Doug. "Which I'm guessing is what you're going to do."

Willow stood motionless for a moment, frozen in time. Then, ever so slowly, she let the gun fall to the floor.

"I can't," she whispered. "I'm sorry."

"That's better," said Doug.

He calmly drew his own sidearm and shot Willow in the chest.

The two Confederation Fleet techs had picked up something odd on their scanners. One wondered to the other why those other troops had been so intent on showing them whatever dirty pictures they'd had. What a weird day. First that, now this.

They marched up the ramp, scanning. Were those life signs? Hard to tell, these sensors weren't great.

What was that right up ahead? One tech turned to the other to ask.

A man leaped out at them, a bat raised over his head.

"Yaaaah!" he cried, chugging towards them.

The techs shrugged, drew their sidearms, and fired.

The bullets bounced off him, leaving a shimmering, yellowish glow behind where they'd hit.

Anthony swung the bat before they had a chance to react. Once, twice. The surprised techs collapsed, unconscious and bleeding, to the ground.

"Heh," he said. "Nice of the thing to work this time around."

"Jesus," said Roger, running up behind him. "Did you do this?"

"Maybe," grunted Anthony. "But I'm not cleaning them up." He handed the bat to Roger. "I'm going to go lie down. You do it."

Roger held the bloody bat at arm's length between thumb and forefinger, like a kid picking up a worm. Where had Anthony even found it?

◂▸►◂◂▸

Willow crumpled without a sound. Jill screamed. Emily let go of Dee's hand and dashed over to Willow's side.

Dee flared back to life. Her furnace burned hot and clear as rage took over.

"Ah!" cried Brian, dropping the suddenly scorching girl.

"Doug," said Dr. Rivers, pointing.

Dee stood, wobbling a little, arms outstretched. She fixed her gaze on Dr. Rivers.

"You," she seethed.

"Doug!" said Dr. Rivers, a little more urgently.

But Doug was busy admiring his handiwork. Emily had her hands pressed against Willow's chest, but she was losing blood fast. Jill had knelt by her, as well. They poured their energy into her, but they were losing the battle.

Dee had lifted off the ground.

"Dee," whispered Renna.

Dee glanced down at Renna, eyes filled with fury and hate. She flew.

"*Doctor Rivers*," she said, and her voice was the sound of a roaring, cracking fire.

The soldiers aimed their rifles—and then dropped them, backing away as they congealed into puddles of melted metal on the ground.

Fire streamed from Dee's hands and feet. Renna, Penny and Brian backed away, clustering around where Willow had fallen.

"Dee," said Dr. Rivers, hands outstretched. "I took good care of you. I wanted to help you! You could live a normal life with the serum, right?"

"Dee..." said Doug calmly. "Sky Ranger is alive, he's fine. You can even talk with him if you want."

Dr. Rivers approached her. "You should come down. I promise, no more injections. But there's no way out of this base."

Flames leapt and crackled around Dee as she hovered high above Dr. Rivers and Doug.

The needle plunged into Dee's eye, over and over again.

"Dee," begged Dr. Rivers. "Please."

A terrible scowl spread across Dee's face.

"Burn," she said.

Dr. Rivers and Doug howled and cried as their bodies erupted into twin pillars of flame.

A split second later, they were nothing but ash. Dee stretched her arms out at the soldiers standing before her.

"*Burn*," she said.

Terrified, they backed away. Some turned and ran.

Tongues of flame licked out after them. One dissolved in a tower of whirling fire.

"Dee!" cried Renna. "Enough! Please!"

"Burn!" cried Dee. Another soldier died as Dee's fires consumed him. Dee's skin, clothes and hair started to crack and smoke. "*BURN!*"

Penny didn't hesitate. She threw herself atop Dee, grabbing her with both hands, trying to drag her to the ground. "Stop!" Penny cried. "Dee! *Turn it off!*"

Her skin was painful to touch. Flame leapt up all around Penny. It licked her hair, scorched her skin and hands. She screamed in agony.

"Dee!"

Dee gasped, and fell back down to the floor. Her fires died, extinguishing themselves as quickly as they had burst forth.

Penny rolled onto the floor, smoking and blackened. Her eyes were open, unblinking, and sightless. Her chest was still, and her fingers curled.

"Oh!" Dee cried. She reached out. "Oh! I'm sorry!" she wailed.

Emily stumbled to Penny's side. She wasn't breathing.

"Dee," Renna exclaimed. She gathered her up in her arms. She was still warm, but had started to shake uncontrollably. "Dee, Dee, are you okay?"

"I—I—" Dee stammered, as the horror of what she'd done sank in. "Oh,!" She buried her head in Renna's shoulder. Brian looked on, unsure of what to do next.

"She's burned," said Renna, with wonder. Dee had never gotten even a sunburn, not even back on Terron.

The last of the soldiers had fled the room. They were alone.

"We should go," Brian said. "We have time. Now."

"We can't leave them behind," said Renna.

"We won't. We'll bring them. But we can't stay here," he said.

"Penny," begged Emily. "Come on, I know you can heal. Come on, please."

She placed a hand on Penny's scorched forehead—and was sucked into the whirling vortex of Penny's pulsing, flowing energy.

It was like reaching into a whirlpool. Emily dragged herself out, gasping and drained. Had Penny *taken* energy from her?

Penny blinked, and her chest rose and fell. Emily, relieved, sighed.

"I'm all right," Penny said, voice like gravel. She smiled up at Emily. "Sister. Thank you. See? I'm okay. How's Willow?"

"Alive," said Emily. "For now."

"We need to go," Brian repeated. "Really."

"He's right, we do," said Penny. "Help me up. I can't feel my legs entirely yet, but I think I can move."

"You're quick," said Jill, admiringly.

"Thanks," said Penny, straining to grin. "I die pretty good. Better'n anyone else."

Willow coughed. Emily dashed back to her as quickly as she could.

"Emily, can you help carry her?" asked Brian. "Renna, take care of Dee. I've got Jill. Penny, you can lean on me, too."

"Sure," said Penny. "Okay."

They stumbled out into the main area. It was deserted again. How long before the whole place was swarming with soldiers? They didn't have much time.

The door opened.

"Ready!" Brian called, raising his gun.

Sky Ranger flew in, looking left and right before seeing them. "Hey!" he said. Draped across his back was Torres.

"You're late!" Brian called.

"You got him!" exclaimed Renna.

"What happened?" said Sky Ranger, wide-eyed, as he saw Penny, Dee, and the bloody mess that was Willow.

"They'll be all right," said Brian. "But we need to go *now*."

"Got it," said Sky Ranger, putting his questions aside. "I'll lead the way." He sped off ahead as they struggled to keep pace.

Brian spoke into a small communicator in his collar. "Felipe! You there?"

"We're here!" said Felipe.

"Get the ship fired up! We're headed your way!"

Lois Lorraine looked at her board. All life signs accounted for. They were on the move at last.

"Operation Seven Six," she said. Heads all over Military Command perked up. Soldiers loyal to House Lorraine quietly left their posts, or pushed a button to black out a camera, or silenced an alarm.

"Headed up to the main lobby," said a voice over the Military

Command network. "In stairwell now. All units to lobby area."

Janeane's calm voice came over the speaker. "All units are to report at once," she said. "To me, boys. Come to me. Listen only to me, come to the lobby. Come to me..."

Lois could hear the waves crashing as she spoke. She closed her eyes. That woman was a marvel, worth every credit she paid her.

She checked. They were nearly at the hangar now.

"Open hangar doors," she said.

Sky Ranger led the group down the hall towards the hangar bay. No resistance. Either the Lorraines were doing a good job of keeping people away or they were headed into another trap.

"There!" cried Brian. Yes! Ahead was the hangar, and in it, a small interstellar ship. The very latest model, Brian noted with satisfaction. Trust the Lorraines to break them out of Military Command in style.

"Get aboard!" said Brian. Roger stood by the entrance, waving them in. No guards seemed to be around. More Lorraine interference?

Above, the hangar door was opening. Blue skies shone overhead.

He ducked inside. The hatch closed.

Brian did a head count. Emily, Penny, Sky Ranger, Renna, Willow, Jill, Dee. Anthony, Roger, James, Felipe, and Broussard were already aboard. Brian made thirteen.

Lucky thirteen.

"Okay!" he called into his communicator. "Go!"

The engines of the ship roared, and with an explosion of fire and a whine of thrusters, the ship lifted itself majestically out of its bay and powered up into the Calvasnan sky, spacebound.

"Away," said Lois. She sighed with relief.

"Still orbital defenses," reminded her father.

"Taken care of," said Lois. "They'll be fine."

The orbital defenses on their monitor flashed green. Clear. Their operatives were erasing all the records of their involvement, even now. It was a brilliant coup for the Lorraines.

"That was a well-executed operation," said Georges. "You have a knack for this."

"Let's hope it does what we want," said Lois.

"It will," he answered. "When have I been wrong? Think of all the territory we'll get from it."

Father and daughter shared a triumphant nod, eyes gleaming with thoughts of land, money, and power.

"Orbital defenses," said Broussard, monitoring his console in the cramped cockpit of their ship.

"I see them," muttered Felipe. "They... oh. They're not tracking!"

"Good," said Brian. "Just like they said."

"Lois Lorraine thought of everything," said Sky Ranger. "Can we get out of the system yet?"

"Soon," said Felipe. "I'm working it out now."

Behind them, Dee was panting and gasping as Emily placed a hand on her.

"You're still hot," said Emily. "You need to learn to regulate a little more."

"I'm sorry," said Dee. "I... I don't know what I did. I don't know how I did it. I... did I really...? Oh God..."

"It's all right," said Renna, her heart breaking. Dee had

been changed. She seemed to have lived a decade in just a few months, and every movement seemed to belong to someone older, someone hurt and broken. "You'll be fine. We're going to Valen. No one will bother us there, we'll be able to live as we like."

"Really...?"

"Yes," said Emily. "The Temple will protect us."

"Or so we hope," said Roger.

But even he couldn't hold back a little smile. *Free.*

"Ready to transit to hyperspace," said Felipe. "All scanners show green. We are clear to go!"

Renna glanced around. Brian stood motionless, considering their options. Felipe was eager to go, hand hovering over the control. Broussard sat next to him, a tired smile on his face. Roger and Anthony stood by, watching the readouts with matching worried expressions. Emily had embraced Dee, who had started to cry with something that might have been relief. James and Jill talked animatedly; Jill was filling him in on what had happened to her. Willow lay alone, propped up against a wall, drifting in and out of consciousness. Emily shot her a reassuring grin, and she nodded back. Penny was touching Dee's shoulder with one hand, and had linked her other hand with Sky Ranger's.

Sky Ranger caught Renna's eye and smiled knowingly.

Rhin, Renna thought. *Family.* Somehow, a ship with all of them together on board felt *right*.

She watched Calvasna receding behind them. The orange sun peeked out over the edge, bathing them in a dirty, dull light.

She wouldn't miss it.

"Take us to Valen," whispered Renna.

The ship shimmered and shot forward, disappearing in a flash of light.

[EPILOGUE]
ONE YEAR LATER

MONICA RANG THE BELL, HUMMING ANXIOUSLY. The door opened, and Monica let out an excited squeal.

"Hey!" she said, giving Penny a hug.

"Hey yourself," said Penny. "We've been waiting."

Monica followed her into the big house—the largest in the tiny village of LaNant.

"Something smells great," she said.

"We've got the good stuff on the stove," said Penny. "Just you wait. You've never tasted anything like it."

"You look good," Monica said.

"I feel good," replied Penny. "Which is pretty amazing."

"So where is he? I haven't seen him except in pictures!"

"With his father," sighed Penny. "Upstairs."

Monica entered the dining room, and was met with a chorus of greetings.

"Hey everyone!" she said.

Brian and Renna sat together, arguing about something. Renna smiled, though, and Brian seemed like he was having a good time.

Felipe and Broussard were doing something to Emily's cats, who had been smuggled aboard the ship by a very reluctant Roger, dangling a piece of meat above their heads and yanking it away when one of them jumped. One of them finally got a claw in it, and dragged it down. Emily scolded them from her seat next to theirs.

James and Jill sat together, sharing little glances.

Anthony sat next to Roger, telling him a story. Roger wore a pained expression.

Willow haltingly got out of her chair and walked gingerly over to Monica. "It's good to see you again," she said, smiling. She had never fully recovered from her injuries, despite everything Emily and Jill and even a few doctors had tried to do. She walked a little hunched over, and she had to watch what she ate. Yet she was a far calmer person than she had been before.

Dee sat at the table, staring thoughtfully at her plate. She'd been shell-shocked and reclusive for a long time, but she'd started warming up to people again recently. Renna often said that she hoped Dee would be back to something like her old self again someday, but she said it with the sort of tone that suggested she never expected it to actually happen.

And, of course, there was Sky Ranger. He floated down the stairs, carrying Amos in his arms.

"Here he is!" he shouted at the top of his lungs.

Everyone cheered.

Penny smiled. "Such a doting father," she observed. "You'd never have known he was capable of it."

"I guess not," said Monica. She still didn't entirely like Sky Ranger. "How is he, then?"

"Doing well," said Penny. "Sky is pretty annoyed that he isn't flying yet. I told him it sometimes skips generations, but he doesn't like to hear that. We don't know much about babies, since we never had them at the Union. We all got sterilization shots, every year."

"Huh," said Monica, distracted by the prospect of seeing a baby again. "Can I hold him?"

"Sky!" Penny called. "Bring him over here!"

Sky Ranger floated gently over to them. "Here," he said. "Good to see you again," he said.

She took Amos from him, and made a long series of cooing, burbling noises at him. "I've got you," she laughed. "Oh, I should steal you away!" Penny and Sky Ranger exchanged a happy glance. Amos did that to people.

"Oh, I forgot," said Monica after a while. "I have something for you. There are two letters, in my bag."

Letters? thought Penny, suddenly feeling sick. *Oh no.* No one sent letters, except for...

Penny undid Monica's bag and withdrew them. One of the letters read, simply, "Sky Ranger III – 8/12/2111." The other read "Brian and Renna Gannett – 8/12/2111."

She handed one letter to Sky Ranger, and the other to Brian and Renna. Brian opened theirs at once, and his face turned pale. Renna read alongside him, and then the two spoke in hushed tones.

◄►►◄◄►

Sky Ranger took his letter up to the roof to read. Who sent letters? He had no idea. But he opened it anyway.

The writing inside was in an elegant script, and the date was ten years earlier.

Written January 7, 2101
To be opened by Sky Ranger III, August 12, 2111

Dear Sky Ranger III,

Hello!
You know me, though we've never met. I'm Val Altrera. I

left Earth to found this colony, and, yes, like you, I'm an extra-human. It's odd, I don't get to talk to many others of my kind! At least, not directly.

I've watched you from the past. My gift, as you know, is to see the many possible futures that exist. I know I have very little time left to me, and I know I won't be able to meet you in person. So I've sent this letter to you instead, to be delivered ten years from now.

I'm writing because I have a task for you. When you're ready, come to the Temple at West Arve. Bring your son, and bring Penny Silverwing. I know you have done marvelous work. Your scales are much more in balance than they were, but you have work left to do.

I know you will do well. Please be good to Penny, and to all of your friends. You will need one another in the years and decades to come.

All of my love and respect,

Val

Sky Ranger folded the letter and put it back in his pocket.

He frowned. What had to be done? Why was someone who had been dead for a decade bothering him? Was it something to do with Torres, who was currently being held at Clearfield Temple? Or something else?

He felt a light breeze and looked up. Penny hovered anxiously next to him.

"What is it?" she asked.

He showed her the letter. She scanned it quickly and nodded.

"Thought so," she said. "Okay. Soon, then, we'll go." She handed the letter back to him. He folded it up and put it in his pocket.

They listened to the shouts and laughter coming from downstairs.

Destiny could wait. He grabbed Penny's hand, and the two of them flew back down to the ground floor. Today, right now, Sky Ranger and Penny would eat dinner with their family.

Susan Jane Bigelow is a native New Englander
and librarian with a passion for books,
computers, and writing.

She lives in northern Connecticut
with her wife and cats.

Keep up with the author online:
http://susanjanebigelow.wordpress.com
Twitter: @whateversusan

CPSIA information can be obtained at www.ICGtesting.com
Printed in the USA
BVOW071409270112

281519BV00002B/1/P